PRAISE F

MW01690402

'A relatable but emot
*Strangers* features me
climax.'

'A shocking glimpse into the fault lines and deceit that have corroded a marriage. Both emotional and spine-chilling. A marvellous read.'
Lynn Curtis, Fiction Editor, formerly of *Woman's Own*.

RECIPIENT OF THE *READERS' FAVORITE* 5-STAR AWARD

*Readers' Favorite* editorial review comments:

☆ 'This is one of the most exciting suspense thrillers I've ever had the pleasure of reading.'
☆ 'A thrilling and satisfying read…'
☆ '*Husband, Wife, Strangers* by Robbie Vale is wonderfully written…'
☆ 'Vale utilises suspense to great effect…'
☆ 'The author's depiction of the characters' internal struggles is stellar.'
☆ '*Husband, Wife, Strangers* is filled with tension…'
☆ 'The author infuses the writing with humanity and permeates it with realism.'
☆ 'Robbie Vale's exploration of themes of grief, betrayal and the fragility of marriage is profound.'
☆ 'The prose is clean, deftly balancing engaging dialogues with terrific descriptions.'
☆ 'Highly recommended…'

Robbie Vale is the author of emotionally gripping suspense novels. His titles include:

*Husband, Wife, Strangers* (2025)
*The Secret Life* (2026)
*The Dream Job* (2026)

For more information, news about forthcoming titles, a free short story and lots of bonus materials, go to robbievale.com or scan the QR code below.

# HUSBAND, WIFE, STRANGERS

ROBBIE VALE

Copyright © 2025 by Robert Vale, writing as Robbie Vale.

The moral rights of the author have been asserted.

All characters and events in this publication, other than those in the public domain, are fictitious. Any resemblance to real persons, living or dead, is purely coincidental.

Published by Toucan Press Ltd., a company registered in England and Wales.
9 Chapel Street, Mumbles, Swansea, SA3 4NH.
Company number 16397112.
Email: contact@toucanpress.co.uk

All rights reserved.
No part of this publication may be reproduced, or transmitted in any form or by any means, without the prior permission in writing of the publisher, nor be otherwise circulated in any form of binding or cover other than that in which it is published and without a similar condition including this condition being imposed on the subsequent purchaser.

For Heather

# *HUSBAND, WIFE, STRANGERS*

Robbie writes the sort of books he loves to read. He calls them emotionally gripping suspense novels. Well-crafted, entertaining and relatable stories that evoke powerful emotions as the suspense slowly builds. Stories set in interesting places populated by characters you believe in and care about. But there has to be a credible, evolving and compelling plot, with a dramatic climax. Not to mention a satisfying ending.

Expect to meet people you can relate to, ones you could even know. People dealing with very human problems – past mistakes, messy relationships and personal dramas. Impossible choices and mounting jeopardy. Problems that grow and threaten everything they hold dear, including life itself.

Some of these characters you will love – you will laugh with them, cry with them, and wrestle with their dilemmas. You will unearth their secrets and share their fears. Urge them to take a different course, or plead with them to walk away.

Others you will come to dread as you uncover the circumstances that defined their lives and caused them to pursue their twisted goals. Goals that seem perfectly reasonable to them, but the pursuit of which will heap appalling suffering on others.

To learn more, go to robbievale.com

# PROLOGUE

It was quiet. Louisa lay still, blinking at a scuff mark on the skirting board inches from her face. She made no attempt to move, intent on processing where she was and what had just happened. She rolled her eyes around, realising that her head was resting on the cold floor tiles at the bottom of the stairs, while her body lay splayed out behind her on the lower treads.

She presumed she had fallen the length of the long single flight and was now lying on her side, her right arm stretched out beyond her head.

That was it! On TV, they always made you wiggle your toes. If you could, you hadn't broken your back. She tried. It worked. But her head hurt like hell, and she had no means of assessing the injury. Blood trickled into her eye. Although in an awkward position, her left arm felt unencumbered. Perhaps she could use it to help lever herself down onto the hall floor. The attempt caused an explosion of red light before her eyes, followed by a shock of pain the like of which she had never experienced. She froze, clenched her teeth and breathed deeply through her nose, trying to ride the wave of nausea that was intent on drowning her, rendering her unconscious.

Was she fainting? No, it was passing, but there was something very wrong. She made herself a promise not to move that arm again.

A little rest, that was the thing. She tried to work out what had happened. It was a fall, obviously, but what had caused it? And then she froze as, from behind her, she heard the unmistakable squeak of the eighth tread. And it all came rushing back…

# 1

# LOUISA

Louisa held the front door open as she studied his face. She could almost see Peter's methodical mind working. A tap of his jacket pockets. Wallet, passport…

'Got everything?'

'I think so. I'll be off then.'

She angled the side of her face in his direction and was rewarded with a brief kiss on the cheek. She watched him descend the two stone steps and crunch across the gravel. An unremarkable figure, the epitome of the conservative, late-forties male, albeit one in reasonable condition. The only evidence of middle age was a modest swelling around the waist, the greying at his temples advancing up his orderly haircut. He turned right onto Lonsdale Road, gave a brief wave and was gone.

She shut the door behind her, leaned against it and gazed unseeing down the hallway and towards the kitchen. She supposed her relationship with Peter was typical of the one any brother and sister in their late forties might enjoy. Amiable. Respectful. Civil enough.

But Peter Hedley wasn't Louisa's brother. He was her husband.

***

She looked at her watch. Two o'clock. She decided to make the most of the blazing Sunday afternoon and stroll towards the river, follow the Thames Path south, and then turn up the High Street to Barnes Pond. Rest there a while, watch someone else's children feed the ducks, then make her way back home through the suburban streets. She might sit in the walled garden for a bit, enjoy a glass of wine in the sun. Hopefully catch Sophie on the phone.

She glanced down at her tatty shorts and faded top. Deciding she would swap them for a casual summer dress, she trudged slowly up the steep flight of stairs leading from the hall. That was the trouble with tall ceilings, she mused. Further to climb. Ten minutes later, she was on her way.

As she walked, she looked up at a plane descending over West London towards Heathrow. Soon her husband would be wedged into one, and heading in the opposite direction. To Amsterdam. A journey he had been making back and forth for nearly ten years now. And during that time, decay had set in to their marriage. Nothing catastrophic, no sudden breakdown. Just an inexorable decline into something that was nothing like the loving union she had hoped for. Yes, the early years had been fine, if not spectacular. Peter was never going to be the most romantic man around. By and large, he preferred things to people. His work as an engineer suited him well.

And, if she was honest with herself, Louisa knew that she too tended to gravitate towards the organised, the disciplined. At least in the stuff that mattered. After all, you didn't get to be the finance director of a decent-sized business for no good reason. But that didn't mean she couldn't enjoy some fun, some spontaneity. When circumstances allowed, of course. She longed for a more exciting relationship with her husband, something to rekindle the memory of them as the carefree lovers they once were. And with Sophie away at university, why the hell not? Surely romantic life, passion even, didn't end at forty-eight?

But this weekend had been tedious. Her husband had come through the door at around eight-thirty, like he typically did every other Friday evening. A glass or two of wine, some mundane chat about not very much. His face remained expressionless when she told him about that afternoon's heated argument over Zoom with Christine. The outsourcing project. Her American boss was pushing it so fast it was bound to fail. Peter just nodded vacantly, offering neither advice nor encouragement. It was like talking to the wall.

The ready meal had been followed by more wine. Then it was off to bed. Sometimes they had sex on a Friday night, sometimes on a Saturday. Never both. Increasingly, not at all. This weekend, he had made no move towards her and she, still jangling from the clash with her boss, had decided not to initiate anything.

They used to have a system. Years ago, she had sat up in bed, cross-legged, both of them laughing as she scribbled away in her A5 Black & Red notebook. Together, they had enthused over the ways they liked to do it, deciding to allocate each variation a number. Then they would take turns to shout one out, following which they would scramble into position, like springtime bunnies that had just discovered what fun they could have together.

The only rule was that you had to go along with it – the exercise made all the more amusing when their memories of what the number represented differed. At this point, a panting and rosy-faced Louisa would reach for her notebook to settle the argument.

But now it was all so bloody mechanical. A bit of the usual foreplay, followed by a muttered suggestion from Peter as to how they might position themselves, never countered by her. She had even stopped making the appropriate noises. What was the point?

By five o'clock, she was home from her walk. Another long and lonely evening stretched ahead. It would be two weeks before she saw her husband again. This wouldn't do. Her previous attempts to engage him in a serious conversation about the state of their marriage had failed, but she wasn't prepared to live the rest of her life like this. She would force things to a conclusion. One way or another.

***

Monday was a pleasant early-June day, so she chose to walk to Barnes Bridge station. From there, it was an easy hop to the drab office blocks of Brentford, with their questionable views over the choked Chiswick flyover. The train journey was generally okay, with most of the other commuters heading into London rather than out of it.

Her phone buzzed on the way. Asha. Louisa's smile as she opened the message quickly turned to a frown.

Hi babe, can we meet up first thing? Important. Costa @8.15?

Her friend always called her 'babe'. Always had, always would. They had met at boarding school; Louisa was fourteen and had been sent there in preparation for the serious business of GCSEs and A levels. Her father was a senior figure in the Foreign and Commonwealth Office, and his job had taken them to successive European capitals. She had been shunted around several international schools until some educational continuity was called for.

Louisa and Asha had hit it off straight away. They had bought a pack of cigarettes and smoked away furiously in a corner of a park before Louisa had thrown up, Asha sliding her arm comfortingly around her new friend. Asha's dad was a Ugandan who, as a young man, had fled to Britain to escape the hideous regime of Idi Amin. He had married an Egyptian woman, started his own importing business and done very well. Together, Louisa and Asha had gone on to Bristol Uni, Louisa studying accounting and management, Asha law. They used to argue over which course was the more boring.

The year after graduating, they were both working in London – Louisa studying for her accountancy exams, Asha her Institute of Personnel and Development qualification, having concluded that the law was not for her. It was there that they teamed up with a few strangers to share a crummy house in Shepherd's Bush. For no good reason, the little group had christened itself 'The Rat Pack' after the famous Hollywood gang of entertainers from the fifties and sixties. Besides Louisa and Asha, there were Robert and Peter, who had similarly been at uni together – Leicester in their case.

Siân, the fifth member of the household, had gone off to the States to marry a disgustingly wealthy businessman from Texas. The union had lasted about nine months before she discovered his penchant for snorting cocaine off the prone bodies of young prostitutes. Siân now lived in Hampstead with her second husband. Also very wealthy, if not quite so disgustingly.

They were all confident, intelligent, and – Louisa thought, with the benefit of hindsight – a bit arrogant. Their lives appeared to stretch seamlessly ahead of them, awash with possibilities.

She glanced fleetingly out of the train window, the panoramas of those early years since replaced by views of suburban back gardens, before Brentford station signalled the start of another working day.

Now Asha and she were both employed by the UK arm of the same company, a large American pharma business based in Atlanta. Asha was the HR director, and Louisa finance director. Still the dream team. Still the best of mates.

Louisa turned back to her phone and skimmed through Asha's message again. No question, the tone of it was all wrong. Something was definitely up.

***

Asha was already at a table with two coffees in front of her. They exchanged their customary hug.

'Wow, love the braids,' said Louisa. 'You do that yourself?'

Asha laughed her big, expansive laugh. 'Hell, no, girl, you know I don't have the patience for that sort of thing. A little salon near home.'

'Does Samuel like them?'

''Course he does. He loves everything about me.'

Louisa grinned. Asha nodded to a chair. Her smile had gone.

'We need to talk, babe.'

'Why? What's happened?'

'I guess it didn't go so well with Christine? Your video call on Friday.'

Louisa reached into her bag, took out her Black & Red notebook and snapped off the elastic strap.

'She's being reckless, and I told her so. Why, has she talked to you about it?'

Asha took a deep breath. 'She thinks you're an impediment to the project. To the company's progress.'

Louisa felt her stomach go into freefall. This was not good. Not good at all.

'An impediment?'

'I quote, my love.'

'Well, if she presses ahead the way she's proposing, the whole thing will fall flat on its face. And I refuse to lead the UK finance department into a disaster.'

Asha winced. 'Well, that's the thing. You won't have to. I'm sorry, babe, but she wants you out.'

Louisa sat blinking, expressionless, whilst her habit of self-control fought against the whooshing sensation of shock that started in her stomach and surged up through her chest. The only outward sign of the battle within was a barely perceptible intake of breath. The blankness on her face gave way to a weak smile. An unconvincing one.

'You're kidding? She can't do that.'

'I'm not. And she can.'

Louisa felt shock giving way to defiance. This could not be happening to her. She had always been the one who chose to leave a job, not the other way around.

'So that's it?'

Asha screwed up her face and nodded at the coffees. 'Let's finish these and adjourn to my office. Then we can run through your options.'

***

Louisa gazed out of the window, drumming her fingers on Asha's table. That gutless bitch. If Christine wanted her out, she should bloody well call Louisa herself and deliver the news personally. Not have Asha do her dirty work for her. Louisa decided she would continue to perform her duties until that happened. She looked up as her friend returned with more coffee. Shortly afterwards, they had a plan. Louisa looked at her notes as she summarised.

'So, you email Christine and tell her that I will only accept a termination from my boss. She calls me and pulls the trigger herself. They're five hours behind, so almost certainly this afternoon. I then brief my team and clear my desk. You put together a compromise agreement. Assuming we can agree on the terms, we both sign.'

'Yes, but you need a lawyer to advise you,' said Asha. 'Straight away. We'll cover the costs, but if you don't get legal advice on the compromise agreement, it may not hold water should you subsequently challenge it.'

'Got it. And then that's me done, is it? Fourteen years and two promotions with this company. Goodbye, Louisa.'

Asha grimaced and patted her arm. 'Hey, I know it makes no sense, and it's going to hurt. But you're strong and you will recover from this. Trust me.' She smiled. 'And I happen to know that HR will give you a glowing reference. You still have your best years ahead of you. Then, when you've had enough, you can take on some non-executive work. You're good enough. You know that.'

Louisa smiled. 'Thank you.' She leaned across and cupped her hand over Asha's. 'And thanks for being a friend. Now, you'll have to excuse me. Until that psycho calls me, I have a finance department to run.'

Asha grinned. 'Go kick some butt, babe.'

***

Louisa put down the hairdryer and brush, lifted the hair off the back of her neck and fanned herself with her other hand. She moved her head around as she inspected the result: the slightly offset soft parting, the informal style swept back at the sides, her ears partly exposed. The fair hair gently flicked together at the back – like 'a somewhat unruly duck's arse', as Asha had once described it.

Louisa breathed out. It had been hot in the hall, and she had pushed herself hard at aerobics. Almost as if she had to get into peak condition to face the challenges ahead. The walk back home and the shower that followed had given her time to think. To reflect on the day and on the uncertain future that awaited.

She was proud of her conduct that afternoon. She had retained her civility in the discussion with Christine, despite making clear her disappointment at the way her boss had handled events. She then called her team together, stood in front of them in the open office and explained in clear and unemotional language why Christine wanted her out. It was okay, she had insisted, a fundamental but professional disagreement as to the way forward. Wide eyes stared back at her. She wished everyone the best, made a half-hearted promise that they would all have a farewell drink together, and hugged far more people than she could ever remember being friendly with.

Louisa had then made her way back to her office and packed her belongings into a banker's box. Asha promised to deliver it to her later that week. Only then had she cried, before composing herself and making her way out of the building and into the wall of traffic noise that poured down from the elevated section of the M4. Just another anonymous face in the crowd. Nowhere to be, no one waiting for her at home. She had never felt more alone. Her marriage was in trouble, her professional life at an abrupt and damaging halt.

But now, as she stared at her reflection in the mirror, it hit her. Maybe there was a way to address both issues at the same time. Of course. Why not? Louisa headed downstairs in search of her notebook and pen.

# 2

# WIM

Wim strolled past the reception desk and emerged into the warm evening air. He exchanged some brief chat with a couple of colleagues outside the office, and then walked to the metro station. There, as was his habit, he picked up a copy of the free newspaper before boarding his train for the short journey back towards the city proper. If it was raining, he might take a tram at the other end, but with weather like this, the twenty-minute walk home through the streets of Amsterdam would be a pleasure.

He glanced at his watch as he neared the apartment. Five-fifty. He was feeling hungry and wondered what they might be eating for dinner. He would find out soon enough – like many Dutch families, they invariably sat down to eat at around six. Wim appreciated a bit of routine, of structure. It seemed to work for the girls, too.

He was happy to get stuck in and quite enjoyed cooking, just so long as he had a recipe in front of him. But Caria was way better at it than he was. And her job meant that she was there for when the kids arrived home from school. Yes, their family life was good, even if he was desperate to provide a bigger and better apartment for them all. Theirs was pleasant enough, but there wasn't enough room, and the place tended to descend into chaos. Wim longed for something bigger – a bedroom each for the girls, a second bathroom. More space for relaxing. But neither did the family want to give up the Amsterdam lifestyle, and Wim sometimes found himself eyeing the details of the wonderful apartments to which he aspired. Something in the calm and affluent Museum Quarter perhaps, or close to Vondelpark. That would be quite special.

But the cost of either renting or buying a place that would fulfil his ambitions was huge. Something to which Wim was giving serious thought. Yes, you had to work hard to do well, but you needed to be smart, too. Very smart.

But for now, he walked down their street, right in the centre of the colourful district known as De Pijp. The architecture was typically Dutch, with the gabled and terraced buildings mostly divided into apartments. The odd shop front or café brought variety and a sense of purpose to the bustling scene. The trunks of intermittent and heavily pollarded trees jutted out into the road, interrupting the lines of parked cars shoehorned down one side of the narrow thoroughfare, but there was little traffic to spoil the pleasant vibe. Bikes, on the other hand, were everywhere.

Wim's smile grew wider as he approached their building. It was set back from the pavement, with a steep set of suspended stone steps leading up to the communal front door. Their apartment was on the entry level, with two others above. Metal stairs led down from the street to the basement beneath, home to a bicycle repair business.

As he reached for his key, he could see the proprietor of the café opposite serving a customer at one of several small tables on the pavement. The man looked up and smiled in recognition, Wim half-raising an arm in response.

And there was the young woman who ran the cycle repair shop. She was at the kerb, bending over and inspecting a bike with a customer. Dressed for the warm weather, her bare legs seemed to go on forever before disappearing into a tight-fitting pair of faded denim shorts. A reminder that the Dutch were the tallest nation on earth. She was undoubtedly very attractive, but Wim didn't care about that. Because so was his Caria.

'Papa, Papa!' Laila hurtled towards him and threw her arms around her father's leg.

'Hey, little one, how are you? Have you had a fun day?' Wim scooped her up and leaned towards Caria, wrapping an arm around her as they dodged Laila's head whilst trying to exchange a kiss.

Seconds later, another girl emerged from a bedroom, her arms extended, swaying around as she part-danced towards the little group.

'Sibel, sweetheart, come and give me a hug.'

The girl obliged and rested her head on Wim's stomach, still moving to the pop music emerging from the room behind them.

Enquiries about school were answered with a mixture of enthusiasm and indifference, before Wim hurried off to change out of his work clothes. The chicken kebabs, rice and salad were nearly ready. A buzzing from his pocket caused him to study his phone, before frowning and setting it aside. It could wait. He had his ladies to attend to, and they came first.

Dinner was followed by them all walking to the nearby park, after which it was back to the apartment to prepare for Laila's bedtime. Once home, she jigged up and down and gazed up at her father, a pleading expression on her face.

'Please, Papa, will you read me some more of *Reynard the Fox*? Please, please?'

Wim smiled down at her. 'Of course, but clean your teeth first and then jump into bed. That cunning fox doesn't like little girls who don't clean their teeth. He'll eat you all up. Grrrr!'

Laila squealed and clenched her fists under her chin. Caria frowned at him.

'Those old stories do sound rather gruesome, my love. You'll give her nightmares.'

'Nonsense.' Wim grinned. 'They've been around for a thousand years. Reynard's cunning, that's all. He knows how to get what he wants.' He extended a hand and rubbed her hip, his eyebrows raised. 'As do I.'

Caria lowered her voice. 'Just don't scare her, okay? Or you'll be sleeping on the sofa.' She removed his hand. 'Alone.'

***

Laila sat up in bed, studying the large, square book. She pointed to the picture on the cover.

'So there's Reynard, with his paw resting on the back of another animal in a red coat. But who is he, and what is he looking at?'

'Well,' said Wim, 'that's Tybalt the cat. See his tail? And Reynard is about to trick him.'

Laila moved her finger. 'So what's that?'

'It's a rope. A noose.'

'A noose? What's it for?'

Wim soft-pedalled his answer, mindful of Caria's warning.

'Well, Reynard has a clever plan to deal with his enemy, once and for all. We'll find out what it is when we get there in the book.'

'Papa?'

'Mmm.'

'Are you clever, like Reynard?'

Wim smiled. 'Well, I have to be. Because that way I can take care of you, your sister and Mama.'

'Good.' She grinned and snuggled down in bed. 'Now, will you read to me, please? I want to know all about Reynard.'

# 3

# LOUISA

Louisa did a great deal of thinking that Monday. Her thoughts had crystallised as the evening wore on. The last remnants of daylight were still visible outside as she lay in bed, staring at the ceiling, apprehension gnawing at her.

She was nervous about Peter's reaction to her being fired. The WhatsApp message had been deliberately vague – she preferred to deliver the news over the phone. But he had yet to call. And without fully understanding why, she was equally anxious about sharing her clever plan to save their marriage. She needed to do some research before taking him through that.

When Peter had started working in Amsterdam, they used to talk every day. But the habit had lapsed. What was the point if they had nothing to say to each other? But now she needed him, and cursed the distance that had grown between them. Hopefully, it wasn't too late to fix that.

She suddenly realised that the alarm was set for six-thirty the next morning and reached out for it, before changing her mind and withdrawing her arm. The idea of switching it off made her feel guilty.

***

Louisa smiled with relief as she looked at the name of the caller. It was Asha. She had expected to hear from Peter by now and wasn't looking forward to the discussion.

'How are you doing this morning, babe? I thought I would check up on you.'

Louisa smiled. 'In case I've topped myself or something?'

'Well, unless I'm very much mistaken, you haven't. Right?'

The banter continued until Asha suggested she call round the following day with Louisa's box of stuff from her office.

'Well, it's sweet of you, but I don't want to mess up your evening.'

'No problem at all. Samuel has his writers' group and I'll have the car with me, so why not?'

'Well, in that case, come round for dinner. Nothing fancy, but I'd appreciate the company. I've been doing some thinking and want to share my ideas with you. I'll make sure I have plenty of your favourite tipple handy.'

That familiar ear-splitting laugh. 'How can I refuse the promise of a ginger beer? Samuel can fix his own supper when he gets home. I'll leave here around six if that's okay. Should be with you by half-past.'

The arrangements made, they rang off. There were three people that Louisa needed to speak to that day. Her brother Michael, who had recently dropped a bit of a bombshell with an unusual request. Her daughter Sophie who should be made aware of her mother's unwelcome state of unemployment. And a lawyer, because Asha said she had to have one to go over the anticipated compromise agreement. She would use the firm that looked after her mother's affairs.

She sighed as she reached for her phone. Better start with Michael.

***

His voice sounded groggy. 'Yeah…? Oh, Sis, it's you.'

'Michael, you sound awful. Are you alright?'

'Uurgh. Just a bit fuzzy, that's all. Still in bed. What time is it?'

'It's nine-thirty. On a Tuesday morning. Can you talk?'

'Let me have a look.' A stifled snigger. 'Yes, I can, Sis. I'm all alone here. No gorgeous man next to me this morning, I'm afraid.'

Louisa rolled her eyes. His mischievous attempts to embarrass her had long since failed to have any impact. But still, he persisted. Refusing to play along, she launched into the point of her call.

'So, Michael – your request. I've been thinking hard about it, and I'm worried. It's not every day a brother asks to borrow twelve thousand pounds from his sister, and I need to know that you're not in any trouble. So how about I come round a bit later, and you can explain it all to me?'

'Oh, crap. Actually, Sis, the place is a bit of a tip, so let's meet in a café. But aren't you working?'

'I'm not working, no.' Louisa sighed. 'I'll tell you about that later. But I would rather come round to yours, if that's okay?'

'Hmm. So you can check up on me, is that it?'

'I'm concerned, that's all. But don't worry about spring cleaning, I want to talk to my brother, not inspect his flat.'

'Studio darling, studio. You flatter the place.'

'Whatever you prefer. Does midday work?'

***

At eleven-fifteen, Louisa stepped off the train at Clapham Junction. She would take advantage of the weather and walk across the common to her brother's address. Thirty-five minutes later, she made her way down the steep concrete steps from the street and tapped on the window of his basement studio. She could see a grinning Michael make his way to the door. It was a low door, she could just get through it without ducking, and she wondered how often her brother would have banged his head on the frame when he was a little the worse for wear. Either from alcohol, or the recreational drugs in which she was sure he dabbled.

They embraced, Louisa instantly comparing the warmth of the greeting with the unemotional parting from her husband on Sunday. She accepted the offer of a coffee, her eyes moving from the collection of dirty mugs in the stained sink, to where Michael ferreted around at the back of a cupboard for some clean ones. He then reached into the fridge, Louisa trying not to stare at the bare shelves within, as Michael sniffed cautiously at a small container of milk.

He grinned at her. 'I think this is okay. I don't want to poison my sis, now do I? Not when she's about to help me out.'

Louisa took him in as he finished making the coffee. The slightly unnatural-looking sandy hair was flicked back over the top of his forehead, the hint of a badly executed DIY colouring job about it. The bags under his eyes suggested some poor choices around lifestyle, but there was nothing new about that. The turquoise T-shirt was faded and creased, worn with cream linen cargo pants beneath which bare feet padded over the worn vinyl flooring of the kitchenette.

But Louisa took comfort from the radiance of his smile, and the eternally optimistic outlook that, despite his challenges around money, her brother always seemed to exude.

The small talk was punctuated by sips of instant coffee, both of them aware of the elephant in the room. Louisa took the initiative.

'Michael, this loan. I don't want to pry, but I would like to know what it's for. I think that's reasonable, don't you?'

Her eyes flicked between him and their surroundings. 'I'm concerned about you.'

'Of course.' Michael lowered his mug. His face wore an unconvincing smile. 'Well, as I explained, I owe this friend of mine... well, associate really... twelve thou'. And he's getting all arsey about it, quite unpleasant really. I just want to pay him back.'

'Okay, but why do you need cash? What's wrong with an electronic transfer?'

Michael grimaced. 'The problem is, the bank is insisting I clear my overdraft. So if I pay the money into my account, they'll no doubt use a chunk of it to do just that – before I can get hold of the cash. Do you see?'

Louisa sighed as she studied his face. Her big brother. Four years older than she was and, financially at least, a mess. She leaned into him.

'Are you in trouble, Michael? Is anyone threatening you?'

'Oh, Lord, no. Don't worry, Sis. I just want to clear things up. Get this man off my back.' He giggled and raised his eyebrows. 'So to speak. You know my scriptwriting work is erratic, to say the least. But I am hopeful on that score, so please don't fret about your money.'

'That wasn't my chief concern. It's you I worry about. Look, I'll do as you ask, but perhaps you need a bit more stability in your life.' She shrugged and glanced around her. 'Financially and otherwise. Your health, what you eat...'

The answering nod was exaggerated. 'I know you mean well, and I shall try, I promise. And paying off this debt will relieve the stress I've been under, so thank you for your help.'

Despite the lack of conviction in Michael's assurances, Louisa nodded.

'Good. I'll talk to my bank. I'd be amazed if I can just march through the doors and withdraw twelve thousand in cash, so I'll let you know the plan once I've spoken to them.

But you'll need to come to Hammersmith. There's no way I'm hauling it halfway across London, and neither am I keeping it in the house.'

'Oh, you are a love. Thank you, Sis. Twelve big ones, yes?'

'As requested. But you must promise me, Michael. Not a word to anyone about where it came from, okay? Peter would go berserk.'

'He's such a stiff, my brother-in-law. And not in a good way.'

A reproving sigh from Louisa. 'And, remember, it's a loan. Six months. No more.'

'Got it. Now, tell me, why aren't you at that stress factory of yours? A day off, is it?'

Louisa winced. 'Ah.'

She went on to tell her brother all about her sacking. His reaction was one of disbelief. Louisa pulled a face.

'Yes, that's how I felt too. It's never happened to me before.' She took a deep breath and lowered her eyes. 'Maybe I was over-confident, had too much faith in my value to the company.' She raised an eyebrow. 'Payback for your arrogant little sister.'

Michael leaned forward and shook her knee. 'No, don't you dare say that. You've bust a gut for that firm. Your boss sounds like a complete cow, she doesn't know what she's doing. You're better off out of it. Why not take some time off, and think carefully about what you want to do with your life?'

Louisa smiled at him, grateful for the sympathy, the unconditional support. Not to mention the good advice. Advice she was already working on. She felt her eyes filling, something that was not wasted on Michael.

'Hey, Sis, you'll be fine, I promise. Now come here and let me hug you. You look like you need one.'

They stood up and embraced, Louisa relishing the closeness. She could have been a small child again, her big brother protecting her, making it better. The emotion was quickly replaced with laughter as Michael held her at arm's length and grinned at her.

'Fuck 'em, that's what I say. It's their loss.'

But her amusement quickly faded when he asked about Peter's reaction. She tried to keep the response breezy.

'I've messaged him, but we've yet to talk.'

***

Sophie's voice was tight when, that afternoon, she responded to her mother's voicemail.

'Oh my God, Mum. Are you okay? That woman… how could she? Just because you disagree on something. That's bullying. Intimidation. You should sue the bitch. Look, is Dad away this weekend?'

'He is.'

'Well, in that case, why don't I come home? We can get pissed together. And I can tell you about my summer job. I'm going to be working on the Isle of Wight ferry!'

Louisa contrasted her daughter's speedy reaction with Peter's failure to get in touch. The concern for her mother. The care. She also reflected on Sophie's enquiry about her father's whereabouts. It was almost as if she were trying to avoid him. Maybe she, too, found him increasingly hard work. Distant and oblivious to anyone's concerns but his own.

Louisa realised that, without work, she'd have the time to shop and cook properly for her daughter, perhaps think about an outing or two. But in the meantime, she was working on her plan.

***

Louisa eyed the clock in the corner of her laptop screen. She needed a break from her research. She sat back and ran her fingers over the battered edge of the desk. She loved it. The pale yew wood, the clean and simple lines of a design that had swept aside the Victorian behemoths of the preceding period. It was a shame she didn't use it more often. Maybe that would change now.

She raised her eyes, gazing out of the wide bay window. To the view that, despite the tranquillity within the solidly built house, kept its inhabitants connected to the outside world. The gravelled courtyard driveway with its splashes of emerald moss invading the perimeter, the holly tree towering over their scruffy VW Passat. The messy stains on the bonnet beneath the branch where the blackbird habitually sat and sang, or feasted on the red berries that adorned the tree in late autumn. The burned orange brick of the street wall, for the most part hidden by pleasantly untamed evergreen shrubs, with tendrils of ferns unfolding through the lower limbs like emerging aliens. And beyond their miniature jungle, Louisa could glimpse the green expanse of the playing fields on the far side of Lonsdale Road.

The calm, the peace, only the murmur of traffic beyond the comforting embrace of these walls to remind her that they lived just a few miles from the centre of one of the world's great cities.

She rose and turned to face the sitting room, admiring it as she often did. The tall ceiling, the Edwardian fireplace surround. The essence of timeless period architecture. The floral-patterned armchair where Peter would doze in front of the horse racing on the TV. Two sage-green upholstered sofas, the back of one adorned with the folded tartan rug that Sophie liked to drape over herself, twirling the tassels between her fingers as she recovered from the excesses of the night before, whilst regaling her mother with tales of her escapades.

Louisa made her way out of the sitting room and into the hallway. The long flight of stairs soared upwards, the tessellating tiles at its foot illuminated by the soft light bleeding through the stained-glass windows on either side of the front door.

It was a beautiful house. She was a lucky woman, and she knew it. Okay, the job thing was a big shock. But she would get over it and move on. What did they say? What doesn't break you, makes you stronger. Stuff her ungrateful boss – Louisa would not allow this setback to ruin her career.

But her marriage… Her shoulders slumped. She had promised herself it would change. But what if it didn't? What if she reluctantly concluded that Peter and she would have to separate? The house would have to go, for sure. She recoiled from the horrible idea of carving up their assets. Ripping their lives apart. The pain and confusion. No, the relationship was worth fighting for, even if it meant taking a few risks.

She made her way into the kitchen to make a coffee. They called it the kitchen, but that didn't do it justice. The rear of the ground floor had been extended outwards, as was the case with many houses on their road. Now the huge, light-filled space was home to a dining area at the back, a living area to the front, and the kitchen and its island to one side. A real family space, with the peaceful sitting room typically only used as a study, or for indulging oneself in front of the fire on a lazy winter weekend.

She flicked the kettle on and reached for a coffee bag. Eyes closed, she held it to her nose and inhaled. She used to hate coffee, but had developed a taste for it whilst in the Rat Pack house in Shepherd's Bush. Tea was what your gran drank, coffee was cool. And at the time, she had so wanted to be cool. To attract the attention of her housemate, Robert. Pathetic, of course, but something had worked.

Because for nine glorious months they had been together, Louisa creeping into his room at night to share his bed. He was kind, tender, and made her laugh. Handsome too, his tall frame topped by lustrous brown hair that contrasted with piercing blue eyes. Eyes that Louisa was sure were looking through hers and into her soul as he lay on top of her, moving ever so gently. At the age of twenty-two, she was in love, and had wondered if they might eventually end up together.

But Robert had stayed true to his plans for the future and taken a job in Canada, with Louisa increasingly shunning food and the sympathies of Asha as the terrible day approached.

Following his departure, she started eating again, but their little group quickly disbanded as life took them in different directions. And then, a few years later, she bumped into Peter, Robert's old friend and their former Rat Pack housemate. They struck up a relationship, and things started to get serious. He seemed solid and reliable, nothing like the unconvincing boyfriends Louisa had motored through in the time since Robert had disappeared from her world.

Maybe here was someone with whom she could spend the rest of her life, she had mused. Build a home and have children. Was it love? She liked to think it was, even if this partnership was more *practical*, and lacked the euphoria that she'd felt in the company of Robert.

The following winter, she and Peter moved into a flat in North London. Louisa's parents' disapproval was tempered by the subsequent announcement of their daughter's engagement that autumn, with a wedding planned for December of the following year. No more living in sin for Daddy's girl, then. Louisa often wondered if her decision to marry had been hastened by her parents' attitudes.

A major row looked like ending the relationship six months before the big day, Louisa explaining to her friends that it was all over with Peter Hedley. She had packed a suitcase and invited herself to stay with Asha, sleeping on an airbed whilst she considered her options and tried to summon the courage to tell her parents.

But fate had dealt its hand, Robert calling Asha to say that he was back in the UK for a few days, and did she want to meet up? Asha was pleased to agree, explaining that she had an unexpected visitor. Louisa had felt a surge of apprehension when they insisted she should join them, unsure whether a meeting with her old flame would make her feel better or worse.

Either way, the airbed remained unused that night, as, following dinner in a Turkish restaurant, Asha travelled home alone, while Louisa and Robert hastily checked themselves into a cheap Paddington hotel.

Shortly afterwards, Robert was back in Canada, and Peter reappeared. His admission of responsibility for their quarrel was accompanied by declarations of remorse for his behaviour. Louisa felt remorseful too – for her reckless one-night stand with Robert, coupled with her failure to divulge it to Peter. But then again, they had broken up at the time, it wasn't his business, and she was allowed. Best move on. She and Peter were quickly and convincingly reconciled – so much so that her usual insistence on condoms was, on that occasion, replaced by an assurance that she was right at the end of her cycle and their use was unnecessary.

They were married as originally planned in December, her father stoically hiding his disapproval of the bump now visible at his daughter's waistline, as he escorted her towards the beaming registrar.

***

Just after three o'clock. Louisa looked at her husband's name on the screen of her phone, wondering why it had taken him so long to call her back. She hesitated for a second before picking up. What was the matter with her? Was she scared of him or something?

The small talk was brief. But then, it always was. Peter came straight to the point.

'So what's up? Something about work, you said.'

Louisa explained.

'Fuck! Shit… Why didn't you say in the message?' It went quiet for a moment. He spoke again. 'Christ, you must have seriously pissed off your boss. What about the payoff? Have they put a figure on the table?'

Louisa took a deep breath. 'As in, "Oh my God, darling. Poor you. Are you okay?"' She rolled her eyes. 'I do have feelings, Peter. You might at least ask me how I am.'

He sighed. 'Sure. Sorry. It's just a bit of a shock, that's all. Are you okay?'

Her voice was clipped. 'I'm fine.'

'So what happens now?'

They spoke about the next steps, the intended compromise agreement and the need for her to get a lawyer. Louisa swallowed and pitched her idea.

'But I was thinking… Why don't I come over to Amsterdam for a few days? I was looking at the weekend after next. You could maybe take the Thursday and Friday off, and we can have a bit of fun together. Meanwhile, I can give some thought as to what I do from here. Career-wise.'

'Well, that shouldn't take too long, should it? You need to get another job, and soon. You'll have to get on to some headhunters and get your CV into shape. And sort out your LinkedIn profile. Most executive search firms default to that these days.'

'Yes, of course. But this is a good opportunity for a rethink. A new direction, perhaps?' Louisa felt the tendons in her neck stiffen as her face involuntarily tensed. 'Maybe one that would enable us to spend more time together.' She moved quickly on. 'And anyway, it's years since I've been to Amsterdam, and I could do with a change of scene. So why not?'

There was a pause before Peter replied. When he did, his words were measured.

'This all sounds rather irresponsible, don't you think? Rather than me bunking off work whilst we fritter our money away in Amsterdam, we're going to have to be careful. The priority has to be you getting another job. One that pays as well as the one you just lost. Then perhaps we can relax a bit.'

Louisa bit her lip.

'My God, Peter. You haven't even asked about the circumstances of my dismissal, but already you seem to be blaming me. And I'm sure we can afford to enjoy ourselves for a few days!'

Louisa had often thought him tight, but dismissed her husband's frugality as a perfectly understandable by-product of his tough upbringing. Peter's father was a small boy when he came over to England with his Irish parents, just after the war. The family had struggled to make ends meet in the canal-side slums of Birmingham, before the bulldozers moved in and broke up the tight-knit communities. Peter had never forgotten the tales of hostility and hardship, or his family's efforts to anglicise themselves in a desperate bid to maximise the opportunities available to their offspring. Louisa heard him sigh.

'It's not just the cost. There's no way I can take time off next week. So it makes sense to postpone the idea until I can. And we're bound to be a bit stressed with all the uncertainty, so now doesn't sound like the right time, that's all.'

'Peter. You already have your Amsterdam apartment, so there's no extra cost there. You were due to come home that weekend anyway, so instead of buying a plane ticket for you, we spend the money on one for me. I am not stressed, and neither should you be. I intend to take my time to think about what I do next. I need a break. I want to get away. So even if you can't take any extra time off, we can still have the weekend together. I'm coming, okay?'

A pause.

'Right. Fair enough.'

Louisa was keen to bring this strained conversation to a close, but not before she had let her husband know how far short of her expectations he had fallen.

'Good. Thank you. And I spoke to Sophie earlier, by the way. She's been very sympathetic and plans to come home this weekend.'

Peter grunted.

'I'll give her your love, shall I?'

He muttered his agreement, and shortly after they rang off. Louisa scowled at her phone and wondered whether she was wasting her time. Was it too late to save this marriage?

# 4

# PETER

Peter slipped his phone into his pocket and sat back in his chair, his hands steepled in front of him. Shit. This wasn't in the plan. None of it. Moments later, he opened his office door and spoke briefly to Grietje, the assistant who looked after him and his team. He stalked over to the lifts, his face like thunder.

Once outside, he wandered in the direction of the Bijlmer Arena concourse, the transport hub that served the office blocks and commercial premises to the south-east of Amsterdam. There he bought a coffee from a little cart, which he sipped whilst sitting on a bench, staring ahead, oblivious to the sights and sounds around him.

This was a shock. His super-dependable wife sacked, her big salary… gone. And now these crazy fucking notions about swanning around in Amsterdam. Like some directionless, dippy airhead, trying to *discover* herself. Getting straight back into work, that's what she should be doing. They *needed* the money, after all. These were their biggest-earning years, and his plans depended on two fat salaries, not one. For now, anyway.

And coming to stay with him, disrupting his life whilst

she avoided the task of sorting out her own? Christ. What was she thinking? She had been fired, for God's sake. Hah! What would *Daddy* have made of that? Stuck-up old bugger, good job he was no longer around to witness his little girl's fall from grace. And what of her mother, Barbara? Just as well she's mad as a box of frogs, because in the past she'd had a way of conveying how very disappointed she was about certain choices Louisa had made. How much longer was the old goat going to drag on for anyway? That bloody home was burning through her cash at a frightening rate. Pleasingly though, she had plenty of it.

Neither of Louisa's parents had liked him, Peter mused. He pictured Barbara, a gentle frown on her face, as her daughter described her new man to her mother. The one she would subsequently marry. 'An *engineer*, did you say, Louisa? Don't they mend ovens or build roads – something like that? Oh, dear.' Well, she'd had to get used to it, the old bag, because by then he and her daughter were an item. And there was no way she could force them apart.

Peter's thoughts returned to the present. What to do about his wife's visit? Shit, shit, shit. He had to get busy. He looked at his watch, tossed his coffee cup into a bin and strode back to the office. He needed to brief Grietje. She might have to work late.

# 5

# LOUISA

Louisa sat nervously in the busy Hammersmith café, her cappuccino untouched in front of her. She glanced around, wondering if any of her fellow patrons had followed her from the bank just along King Street, well aware of the plastic carrier stuffed with twenty-pound notes now weighing down her capacious tote bag. None of them gave the impression that they were about to mug her, but despite that, she smiled with relief as, moments later, Michael arrived. Amazing how he can be on time when it matters to him, she thought.

Louisa took in her brother's appearance as he approached the table. The beige linen shirt, creased and unbuttoned, covered a pale T-shirt worn with slightly grubby white jeans and a pair of distressed deck shoes. A rainbow-coloured cheesecloth scarf was looped loosely around his neck. Despite the warm weather, Michael always wore a scarf – his trademark accessory. A dark blue canvas satchel hung over his shoulder. Louisa couldn't help noticing that it looked limp and empty. For now, anyway.

His smile was genuine, exposing even, white teeth. They were lucky, she thought, they both had nice teeth. She stood up as he held out his arms to engulf her in a tight hug.

'*Daaarling* Sis, how *aare* you?'

Louisa's forced smile disguised the anxiety she felt within. As if in secretly handing over a serious wad of cash to Michael, she was doing wrong. Loaning her brother money for God knows what. Would it help him, or merely accelerate his decline into financial ruin? And at the same time, she was deceiving her husband, who knew nothing of this.

Louisa took a deep breath before replying. 'Fine, Michael, fine. You look well, I must say.'

He kept one hand on her arm. 'One tries, my love, one tries. Anyway, let me grab a coffee and I'll be right with you.'

A couple of minutes later, they were sitting opposite each other, exchanging small talk, Louisa aware of Michael's eyes repeatedly straying towards her bag. She didn't think he would concentrate on much else until they had fulfilled the purpose of their rendezvous.

She sighed and said, 'Before you explode with anticipation, I have something for you.'

Michael looked around cautiously before taking the plastic bag and easing it into his satchel. 'You're a brick, thank you.'

'It's okay, Michael, but remember what I said. This is a one-off favour. Do you understand? No more.'

'Of course.' He smiled. 'And thank you, my love, you have rather saved the day, you know. Now, tell me what's going on with you. Any job offers yet?'

'It's a bit soon for that. I need to formally end things with my old employers first. There's a settlement to agree, but I have the services of Mum's lawyers to help me with that.'

Michael shook his head. 'Those horrible corporate types. I don't know how you put up with it. That's one reason why I like scriptwriting. No nagging boss telling me what to do and how to do it. Perhaps that's why it only pays a pittance.' He rolled his eyes. 'And sometimes nothing at all. So, what will you do now?'

Louisa chose her words carefully. Anything shared in confidence with her brother tended to become common knowledge very quickly.

'Well, I don't know yet. But it might involve me looking at opportunities further from home. So, I do need you to increase the frequency of your visits to Mum. You hardly see her, Michael, and it's not right. It's a condition of that cash currently sitting in your bag, okay?'

He held up his hands in resignation. 'Sure. No problem. Even if she has absolutely no idea who I am.'

'She has no idea who anyone is most of the time. Once a week, then? Can I rely on you?'

'For you, darling – once a week it is. So what about these opportunities further afield? Sounds exciting.'

'Oh, nothing concrete, just some ideas that could signal a change of direction for Peter and me.'

Michael patted her arm. 'Ooh, I see. And what does he have to say about that?'

'We haven't talked about it yet. I'm still in the research phase, shall we say.'

'So he doesn't know?'

'Not yet.'

Michael raised his eyebrows. 'That's brave of you. Peter doesn't strike me as a man who likes surprises.'

Louisa forced a smile and studied Michael's face as he sipped his coffee. He was no fool when it came to reading her husband. She wondered if she was making a mistake by not sharing her idea with Peter from the outset. But surely it would be worth it, if her scheme to save their marriage worked. Better to put together a concrete and workable plan before presenting it. Less opportunity for Peter to dismiss her thinking as the ill-conceived ramblings of a rudderless scatterbrain.

***

Asha pushed away her plate and nodded appreciatively at Louisa.

'Thank you for this evening. That was really good. I thought only men did barbecues.' She mimicked beating her chest. 'The big macho hunters cooking meat for their little *wimmin*. But this sister is doin' it for herself.'

'I'm glad you enjoyed it. But this sister has no bloody choice most of the time.'

Asha grimaced. 'I know, my love. It can't be easy. So, how has Peter taken the news about your situation?'

'He was shocked, I guess.' Louisa smiled in resignation. 'As I was. He immediately started on about the money side of things, the need for me to get another job without delay. That sort of thing. Almost as if it was my fault.'

'Well, hopefully, he's going to give you the support you need. And deserve.'

Louisa stared at the floor while she considered this.

'I dunno. It's a bloody mess, frankly. *We're* a bloody mess.' She lifted her head so she could meet Asha's questioning gaze.

'I was only thinking on Sunday, when Peter went back to Amsterdam, just how crap our married life has become. We're hardly ever together. And when we are there's no romance, no excitement. I know I've moaned about it in the past, but this time I'm serious. It can't go on. And, strangely, maybe me losing my job could be the perfect opportunity for us to sort out our marriage.'

Asha leaned in and patted her hand.

'Sorry – I hadn't realised things were so bad. What are you thinking?'

'Well, I have yet to put this to Peter, but now I'm unemployed, maybe I could spend time in Amsterdam with him… look for some work out there. Something temporary, or part-time, or maybe work that I could do remotely from the apartment. It must be worth exploring, right?'

'Why not? It's a great idea. Kill two birds with one stone.'

'Exactly. So, I'm going to spend a couple of days over there the weekend after next, by which time I'll have done some research on job opportunities.'

Asha held up a finger.

'Well, in that case, I'm going to introduce you to a recruiter who works in the Netherlands. She does quite a bit with international companies, and she may be able to give you some advice. Or even help you find something.'

'Oh, wow, thanks. That would be great. You're a pal.'

'I feel awful about what happened. I never thought I'd have to tell my best friend she's being let go. I'm so sorry, babe.'

Louisa put a hand on Asha's knee and shook it gently. 'Hey, it's not your fault, is it? It's that… woman in Atlanta who decided to fire me.'

'I know, but it does make me think about my own job. When I went into HR, I thought I would be spending my time helping to create a truly awesome workplace. One where people can feel happy and give their best. In truth, I have very little input on shaping things. All the policies come out of Atlanta. I'm not enjoying my job these days. Not one bit. And your departure is the last straw.'

***

By Thursday afternoon, and after many hours at her desk, Louisa's notebook was filling up with background information and new avenues to explore in the Netherlands. An email exchange with Asha's contact in Amsterdam proved useful. But despite her optimism, there were still big gaps in Louisa's knowledge, and she wasn't yet ready to share her ideas with Peter.

On another call, he reiterated his concerns, all of which were financial. The need for her to replace her income. Quickly. To update her CV. And had she made a list of recruitment companies? What about the severance agreement? Did she have a lawyer yet? What about her shares and share options? The list went on. But there was nothing about her, how she was feeling. No comfort, no reassurance. It was all money, money, money.

Louisa was pleased to end the fraught discussion and spent the next ten minutes staring out at the garden. Her doubts had resurfaced. Was there any way back for them? But then she remembered the promise she had made to herself. If their marriage was going to end in failure, then she had to be sure that she had given it her best shot.

***

Louisa put the shopping bag into the boot of the Passat and headed back from Barnes village to home, humming along to the radio as she drove. Sophie had called yesterday to say she would arrive on the Friday evening if it suited her mother. It suited Louisa very well. She was dying to see her girl, and the idea of having her to herself for two whole nights had lifted her spirits.

Louisa decided she would cook prawn linguine with garlic, tomatoes and parsley. All would be prepared by the time she collected Sophie from Barnes station at twelve minutes past seven. Assuming there were no delays, of course.

But first, she would have a quick spin around the top floor. Towels into the bathroom. A bit of dusting, hoover Sophie's bedroom. A pause as she fondly examined one of her daughter's athletics trophies. The four hundred metres hurdles. Louisa could never work out how you cleared those bars at such speed. They frightened her, but evidently not her gutsy daughter. She reached for her duster again and carefully wiped the shield, before placing it back next to a photo. Sophie and her hockey teammates, all proudly clutching their medals. She would have been seventeen then.

Louisa lifted her eyes and stared into space. Whatever happened now between her and Peter, she could take comfort from the fact that Sophie, her only child, had turned out alright. Better than alright, come to think of it. She sighed, was back in the moment and resumed her tasks.

Everything went to plan, and by seven-thirty mother and daughter were both standing in the kitchen, clutching glasses of wine. Sophie leaned back against the island, very much at home. Louisa smiled, keen to take her in, but without giving the appearance of a mother checking over her student child. Making sure she was alright, feeding herself properly…

Sophie looked well. Her blonde shoulder-length hair was thick and lustrous, the parting having migrated a little further to the left. To the sides of her pale blue vest top, pink bra straps contrasted with tanned shoulders. The leanness of her frame was accentuated by a filmy print skirt, worn low on the hips. But for Louisa, her only child's best attributes remained that wide, candid smile and those gorgeous eyes of forget-me-not blue.

Louisa put her glass down and wrapped her arms around her daughter, Sophie returning the tight hug. They stayed like this for a few seconds before the girl spoke.

'You okay, Mum?'

They separated.

'No, not really. It's been a tough week.'

Sophie breathed in deeply. 'What will you do?'

'Still thinking it all through, my love. But I'll be fine, don't you worry. I'm going over to Amsterdam next weekend to stay with your father. Take some time out to decide what I want to do next.'

'Great! Hopefully he's pleased about that. Is he looking after you?'

Louisa tried, really tried, to make her response a reassuring one. 'Of course! We'll have some fun.'

Sophie was blinking, her forced smile a mirror of her mother's. Louisa's heart skipped a beat. She was a poor actress. They both knew the truth. Quickly, she changed the subject.

'And how's your social life? What have you been up to? Anyone special on the horizon?'

'Well, now, that's one reason why I was hoping for a little tête-à-tête.' Sophie pulled out a stool and sat down. She stared straight at her mother, took a deep breath and then exhaled suddenly. 'There is actually someone really nice. And she's a she. I think I'm bi, Mum.'

***

They had another hug, topped up the wine glasses, and now sat facing each other.

Sophie frowned. 'So you already suspected that might be the case?'

'Yes, I did.'

'Wow. Amazing.' The girl grinned. 'And I thought I was being so low-key about it all. Discreet. Not sure why I needed to be, frankly. So… I still like boys, and I have no idea how this will all play out, but for now, the attraction to Emma is clear. It feels right.'

'And that's absolutely fine,' said Louisa. 'Be who you are, my love. Happiness is everything.' Too bloody right, she thought. 'Your gran, bless her, always used to say: "Sod the lot of them. Take me as I am, or go to hell."'

'She's a star.' A sorrowful expression crossed Sophie's glowing young face. 'Or was, anyway.' She smiled. 'I know, why don't I come and see her with you? I haven't been for ages. We could go on Sunday morning.'

'Well, that's very thoughtful of you. Thank you.' Louisa frowned.

'What?'

'What we've been talking about. Your dad…'

A look of resignation replaced Sophie's smile. 'Well, he has to know, I suppose.'

'Would you like me to soften him up a bit? You know, gently lead into the subject and let him know that you're… exploring your feelings?'

'Oh, yes, please.' Sophie winced. 'I don't think he's too bothered about me anyway. And this won't help, will it?'

'Now, don't be silly.' Louisa hoped her gentle scolding sounded convincing. It seemed that it wasn't just his wife who felt Peter didn't care about his family.

***

Louisa laid a hand on Sophie's arm as they eyed the nursing home from the car park.

'She's got worse, I'm afraid. She may recognise you briefly, she may not. Don't be upset. She just likes the company. Rattles on about all sorts of stuff from the past. But then she gets worn out. Struggles to breathe.'

Sophie nodded. 'Got it. Does Uncle Michael visit Gran much?'

'Not as often as he should. I had a bit of a pop at him about it this week.'

'Ah. And how is he?'

There's no way I'm going to tell you about the loan, thought Louisa.

'The usual. But that's the Michael we know and love.'

Sophie smiled whilst raising her eyebrows. 'So you have a gay brother and a bi-sexual daughter. Interesting family, isn't it?'

Louisa laughed. 'Come on, you, let's get on with it.'

Five minutes later they were all seated together, Louisa watching as Sophie perched on the edge of the bed and tried to interact with her grandmother.

Barbara Bruce-Gardiner was seemingly lost in her own parallel world as she muttered about her childhood home in Norfolk. Something to do with the gardener. And his shed. Louisa looked alarmed and hoped they weren't going to learn anything shocking. She studied her mother. The grey hair was dishevelled, a function of her habit of rubbing her head as she wandered her room, trying to find things from her past that were no longer there. Her blouse was soiled with a few little food spots, presumably acquired at breakfast. It was all such a contrast to the beautifully presented woman she once was, the consummate diplomat's wife.

Louisa breathed deeply and patted her mother's knee, reflecting on the twists and turns that life takes. The roles rotating as one generation fades and the next rises in its place. When she was small, she was in awe of her parents – in truth, she had been a little afraid of her father. His life had been governed by a sense of discipline, service and convention, his wife an apparently willing participant in a rigorous adherence to his rules. Had she really been happy? Hard to tell now. Only in her teens had Louisa started to question how things worked at home, even if she lacked the courage to voice her concerns. By this time, she had unconsciously begun to emulate some of the habits that had served her father well: the ability to organise, the discipline to see things through.

But she knew she wanted a very different marriage from that of her parents, and her love affair with Robert showed that it should be possible. However, the succession of unsatisfactory boyfriends that followed their break-up had dented her confidence. Her subsequent marriage to Peter was the result of much soul-searching, and she still sometimes wondered to what extent her decision was based on a determination to demonstrate to her parents that she was capable of forming a partnership that was nothing like theirs. Funny how things had worked out.

Louisa headed for the bathroom, returning with her mother's hairbrush. The mother becomes the child, she thought, as she gently stroked Barbara's thin, grey hair. She looked at Sophie and wondered whether, at some point, her daughter would be doing the same for her.

Louisa wiped her brow with the back of her hand. 'I'm just going to get the key to the french doors,' she said. 'It gets so warm in here. But we must remember to lock them afterwards and give the key straight back.'

'Quite right.' Sophie nodded at her grandmother. 'We don't want her legging it down the M3.'

Louisa smiled, laid down the brush and headed for the door.

***

Dropping her daughter back at the station had been painful. Louisa shut the front door behind her and stood motionless in the hallway, the silence here all the more apparent because of the buzz, the sense of renewed hopefulness, that had accompanied Sophie's brief, but oh-so-welcome visit. Everything about it had been perfect. The Friday meal washed down with a bit too much wine, the riverside walk on Saturday, and dinner out in Barnes the same evening… it was all wonderful.

And the closeness she'd felt to her daughter. The hugs of understanding, of unconditional love, as Sophie had looked her in the eye and boldly explained her sexuality to her mother. The fact that she felt able to do that only made their bond stronger. In nineteen short years, the child Louisa had carried had morphed into a capable young woman, intelligent, caring and loving. Even her degree course was a practical expression of concern. Marine biology with oceanography. Because the seas *mattered.*

Overcome with love and pride and missing her daughter's lively presence already, Louisa stood in the hallway and cried. She knew that she owed it to herself to resolve her issues with Peter. But now there was an even stronger imperative. She owed it to Sophie, too. Because if she, Louisa, allowed herself to live a lie, to tolerate a rotten marriage, then she would have failed to demonstrate the courage and determination that were already evident in her daughter. And she was not going to let her child down.

Louisa made her way to the kitchen, poured herself a glass of wine and reached for her phone. It went straight to voicemail, so she left a message. She understood and accepted that during the week. But on a Sunday evening? What the hell was Peter up to that prevented him from answering his phone, even if only to say that he would call her back in a minute? She looked at her watch. She was ready to let him know what she had been planning. Bring it on.

# 6

# WIM

Wim winced as he watched Laila hanging upside down from the climbing frame.

'I wish she wouldn't do that. What if she falls?'

Caria smiled. 'It's what playgrounds are for. Don't look if it frightens you.'

He glanced at his watch. 'Anyway, we should be going soon. It's nearly Laila's bedtime.'

'She's fine. They're having fun, enjoying the weather. Just relax.' Caria sat forward on the park bench and peered at his face. 'Are you okay? You seem anxious.'

Wim slid his arm around her, pulling her in. 'Just thinking about the apartment. We need something bigger, we need more room.'

'It's nice enough. One day, maybe. There's no rush.'

'I disagree, we need it now.' He nodded to the girls. 'They are getting bigger, they should have a bedroom each. And you and I need a bit more privacy, our own bathroom – instead of sharing with those two.'

'Patience, my love.'

Wim wagged a finger. 'No, I don't want to wait forever. It's now that we need the extra space. I want to do it. For you.' He nodded towards the play area. 'And for them.'

Caria kissed his cheek. 'If you say so. Come on, then. Let's get them back.'

They wandered over to the girls, and amid protests, the little group set off for the apartment. Laila lagged behind, dragging her feet.

Wim held a hand out to his daughter. 'Laila, don't do that, you'll ruin your shoes.'

'But I'm tired. Papa, will you carry me, please?'

He smiled. 'You're getting too big.'

Laila stood still, her head drooping, shoulders slumped. Her 'sad orphan' act, as Wim called it. She gazed at the ground. The words were softly spoken, the tone pleading.

'Please, Papa?'

'Oh my God, Laila. Okay, for now, I'll carry you. But you're getting too heavy for this.' Wim scooped her up and grunted as he set her on his shoulders.

Laila giggled. 'Yey! Thank you, Papa. Papa, will you read me *Reynard the Fox* when I'm in bed?'

'Not tonight, little one. It's getting late, and you need a shower.'

'But I want to know what the cunning fox does next. He always finds a way to get what he wants.'

'Yes, he does,' said Wim, his thoughts returning to the apartment, to his plans for his little family. 'He certainly does.'

# 7

# LOUISA

It was nearly eight o'clock that Sunday evening before Peter called back. By that time, Louisa had worked herself into a state and was on her third glass of wine. She could tell he was outside – taking a gentle stroll, apparently. After describing her weekend with Sophie, Louisa gave up on learning much about his and explained her thinking.

'Look, Peter, we have to confront the truth. Our marriage is in trouble, and rather than making meaningless promises, we need to actually do something about it. That means living as the man and wife we used to be. And that means living together.'

'But that's not possible, is it? I work here, and you'll be getting another job in the UK.'

'Well, I've been thinking about that, and in future, I want to spend as much of my time as possible in Amsterdam. With you. I could either get a job with a Dutch company, or a UK one that will allow me to do most of my work from home. Or even some freelance stuff.'

Okay, she continued, it was more difficult since Brexit, but neither was it impossible. Peter's Dutch residency status should help. And Michael had agreed to step up his visits to their mother.

Louisa didn't need to see her husband's face to sense the frustration in his response. He tried to separate the two issues. Yes, they needed to sort out their marriage. That would start next weekend with her visit.

But the idea of her working in Amsterdam was ridiculous. Instead of sitting at a desk whilst gazing out of the window of some clichéd canal-side apartment, she needed to focus on replacing *all* her lost income. They had a mortgage to pay off. They needed to set aside lots of money to fund their old age. And it wouldn't work if she went 'off the rails' like this.

Louisa screwed her eyes shut and took a deep breath. How patronising could he get?

'Don't you dare accuse me of going off the bloody rails! I'm here all alone, every evening, every night, other than on your occasional visits home. It's not what I signed up for, and it has to stop. So, either we go with my plan or you find a job back here. Because if we can't *live* as husband and wife, then we can't *stay* as husband and wife.'

She heard Peter sigh. 'You're doing it again. You've clearly forgotten, but we've had this conversation before. There's no way I'd be able to get a similar role back in the UK.'

'I don't see the problem. You could take a drop in salary and still be better off. By the time you've paid for the apartment and travel, what's left isn't brilliant, now is it?'

There was no mistaking the shift in Peter's tone. The resignation had given way to hostility.

'Oh, Christ, so that's it! Here we go again. Demean my efforts, why don't you? Do you know how much that hurts?'

'Don't change the subject! And I've never demeaned your efforts.' She hadn't wanted to go this far, not straight away, but it looked as if she had no choice in the matter. 'Peter, you're my husband. Naturally, I want us to be together. Either this becomes a proper full-time relationship, or we need to go our separate ways.'

There was a stunned silence at the other end of the line. When he spoke again, he'd dialled back the anger and appeared to be attempting to sound reasonable.

'Look, you've had a shock. I get that. But you're blowing things out of proportion. We can sort this out when you come over. Loads of people struggle with a long-term relationship. We're no different.'

'Peter, I've explained my position. Either we work together on this, or it's over.'

'Okay. Let's call a truce and pick it up next weekend. And Michael… You said he could step up and help out more with Barbara. And so he should, but I hope you haven't told him about our problems? You know what he's like, gossiping away like some old busybody.'

'No, of course not. But if I am going to spend more time with you over there, I need him to visit Mum much more. Otherwise it would be very difficult for me.'

There was a pause before he spoke. 'Yes, I get that.'

'Right then. I'm going now. I don't know how we've grown apart the way we have, but it hurts me. It hurts me very much. Peter, I want to say I love you. I used to say it often, and you would say it back to me. One day, quite soon, we are going to say it again and mean it. Because the alternative is too horrible to contemplate. At least, it is for me. Think about that, won't you?'

# 8

Five days was more than enough time to prepare for a weekend visit to Amsterdam, make the travel arrangements and collect together what she would need. The hard part was working out how to get through to Peter. How to make sure that he was as committed as she was to reviving their marriage.

Louisa fired up her computer and started Googling: *How to save your marriage.* Here we go. It was clear from the outset that the opening results were sponsored:

*Invest now in our ten-week loving relationship program.*
*Save your marriage in six steps.*
*Sign up for our Partners for Life course today.*

Hmm. All of them promised amazing results. All of them required you to have your credit card handy.

The other, non-commercial links all suggested different ways to approach the problem. There were, however, a few common themes. You both had to *want* to save the relationship. Fair enough. You (yes, *you,* Louisa) needed to recognise that however wonderful you thought you were, your spouse evidently had some issues with you. Oh, and you had to talk to each other. No shit.

Louisa gazed up at the corner of the room. She wondered

what Peter would say about her, if he were speaking honestly? She could ask him, of course, but suppose he wasn't prepared to come clean? What did she do that turned him off her? What wasn't she doing that he wanted from her?

By lunchtime, she felt she was making some headway. At least she knew the things she wanted to raise with him, the issues she needed to explore. If he could be as candid, maybe there was still hope for them.

***

It was always the same with airports, you had to walk bloody miles. Correction – kilometres. Schiphol was no different, even if it seemed more modern and less tired-looking than Heathrow. The wheels on her bag buzzed along behind her on the metal slats of the moving walkway. Business people charged past on their way back to their loved ones. Out of my way, I'm nearly home! A typical Friday evening.

It had been some years since she had last undertaken this journey. Maybe it would become commonplace in the months ahead. As she stepped into the arrivals hall, it felt like everything depended on how the next two days went. This was ridiculous.

There he was. Must be optimistic, so a big smile from her. A raising of the eyebrows from Peter, a nod of the head. Yes, he too was smiling. Thank God for that. She looked down at his hands and felt a fleeting wave of disappointment. Stupid really, but as she had gazed through the aeroplane window at the huge wind turbines in the North Sea, she had briefly dared to wonder if her husband might greet her with some flowers. Nothing fancy, just a little bunch would have sent a signal. An important signal. She scolded herself: don't be silly, you know he's not that sort of man.

They stood, face to face, he seemingly unsure of what sort

of kiss she was expecting. Louisa had given this one some thought. She stopped right in front of him and leaned in, chin forward, lips slightly parted. She looked directly at his mouth. He understood.

The softest of touches, but held for a second. The hint of a peace overture from both sides. Each of them took a step back.

'Shall we go?' she asked.

They boarded a train beneath the airport. Peter stowed her wheelie case and sat down next to her.

'It's about fifteen minutes to the station. The one I use for the office. Bijlmer Arena. From there we get the metro to Amstelstation. Five stops, then a short walk to the apartment.'

'It's been so long, I don't even remember how to get there.'

'Sure. But it is a different place from when you were last here.'

Louisa stared blankly at him. 'What do you mean? I didn't know you had moved. You never told me.'

'I'm sure I did. You know what you're like.'

'I don't think so. And, Peter, I should *know* where you stay in Amsterdam. I should have your address, for goodness' sake.'

He smiled. 'No problem, we can soon fix that.'

Louisa turned away, staring out of the window. Why on earth would he move apartments and not even tell her?

***

Thirty minutes later, they were halfway up an external concrete stairway. As he fumbled for the keys to the first-floor apartment, Louisa looked over her shoulder, up and down the drab street. In every direction, there were characterless three-storey buildings built out of pale grey brick. Flat roofs. Not exactly the gabled canal-side houses of Amsterdam that the tourist images conjured up. It would be a bit depressing to spend all day here. Never mind.

The inside was rather better. To the left of the entrance door, there was a tiny kitchen area. Louisa glanced at the toy-sized sink, the two-ring hob. You'd struggle to prepare a Christmas dinner with that, she thought. To the right, the living area was home to a modest table with four dining chairs, alongside a slim wall unit that housed a TV. Facing it was a sofa, and wedged into the corner was an easy chair with wooden arms. Hardly luxurious, but functional and comfortable enough. Useless for a family, reasoned Louisa, but perfect for someone on their own in the city. Someone like Peter. To one side of the wall unit, a cramped lobby gave way to two doors.

She pushed open the first and peeped into the bathroom. Basic, but bright and clean. It reminded her of one of those inexpensive chain hotels.

The second door was wide open. Louisa felt like an intruder as she stared at the neatly turned-back double bed. The one where her husband spent most of his nights. But not with his wife. She scolded herself as her eyes instinctively fell on the pillows, as if looking for evidence of more than one occupant. But she had a plan. Tonight, in this room, she would try and rekindle some of what they used to have.

'What do you think?' He put her case on the single chair.

'It's fine for one, I'm sure. The area is a bit tedious though.'

'It is. But it's convenient for the office, and you can be in the old centre in twenty minutes if you want.'

'Peter, are you happy here? It's just that the place is so sterile, there's nothing to connect it with you.' She held up her hand. 'But I have something that might help to remedy that.'

He raised his eyebrows. 'You've brought something for me?'

'Yes. A few things. Let's see, shall we?'

She opened her case and produced a framed photograph of them, taken a few summers ago on a trip to Wimbledon. Semi-finals day, corporate entertainment at its best. She was wearing a floaty dress and Peter looked tanned and relaxed for once, sporting a lightweight linen suit and open-neck shirt. Very summery. She nodded at the empty bedside unit. 'You don't have to, of course, but I thought it might be nice.'

'It's perfect, thank you.' He glanced at the photo before setting it down where Louisa had intended.

'And this is for you as well.'

Peter carefully eased the tissue wrapping off, as if he were going to save it for something else. He held up a colourful shirt, the sort of classy but casual wear that Louisa occasionally bought him for holidays, in the hope it might encourage him to loosen up a bit. He smiled.

'Wicked. Thank you. I have no idea what it cost, and nor do I want to know.'

'I also have something else you might like, but this is for tonight, okay?' She held up a little cami top in dark burgundy silk, then some matching shorts. Raising them to shoulder height, she turned her head slightly and arched one eyebrow at him. 'Well?'

Peter blinked repeatedly. 'Super… very nice. Right!'

Louisa thought his response awkward. She wondered if she might be building up the weekend too much, setting lofty expectations and embarrassing him with her careful preparations.

Confirmation that this might be the case followed. Peter's face wore a pained expression.

'I don't have anything for you, I'm afraid. But I do plan on treating you to a decent dinner.'

'Thank you. We're going to have a nice evening together, and then tomorrow we can stroll around Amsterdam and have a good talk. Okay?'

***

'Will you zip me up, please?'

He moved behind her. She waited in vain for a comment about the dress.

'It's new. Apparently, the colour is called vetiver. Do you like it?'

'I do. A sort of greeny-brown. Reminds me of lentils. Nice fit. But the shirt and everything else – let's just make sure we go easy on the spending until you get sorted out.'

She turned to face him. 'Not tonight, okay? Tonight we enjoy ourselves.'

Peter shrugged.

She beamed. 'Now, time for that restaurant.'

It had taken about ten minutes to get there on foot, Louisa walking carefully in her heels. The restaurant itself was just right, not too casual, but neither was it stuffy. They talked about all sorts of things over dinner, avoiding anything controversial. Such as her job. Their marriage.

She drank a couple of glasses of white wine, Peter's intake of red was modest. Louisa wondered if he was avoiding drinking too much, in order not to disappoint back at the apartment.

Once there, she poured them glasses of water and carried them into the bedroom.

She leaned her head forward and pushed her hair up for him. She could feel his hands at work. She eased the dress down, stepped out of it and reached for a hanger from the wardrobe, thinking how bare it was. Maybe she should take him shopping for some new clothes. He was unlikely to do it on his own. As he undid his shirt, Louisa smiled and retrieved her lingerie from the case.

'Give me a minute.' She headed for the bathroom.

On her return, Peter was lying in bed, messing with his phone.

Louisa paused in the doorway, hands on hips. 'Ta-dah.'

She was hoping for a bit more than raised eyebrows and a knowing nod, but at least he put his phone down. She made her way over to the bed without comment, determined not to spoil the moment. Tonight would be special, different. She would surprise him, and rekindle some of the adventurous spontaneity that had characterised the earlier years of their marriage. It would be a marker, a statement of intent, of willingness and desire to breathe new life into an important part of their marriage. And, hopefully, he would appreciate her efforts and start to demonstrate some enthusiasm for the changes that lay ahead.

***

A little later, they were both lying on their backs, staring up at the ceiling, a faint smile playing on Louisa's lips. She turned to Peter and snuggled into him.

'Enjoy it?' she said. 'You naughty man.'

'Mmm,' came the reply. 'Oh, yes.'

With that, he lifted her arm off his chest, pulled away from her and padded off to the bathroom. On his return shortly afterwards, Louisa pushed herself up from the bed.

'My turn. Won't be long.'

She collected her discarded shorts from the floor and stepped across the little lobby. She emerged a couple of minutes later, naked, hoping for a cuddle to round off their lovemaking. Peter was lying with his back turned to her, clad in his briefs. The lamp on his side of the bed had been switched off.

Louisa felt like a balloon that had just been pricked. She got into bed next to him, staring down at his motionless form. She willed him to roll over; she wanted to be held, to feel the tenderness that was supposed to accompany sex between loving couples. She wondered whether to whisper to him, or perhaps spoon up against him, feel his body against hers. He didn't move.

Frustrated, she went over to her case and found her nightdress. She got back into bed, reached for the lamp and flopped back, blinking into the darkness. Had they just made love? Or had they merely had sex? Peter had clearly enjoyed it, been a keen participant. And there was no doubt that he was pleasantly surprised by his wife's willingness to push the boundaries in the pursuit of pleasure.

But was his enjoyment based purely on the form and feel of the flesh before him, with no emotional attachment to the woman within? There had certainly been lust, sexual gratification… but love?

Or perhaps he was doing it because it was expected of him? A duty. And it was easier for him to go along with it, rather than confront the truth. That she no longer interested him.

Louisa lay awake for a long time, thinking. Her only conclusion before she eventually drifted off to sleep was that it was too soon to give up.

# 9

# PETER

Peter awoke early. He could hear Louisa's rhythmic breathing on the pillow next to him. He didn't look over at her, preferring that she continue to sleep whilst he did some thinking.

Thus far, everything seemed to have gone broadly to plan, even if he needed to work harder on reassuring his wife, winning her over. And to do that, he had to set aside his resentment at her interference in the life he had made for himself here.

He carefully reached for his watch. Give it an hour, and he would bring her coffee in bed. That should get the day off to a good start.

***

'Wakey-wakey.'

Peter stood by the side of the bed, a mug in each hand. He put one down next to Louisa. He watched her roll onto her back, rub her eyes and shuffle up in bed, a faint look of surprise evident on her face.

'Mmm. That's a rare treat,' she said.

'I think you deserve it after last night.'

She raised her eyebrows. 'I'll bear that in mind.'

Peter gave a sheepish grin. 'I must have been knackered though, I think I went straight to sleep.'

Louisa reached for her coffee. 'You did, but no matter.'

'Sorry about that.' He sat on the bed next to her. 'Anyway, what about today? Your call, but I have some ideas if you'd like to hear them?'

'Okay, tell me.'

'Over breakfast. There's a nice little café that I've heard about. It's quite famous. We can walk it in fifteen minutes.'

# 10

# LOUISA

Louisa stood under the shower and reflected on the evening before. As she had lain in bed, Peter snoring softly by her side, the doubts had continued to gnaw away at her. No welcome flowers, either at the airport or in the apartment. No little gift or token to show he had thought about her, that he was eagerly awaiting her visit. He hadn't reached for her hand on the way back to the apartment. Neither had he made any attempt to hold her close after their bout of lovemaking – or sex, rather.

But this morning, so far at least, he had been warm and conciliatory. There was the prospect of a leisurely breakfast, over which he was going to suggest some things they might do together. Perhaps he had just been tired last night, maybe she was being oversensitive. Well, she'd see how the day went. Because whatever else was going to happen, at some point she would sit him down and gently but firmly explain the two conditions that must be met if their marriage were to continue.

***

The café was unpretentious. Casual, but with a distinct Amsterdam vibe. It was quiet at this time on a Saturday morning, and Louisa's eyes switched between the menu and Peter's face as he explained the offerings to her.

A lethargic young man came over to take their order, Peter joking with him in Dutch and receiving a rueful smile in return.

Louisa cocked her head and leaned forward as the waiter retreated.

'What was all that about?'

Peter grinned. 'I told him he looked like he might have had a heavy night, partying.'

'That's exactly what I thought. And had he?'

'Yup. Another crazy young Dutchman.'

Louisa nodded in appreciation. 'It's a fun city. And your Dutch is very good. Well done you.'

Peter gave a modest shrug. 'If you want things to work out for you here, you must learn the language. It's important. Otherwise you're just another expat passing through.'

He gazed out of the window, Louisa watching him, thinking how invested he was in his Amsterdam life. She too, would need to make a big effort if she was going to share it with him.

Breakfast over, they headed towards the Albert Cuyp Market, where they mingled with the crowds – an eclectic mix of locals and tourists. They wandered amongst the many stalls that sold everything from food, clothing and housewares to the inevitable tourist gifts. Louisa stopped to inspect a tiny pair of ceramic Dutch clogs mounted on an orange ribbon.

She smiled at Peter. 'Aren't these cute?'

He winked and reached for his wallet. 'They are yours.'

'Thank you, Peter.' She kissed his cheek and watched him hand a ten-euro note to the vendor. More smiles and chat in Dutch. The clogs were passed to her in a small paper bag. She hooked her arm through his as they walked on.

'You like it here, don't you?'

'Sure. It's a great place. It works for me.'

Me. It works for *me*. Louisa said nothing, waiting and hoping that he was going to open up about her coming to live there, too. She was desperate for him to say that was what he wanted – for her to be with him in this wonderful city. Because everything she had heard so far suggested the opposite.

She bit her lip and changed the subject. For now, anyway.

'So what's next, tour guide?'

Peter nodded ahead of him. 'De Negen Straatjes. It's a little enclave of quaint and authentic Amsterdam streets. Perfect for just wandering around, soaking up the atmosphere. And the obligatory canal tour after lunch. You just have to do that.'

They set off. The opportunity for Louisa to explain her conditions for them remaining together came as they sat outside a café, enjoying the sun, cold beers in front of them. Her gaze kept shifting between the glass she was pointlessly rotating on the table and Peter's blank face.

The first imperative was clear enough. They had to spend the bulk of their time in the same place. And that meant either she must live in Amsterdam, or he back in the UK. Yes, one or the other could flit backwards and forwards as necessary, but most of the time they would be together.

The second was also straightforward. To explain, anyway. He had to be sure he loved her, that he *wanted* them to be a close and loving couple, more intimate and more fun. They would each need to prioritise pleasing the other. Because, as Louisa patiently explained to her husband, simply being together wasn't enough. Without love, it was pointless.

Peter sighed. 'Let's deal with your second point first. Of course I love you. I know I'm not some sloppy romantic, but you are blowing the issue out of proportion. Yes, I will try harder, and yes, I can do more. But you banging on about it all the time just makes it worse.'

'Peter, we've been here before. I am not blowing it out of proportion. I don't see any *evidence* of your love. The little signs that show you are thinking of me.'

'Christ, you've been on the bloody internet, haven't you? Some sodding agony aunt's idea of what a perfect marriage should look like. So, I'm sorry you think I'm ignoring you. And now, if I do perform some little... some little act of kindness, you're going to think I'm only doing it to please you. That I don't mean it. I can't win, can I?'

Louisa shook her head and looked away, staring at the ridiculous number of bikes chained to the adjacent railings. It was quiet for a couple of minutes before she turned back to him.

'Will you try? If I promise to stop going on about it, will you show me your love? Prove to me I'm wrong?'

Louisa could hear the resignation in his voice. 'Yes.' Why did he always give the impression she was forcing his hand? But perhaps he could be more whole-hearted on the other point. Physically being together. In the same place.

'Peter, it's been like this for nearly ten years now. I hardly see you. While everyone else seems to be working more and more from home, you're doing precisely the opposite. We need to be together. I could come to Amsterdam, or you could spend more time in the UK.'

She hated the way that trying to sort out the problems with their marriage made her out to be the one who was always criticising, finding fault with their situation. But surely it was better to be like that, than to remain seemingly indifferent to whether they were together or not. She raised her hands in frustration. 'I don't much care which it is, but it must be one or the other.'

'But you need to work. To replace the lost income. You can't do that here.'

'Well, of course I can. I've looked into it.'

'Yes, but not for the big bucks you were on before they kicked you out.'

*Kicked you out?* Hardly a ringing demonstration of support. Louisa breathed in deeply, forcing herself to ignore his caustic remark.

'I can still earn enough. We're hardly short. And while we've never relied on it, you know that when my mum passes, there's a big legacy there. It will make a massive difference to us in our old age.'

Peter grunted. 'But your flaky brother will get half of that, won't he? Though God knows what he'll do with it. I expect most of it will go up his nose.'

Louisa shook her head. 'Peter, please don't. Michael may be flaky, as you put it, but he's still my brother. And he's not a drug addict.'

'You sure about that? And what about Barbara? She's used to seeing you twice a week. You can't abandon her.'

'Thank you for your newfound concern for my mother. But as I explained on the phone, Michael has agreed to step up and visit more often.'

'Your ever-reliable brother? Good luck with that.'

They sat silently, sipping at their beers, watching the world go by.

'And what about Sophie?' said Peter.

'She'll be fine. We had a chat about it last weekend, when she came to stay. She doesn't come home that often and starts her summer job on Monday. We can work around her. And if I come to Amsterdam, she can visit us here. She'd love that.'

Louisa took another deep breath. 'And on the subject of Sophie, you need to talk with her more. Call her sometimes, just to have a chat. She's changing, Peter, working out who she is. You might be surprised.'

A frown. 'What do you mean?'

Louisa held her breath for a second. 'She has a girlfriend.'

'I'm sure she has.'

'No, I mean a *girlfriend.*'

Peter stared at her, his jaw slack. A shake of the head. 'She's a lesbian?'

'She said she thinks she's bisexual.'

Peter slumped back, exhaling deeply. 'Jesus, your lot.'

Louisa was about to remonstrate with him: *Yours too, Peter*. She bit her lip and was rescued by a buzz from her phone. She studied the message.

Peter raised his eyebrows. 'Everything all right?'

'Michael. He wants to buy me dinner when I get back.' She blinked repeatedly, knowing her next words would invite derision. 'Says he has an idea.'

'Oh, Christ. That's all we need. Your brother with an idea. When? Where?'

'Thursday. That Spanish restaurant in Clapham. The one we all went to over Easter.'

'Just make sure he pays his way. Bloody sponger, your brother.'

Louisa shook her head. She didn't say anything, reflecting on the money she had loaned Michael ten days ago. Twelve thousand pounds. She hoped everything was okay. Peter would never forgive her if he found out.

'Anyway, back to us. Aside from me coming to Amsterdam, have you thought about working from home more?'

He shrugged. 'It's possible, I guess, if not ideal. I would need to talk to my boss.'

Louisa put on a pleading look. 'Would you do that, please? Let's investigate all the options. Then we can go with the one that works best. For both of us.'

***

That evening, they took the Metro into the centre and dined at an Italian restaurant. As on the previous night, it was unpretentious, but the food was good. And once more Louisa found herself the instigator of most of their chat. But there was something she wanted to ask him, something that had been playing on her mind.

She cleared her throat, studying her husband's face intently as he forked spaghetti carbonara into his mouth.

'Peter, can we go and see the red-light district, please? I understand it's quite safe – very touristy, in fact. I'd like to visit it whilst I'm here.'

He put down his fork.

'Really? I don't see the attraction, to be honest. Gangs of blokes, stag nights, that sort of thing. All rather seedy.'

'But I read about it when I was investigating things to do in Amsterdam. Apparently it's very well policed, and it seems silly not to take a look now that we're here. Unless of course you're tired of it? I'm sure you will have taken some of your business contacts there.'

'Ha-ha.'

She watched his face carefully. 'So? Can we, please?'

He gave in without much of a struggle, and a little later they were weaving through crowded and noisy streets. Fascinated, Louisa peered around her, without trying to make it look obvious. Peter made no attempt to take her hand, so she took his, as if to deny any of the women in the windows the notion that he was there as a potential customer. *He's mine.* Well, I think he is, anyway.

Peter had been right about the gangs of men, some not so young, even if they appeared to be generally well-behaved. As her internet site had suggested, it was clear that many of the visitors were, just like her, curious tourists. The working women avoided making eye contact with the gawping couples, but several times Louisa saw one of them beckoning subtly towards an unattached man. Suddenly, she froze and gripped Peter's hand, hissing in his ear.

'Look, that man's going in. There!'

'Don't stare, for God's sake. It's not polite.'

'Well, excuse me.' She hesitated before turning to face him. 'How much is it? How long do you get?'

The laugh was abrupt, cynical. 'Trying to catch me out, are you?' He studied her face; she looked back at him expectantly.

'I *understand* that it's typically around a hundred euros. That's for about twenty minutes.'

'Gosh, it's not long, is it? And is there a choice of... activities?' Her eyes were wide.

Peter's face was expressionless. 'Apparently, they are very small rooms. Rather bare. A plastic-covered bed. Like in a doctor's surgery. The woman will pretty much do what you want. Show you her genitals, let you fiddle with her. Then suck you off, or you can fuck her over the side of the bed. Or a bit of both, I guess.' He scanned her face. 'Have I shocked you? Is your curiosity satisfied?'

Louisa stared back at him. No hint of a blush. She was deadpan.

'That's pretty much what I thought. What I read on the internet. Thank you for showing it to me.'

She smiled, her eyes scanning his face. Yes, she had wanted to see the red-light district, and why not? It's what tourists do in Amsterdam – well, some of them anyway. But she had also wanted to see Peter's reaction, both to her suggestion that they visit it, and the place itself. Was he familiar with it? Did he know his way around more than a casual visitor might? The red-light district was a distinctive feature of Amsterdam, and her husband, it seemed, was a big fan of the city's liberal and easy-going lifestyle.

She decided she wouldn't quiz him on it any further. The mood between them today had been more relaxed, so why spoil things? Tomorrow they'd planned a walk and a late brunch before she took her afternoon flight back to London.

Their weekend together had got off to a rocky start, it was true, but Louisa felt she had cleared the air between them. Peter could now be in no doubt that she wanted to be with him, sharing his daily life. And with Asha's introduction, she was hopeful she could find work here for herself.

***

Louisa stared once again at the incredible number of offshore wind turbines as the plane gathered height out of Amsterdam. A flurry of activity to try and save the planet from the worst of global warming. She wondered if Sophie would ever have children, or whether she would baulk at the idea, her fear for the earth proved all too true. It was understandable that any responsible young person would think twice before bringing another soul into the world.

Louisa often regretted never having more children. But Sophie's birth had been via a caesarean, and the uncontrolled bleeding that followed had resulted in an emergency hysterectomy. The choice denied her.

The turbines disappeared beneath the clouds, and Louisa's thoughts turned back to the weekend now drawing to a close.

She was pleased on two counts. There could be no confusion in Peter's mind about her two demands. A normal, loving marriage, and for them to spend most of their time together. Or she would end it. There was no ambiguity, no hesitation. He knew the score.

In addition, her brief but enjoyable brush with Amsterdam had left her feeling excited about the opportunity to base herself there. Whether on the payroll of a local employer, or working remotely for a UK entity. She was up for it.

So, those were the positives. But it hadn't all been a bed of roses. Try as she might, she saw no evidence that Peter's attitude towards her had been changed by their weekend together. He didn't suddenly wake up, realise what a miserable boor he had become and, amid floods of tears, commit himself to returning their marriage to the sunny uplands where it had once contentedly basked.

And he still seemed convinced that Louisa should stay in London, where once again she would command a big salary. She, however, was very comfortable with the state of their finances, and the idea of earning less to enjoy a better quality of life with her husband seemed perfectly okay to her. And there was always the possibility of downsizing at home. It was a large house and with its four bedrooms and three bathrooms could easily accommodate a sizeable family. She toyed with the idea of getting a valuation.

The Amsterdam apartment was the biggest disappointment. After the spacious house in Barnes, she recoiled from the idea of spending her days in its dull, cramped confines. She struggled to understand how Peter could cope with endless evenings on his own in such a characterless place.

No, if she was going to spend the bulk of her time in Amsterdam with him, they would need to find something much more appealing. So, irrespective of her husband's reservations, she would start familiarising herself with what was available. Louisa liked to have a mission. That would be her next one.

# 11

# WIM

Wim had decided that a treat was in order for his family. He mounted the steep steps to the apartment and let himself in, just managing to lower his backpack to the floor before Laila launched herself at him.

'Papa, Papa!'

'Uurgh!' He winced as the little girl slammed into his thigh, throwing her arms around him. She was followed by the calmer and older Sibel, who as usual enveloped his waist, carefully and gently, as if he were made of some fragile material that could snap at any time. The girls were so different. He looked up and smiled at their mother.

Caria slowly blinked her eyes at him, keeping her arms folded, well used to waiting her turn in the flurry of greetings. The initial rush of childish chatter over, she exchanged kisses and hugs with her man.

'How was it?'

'Ah, the usual. Nothing has changed.'

'You're very kind, you know. A good man.'

Wim gave a weak smile. 'It's my duty, that's all.'

'Still. Others might not be so caring,' said Caria.

Wim shrugged. 'It is what it is. Look, let me get changed

and then I'm taking us all out to dinner, so have a think about where you would like to eat.'

***

Later that evening, Wim lay back on Laila's bed as she shuffled herself up between his outstretched arm and his chest. He turned to face his daughter.

'Did Mama read to you whilst I was away?'

'No, Papa, I waited for you.' She turned the square book over and inspected the cover. 'Only *you* can read me *Reynard the Fox.*' She studied her father's face. 'It's special, for me and you.'

'Okay, but you and Mama could have a special book as well, you know.'

'Mmm.' Laila appeared to give this point some thought, before returning to *Reynard* and opening the pages to where her bookmark lay.

Wim eyed the text, then her. 'So where are we?'

Laila jabbed a finger. 'Here.'

'Yes, I see that. But what had happened the last time we read the book?'

Laila shuffled in irritation, as if dealing with an inconvenience. She looked away, her face creased with concentration. 'Um, er… ah, I know! Reynard was teaching Greedymind to fish. But he was mean to her, and tried to kill her.'

'Hmm. He is a very cunning fox, that one.'

'Yes, but he shouldn't kill the other animals, should he, Papa?'

***

Wim looked over his shoulder, running hard but appearing to make no progress. Behind him, the animals were gaining ground. He could hear them shouting and screaming after him.

'Liar! Cheat! You deceiver! Greedymind the she-wolf has told us everything.'

At the front of the pack was Greedymind herself, teeth bared. 'Stop him,' she was crying, 'he tried to kill me!' They were on him now, and he felt himself pulled to the ground as fists and clubs rained down on him. Someone had his elbow and wouldn't let go. He tried to push them off.

'Wim, Wim, it's okay… Shush, it's okay. Quiet now, you'll wake the girls.'

Caria's hand was on his arm, shaking it. He sat up, gripping her wrist.

'Wim,' she hissed, 'let go, my love, you're hurting me.'

He froze for a moment before looking all around him and then collapsing back onto the damp pillow.

'Uurgh. My God.' He turned his head to her. 'Are you okay?'

'Better than you, I think. Let me get you some water. What were you dreaming about?'

'I was…' He stopped speaking, having thought better of it. 'Nothing really, just some nonsense.'

***

In the morning, he awoke with a start and lay there, recalling his dream. It seemed so real. He flopped an arm onto the pillow above his head. It still felt damp, whilst the sheet over him was crumpled and smelled of sweat.

He swallowed, playing over the scenes that had unfolded so horribly during the night. Might there be some meaning in them? Gradually, the violent images were replaced with thoughts of his predicament. His eyes moved restlessly but without seeing, for his mind was elsewhere. Now it was racing, ideas coming to the fore, presenting themselves to him, jostling for position. Perhaps his dilemma could be turned to his advantage. Yes, why not? The corners of his mouth began to twitch as a new and better plan formed in his mind. A bold plan, a plan of consequence. A *cunning* plan.

Concentrating, he played through all that he must do. Then he focused on how it could be brought about. Satisfied, he closed his eyes. And over there – yes, now he could see Reynard watching him. The handsome fox was standing on his hind legs, the bronze-coloured fur concealed beneath a long, dark tailcoat. He held his front paws crossed in front of him. There was a faint smile upon his vulpine face, and he was nodding his head in approval.

# 12

# LOUISA

'Hi, babe, it's your big sis calling to check up on you.'

Louisa grinned. 'Morning, Asha, and how are you?'

'Well, I'm fine, my darling, just fine. And how was your weekend? Non-stop fun and lovin', I'm hoping?'

'I'm not sure I would go that far, but it was very informative and I can see why Peter likes it there. If you're up for lunch sometime this week, I can tell you all about it.'

Arrangements made, they rang off. Louisa would drive over to Brentford tomorrow, pick up Asha and take them over to the garden centre café at Syon Park.

***

With the Monday chores behind her, Louisa made herself a coffee, sat down at her laptop and started Googling.

Her first inclination was to try and get a sense of the areas in Amsterdam where she and Peter might want to look for a place together. No point in finding a fab apartment, only to discover the location didn't work. She knew where Peter's office was – he took the metro to Bijlmer Arena, but the area was out of the city and looked to her to be entirely commercial. The Google street view confirmed it. Wide roads arranged in a grid and lined with modern office buildings. She even found Peter's.

After studying various online maps of the metro and the city, the conclusion was clear. Either they should look down the eastern side of the central area, or Peter's journey to work would become more complicated.

An hour later, Louisa pored over some print-outs and highlighted areas where she could start a search. Then back to the computer. There was a huge choice of apartments, but her eyes widened as she looked at the rents being asked. She had no idea how much more they would have to pay compared to Peter's current place, so Googled that address in the hope that the internet would throw up the price at which it was being offered when he took it on. A useful point of reference.

She quickly found the apartment and clicked through the pictures. She rather enjoyed the voyeuristic tour, the corners of her mouth twitching at the sight of the bed.

Now for the details. The apartment could be rented for anything from seven days. The price quoted was indicative, the actual cost would depend on how long it was let for.

She input some dates to try and firm up on the price; apparently it was available from next week. Clearly there was an error on the site, in addition to which the rent seemed very high. Presumably, that was for a very short let, Louisa couldn't imagine Peter paying *that*. However the error had come about, she wasn't about to learn the price for a longer-term tenancy. Frustrated, she resumed her search. She found plenty that would be of interest, and hoped that, like Peter's apartment, the photos were an accurate representation of the interiors.

The possibilities were all written down in her notebook. She had reached the last page of it and glanced over to the bookshelf. A brand new and unused one sat there, awaiting its turn. Next to it were sixty-seven full ones, lined up in a row. Black & Red, A5. The design had hardly changed, although she had transitioned from hardbacks to softbacks with an elastic strap. All her notes since she had started her search for her first trainee position in accountancy, so many years ago. She made a point of never commenting on people in those books. It was a bit like social media. Don't post anything that you would have a problem with, ten or twenty years from now.

She smiled as she tried to identify the only one that contained material that might be faintly embarrassing. She imagined a much older Sophie leafing through her late mother's notebooks, wondering what to do with them. Her eyes would widen as she read the numbered list of favourite positions, gleefully compiled in bed before Sophie was even born. Kids never believed their parents had sex, let alone enjoyed it.

After another hour her brain was scrambled, and she took a break. She leaned against the island in the kitchen and, sipping a cup of tea, looked out on the garden. Whatever they ended up with, she would make sure it felt like their place. Their home away from home. She had been surprised by how sterile Peter's apartment was. More like a hotel, really. So transient-seeming. Her mind returned to that listing on the website, a sense of unease overcoming her. Less than a minute later she was back in the sitting room, gazing at the web page. Two minutes after that, she was talking to a woman who laughed when Louisa politely asked if she could speak English.

'Certainly, *mevrouw*. I could not otherwise do my job.'

Louisa explained her interest in a certain apartment that she had come across on the website. The woman took the details and gave her a brief description. Louisa made no mention of the fact that she had spent Friday and Saturday night there with her husband.

'So, it says it's available from June the twenty-third. Is that correct?'

The woman's accent was typical of the people Louisa had encountered these past few days: slow and unhurried with a marked sibilance on the letter 's'.

'Yesh, that's correct. It's intended for short lettings, so it's fully serviced. Cleaning, all facilities included, a weekly change of bed sheets, towels and so on.'

'Ah, I see,' Louisa lied. She didn't see at all. She needed certainty, but neither did she want to antagonise this woman. She knew that Dutch people could be very direct.

'I am sorry, but would you mind just checking? I would like to be sure that it is available as you said, and whether it could be let for a longer period. Say one year?' She could sense the letting agent's frustration.

'Hold the line.'

Louisa took a deep breath, staring out at the holly tree.

'Hello?'

'Yes, I'm here.'

'I have the file in front of me, *mevrouw*. As I said, the current arrangement ends on June the twenty-third. It's empty after that. For how long would you be interested in renting it?'

Moments later, a frowning Louisa put her phone down. So where would Peter be living from now on? He had made no mention of an imminent change of apartment, and neither had he told her that he had moved from his previous place. It made no sense. But more importantly, why the hell would he keep this sort of stuff from her?

# 13

The garden centre café was busy, and they were lucky to get a table. Louisa studied her friend as Asha chatted to the waitress. The braids were still very much in evidence, a few beads contrasting with the dark hair that waved past high cheekbones and down over her shoulders.

Asha smiled after the young woman. She was always smiling. Perpetually cheerful, constantly looking for the best in people, whatever the situation. She turned back to Louisa.

'Nice girl. Now, I know we don't want to talk shop, but just to let you know: we should have a draft compromise agreement later this week. You'll need to put it in front of your lawyer.'

'Okay, thank you. And how are things back at the office? You seemed a bit depressed with it all when you came round for dinner.'

'No better, it's not going to change. And with you gone, I'm not sure I want to stay. I think I might start looking around too.'

'For what sort of thing?'

'Well, HR of course.' Asha smiled broadly. 'It's what I know. But I want to be with a company that puts people at the heart of what it does.'

'Rather than kicking them out if they refuse to knuckle under to bullies?'

Asha grimaced. 'You got it, babe. Anyway, let's talk about you. How's the grand plan to fix your marriage and find work in Amsterdam?' The look she gave Louisa was suggestive. 'And how was the romantic weekend?'

Louisa held her breath for a moment, her chin high, the eyes gazing off to one side rather than meeting her friend's. 'The weekend was… interesting, I would say.'

Asha gave one of her big laughs. 'I'm intrigued. Tell me all.'

Louisa gave her the whole story. She started with an account of the practical stuff. What they did, where they went. The comfortable but tiny apartment, the uninspiring street on which it was located.

And then she went on to describe the talks they had had. Her conditions for them staying together. Peter's apparent agreement that he needed to change, to try harder, but with little evidence that he was yet doing so. Their discussions about either Peter working more from home, or she from Amsterdam. His lukewarm reception of her proposal that she should move there and join him.

Louisa talked about her investigations into an apartment that might suit them both, and then the discovery that had kept her awake for much of last night. She leaned closer to Asha as she related the discussion with the woman from the letting agency. The revelation that Peter's apartment was on a short let. He hadn't told her that he had recently moved in, and neither had he told her that he would shortly move out.

Asha's shrug of the shoulders was not unexpected, her reaction unconcerned.

'Maybe it's just a mix-up, babe. Someone must have their facts wrong. Ask him.'

'Hmm. As obvious as it sounds, I'm not going to do that.'

'Why on earth not?'

'Because…' Louisa hesitated. 'I feel awful for this, and it

may say more about my marriage than anything else, but I want to wait and see what he tells me.' She forced a smile. 'If he's still in the same flat after June the twenty-third, I'll know it was a mix-up on the part of the agency. No problem.'

'Sure. Mystery solved.'

'But if he tells me in the meantime that he's moving out, then I'll find that very strange. I don't even know when he moved in, and why take the place short term? He should have told me everything at the time.' She shook her head. 'The whole thing is very odd.'

'Just a bit. But I'm sure all will become clear.'

'Yes, but there's another possibility, isn't there?'

Asha's eyebrows were raised. 'What's that?'

'Well, if I subsequently find out for myself that he's moved out, and he hasn't told me… then I don't know what I'll think.'

'But short of asking him, how will you find out?'

'Because that recruiter you put me on to – she emailed me this morning. There are a couple of opportunities she's working on that she thinks could be of interest. She suggested Zoom, but I want to visit Amsterdam again. Soon. And I don't intend to give Peter very much notice at all. I want to know what the hell is going on with him.'

***

Peter called her that afternoon. It was the first time they had spoken since she left him on Sunday, and Louisa was alert, her radar tuned for any signs that would indicate he was ready – no, *keen* to invest himself in their marriage. That he loved her. That he wanted them to be together.

So far, there had been nothing. As a result, their conversation was strained. She asked him, once again, if he was committed to making the marriage work. Once again, he assured her he was. She asked him how he intended to show it.

'Louisa. It's Tuesday. You only got home on Sunday. There's not a lot I can do from here, now is there? Please. Be reasonable.'

She closed her eyes tightly before moving the conversation on. Peter asked about her settlement from the company. She told him that she should get a draft agreement that week.

'Let me know when you do. We can go through it together.'

She sighed. 'I will.'

'Oh, are you still meeting your brother for dinner on Thursday? Any news from him?'

'Yes, he confirmed today. And in case you're worried, he's insisting on paying.'

'Good. Still going to that Spanish place in Clapham?'

'We are, yes. Oh, and have you spoken to Sophie? You said you would.'

'Not yet. Been busy.'

'She started her new job yesterday. On the ferry. She messaged me to say so far, so good. Talk to her, Peter. Please.'

They ended the call, Louisa wondering why, when it came to her husband, everything was such hard work.

***

It was only a few stops. She couldn't remember where she had heard it, or why she had remembered it, but Clapham Junction was apparently one of the busiest railway stations in Britain. Louisa made her way out onto the noisy street, clutching a map printed from the internet that afternoon. She was comfortable using the navigation on her phone, but savvy enough to know that the device would probably be ripped from her hands within minutes, were she foolish enough to hold it in front of her as she wandered along.

She found the restaurant easily enough, eyes darting in search of her brother as she entered. It would have been a pleasant surprise if he'd been on time, but no, he was running true to form. She gave Michael's name to a beautiful raven-haired woman sporting tall black heels, a luxuriant ponytail and a tight-fitting white blouse. Decidedly Iberian. Louisa was led to a table and took the seat with a view of the door.

Ten minutes later, she smiled at her brother and then rolled her eyes at the lame excuse he offered for his tardiness. Greetings and apologies dispensed with, Michael reached for the wine list.

'I don't know about you, Sis, but I'm gagging for a drink. White okay, is it?'

Louisa nodded and Michael's eyes flicked over the card with its boozy offerings. He turned impatiently in his seat to attract some attention from behind him. The beauty arrived, Michael instantly engaging with her and making her smile.

The wine ordered, he turned back to Louisa. He leaned in, eyebrows raised.

'Isn't she *gorgeous*? My God! And those breasts.' He raised his hands in front of himself in a cupping action. 'So deliciously pointy… She could even make an old queen think again, that one.'

Louisa shook her head and took him in. The trademark scarf. This one a plain turquoise colour, cheesecloth or something similar. A pale yellow lightweight jacket over a white shirt. Mercifully, there was no evidence of another do-it-yourself hair-colouring job.

The wine arrived and was declared a success, they exchanged small talk over the menus, and shortly afterwards the food was ordered. Michael asked about the Amsterdam trip and received a sanitised account. He was aware of Louisa's frustrations with the demands of Peter's long-distance job, but that was it. There was not, and never had been, any indication of more profound difficulties. Louisa found it a bit sad that she couldn't confide in her brother, but neither could she work out if it was the sort of thing that sisters and brothers would talk about anyway.

'And how's my favourite niece? Has she started her summer job yet?'

Louisa smiled. To her lasting regret, Sophie was Michael's only young relative.

'She has, yes. On the Isle of Wight ferry.'

'I remember you saying. Good for her. Sounds like fun – all those sailors. Maybe I should join her.'

'Well, you might as well know, although please don't make a fuss about it, but she thinks she may be bi. She has a girlfriend.'

'Oh, love her. If she were here, I'd give her a big hug. She's a gutsy girl, that one. Not sure if her father will approve, though.'

Louisa blinked. Sometimes, despite his frivolous approach, Michael surprised her by showing how much he took in.

The evening wore on, Louisa wondering when her brother was going to share his 'idea' with her. When he was going to get to the point of their rendezvous. She didn't have to wait long.

Michael pushed his plate away from him and filled their glasses.

'Now then, Sis, thank you for coming along tonight. So, I have this plan I want to share with you. I want to go off to India for a bit. To Goa. I think I need a break, a proper change of scene. My brain has dried up and I haven't sold any work for *ages*. Hence the debt with which you kindly helped me.'

Louisa looked at him. She wasn't sure what was coming next, but if he was going to ask her for another loan, she knew what the answer would be.

'I see. So, what's stopping you?'

'Ah.' He smiled to disguise the pained expression on his face. 'Well, that's the thing. Money. It always comes down to that, doesn't it?'

He closed his eyes and held up a hand. As if he had anticipated her concern.

'But don't worry, I'm not going to ask you for any more help. In fact, this way I could give you your twelve thou back straight away.'

Louisa shook her head slightly. 'I'm not with you.'

'Well, the obvious thing is for Mum to lend it to me, isn't it? Now, she's not going to get it back, of course, but when the time comes, we can adjust what you and I get from her estate. So it makes no difference to you in the long term. Clever, eh?'

Louisa sat up and breathed deeply, studying her brother. He was no longer meeting her eyes. They both knew the score. On the death of her husband, and in a rare moment of lucidity, their mother had set up powers of attorney and a new executor for her will. Very sensible, absolutely the right thing to do.

But whilst she loved her son, Barbara Bruce-Gardiner was well aware of Michael's recklessness. His poor habits with money. So she had given him none of the authority that now resided with Louisa. She was the one who managed her mother's affairs for her, and held the powers of attorney that governed decisions around her care and finances. Michael had no legal role to play in the process. So it was Louisa, and only Louisa, who could accede to his request.

'I see. And did you have a figure in mind?'

He gazed back at her defiantly.

'One hundred thousand.'

'My God, Michael, what the hell do you need that much for?'

'Sis, I'm fifty-two. Yes, I want to write my scripts, but

I don't want any pressure. And I want to have a bit of fun. Before it's too late. So, I was thinking about moving out there for a while. It's very cheap to live, you know. If I sell some work, great.' He shrugged. 'But it's not the end of the world if I don't.'

He reached for the wine bottle. 'So what do you say?'

Louisa studied his face for a while. 'I say… I need the ladies. You'll have to excuse me a moment.'

***

A few minutes later, Louisa had retaken her place opposite her brother. His smile was unconvincing; she could see the anxiety behind it.

'Michael, the problem… the problem I've got, is that this isn't really my decision.'

He held up a finger, his mouth half-open, ready to protest.

'No, wait. Let me explain. I have powers of attorney. That means I am, in effect, supposed to take the decisions that Mum would have taken herself, had she been able.'

'Of course.'

'So, what I have to do, what we both *need* to do, is anticipate whether Mum would have agreed to your request.'

Michael puffed himself up, as if about to deliver a profound and far-reaching verdict on a matter of national importance.

'Hmm. The thing is, Sis, we shall never know the answer to that question. And that is why you must look at it from all angles. Be reasonable. But what I would say is that it makes not a jot of difference to either Mum or you. So in that case, surely it's easy for you to say yes.'

'Really?'

He nodded. 'I think she would want me to be happy, don't you?'

'Of course I do.'

'Well then?'

'Michael, you have put me in a difficult position. Despite what *you* say, I have to try and anticipate what *she* would say. What she would do. I hope you can see that.'

'Not really, no.' A pause. 'So what happens now?'

'I need to think about it.'

'Okay.'

He turned around again and held up his finger. The beauty arrived.

'My bill, please, sweetheart.' He reached out and laid a hand on her arm. 'And then I'm going to take my little sister here to Bar Seventeen, just around the corner, where I shall try and get her a bit drunk. You see, I need a favour from her.'

The waitress looked at them each in turn. Louisa arched her eyebrows as if in light-hearted dismissal of his comment. It concealed the turmoil raging inside her. What the hell did she do now?

***

Louisa's first sip of wine was accompanied by a furtive glance around her. 'I'm not so sure this was a good idea, Michael.'

'Nonsense, my darling. We need to loosen you up a bit. Expose you to cosmopolitan London. Instead of that boring middle-class enclave in which you reside.' He made a noise like a sheep. '*Baaarnes.*'

'But Michael… I'm not sure I fit in here. The people… they're all men.'

'No they're not. You're not a man. And what about that one over there?' He flicked his eyes to his right.'

'Frankly, I'm not sure.'

He giggled. 'Neither am I.'

With that, he stood up, his face beaming. 'George, my love.' He held out his arms and embraced the man now standing in front of him. Introductions followed. George seemed very pleasant and chatted for a few minutes before leaving them to it. Louisa was aware of Michael occasionally nodding to someone or other in the busy bar. He seemed to recognise quite a few of the patrons.

They had avoided any further discussion about the loan and got through two drinks each, the second round against Louisa's wishes. She looked at her watch and tapped her fingertips on the table.

'Right, I'm off. Train to catch. And thank you for dinner, it was really good.'

They headed outside together, Louisa aware of the odd stare in her direction.

Michael nodded over his shoulder. 'Shall I walk you to the station?'

'Thank you, but it's only two minutes, busy streets and all that. I'm fine.'

'Any thoughts? My request... Will you think seriously about it?'

Louisa shrugged. 'Michael, I have been thinking about it. And I doubt Mum would approve. If it were for a house or something, then yes, I believe she might. But to spend all that money on supporting some hippy lifestyle... I'm not sure she would go along with that.'

'I see. So it's a no, then.' His face screwed up. 'But if I were to buy into your notion of responsibility, your idea of some fucking middle-class utopia... owning your own house, all that crap... that would be okay, would it? Then I could have the money?'

'Look, I'm just trying to...'

'Oh, please. All you're doing is applying your own bloody value system to me. And I don't buy it. You're punishing me because of what I am. Because we're different. How dare you?'

'Michael, please, this has nothing to do with...'

‘Oh, spare me.’ He turned to walk away, before stopping and wheeling around to confront her.

‘It’s nothing to you. It can make no conceivable difference to your cosy, complacent circumstances.’

He wheeled away again, calling over his shoulder, ‘Goodbye, Louisa.’

She raised one hand as if to protest, to challenge him. But what was the point? She knew him well enough. For now, he was angry and upset. But they always made up. She would call him tomorrow and repair the damage. And quite possibly tell him she would go along with it.

***

Louisa sat with her head resting on her hand, the lights of suburban London flashing past as the train rumbled back towards Barnes Bridge. She nearly missed her stop, engrossed in the argument raging in her mind. Michael was right, of course. There was no legal downside should she go along with his idea. An agreement could easily be drawn up, and he could borrow the money. Then, on their mother’s passing, an adjustment could be made to the distribution of her estate.

Louisa descended the steps from the station platform, gazing at the great waterway that split London in two. She took a quick look at her watch. A ten-minute wait if she chose to get the bus. Sod it. It was dry, a pleasant enough night. The walk would give her more time to think. Twenty-five minutes later, she turned the key in the front door and prepared for bed. Twice she looked at her phone and thought about messaging Michael. Either to try and get him to understand, or to agree to his request. But the whole point of a power of attorney was to represent the wishes of the person concerned, not to subjugate them to your own. And Louisa wasn’t sure her mother would have readily lent her son one hundred thousand pounds to fund a questionable lifestyle in India. But then again, with his happiness at stake, she may well have been persuaded.

Louisa hated that the decision had been put on her. But she had accepted responsibility for managing their mother's affairs, and had both a legal and a moral obligation to discharge it. She could either knowingly go against her mother's likely wishes, or seriously disappoint her brother.

She sighed, turned on her side, and for the first time since losing her job, switched off her alarm.

***

That moment of disorientation as sleep is suddenly and involuntarily replaced by consciousness. It only takes a second, but the confusion seems to last much longer. A banging was going on somewhere, but Louisa couldn't work out exactly where. Was it in her dream? No, surely not. And then her eyes snapped wide open, her mind started to race. There it was again. This was real. That was it – someone was at the door. More banging, urgent now. Christ, what was going on?

Louisa jumped out of bed, cursing as she glanced at the alarm clock. Just gone nine. She grabbed her dressing gown, stuffing toes into slippers that were determined to get away from her. She descended the long flight of stairs, gripping the bannister.

Did she overdo it last night? The intruder alarm protested as she cleared the last couple of steps. Night mode. Shit. Right, focus on the panel. She carefully pressed the four numbers. Relief. Another expletive as she looked around. Keys, keys, where were the bloody keys?

She shouted: 'Hold on, nearly there.'

Finally, she stood to one side of the open door, blinking through her frown. A man and a woman. The man in a jacket, trousers and tie. The woman in police uniform.

Blood rushed to her brain. She gripped the latch handle tightly. Oh, God. Not Sophie, please, no.

The man tapped the bell push. 'Sorry about the banging, I don't think this works. Mrs Louisa Hedley?'

She swallowed. 'Yes.'

'Detective Inspector Lloyd Griffiths.'

He thrust a police ID card in front of her. She took a cursory glance, but didn't give a damn about his name and rank. Panic was welling up inside her, her heart beating fast.

A nod to his colleague. 'This is PC Ruth Thompson. Can we come in, please?'

'Yes.' She stood aside, already pleading with them. 'Sophie… Is Sophie alright?' The pitch of her voice rose. 'Tell me, is she okay?'

'Sophie?'

'My daughter.'

'This isn't about her.'

The wave of relief she felt then… followed by a feeling of intense guilt. Because whatever else they were going to tell her, it couldn't be worse than that.

'Come this way.' Into the kitchen. She hurriedly glanced around, hoping not to see an empty wine bottle.

Louisa pointed to the sofa. 'Please.'

They all sat, she on the edge of her chair, eyes flitting between them. The police pair taking out notebooks. She pulled her dressing gown around her knees, set them sideways on and pressed them together. *Get on with it.*

'What's this about?'

'Is your brother Michael Bruce-Gardiner, of 47A King Street, Clapham?'

'Yes, he is.'

'Mrs Hedley, I'm very sorry to tell you that your brother is dead.'

# 14

For some time afterwards, Louisa reflected on her reaction. She felt guilty about it. She could imagine a couple of different scenarios. Instant grief and tears, accompanied by the inevitable barrage of questions. Or disbelief, denial even, the truth not sinking in for a while. She didn't choose the latter, it just happened. She was with her brother only last night…

Her incredulity manifested itself in a thin smile, accompanied by a shake of the head.

'I don't understand. That can't be right. What happened? And what makes you think it's Michael?'

Only as the details emerged did other emotions start to crowd in. The PC moved to the kitchen island, returning with the roll of paper towel. She tore off a couple of sheets and held them out. Louisa looked up, smiling through her tears at this simple act of kindness.

But the facts were appalling, Louisa shaking her head in disbelief as the full horror of his death was exposed. Michael had been attacked with a knife as he walked across Clapham Common in the direction of his flat. Several stab wounds from behind. One from the front. Straight to the heart. Death was pretty much instantaneous.

'He wouldn't have suffered.'

Oh, that's all right, then.

DI Griffiths leaned forward. 'Mrs Hedley, this is a murder investigation. We have closed off parts of the common, there is a search going on right now and we shall shortly get divers into the ponds there. But we need to try and establish why this happened, as soon as possible. And then hopefully we'll get to whoever was responsible. Are you okay to answer some questions now? To help us?'

'Yes, of course.'

The constable patted her arm. 'Shall I put the kettle on?'

For the next hour they sat and talked, Louisa painting a picture of her brother and his lifestyle as best she could. Her guilt grew as she realised just how little she knew about the company he kept. His friends, who were they? Any lovers on the scene? Had he fallen out with anyone?

She was able to contribute more about his work and financial situation, aware that it didn't make for good listening. His meagre income and his inability to manage money. His debts. Her loan, in cash, to enable him to clear them. His plan to go abroad on the proceeds of a further loan, a big one, from their mother. Their argument outside the bar last night. Michael storming off.

All the while, the two people opposite scribbled away furiously in their notebooks, probing, checking facts. And then there was more about Michael's relatives. Where was her husband yesterday evening? How did he and Michael get on? The daughter she mentioned when she first saw them at her door. Sophie, was it? What about her? Anyone else? The interrogation seemed endless.

Having exhausted his questions about the family, the inspector returned to the events of last night. Had Michael argued with anyone in the bar? Did Louisa notice anyone watching him? At what time had they parted? Did she see anyone following him as he stormed off? And then questions aimed at establishing her movements. Had she gone directly to Clapham Junction? What time train did she get? Could anyone verify her whereabouts?

Louisa spoke patiently, her voice heavy with resignation. 'Look, I parted from my brother as I explained. I went directly to the station. I waited maybe five minutes for a train. Until just after eleven, as I recall. I got off at Barnes Bridge and walked home. And that's it.'

'Thank you, Mrs Hedley. I hope you understand that we must ask these things.' The inspector looked at his colleague with raised eyebrows. 'Now, we need to explain to you what happens next. The police process, the coroner. That sort of thing.'

***

Louisa's terrible sense of loss was matched by several other pressing concerns.

Try as she might, she couldn't get the idea of her brother's last seconds from her mind. The post-mortem would likely confirm that he was stabbed multiple times in the back, before one final knife wound to his chest. Straight into his heart. To make sure. This wasn't a mugging. Neither was it an altercation that had got out of hand. This was an assassination. Deliberate and cold.

Did Michael see his assailant? And if so, did he recognise him, or her, maybe? A second or two of confusion as, paralysed with shock, he stood motionless, his back arched, arms lifted from his sides, his brain desperately trying to process what was going on. And then a figure appearing in front of him, their eyes locking before an arm lunged forward, Michael watching in disbelief as the blade disappeared into his chest, only to reappear a second later. Then, sinking to the ground, his consciousness already receding behind the creeping mist that delivered him into oblivion.

The overwhelming guilt she felt at their bitter parting... She played back his last words to her as they argued outside the bar in Clapham. Words of anger, bitterness even. Now she would never be able to put her arms around him again, to comfort him. To make it better. Her stupid, soft, big brother. Michael didn't harbour grudges, he wasn't like that. They would have made up. But now he was gone forever, the opportunity lost. And they didn't part as friends. Because of her, and her priggish attitude.

So, as she stood in the shower, Louisa wept aloud, a shuddering outpouring of grief. Michael was harmless. He was kind. He didn't deserve to die like that. And she would miss him terribly.

***

A little later, Louisa opened her notebook to make a list. It was what she did, and routine was comforting at a time like this.

Two-thirty today, the mortuary. To identify the body. She didn't know if they would already have done the post-mortem.

Call Peter.

Call Sophie.

Call Asha.

The police would want to hand over Michael's meagre possessions once their investigation work had been completed. Someone would need to sort out his affairs. Best speak to the solicitor about that.

Their mother. No, *her* mother. Michael was gone. Barbara would have to be told, even if she was unlikely to understand what had happened, to really register it. But in a rare moment of lucidity, she might ask after her son, enquire as to when Michael would visit again. And however painful it might be,

Louisa didn't think she had the right to deceive her. But she would soften the news if she could. Say it was a heart attack, perhaps? Yes, that might be a good compromise.

And so it began.

Peter called back first. His shock and concern were clear. He asked how she was. He said he would check flights. He messaged soon after – he would be home that evening. Louisa was grateful.

Asha picked up straight away. She insisted she would come around now, accompany her friend to the mortuary and stay with her until Peter arrived. She turned up within the hour and immediately began dispensing both emotional support and practical help. She made lunch with leftovers from the fridge. Louisa thanked her friend profusely, reluctantly lifted her fork and then returned it to the plate. She covered her face with her hands, rocking slowly back and forth in her seat.

Shortly afterwards, they left for the mortuary, Asha driving as Louisa gazed out of the car window, occasionally wiping away a tear with the palm of her hand. She played back to herself everything the police had said.

They believed that this was an attack by someone who knew Michael, and for whatever reason, wanted him dead. They had made it a priority to try and identify and interview everyone who was in Bar Seventeen last night. Louisa hadn't argued – even if she didn't think her brother capable of falling out with someone so badly that they would want to kill him. He was more likely to walk away than to bring a quarrel to a dramatic and ugly conclusion. That was why she was sure that, one way or another, they would in time have recovered from the row over the money he wanted to borrow from their mother.

But whilst she was less than convinced by the police theory, she couldn't come up with an alternative, other than this was a random killing by a crazed psychopath.

Quite possibly a homophobic one – the bar they had visited was popular amongst the gay community. Someone who harboured a grudge could easily have followed Michael across the common and plunged the knife into his back in an act of hatred. It wouldn't be the first time people had been targeted because of their sexual orientation, and neither would it be the last. Louisa's eyes widened as she wondered whether Sophie, too, would come to experience the hatred of Neanderthal bigots.

Her daughter called a little later, straight off the ferry where she had been serving in the café. She was deeply upset. Despite her mother's protests, she too insisted on coming home. She would catch a train in the morning. She subsequently messaged to say she should arrive at Barnes station at twelve minutes past eleven. Louisa insisted on coming to meet her. She didn't know why, but she preferred to greet Sophie alone. Mother and daughter, united in grief.

Peter arrived at around ten-thirty that evening, at which point Asha promptly excused herself and headed off. Louisa poured herself and her husband a brandy. Even though she didn't like the stuff, it seemed a more appropriate drink than wine. They sat at the kitchen island, playing over events and speculating as to the identity and motivation of the killer. They agreed they would visit Louisa's mother the following afternoon and undertake the dreadful task of trying to explain her son's death to her.

Louisa toyed with the idea of telling Peter about the loan to Michael. She looked at him over her glass before deciding not to. Her decision was accompanied by a sense of guilt, of failure. Her failure in not having the courage previously to tell him that she intended to lend her brother some money. Her cowardice in not coming clean now. What did it say about their marriage? About them? Then her heart skipped a beat. Christ, the police knew all about the money. She would need to make sure that they never mentioned it during any discussion with her husband.

***

Louisa was clearing away the breakfast things when her phone rang. Detective Inspector Griffiths. A brief exchange followed, the officer explaining that he would like to update Louisa on the case, and to speak to her husband if he was now home. Agreement was reached that he would visit that morning, Louisa stressing that she would need to leave the house just before eleven o'clock to meet Sophie off her train. The inspector said he understood, he would arrive at ten.

Before ending the call, Louisa leaned forward and peered down the hall. No sign of Peter, he had gone to shower. She made her way over to the window and whispered into her phone, stressing that Peter was not to learn of the loan to her brother. An uncomfortable pause was followed by DI Griffiths' cautious acknowledgement of her request.

The policeman was punctual. He was accompanied this time by a stern-looking woman in plain clothes whom he introduced as Detective Sergeant Jess Lynch. Peter joined them as Louisa made coffee, the inspector updating them on the progress of the investigation.

They remained convinced that Michael's murder was premeditated and carried out by someone who knew him. Consequently, they were trying to identify all the patrons of Bar Seventeen on Thursday evening. Good progress had been made, but a television appeal would go out that evening on the London TV news bulletins, asking anyone who was there that night to come forward. There was no CCTV camera covering the entrance, but there were two inside, and the recordings should prove useful.

DI Griffiths then handed over to DS Lynch, who had

some questions for Peter. She wanted to know where he was on Thursday evening. He explained his job was in the Netherlands, and then reached for his phone. He flicked at the screen before holding it up.

'Here we go, the boarding passes. Heathrow to Schiphol with BA on Sunday, the fourth of June. Then back to London yesterday evening. On hearing the news. Also with BA.'

'I see,' said DS Lynch. She smiled a cold and unconvincing smile. 'I will need to see your passport, if I may.'

'Of course.' Peter shrugged. 'I'll get it now.'

An uncomfortable silence settled on the group whilst Peter disappeared upstairs, returning moments later. DS Lynch raised her phone and photographed the front page, before leafing through the passport and taking a couple more shots. Eventually, she held it out to him, her eyebrows raised.

'And is there anyone who can verify your presence in Amsterdam?'

Peter looked surprised. 'Any number of my colleagues, I guess. The immigration people. And BA, of course.'

The sergeant scribbled away, then scowled a little as she queried the length of time he spent away from home. It seemed unusual. Peter smiled as he explained Louisa's visit to Amsterdam the previous weekend.

The sergeant appeared satisfied. 'Ah. I see.'

Louisa drew a slow and deep breath. No, you don't. She studied the policewoman's face, wondering whom she might have in her life. A husband, partner, lover, perhaps? Was DS Lynch's relationship with them any better than Louisa's with Peter? Would the sergeant go home, after a long and fraught shift dealing with the dregs of society, to someone who would be genuinely pleased to see her? Someone who would hold her, kiss her, show her real love? Louisa hoped so. Her job couldn't be easy.

The object of her scrutiny then went on to question Peter

about his brother-in-law. What was he like, did they get on? Did Peter think Michael was in trouble?

Peter shrugged. 'Trouble? I don't think so. What makes you think that?'

Oh, Christ. Surely not. The surge of panic seemed to start in Louisa's abdomen, then come rushing up through her chest before filling her head. She thought it was going to explode.

DS Lynch took a deep breath. A gentle frown creased her forehead, as if she were accusing Peter of some indiscretion.

'Well, your wife's loan to Michael for a start.' She looked at her notes. 'A loan of twelve thousand pounds, in cash. Apparently, he needed the money to clear some debts. Perhaps he was being threatened. But we don't know who that money went to. Any ideas, Mr Hedley?'

# 15

Louisa was frightened by the ease with which Peter coped with such an unexpected and shocking revelation. It would have been magnificent had it not turned her cold. She'd had no idea he was such a convincing actor.

His smile looked so natural, but to her all the more menacing – because she knew how furious this discovery would have made him. He turned to Louisa, his eyebrows raised slightly, then reached out and patted her thigh.

'Well, Michael was a very lovable character. We shall all miss him terribly. But I have no reason to suppose he was in trouble or being threatened, though I think my wife would have a better idea than I. Any thoughts, darling?'

Louisa swallowed. She didn't want to; she knew the involuntary action wouldn't have been lost on her husband. Shame threatened to suffocate her. And there was something else… fear. She could see Inspector Griffiths' gaze shifting between herself and Peter.

She couldn't look at her husband. She didn't want to look at DI Griffiths. She wasn't going to look at Sergeant Lynch. Instead, Louisa fixed her eyes on a magazine on the coffee table. As yet, unread.

Her voice sounded small. 'My brother wanted to borrow twelve thousand pounds. He owed someone money. I don't know who to, I didn't ask, and he didn't volunteer a name.

But he wanted it in cash. He explained that if the loan was paid into his account, the bank would use some of it to clear his overdraft.'

DS Lynch didn't flinch. She looked at her notes. Her tone was very matter-of-fact.

'He is overdrawn by nearly five thousand. He's maxed out on two credit cards, with a combined outstanding balance of fourteen thousand. So, nineteen thousand in debt, plus any other commitments we don't yet know about.' She flicked an insincere smile at Louisa. 'And the personal loan you say you made him, of course.'

Bitch. Louisa's earlier concern for the state of the policewoman's love life had vanished. And what the hell did she mean by questioning the loan to Michael? The personal loan you *say* you made him. Why doubt that?

DS Lynch's eyes moved between Louisa and Peter. 'Have either of you any thoughts on his financial situation?'

A few minutes later, Louisa showed the visitors to the door. She glanced at her watch. Ten minutes before she needed to leave to meet Sophie. She looked down the hall, to where she knew Peter was waiting. She had to take the worst of it now, before her daughter came home. She made her way slowly into the kitchen. He was leaning against the island, arms folded, a look of disgust on his face as he eyed his wife.

'You know what? All this crap about our marriage, how distant we are – and according to my wife, it's down to *me*.' He poked a finger into his chest and leaned in towards her. 'Nasty Peter.' He jerked his head. 'And here *she* is, lending our money to her useless fucking brother, when any sane person would know that he'd piss it up against the wall in five minutes. And then hiding it all from her husband. Deliberately setting out to deceive me.'

This was Louisa's one chance to turn the tables. Best take it now. She hissed at him, 'Don't you dare, Peter. He's dead.

My brother is dead. And it was my money, it came out of my savings account. I'm allowed to help my brother with my own money.'

Peter raised his hands. 'We always said that everything that we have is ours.' His voice was calmer now. 'Has that changed? Are we now going to draw a line between what's mine and what's yours?'

'No, of course not. We share.'

He gazed out over the garden. 'Right. Good. I know you were trying to help Michael, and I understand that.' He turned back to her. 'But please remember that neither of us is perfect. I'm not, you're not.'

He glanced at the kitchen clock.

'You'd better get Sophie. We don't want her to see we've been fighting.'

Louisa willingly agreed. She picked up her bag and keys and hurried out.

***

In the few minutes it took to drive to the station, Louisa played over the scene that had just unfolded. She was not surprised by Peter's vitriol, his sneering condemnation, not only of her poor judgement, but her dishonesty. It hurt her to acknowledge it, but he was right. She had deceived him.

But she was surprised by his apparent desire to set the episode aside. To make sure things were calm when Sophie arrived. He had previously made no attempt to hide his grumpiness in their daughter's company, but Louisa was relieved and grateful he was doing so now. Perhaps he was capable of empathy. Maybe there was a glimmer of hope after all.

As usual, parking in the wooded lane by the station was a nightmare. Louisa tended to use the stop at Barnes Bridge, it was a shorter walk home. But trying to park there was even worse, so this was where she and Sophie would meet. Louisa just managed to find a space and was hurrying towards the station entrance when she heard a train pulling out. Seconds later, her daughter appeared, a backpack slung over her shoulder. The hugs and tears lasted a while, Louisa had never been so glad to see her. She didn't think she would ever forget the cold fear she had felt when she opened the door to the police the day before.

# 16

# PETER

Peter was deeply impressed by his Herculean efforts to control his anger. It would have been so easy – and entirely justified, surely – for him to have gone nuclear about his wife's stupidity in lending Michael twelve thousand pounds. The loss of the money was bad enough, but the fact that she *deliberately* kept the loan from her husband... Christ. A fine example of her capacity for deception.

And yet she was always banging on about *his* failings. Well, lady, one day *yours* are going to come out – and in spectacular style, he thought. But in the meantime, there was nothing to be gained by making the police aware of the huge rift between them. Neither did he want Sophie to witness their troubles. A bit of blissful ignorance would be just fine.

So in the meantime, he would do all the things that a good, caring husband would do. He would support his wife, demonstrate his devotion to her, and all would be well. This afternoon, he would accompany her as she broke the news of Michael's demise to her mother.

***

Peter eyed the nursing home from behind the steering wheel of the Passat. He hated the place with a vengeance. Just the smell of it was enough – overcooked cabbage mingled with the odour of God only knows what else. He turned to Louisa; she, too, was gazing at the building, making no attempt to get out of the car. Her anxiety about the task ahead was obvious.

'How will you do this?' he asked.

'I really don't know. Just tell her, I suppose, and give her the chance to come back to it if she chooses. But we need to talk to the staff first, explain what's happened. They'll have to deal with any subsequent fallout.'

Thirty minutes later, they were in Barbara's room, where Peter sat on a corner of the bed, hands in pockets, like a sullen schoolboy undertaking an unwelcome visit to a stern maiden aunt.

He watched Barbara Bruce-Gardiner shuffling around her room, as usual engrossed in a vain search for something. The wispy hair was everywhere, the T-shirt stained. The baggy jogging pants were embarrassingly low on her hips. My, how the mighty are fallen, mused Peter, as Louisa hoisted them up for her mother. He grinned to himself – the old girl would have had a fit at the way she looked now. Like a bloody bag lady. They were so fecking posh, Louisa's parents – so damn superior. And they'd never really liked him, of course. The tiny coughs, or twitching of the eyebrows when he committed some trivial *faux pas*. Putting his knife down on the plate with the blade facing outwards; buttering the whole of his bread roll, instead of tearing little pieces off as he ate.

And it was even worse when they made allowances for him – because his family didn't enjoy the *advantages* that theirs had. He hated being patronised more than anything. Fortunately, they steered clear of any references to his Irish ancestry, other than a description of his background as 'quaint' when Barbara had once quizzed him about it.

Peter watched silently as Louisa tried in vain to attract her mother's attention.

'Mum? Mum. Sit down a minute. You have to listen to me.'

The bewildered woman stared back at her. 'What is it? I'm busy. There's no peace here, you know. And those aeroplanes, day and night. The poor souls...'

Her voice faded as she looked into the corner of the room. She had been born just before the war and raised in Norfolk. She had often recounted tales of the hordes of bombers that used to fly low over their beautiful house, she standing on the terrace and watching in awe as the sun went down behind her. The engines struggling against a full payload of bombs, the noise deafening, the house shaking beneath them. The slow, bloated planes lumbering east in tight formations; great, fat targets for the anti-aircraft guns and fighter planes that lay in wait. And then their poignant return, many hours later. Straggling, limping home. The lucky ones, anyway. Always fewer in number, often with parts hanging off or missing, smoke trailing from torn metal. Exhausted crews, their relief at having survived one more mission offset by the anguish of losing brave friends. Beer and bravado masking the dread of having to do it all again, very soon.

The handsome man Barbara had married worked in the Foreign Office. William Bruce-Gardiner became a highly regarded senior diplomat, his life dedicated to fostering Britain's international relations. A gifted child of the first half of the twentieth century, he wasn't shy about reminding his children that diplomacy was preferable to what tended to follow when it failed.

Louisa tried again with her mother, easing her into the tall armchair and kneeling before her.

'Mum, listen. I'm sorry but I need to tell you...'

Peter watched as his wife lowered her head, her shoulders

jerking. Moments later, she looked up and tried again, wiping the tears from her eyes with the back of her hand.

'It's Michael, Mum. I'm afraid he's passed away.' She patted Barbara's hand, the skin paper-thin with age. 'He's gone, Mum… gone to be with Dad. Do you understand what I'm saying? Your son, Michael?'

Barbara's head gently wobbled up and down as, expressionless, she scanned Louisa's eyes for what seemed to Peter like an age.

'Don't cry now, there's a good girl. You know Daddy doesn't like it.' Her face lit up. 'You can have an ice cream later – if you're good.'

'Oh, Christ,' muttered Peter. He got up and moved to the french doors, trying the handle. 'It's roasting in here. Can we get these open?'

Louisa spoke over her shoulder. 'You'll have to ask the staff for a key. They can't leave it in the lock for obvious reasons.'

'Right. Back in a sec.'

A couple of minutes later, they were relieved by the gentle movement of summer air through the open doors. Peter nodded towards Louisa's mother.

'Any progress?'

A slight shake of the head. 'I've told her, but… you know.'

'You can't do anything else.'

Louisa looked out onto the garden. 'I think I'll take her for a stroll outside. See if I can get through to her there.'

'Sure. Good luck.' Peter settled himself in the armchair as Louisa helped her mother through the door and into the garden. He pulled out his phone in search of the horse racing. Royal Ascot. He had a few quid invested.

Ten minutes later they were back, Peter cursing to himself as he pocketed his phone. Nearly two hundred down after three races. At least it wasn't twelve grand, he mused. He watched his wife put her hands on Barbara's shoulders and look into her blank face.

'We're going in a minute, Mum. But I'll be back to see you soon, okay? Now, let me help you to the bathroom before we leave.'

She grimaced at Peter. 'You might want to excuse yourself at this point.' She nodded to the garden doors. 'Will you lock them, please?'

'Right.' He stood up and did as he was told. 'I'll leave you to sort your mum out and go and drop off the key. See you at the car.'

Peter's attempted goodbye to his mother-in-law didn't register, and he left them to it, smiling to himself as he left.

The journey home from Sunbury was mostly undertaken in silence. As they turned into their driveway, he finally spoke.

'You're going to have to rethink your plans regarding Amsterdam. With Michael unable to share the visits to Barbara, it's going to make it harder for you to spend time over there, isn't it?'

# 17

# LOUISA

Louisa rebuffed her husband's suggestion of a takeaway on Saturday evening, preferring to cook something herself. To keep busy. She had correctly anticipated that Sophie would join her in the kitchen and that Peter would leave them to it, retiring to the sitting room with a beer. She felt guilty that, right now, she preferred it that way.

Louisa and her daughter prepared a dinner of Asian salmon with stir-fried vegetables and noodles; the silence and calm in which they worked only added to the melancholy.

Louisa fixed her eyes on the knife in her hand as it effortlessly sliced through peppers and spring onions. She tried and failed to erase a scene from her mind in which someone repeatedly plunged a similar one into Michael's back, then calmly walked around in front of him, chose the critical spot on his chest and slid the bloodied blade into his heart. The organ flailing, the slashed ventricles forcing blood not around his arteries, but into his chest cavity and out of the wound, where it pulsed onto the ground below.

Little gasps accompanied Louisa's sharp intakes of breath as she lost control of herself. Sophie wordlessly held her mother tight as their tears dampened each other's shoulders.

On Sunday, brunch was followed by the three of them taking a walk together. They headed towards Hammersmith Bridge, picked up the Thames Path and followed the river downstream before cutting back across Barnes Common.

Louisa was dreading Sophie's departure later that afternoon, less so Peter's. They had all agreed that they would carry on 'as normal' until funeral arrangements were made, but that depended upon the coroner issuing an interim death certificate. Without that, Michael's body could not be released to an undertaker.

Louisa spent the long Sunday evening alone. She wished she had her former job to go to in the morning and dreaded the upcoming week. In the morning she would call DI Griffiths for the promised update.

***

The Monday morning discussion was relatively brief. Griffiths asked her to attend a voluntary interview where he intended to formally record both the facts and the speculation surrounding her brother's lifestyle and the events leading up to his death. She was welcome to bring someone by way of support, or a legal representative if she chose.

Louisa readily agreed to the meeting, even if she was mildly perturbed by the idea of 'formally' recording her contribution. A two o'clock appointment at the police station was agreed.

Her heart sank the next day when she was greeted by the boot-faced DS Lynch, who showed her into the interview room. They were soon joined by DI Griffiths, who worked hard to put her at ease. She was offered tea or coffee, but chose water. Jess Lynch then took Louisa through the formalities, of which there were quite a few. The interview would be recorded, and the equipment was explained to her.

Louisa was there voluntarily; she could leave at any time, but anything she said could be given in evidence. Hence the need for absolute truthfulness.

Most of the questions came from DS Lynch, with DI Griffiths interjecting from time to time. Louisa's interviewer seemed keen to explore the subject of the loan to Michael. Why was it in cash? Could she verify that she had given the money to him? Louisa didn't understand this last point and said so. The sergeant responded that they only had Louisa's word that the cash had gone to her brother. Might it have been put to some other use? Louisa shook her head.

'I really don't get this. I was hardly going to ask him for a receipt, was I? I transferred the money from my savings account to my personal bank account. The one I use for buying presents for my husband, gifting Sophie a little something now and again. That sort of thing. Normally there's just a few hundred pounds in it. I withdrew the twelve thousand in cash, as previously agreed with my bank, and then walked directly to the café where I met Michael for coffee. And that's when I handed it over. I can show you the transactions on my banking app if you like.'

DS Lynch was watching her intently. She sniffed. 'Okay, we can come back to that.'

Louisa was getting anxious. 'Come back to what?'

DI Griffiths held up his hand. 'Let's move on, shall we? And by the way, my apologies for our referencing the loan in front of your husband. My error. Was he very angry?'

'Why do you ask?'

A shrug. 'No reason really. It's just that you were very keen that he didn't find out. But he didn't seem overly concerned. Unless he hid it well, of course.'

Louisa returned his shrug without commenting. DS Lynch continued.

'Can we talk about your mother, please?'

'My mother?'

'Is she wealthy, Mrs Hedley?'

Louisa was surprised to be asked this. 'Well, yes, I suppose she is. Why?'

'So, if you totalled up her savings, investments, that sort of thing, what would they be worth? Broadly speaking.'

Louisa raised her eyebrows. 'I would need to check. But around two million, I would say.'

'I see. And who are the beneficiaries in her will?'

'There's a legacy to her grandchild… she only has one. My daughter Sophie. The rest benefits my brother and myself, so…'

Louisa stopped, the blood surging into her head.

'My God. You can't be… are you suggesting that I murdered Michael so that I can benefit from his share of my mother's estate?'

'Is that what will now happen?'

Louisa blinked at the sergeant. 'I suppose it is. But, please, answer my question. Do you seriously believe I might have killed my own brother?'

'Of course not,' said DS Lynch. She leaned back, forced into giving an unconvincing smile, her hands steepled together.

Louisa nodded.

'But I do think you might have paid someone to do it for you, Mrs Hedley. For twelve thousand in cash, perhaps? Twelve thousand pounds that appears to have vanished without trace.'

# 18

The journey back from the interview took place in a kind of haze. Louisa was shocked, frightened. The police had concluded that she had a good motive for killing her brother and were choosing to believe that the twelve thousand pounds she had withdrawn from her account had been used to commission his murder. The fact that Louisa had attempted to keep the 'loan' from her husband made it look even worse.

But surely, she reasoned, they must be able to see that she loved Michael. They must be able to tell that she wasn't the sort of person who would kill her brother to profit from an inheritance. This was bloody ridiculous. How dare they? Well, the best thing she could do would be to co-operate fully with their stupid line of enquiry, whilst insisting they vigorously pursue any others. Because Michael deserved justice. He needed it. As did she.

By the time she got off the tube at Hammersmith, her fear had morphed into anger. She didn't think she would feel like cooking that evening, so made her way to the Marks and Spencer food hall just along from the station. She eyed the shelves full of chilled ready meals. 'Serves one'. Well, that's a change, then. Another solitary dinner, a sad reminder of her single life, interspersed with occasional and fleeting visits from a man whose love she doubted.

Not exactly what she had expected from her marriage.

And now, alone, she had to deal with the suspicions of the police. In any normal relationship, she would be accompanied by someone who would wrap their arms around her and share the burden. But Peter had headed back to Amsterdam at the first opportunity, his actions speaking far louder than the thin words of comfort. Managing the grief on your own was bad enough, but to be the prime suspect in Michael's murder was, well…

Twenty minutes later and as she trudged into their gravelled forecourt, she could see two bunches of flowers on the doorstep. She opened the front door, sorted out the alarm and, one bouquet at a time, took them into the kitchen.

The first was from Asha. Of course. Louisa smiled, grateful on two counts. For the flowers, naturally, but also for the excuse to call her friend. She so wanted to talk to her, to share her unsettling experience at the hands of the police. To hear a reassuring voice.

The second was from Robert. Her heart fluttered. The note on the card attached to his flowers was kind and heartfelt. He said he had heard the terrible news from Asha, who had messaged him on Saturday. Louisa knew that he understood the pain of losing someone close only too well, his wife having lost her battle with cancer some years before. He now juggled his role as father to two charming kids with the management of his growing business.

As former members of the Shepherd's Bush Rat Pack, both Asha and Robert had agreed to become godparents to Sophie. Nothing religious, and Louisa had partly explained it as a way of cementing the adults' friendship and commitment to each other. But deep down, she had another motive. Reflecting on her childhood and teenage years, she felt she had benefitted considerably from the presence of a brother. But Sophie was destined to remain an only child, her mother's hysterectomy had seen to that.

So the idea of having two guardian angels in Sophie's life seemed to offer a degree of compensation for the lack of a sibling. And it had worked. Sophie had grown up happy and well adjusted, with the friendly support of two caring godparents. Asha and Sophie adored each other, even if the contact between them had tailed off with Sophie's majority and departure for university.

Robert, too, had done his bit. Sophie's birth had preceded that of his children by some years, but Louisa had always been touched by his determination to pay attention to his charge, and show genuine interest in the little girl. That concern had never faltered, despite Peter having long ago distanced himself from his one-time best friend. Louisa remained unclear as to the reason for that, but neither was she inclined to question her husband about his abandoned friendship with her former lover.

The reason was simple. Peter was unaware of the one-night stand she had shared with Robert, and the guilt Louisa felt about it still haunted her. Not because she was cheating on him when it happened – they had, after all, broken off their engagement at that point. Rather for what her willingness to jump back into bed with her old flame said about her true feelings. Might they have ended up together had Robert not returned to Canada? Or was their night of passion merely an exercise in nostalgia, an opportunity seized in the heat of the moment? And the angst was compounded by the fact that she chose not to tell Peter about it when they got back together and resumed their engagement.

But, as always, she dismissed this anxiety. Louisa preferred not to dwell on the episode. It was history.

She unwrapped the bouquets and began filling two vases with water, breaking off from her efforts to answer a welcome call from Sophie. She, too, had received flowers from Robert, together with a message expressing his shock and sadness at the loss of her uncle. Louisa chose not to burden her daughter with her earlier dreadful experience at the hands of the police officers, and the conversation principally revolved around the more practical aspects of dealing with sudden death.

Having completed the flower arranging, Louisa reached for her phone and settled onto the sofa. Time to get a fix of Asha. Profuse thanks for her friend's flowers precipitated another bout of weeping, Louisa's frustrated apology earning her a stern ticking off.

'For heaven's sake, babe, it's natural. You have to let it all out. It ain't healthy otherwise. Now, tell me all.'

So she did, bringing Asha up to speed on the weekend: her mother, Sophie, Peter, the damned detectives and Robert's flowers. Asha listened intently, her frustration at the police tempered by her customary common sense.

'Honey, it's good they are looking at everything. I'm no expert, but you keep hearing that most murders are committed by people who knew the victim. So they're bound to focus on you and Peter to start with. They're doing their job, right? I'm sure they'll back off in time.'

'Thank you, my love. Wise as ever. I was bloody angry earlier, but I can see why they would have me firmly in their sights. It's just galling that they're wasting time on me, when the real killer is out there somewhere on the streets of London.'

'It is. I feel for you, babe.'

'Thank you. Oh, and by the way,' said Louisa, 'the draft of the compromise agreement arrived on Friday. Unsurprisingly, I have yet to study it. Anyway, how are you? How's work?'

'Same as, I'm afraid. I need to get off my backside and do something, though. You know what it's like. Easier to talk about it than to act.'

After they rang off, Louisa stared out of the window, reflecting on Asha's lack of surprise that her friend should be heading the list of potential suspects for Michael's murder. The more Louisa thought about that, the more anxious she became. The next knock on the door could herald her arrest.

***

On Tuesday morning she received an email from the Amsterdam recruitment consultant. Of the opportunities that she thought might be relevant to Louisa, one in particular was starting to crystallise. Louisa readily agreed to the suggestion of a Zoom call, and that afternoon at three o'clock, she sat in front of her laptop, notebook and pen at the ready.

She was relieved that the technology worked and took an instant liking to Janna. Louisa explained her situation, leaving nothing out concerning the circumstances of her departure from her most recent job. She was adamant:

'I will always do what's right. I was fourteen years with that company, and they saw fit to promote me twice. But I won't simply roll over in the face of a misguided woman trying to put her own ambition ahead of a successful outcome to a key project. If she tries to rush everything, it will lead to failure.'

Janna laughed. 'It happens, Louisa. So, what now?'

She described Peter's Amsterdam role, and the fact that *they* were keen to spend more time together. She hoped that this would be the only lie she would tell Janna.

'Okay. Let me outline the position that I think is about to be confirmed. I can't name the company, but if they want to meet with you, then we shall have you sign a confidentiality agreement.'

The job sounded perfect. A one-year project with a pan-European business that was poised to install new accounting software across its operations. Lots of Zoom meetings with the company's financial managers, the software provider and a 'big four' consulting firm that had been brought in to help. While the company's head office was in the south of Amsterdam, the work could be done from pretty much anywhere. Louisa smiled as it was explained that the client was looking for someone who was disciplined, organised and thorough.

Janna was hoping for confirmation of the assignment later that week. Could Louisa get over to Amsterdam without delay once it was?

'Ah, let me see. You might lose the video while I look at my calendar.'

This was weird. Any normal person would have explained the dreadful circumstances of her brother's death. That they were grieving. That there was so much to sort out. The coroner, the undertaker, the police, her brother's affairs. Arrangements to be made. So, regrettably, the idea of travelling to Amsterdam now was ridiculous.

However... Louisa had long ago decided she wasn't normal. She dreaded the idea of sitting around while circumstances beyond her control played themselves out. And here was an ideal opportunity to distract herself. The job sounded perfect, she could do it from either Amsterdam or Barnes. It also offered the prospect of paying a surprise visit to her husband – see how much he liked *that*. And anyway, doing something had to be better than loitering around the house on her own.

'Janna? I'm sure it will be fine. I look forward to hearing from you when you have further news.'

As they ended the call, Louisa thought about what she should share with Peter. She decided that for now, she would talk to him in general terms about her job search, but would keep quiet about the potential interview.

On a call with him that afternoon, she waited until they had exhausted the primary topic of conversation – Michael's death. She then updated Peter on the tortuous discussion with the police, in particular their misgivings about the twelve thousand pounds in cash.

Louisa could hear the sneer in his voice.

'I guess that's what happens when you try and hide things from people. It comes back to bite you, right?'

She forced herself to remain silent. But Peter wasn't done.

'No wonder they're suspicious. But it will all blow over soon enough when they realise there's no evidence to connect you to the crime.'

'Christ, you sound so clinical about it all. I'm under suspicion for the murder of my brother, and you're talking like a lawyer. I don't want it to blow over! I want them to catch whoever did it.'

'Good luck with that.'

'I don't understand. What do you mean?'

'They don't have anything, do they? Have they told you about any leads, or possible lines of enquiry? Have they found the knife?'

'No.'

'There you go. They have nothing – other than you.'

They moved on, Louisa aware of a tightening in her chest as she explained that she had been doing more research into finance jobs in Amsterdam. That she was hopeful of finding one. She was unsurprised by his response.

'Look, it's a bad idea, okay? You can earn much more in the UK. And we would have to get a bigger, more expensive place here if you came over. More flights to pay for. And then there's Barbara and Sophie to consider. It just doesn't make sense for you to relocate at the moment.'

Louisa rested her forehead on her hand, her elbow on the kitchen island.

'Once again, Peter, it sounds as if you don't want me with you. If that's the case, just tell me, because…'

'Of course it isn't. You're always misrepresenting me,

twisting what I'm trying to say! I'm just dealing with the practicalities, that's all. We need to look at other options.'

'Such as?'

'Well, I said I would talk to my boss. See if I can work from the UK more. So I did. He didn't seem to have a problem with it, but there is a reorganisation being talked about. One that could work in my favour. We need to give it a couple of months, that's all.'

'Okay, good. But it may or may not come about, correct? Meanwhile, I plan to spend more of my time in Amsterdam. As we discussed. Look for something temporary.'

'But you're not thinking this through. You were on a big salary. You need to replace it. You can only do that in the UK.'

'You're determined to keep me here, aren't you? Why is my being over there such a problem for you? Got a bit on the side, have you, Peter?'

'Oh, for God's sake. You're just being hyper-sensitive, as usual. I tell you what: if you think that, why not pay a private detective to follow me around? Put your mind at rest. It'd cost a lot less than twelve grand, too.'

'Don't be ridiculous. Or sarcastic.'

'No, *you're* the one being ridiculous. I bust my gut over here, working all hours. It's not easy. But I do it for *us*. Please remember that.'

Louisa fought to prevent her anger from boiling over. Peter was presenting himself as hard done by, when all the time he was the one driving the big decisions. *He* had chosen to work in another country, and then to limit his trips home on the grounds of economy. It was him, for God's sake.

'We both work hard, as you well know,' she began in a level voice. 'But you also know that I am not prepared to tolerate a crap marriage because of it. I would rather have less money and live a normal life with a loving husband. I won't go on like this.'

'Right now, the idea of hard work seems to have taken a back seat to swanning around in Amsterdam on some permanent bloody holiday!'

At that, Louisa finally saw red. 'I don't want a holiday, I want to work! I intend to work. But I want a married life as well. And that's something I'm not prepared to compromise on.'

***

On Wednesday morning, Louisa set off on foot from home to Barnes Bridge Station, took the train to Clapham Junction and from there walked down a busy St John's Road. She stopped off at a Marks and Spencer and fought back the tears as she inspected a bunch of white lilies before making for the checkout. She then headed south-east onto the common, unsure exactly where her brother had met his violent death.

Looking anxiously around, she followed the path alongside a wooded area, with football pitches to her left. And then she saw it. A sign, appealing for witnesses to a brutal attack. The murder of her brother. Peter was right, the police were clutching at straws.

And then, perhaps twenty paces further on, a little shrine dedicated to Michael. Louisa immediately thought of the memorial to Marc Bolan, just a few hundred yards from Barnes Station. That one was permanent, but hard to find – tucked away in the shrubbery alongside a busy road. This one was temporary, but impossible to miss as you passed by. She approached slowly, her heart racing, breath coming erratically.

Clutching her flowers, she eased herself down onto one knee and gazed with gratitude at the impromptu tribute to her brother. People cared enough to bring little tokens of love and visit the place where their friend was brutally murdered.

Michael's may not have been a life of great consequence, but Louisa was comforted to see that it had mattered to others, as well as to herself.

Bunches of flowers lay fading in the warmth of summer. Just like a human life, they were temporary, fleeting. Behind them, a couple of potted plants were faring better. Interspersed with the floral offerings were plastic document wallets, protecting the cards and messages within from the weather. One was from someone named George. Louisa wondered if it was the same person that Michael had introduced her to in Bar Seventeen that fateful night.

She studied the wording, the names, the kisses. The childlike drawings that accompanied some of them. Flowers. A dove clutching an olive branch. Sad faces, mouths turned down, oversized teardrops rolling down cheeks. Some were accompanied by photos of a carefree Michael grinning back at her, condensation already taking its toll on the images. A pale and flimsy scarf, precisely the sort he'd favoured, weaved its fragile way through the sad little tableau.

Louisa put down her offering, rested her head in her hands and wept, the feeling of profound loss accompanied by one of gratitude for the care and compassion of others.

After a couple of minutes, she stood, reached for her handkerchief and wiped her face. Without turning, she took a few paces back to the edge of the path, hands held in front of her, her head bowed. As if at a war memorial on Remembrance Day.

A woman's voice shook her from her trance.

'Are you alright, love?'

Louisa turned to face her, eyes still wet, but a tremulous smile on her face at the kind words of a stranger. She saw an elderly woman, bent over and limping, a lopsided wheeled shopping trolley in tow.

'I'll be okay. Thank you for asking.'

The woman nodded at the flowers and messages. 'Terrible business, weren't it? Terrible. Knew him well, did you, love?'

Louisa sighed. 'Not well enough, I'm afraid.'

***

By Wednesday lunchtime she had heard nothing more from the police. Her relief at not having been arrested was offset by frustration at the lack of progress in finding her brother's killer. She would call them for an update that afternoon. She remembered Peter's analysis of the inquiry. Did they have any leads? Active lines of investigation? What about the knife? Well, Louisa thought, they needed to pull their bloody fingers out. Catch whoever had murdered her harmless brother.

She had at least heard from Janna in the Netherlands, who had received confirmation that the temporary work assignment was 'go'. When could Louisa get over to see her? The response was immediate. If she could get a flight, Louisa would be there on Friday. And then she could enjoy a weekend with her husband. Janna was delighted.

Peter wasn't.

***

Louisa deliberately kept the details vague. 'I know it's short notice, but the recruitment consultant only had confirmation of it today. It sounds ideal, Peter, and I intend to explore it further.'

'But I told you, I think there may be an opportunity for me to spend more time in the UK. That way you can get a proper job there, instead of some temporary thing here.'

'It's for a year, and I can do the work from pretty much anywhere. So if you're able to work from the UK, I will be too. It's perfect. And well paid, which I know worries you.

So, I will arrive on Friday morning, see Janna the recruitment consultant, and then you and I can spend the weekend together in your apartment.'

'I'm afraid there's a bit of a problem with that.'

Louisa resisted blurting out the words. 'I knew it. I bloody *knew* it!' She masked her fury with a bland query.

'Meaning what?'

'Well, it's all a bit of a cock-up. I thought it was a normal let, twelve months plus. And the price seemed reasonable. But it transpires that the agreement we signed means either party can terminate at short notice. As a consequence, it's ridiculously expensive. So I pulled the plug.'

'And how on earth could that happen?'

'The agreement is in Dutch, as you might imagine. That's why Grietje, the assistant in our department, takes care of all this stuff for me. She thought that's what I wanted, a short let, because I had spoken to her about taking a room in a friend's place. More of a friend of a friend, really. Anyway, it's all turned out fine because that's what I've done, now. It's much cheaper.'

'I see. When did all this happen?'

'This week. It's been a bit hectic, as you might imagine.'

'Why didn't you tell me? I find that really odd. Unbelievable, frankly.'

'Give me a chance. As I said, it's only just happened. But it will save a lot of money.'

'Right. Promise me that you'll message me the address as soon as we have finished this call, okay? I never had the details of your last place, and that's not going to happen again.'

'I promise.'

'Good. Well, I'll be there on Friday, as I say. So where's the house? Where shall we meet?'

'It's an apartment. But you can't stay there, I lodge with a family. I only have a small room. Single bed.'

Louisa closed her eyes and took a deep breath. 'So what do you suggest?'

'Well, frankly, I don't see any point in you coming at all. It didn't make sense before, and this just makes it harder.'

'Peter, I'm coming. I have an interview with a recruitment consultancy. If I can't stay with you, then we'll just have to find a hotel, won't we?'

'But what about the cost? We need to be careful…'

The argument rolled backwards and forwards, Peter finally proposing that he would have Grietje book them a room. Louisa had other ideas.

'No, let me do it. I don't want any more misunderstandings. We've had too many of those as it is.'

# 19

# WIM

Wim held his ear to the door as he rapped on it with his knuckles.

'Sibel, please, hurry up. I need the bathroom. I have to get to work.'

A muffled voice came back. 'Okay, okay. Give me a minute.'

Wim heard the sound of the toilet flushing, and taps being run. The lock clicked, and Sibel emerged in her pyjama shorts and top. She was frowning.

'Don't put that expression on with me,' said Wim. 'You're the one holding everybody up.'

Tilting her head forward, Sibel slowly peered to her left, and then to the right. She looked straight into Wim's eyes. 'Everybody?'

'Don't be cheeky, please. It's not clever, it's disrespectful.'

The girl raised her eyebrows, then put her tongue out before scampering off to her and Laila's bedroom, giggling as she went.

Wim watched her disappear before marching into the bathroom and slamming the door. Damn it!

***

That evening, Caria's gaze shifted from the television to Wim, tapping away at his laptop as he sat at the other end of the sofa. She frowned.

'Not work, I hope? You've had a long day.'

'No. Not at all,' said Wim.

'What then?'

'Nothing really.'

'Tell me.'

He sighed and set his computer down. 'Apartments. We can't go on like this, we need more space.'

'But what about the cost? This place is expensive enough as it is.'

'Well, I'm working on it.' He turned the laptop towards her. 'What do you think of this one?'

Caria leaned over and flicked through the pictures before her eyes dropped to the price. She recoiled, a smile of disbelief on her face.

'My God, Wim, have you seen how much they want? We can't afford that.'

'Well, I'm going to make sure we can. You know I have some assets that I shall be able to realise one day, and I'm working on bringing that date forward.'

Caria shook her head in exasperation. 'Assets. Some assets… You've never explained it to me.' She shrugged. 'And that's okay, by the way, it's your business, not mine.'

Wim forced a smile. 'I don't want to bore you with the details, that's all.'

Caria slumped back on the sofa, folded her arms and locked her eyes on the TV. 'Like I said, it's your business.' It was quiet for a minute before she abruptly got to her feet. 'Actually, I'm tired. I think I'll go to bed.'

Wim looked up. 'Give me a minute and I'll join you.'

'I'm tired. Okay?'

He waited for a kiss that failed to materialise. He sighed, closed his laptop and stared into space. It was time the fox got busy. It was time to deploy Operation Reynard.

# 20

# LOUISA

On Wednesday evening Louisa rewarded herself with a glass of wine. Her flights were booked, and she had found them a decent hotel at a good price. The modern building was a stone's throw from the Spaklerweg metro stop, with an easy ride in one direction to the city centre and the other to the Bijlmer Arena station. This was not only the one Peter used for work, but it also had a frequent and fast train connection with Schiphol Airport. Perfect.

She had emailed Janna, who looked forward to meeting her at two o'clock on Friday. Louisa could drop off her bag at the hotel and use the free time before their rendezvous to explore some nearby areas. She wanted to get a feel for where she and Peter might take an apartment.

He would join her at the hotel once he had finished work, following which a short metro ride and a pleasant stroll would take them over the Amstel river to the bustling city centre, where Louisa had booked a restaurant for dinner.

She had enjoyed making the arrangements, her confidence growing as she studied airline schedules and online maps of Amsterdam, with its metro and rail lines. She was getting excited by the prospect of dividing her time between home and the Netherlands. She flopped down on the sofa, wine glass by her side. This could be fun.

But then the guilt kicked in. Her mother. Peter's words rang in Louisa's ears – with Michael unable to fulfil his solemn promise to visit their mother regularly, it was all down to her now. If she were living and working in Amsterdam, that would only be possible every few weeks at best. Was that fair? Was Louisa being selfish? Perhaps she should abandon any hopes of a more fulfilling life until the responsibility was no longer there.

The alternative school of thought was that her mother rarely recognised her now anyway. Furthermore, she would be taking positive steps to save her marriage. What to do? She sighed and reached for her glass.

***

Louisa locked the front door behind her and cursed as she wrestled her wheelie bag across the uncooperative gravel of their front courtyard. The first signs of daylight had just been visible as she showered. Now the early-morning sun was rising as she walked up Lonsdale Road in the direction of Hammersmith tube station.

By seven o'clock, she was by her gate in Heathrow's Terminal Five and sipping a cappuccino. As she studied her updated and freshly printed CV, she became aware of a pair of tan men's shoes planted right in front of her. She shuffled uncomfortably, wondering why someone would invade her space like this. She looked up, and the sensations that flooded her mind morphed in a split second from surprise, to guilt, to delight.

The brown hair, although flecked with grey, was still thick as ever. A light salt-and-pepper stubble did nothing to disguise the dimpled cheeks beneath. And then there were those gorgeous blue eyes, shining at her. Eyes that instantly evoked memories of their intimacy as they slowly made love in his bed, all those years ago.

He spoke first, his smile reflecting pleasure at this chance meeting, but also acknowledging he was talking to a woman who had suffered a family bereavement just a week before.

'Louisa. My God. How are you?'

'Robert,' she said, scrambling to her feet.

'You're the last person I expected to bump into. Come here.'

Louisa was conscious that the ensuing embrace lasted longer than it might have done. She was only aware that her eyes had been closed when they slowly opened to reveal a woman on the row of seating opposite, watching them intently. Louisa took a deep breath and she and Robert stepped apart, hands still resting on each other's arms, reluctant to break contact.

'I'm okay, thank you,' said Louisa. 'A bit shell-shocked, I suppose. I still can't believe it. Poor Michael. And thank you for the lovely flowers by the way, and for Sophie's.'

'Of course. I heard the terrible news from Asha. It's truly awful. And thanks for your message. If there's anything I can do, by the way.'

Louisa shook her head and smiled. 'We're fine, thank you.'

'Okay. But you know where I am…' Robert appeared to shift tack. 'So, you're off to see Peter, I'm guessing?'

'I am, yes. I'll be glad to get away for a couple of days. Escape all the turmoil. But there's another purpose to my visit as well. A possible job opportunity.'

'Wow. Time for a change?'

'Ah, there's a bit more to it than that. You're on this Amsterdam flight, I take it?'

'I am. But if you are as well, let me see if I can get us seated together. Have you got your boarding pass? Oh, and your passport. You wait here with the bags.'

Louisa watched as Robert engaged with a man at the desk, their discussion punctuated by glances over to her. She smiled and held up her hand, just as her phone buzzed to indicate the arrival of a message. She studied the screen in disbelief. Really? She sighed and stared up at the ceiling, before switching the smile back on as Robert returned.

***

'Robert, did you pay extra for this? I'll be very cross if you did.'

They were sitting towards the front of the plane. Business class. Robert shook his head with a smile and moved the conversation on.

'Don't worry, it's great to catch up.' His eyes scanned her face. 'So, tell me all.'

Louisa did. She took him through everything that had happened these past weeks. Losing her job at the start of the month. Then Michael's awful murder, the suspicions of the police. Her plans to base herself in Amsterdam, so she and Peter could spend more time together.

'That sounds great. It seems like a long time since he started his job over there.'

'Ten years, give or take.'

'Wow. Where did that go? Time flies.'

Not for me, thought Louisa. She forced a smile. 'Doesn't it?'

'Peter must be thrilled by the prospect of you joining him.'

Louisa blinked furiously, aware that Robert may have picked up on her hesitation. 'Of course. But it does pose some practical challenges. Not least in terms of visiting my mother. Anyway, enough of my fraught world. Tell me about yours. What takes you to Amsterdam?'

Robert explained that he had a meeting with a client that afternoon, and a further one with a potential supplier on Saturday morning. His events management business was going very well.

Louisa asked after his children, knowing how difficult it would be to give a thirteen-year-old girl and a boy of eight the attention they needed whilst building a business. Since the death of his wife, Robert employed the services of Mary, a widowed live-in housekeeper-cum-nanny. Lily and Josh adored her; apparently the woman rather liked the nickname they had given her: Mary Poppins.

'We don't see nearly enough of you, though,' she continued. 'We used to be really tight, our two families. I'm not quite sure what happened.'

This was a lie. Louisa knew precisely what had happened. Peter's relationship with Robert was a casualty of his declining interest in any form of socialising, the extent of the problem accelerating as he spent more and more time in Amsterdam. But when it came to Robert, Peter's attitude seemed especially difficult to understand. They used to be the best of mates, all through university and afterwards in the Shepherd's Bush house share.

Robert raised his hands. 'We'll have to try and get together soon. If you two didn't see so little of each other, I would suggest the three of us meet for dinner in Amsterdam this evening.'

'Fat chance!' Louisa rolled her eyes. 'Peter messaged me while you were sorting the boarding passes. He's had to go to Italy to manage a crisis there. He won't be back in Amsterdam until tomorrow afternoon.'

Shit! Sometimes, Louisa subsequently reminded herself, you open your mouth before your brain has had a chance to do its job. To consider all the options. No going back now.

'Oh, no,' said Robert, 'That's a real shame. Did you guys have anything planned?'

She and Robert looked at each other. The cards had been dealt. They couldn't be silently gathered up, shuffled and flicked across the table anew.

'Dinner in the centre.'

Louisa smiled, as if in defeat. They both knew where this was going. Robert broke the silence.

'Well, look, I don't know how to put this, but I would love you to join me if you are able. But you may not feel like it, and I certainly wouldn't want to offend anyone.'

This wasn't getting any easier. *And I certainly wouldn't want to offend anyone* was code. *Anyone* was Peter. They both knew him well enough, and there was little doubt that he would indeed become extremely prickly if he heard that his wife and her former lover, his old friend, were having dinner together.

Louisa tried harder this time to consider all her choices before she committed herself either way. Secretly, she would be thrilled to join Robert. When they were a couple, she'd been the happiest she could ever remember, although their subsequent secretive and risky one-night stand in a seedy London hotel had caused her much angst.

She had often wondered how events might have unfolded had he not left for Canada all those years ago. He was twenty-four at the time, she twenty-two. They had never discussed a future together, and whilst she would have been thrilled had he not gone abroad, Louisa understood his promise to himself to see something of the world before settling down. Where he would end up, he wasn't sure. His departure seemed inevitable, and once it happened, she thought he was gone forever. But after a few fleeting visits home (including *the* one after she had temporarily broken up with Peter), he had eventually returned to the UK for good. By then, she and Peter had been married for three years, and Sophie was well into the terrible twos.

So right now, there were a few potential courses of action she might take.

Decline. Robert would understand.

Accept his invitation, knowing that Peter would be seriously pissed off.

Accept, but omit to tell Peter. Naturally, the deceit would require Robert's full cooperation. It would make liars out of them both, and God knows what would happen if Peter ever learned the truth.

Louisa studied Robert's face. Her smile disguised the turmoil in her mind.

# 21

Louisa put down her coffee cup and glanced around at her fellow patrons. A mixed bunch, but with one thing in common. They all appeared to be enjoying the warm summer weather, the company of others, and the relaxed vibe of the canalside café. She smiled. It was rather special.

She turned her face up to the sun, closed her eyes and undertook a lazy review of recent events. The meeting with Janna yesterday had gone well. Louisa was sure that she would have the opportunity to meet with the client company, even if she was a little surprised to learn that they had asked Janna to prepare a shortlist of three candidates.

Never mind that, I'm perfect for the job. But better get used to the idea of competition, she had told herself. Finding the right opportunity won't all be plain sailing.

Then this morning, map in hand, she had wandered the streets of Amsterdam, exploring the centre, surprised by just how compact it was. Compared to London, anyway. There were many more areas a little further out that she would want to investigate, but her feet were getting tired and she was running out of time. Peter should arrive at around five o'clock.

And there was that chance meeting with Robert to think about. The flight over in his company had been a pleasure. Louisa had forgotten what it was like to spend time with a man who wasn't constantly trying to thwart her. That persistent undertow of friction, wearing you down, destroying your enjoyment of life. Destroying *them*.

His insistence that they have dinner together had been tinged with anxiety at the thought of explaining it to Peter. Which she would, for neither she nor her companion had dared to suggest what they were both thinking. Wouldn't it be easier to keep it from him? Not really. To have agreed to do so would have caused Louisa to cross a line, a very clear one. She wouldn't do that, even if she would soon be made to pay for her candour when she told Peter how she had bumped into their old friend – and felt obliged to accept his invitation to dinner.

It had been a wonderful evening, nevertheless. The sort she was desperate to replicate with her husband, if only he would show some interest in his wife. Louisa remembered her promise to do everything to save the marriage. Only when she had expended all her energy on the task and reluctantly concluded she had failed, would she abandon hope. She wasn't there yet.

Robert had insisted they get a taxi back from the restaurant. His hotel was only five minutes or so from hers, and he didn't like the idea of her walking alone from the metro station. He had stared silently out of the car window as they left the old centre behind them, Louisa wondering if he was steeling himself to ensure their parting was devoid of any demonstration of the feelings she was sure they both still harboured.

She didn't think for one minute that either of them would risk moving their encounter into a place they might regret, but was nevertheless relieved to get safely past the parting kiss on the cheek. Robert had climbed back into the taxi and was swiftly gone.

Louisa looked at her watch and beckoned the waiter over.

Best get back to the hotel, Peter would be there soon. She felt her stomach lurch. And before then, she needed to work out how to raise the subject of her dinner with Robert.

***

Louisa took a seat in the lobby and awaited the arrival of her husband. He had called from Schiphol – his flight had landed and he should be with her shortly. Apparently he had everything he needed for this evening in his carry-on bag. No need to return to his room with its single bed in someone else's house. It couldn't be much of a life being a lodger, Louisa thought.

She busied herself with her mobile phone, pointlessly flicking between screens but without paying any attention to the offered content. She took a deep breath, put the phone in her bag and replaced it with a street plan of Amsterdam. She was still studying it when Peter arrived, raising his eyebrows and sighing at the sight of the map. The brief kiss they exchanged was accompanied by her rubbing his lower back, moving her hand around to his side. It was a hint.

*Hold me.*

It didn't work.

Five minutes later they were in their room, where he gave her an account of his trip in response to her questioning. She had to wait for him to emerge from the shower before he asked about her, about yesterday's meeting, about what she had done today.

Keen to get through Peter's inevitable reaction to yesterday evening, Louis started by telling him about bumping into Robert at the airport. She was aware of a brief pause in the towelling of his hair as he digested the news. She told him that Robert had proposed that the three of them should meet up for dinner, at which point she had explained that he, Peter, had been called to Italy. She told him of Robert's refusal to take 'no' for an answer, hiding the fact that she had readily agreed. The coward that she was.

Peter's voice was terse. 'Oh. I see. And did you have a cosy evening together?'

There it was again. That nasty, destructive sarcasm. *A cosy evening.* At that moment Louisa wondered if she was truly wasting her time. Whether she should have put her hands on Robert's face last night as they stood by the taxi, raised herself onto her toes and kissed him full on the mouth. Abandoned her attempts to save her marriage and instead just let herself go. Because she was a woman, he was a man, and for nine glorious months they had revelled in the attraction they felt to one another. As well as on one crazy night following her temporary break-up with Peter.

But instead, she reminded herself why she was there, humoured her husband and stepped back from the edge of the precipice. She would do her best to defuse the situation and ensure they spent a pleasant evening together. Tomorrow they would enjoy a walk around Amsterdam in the morning, and then she would head off home in the afternoon.

Her plan only partly worked. Over dinner, she talked about the meeting with Janna and her excitement at the prospect of securing work here. Peter's response was entirely predictable.

'But we've talked about this already. You can earn much more in the UK, and that's where you should be concentrating your efforts.'

Louisa looked around the restaurant, lowered her voice and leaned towards her husband.

'Peter, I'm trying to address two issues here, not one. If our marriage is to survive, we need to be together. It's not just about me getting work, it's about us being able to live in the same place.'

'Yes, and I have explained that I'm trying to arrange it so that I can spend much more time in the UK. So you need to get a job *there*. That way we can be together *and* save a bloody fortune on accommodation in Amsterdam!'

'But we don't know if that will happen, do we? And as I have said, the role that I'm pursuing can be done from anywhere. So if you do manage to convince your boss to let you work out of the UK, I can do the same.' She opened her hands. 'What's not to like? You seem determined to undermine my efforts to get us back to normal.'

Peter closed his eyes and gently shook his head.

'You're so bloody insecure about us, so sensitive. I've told you before, it just makes it worse. Two weeks ago, our weekend here together… That worked, didn't it? And I'll tell you why it worked. It's because you promised to stop banging on about *us*.'

Louisa picked up her knife and fork and pushed some food around her plate. He was right in that the weekend had worked. From the point of view of sex, anyway. But he had still been far from the loving, engaged partner that he used to be. But perhaps she was being unreasonable. Maybe she needed to be patient, and then the caring and tenderness would follow, assuming she gave him the time and space he seemed to need.

So tonight, she would park her despair at losing her brother in the most dreadful circumstances. Instead, she would concentrate on pleasing her husband in the hope that her efforts at playing the lover would not be in vain. That he would appreciate the connection between pleasure in the bedroom and the fun, romantic life they used to enjoy together. And reward her for it. Because hope was all she had left.

***

On Monday morning the coroner's office called. An interim death certificate had been issued, and Michael's body was ready for release to an undertaker. Louisa wasted no time in contacting the one she had already engaged in preparation for such an eventuality.

By early afternoon a funeral date had been agreed. Friday the fourteenth at Mortlake Crematorium, with the wake at the adjacent Putney Town Rowing Club.

Louisa now gave some thought as to how to communicate the arrangements to Michael's friends. She felt a pang of guilt as the realisation hit that she had no idea who they even were, let alone how to contact them. She cast her mind back to the impromptu memorial on Clapham Common. Surely they would want to mourn him at a funeral service, or at least be given the opportunity? An idea struck her, and she resolved to act on it.

In the meantime, she could tell her family and friends. Including Robert. She wasn't sure why, but knew that Peter wouldn't like that. Tough. Because Robert was both a friend of the family and Sophie's godfather, and she would be there grieving for her uncle.

As these thoughts were going through her head, she heard a knock on the front door. Once more, Louisa felt a surge of anxiety as she eyed her visitor. Detective Inspector Lloyd Griffiths.

'Mrs Hedley. I'm sorry to disturb you, but I need to update you on a couple of things. I was in the area and thought I would drop by on the off-chance.' He looked past her and down the hall towards the kitchen. 'As long as I'm not disturbing you, of course?'

'No, not at all. Come on in. I've just been tying down the arrangements for Michael's funeral. The coroner has released the body.'

'Yes, I heard.'

They were soon seated on adjoining sofas, sipping tea. The inspector looked around approvingly. 'It's really nice, this. The perfect family space. Kitchen, dining table and living room. Very sociable.'

Louisa smiled politely. All she needed was someone here at home with whom she could share it. It was as if her visitor had read her mind.

'It must be hard on you, with your husband away all the time.'

'Oh, we manage.' Louisa set down her cup, anxious to move the conversation on. As she looked up, her heart skipped a beat – the inspector was staring at her, frowning, as if trying to get inside her thoughts. His head jerked a little at the unexpected eye contact, the action of someone who'd been caught out.

He cleared his throat. 'So, first things first,' he said in his official voice. 'We are ready to hand Michael's flat over to whoever will administer his affairs. We understand that's you, but tell us if not. Obviously, the place has been thoroughly searched, but I don't believe it's in too bad a state as a result. His phone and laptop are evidence and will stay with us. Not that the hard drive has thrown up anything relevant to his murder.'

Louisa could see the detective choosing his words carefully. She had no idea what was on Michael's computer and preferred to keep it that way.

'As for the investigation, we have no new leads, I'm afraid. Nor have we found the murder weapon. The television appeal produced nothing other than the usual cranks. We have questioned everyone we can from Bar Seventeen, whether or not they were there on the night Michael died. There will be other friends and contacts, of course, but if we don't know about them, we can't talk to them.'

'I see.' Louisa raised her eyebrows. 'So what about me?

Do you and your cheerful sergeant still think I paid someone to kill my brother?'

DI Griffiths winced. 'We don't *think* you had your brother killed, Mrs Hedley, but neither can we rule out the possibility. That's our job. To keep an open mind.'

Louisa recalled that Peter, annoyingly, had said as much.

'On that, have you had any further thoughts as to who the twelve thousand pounds went to?' DI Griffiths continued. 'Because if we can establish that the money was indeed used to pay off a debt, then we can at least dismiss the possibility of you using it for another purpose. We have you on CCTV on the platform at Clapham Junction at the time of death, so we know it wasn't you who stabbed your brother.'

'Very reassuring. But no, I have no idea who he gave the money to. I guess I'm doomed to remain a suspect after all.'

No response to that. 'Oh, and the funeral. Any arrangements in place for that yet?'

Louisa gave him the details. He made a note, thanked her and stood to leave. He turned back on the doorstep.

'One last thing. My apologies again for the slip-up with Sergeant Lynch. When she mentioned the loan to your brother in front of your husband.'

'Your apologies?'

'Yes. I'm sorry.'

'Hmm. So what did you see, Inspector? What conclusions did you draw about my husband and me when the "slip-up" happened?'

'I'm afraid I'm not with you.'

'Well, here's the thing. I don't believe for one second that it was accidental. You planned it, didn't you? You wanted to see how my husband and I would react.'

DI Griffiths narrowed his eyes. His gaze travelled from her face, down her body and back again. Louisa tensed, uncomfortable under such scrutiny. Was he looking for evidence of something? Trying to intimidate her, perhaps? No, she thought, this was something else. Something she definitely didn't like.

'Are you afraid of him, Mrs Hedley? Does he bully you, control you?'

Another pregnant pause.

'I think you should leave now.'

A slow nod. 'Please call me if you want to talk. Or for any other reason.'

Louisa closed the door after him and slumped back against it, her eyes shut. She breathed deeply, waiting for the queasiness to pass. Had that just happened? A police inspector, a man who was investigating the murder of her brother. Someone who was supposed to be a professional, someone you should be able to trust. And yet there he was, testing to see if she was vulnerable – what – to see if she would fall weakly into his welcoming arms? Was he cynically using privileged information gathered in his police duties, playing on the fact that her husband was rarely home and suspecting he bullied her when he was? Or was he genuinely concerned about her, and she, Louisa Hedley, was guilty of the paranoia that her husband so often accused her of demonstrating. My God.

She straightened up and marched off to the kitchen. She'd had enough of being intimidated. If she had to, she'd stick a bloody great notice on the front door: *No victims here.* She wouldn't be a victim of her former boss. She wouldn't be the victim of Peter's indifference to their marriage, his hostility to her ambitions. And neither would she present as a victim to DI Griffiths and his conniving sidekick.

# 22

At around lunchtime, Louisa called Asha. She wanted to update her friend on Michael, but also had a favour to ask. Louisa moved the phone away from her ear. Asha didn't talk softly.

'So, how are you doing, babe? How was Amsterdam?'

'It was even more interesting than my last visit. Listen, I know you're working, so I won't keep you. But I wondered if you fancied getting together this week for a catch-up?'

'Good idea.'

'Well, this Wednesday is the first in the month. Does Samuel have his writers' group that evening?'

'He sure does.'

'Right. In that case, I'm treating you to dinner whilst he's out. At a restaurant.'

'Sounds wonderful, but we'll go Dutch, honey. Like we usually do.'

Louisa sucked in air through her teeth. 'No, let me pay. Because there's a catch.'

'Which is...?'

'We're going to Clapham.'

'Okaaay. But why would we go to Clapham for dinner?'

'Because there's a gay bar there that I would like to take you to – after we've eaten.'

***

On Tuesday morning Peter didn't pick up. As usual. Louisa left a message and he called back a little later. And as usual, the discussion was hard work, Louisa struggling to extract from him some of the easy chat that ought to characterise the conversation between a husband and wife separated by the demands of work.

She set aside her growing pessimism and explained that she had engaged a funeral director to take care of the arrangements for Michael's service. She had correctly predicted Peter's response.

'And, presumably, we have to pay for all that? What did the police say – your brother has debts of nineteen thousand? Not to mention the twelve he just conned out of you.'

Count to ten. She spoke softly.

'He's my brother, Peter, what else do you expect me to do? We're going to have a proper funeral on Friday the fourteenth. Two o'clock. Mortlake Crem and then at Putney Town Rowing Club. I have no idea how many will turn up, and I'm giving some thought as to how to communicate the arrangements to Michael's friends.'

'Well, that should be different. I've never been to a gay funeral. Hang on a sec.'

She bit her lip. He was obviously distracted by something.

'Okay, just looking at my calendar. It's a busy week, so if the funeral's at two, I'll fly over on the Friday morning. Get an early flight. Should work.'

Louisa gritted her teeth and breathed in deeply through her nose before the words exploded from her.

'Oh, Peter. I can't believe you just said that. I can't! How could you be so heartless, so cold? My only brother is dead. He was murdered, for Christ's sake. Don't you think any wife might expect her husband to be home, comforting her, the night before a family funeral? It's the sort of thing normal people do.'

'Here we go. More drama. Because I happen to take my work seriously.'

'Oh, I have no doubt you take your work seriously – I just wish you would do the same with your marriage. Look, I don't know when Sophie will arrive home or when she will go back to Southampton. But at some point that weekend… assuming you stay that long, of course… we are going to plan how we exit this marriage in a civilised manner. I want a divorce.'

# 23

## PETER

Peter tossed the phone down onto his desk and rapped at his clenched jaw with a knuckle. Shit, shit! He had long believed that a divorce was inevitable. Indeed, it had been part of his plan. But plans change.

He cursed himself as he realised he had failed to placate his discontented wife. Had he been more careful and worked harder at playing the perfect husband, Louisa might have continued to tolerate his absence. And then life could have gone on as it was. For now, anyway.

Okay, her job loss was unforeseen, but it had certainly been avoidable. Typical Louisa, he thought, her and her bloody principles. Why couldn't she have just gone along with her boss's plans, instead of resisting, digging in? Well, this time, her stubbornness had come at a high price.

And, in consequence, she was now planning to come and fuck up *his* life in Amsterdam. Well, that certainly couldn't happen. And neither could a divorce. Right now, that would be a disaster. Which left him with three imperatives if he wanted events to unfold to his advantage.

Firstly, head off the divorce thing. He knew Louisa didn't want it, not really. And a big part of that was because she hated the idea of failure. But she had lost patience with him. Well, he would just have to charm her out of her threat. He could do that, surely? Just be *nice*, dickhead.

As part of that, he would need to be seen to be going along with her plan to come and live with him in Amsterdam. But they both knew that there were challenges to overcome before it could happen. And whilst he would give the impression of working with her, supporting her – some of those challenges were quite significant…

And lastly, there was the money. Didn't it always come down to that? Although she had never acknowledged it, and never would, his wife *owed* him. Peter had long known that one day he would exact payback from her. Tit for tat. Only now the stakes were very much higher than he had initially foreseen. But so be it – Louisa would finally get what she deserved.

# 24

# LOUISA

Louisa's heart skipped a beat as she looked at the name of the incoming caller. Was this fate? Only that morning she had told Peter their marriage was over, and now here was Robert. His voice was soothing and tinged with empathy, as he asked how she was coping.

Louisa let out a big sigh. What she *wanted* to say was that she had just told Peter she was going to divorce him – and did Robert fancy meeting up for dinner, and who knows what else, sometime very soon? She was just figuring out a more anodyne response when he continued.

'Sorry, I expect you're sick of people asking. But look, thank you for the invitation to Michael's funeral. Of course I shall come.'

'Good, thank you. I need you there.' Louisa's eyes widened as she reflected on her unguarded words. She hurriedly corrected herself. '*We* need you there. You're like family.'

'Of course. Now, is there anything I can do? I know it's not easy, with Peter away.'

Anything he could do? Well… She pushed the thought aside. 'That's sweet, thank you. It's been awful. The coroner's office, the police, there's just so much to sort out when someone dies, you have no idea…'

One hand flew to her mouth. She wanted to snatch the words back.

'Oh, God, Robert, I'm so sorry. I didn't think, please forgive me. You know very well what it's like.' Louisa sniffed loudly and jerked her head upright. 'I just seem to be drowning in my own…' She couldn't finish, the words replaced by heaving sobs.

'Hey, it's okay. Take your time, it's alright.'

'Just a sec.'

Louisa put down the phone, wiped her eyes and blew her nose. She took a deep breath, fanned her face with her hands and tried again.

'Right, sorry about that.' She cleared her throat. 'Let's have another go.'

He laughed. 'Good for you. Now, what are you doing on Thursday?'

Louisa's heart jumped. Could he read her mind? 'Why?'

'Answer the question, please.'

'Nothing very much, just ploughing through the list of things to do for the funeral, I guess.'

'Right. Well, we need to get you out for some fresh air. I was thinking Richmond Park.'

They were both familiar with the marvellous green lung to the west of the capital. As lovers, they had often escaped there for some privacy, something that was in short supply in the Rat Pack house. Louisa recalled a hasty lovemaking session, half-sitting and half-leaning on the rough trunk of a fallen tree, her arms wrapped tightly around Robert's neck as she glanced furtively over his shoulder. The journey home had been undertaken with frequent wriggles and poorly disguised scratches of her behind, as she tried to dislodge itchy traces of bark from inside her knickers.

'And there's also something I want to talk to you about, but only if you're up to it, of course. A job opportunity that might be of interest.' He laughed. 'But I'm afraid the assignment is top secret, so you're not allowed to tell anyone about our meeting, or anything to do with it. Deal?'

Louisa could feel the blood rushing to her neck, her cheeks. The opportunity to get out of the house, that was one thing. But to spend some time in Robert's company – right now she couldn't think of anyone else with whom she would rather be.

But this was becoming tricky. On the surface, Robert's urging that the assignment was 'top secret' was just fooling around. But his insistence that she didn't tell anyone about their meeting? Despite the ambiguous wording, she knew exactly what he was saying. Because they both understood it was code for 'we won't tell Peter'. Robert had no idea that Louisa planned to divorce her husband. But he had worked out that she was unlikely to accept his invitation if Peter were to find out. And evidently, Robert wasn't averse to a bit of deceit himself, to make sure Louisa said 'yes'.

***

The following day, Louisa was sitting at her desk in the bay window, when a woman crunched over the gravel and past their tired-looking car. She was admiring a huge bouquet carried in her arms. She looked up and exchanged a smile with Louisa, who rose and headed for the front door.

That was another thing that happened when someone close to you died. All the flowers. She had run out of vases and was wondering what she could put these in, as she exchanged pleasantries with the woman and relieved her of the delivery.

Louisa laid them down on the kitchen island, eased open the little square envelope and removed the card. She reread it as she fished around behind her for one of the stools, sinking slowly onto it. She gazed out of the window onto the garden for a minute, then picked up the card and studied the wording once more.

***

It was a couple of hours before they spoke. Peter sounded a little nervous. 'I got your message, thank you.'

'No, thank *you*. They are absolutely beautiful. I can't recall the last time you sent me flowers.'

'Well, I seem to put my foot in my mouth every time I open it these days, so I thought I would try a different tack. I'm very sorry, Louisa, I know I've been a complete fuckwit lately. You have tried so hard to make things better between us, and I just keep throwing it back in your face.'

'I won't disagree with that. But why, Peter? Why has it got to this?'

'Just me, I guess. But I see it now. And Louisa, don't divorce me. I can change, I know it. Promise me you won't leave? I couldn't cope with that. I do love you.'

***

Louisa sat at the breakfast island with her chin in her hand, staring into space. She turned to look at the flowers. Peter's flowers. Perhaps the message had finally got through to him, her demand for a divorce jolting him into realising just how distant, how miserable, he had become. For this wasn't some calculation on her part, a clever ploy to force him into changing his behaviour. No, her mind had been made up, convinced as she was that all hope for them was lost. Louisa didn't think herself unreasonable. After all, it was perfectly normal to want a husband who loved his wife and showed it.

Without that love and support, there was nothing. And they used to have it, didn't they?

It was hard to remember now what it was like in the first years of their marriage. But the gradual and unrelenting decline into tedium and metaphorical distance had accelerated rapidly with Peter's move to Amsterdam, as if he was glad to be free of her and Sophie. If she was honest with herself, Louisa knew she had left it too long to bring things to a head between them, desperate as she was to spare her teenage daughter the potential trauma of a family break-up.

But Peter's comments earlier had given her hope. Louisa wasn't naïve, but neither had she heard him talk like that before. Maybe it was going to be alright. She would give him the benefit of the doubt. For now, at least.

***

At seven-fifteen on Wednesday evening, Louisa was in the shopping centre at Clapham Junction, watching the passers-by. She didn't have to wait long, Asha came marching up and threw her arms around her friend. She peered into Louisa's eyes with a show of concern.

'Are you okay, babe, are you sure this won't be too painful?'

'No, I don't believe so. We can have dinner, a good natter, and then we can visit Bar Seventeen. It's as I explained on the phone, I want to see if we can talk to some of Michael's friends. Put the word out about his funeral, otherwise they may not know.'

'It's a good thing to do, my love. It would be awful if people wanted to pay their respects but didn't know about the arrangements. And there's nothing worse than a badly attended funeral.'

Ten minutes later they were sitting in a brasserie, a different restaurant to the one where she and Michael had argued that fateful night. She had no desire to revisit it and was well aware that it was only a short walk to the common and the place where he had met his death. She recounted to Asha her visit to Michael's shrine, her surprise at the number of tributes, and the depth of feeling shown towards her dead brother.

'I know our lives were very different, and I do feel guilty for not being involved in his. But, hopefully, we can find out a bit more about his friends when we visit the bar afterwards.'

Louisa was keen to make sure that the conversation did not become one-sided and managed to get Asha to talk about herself. Not least her continuing dissatisfaction with her lot at work, even if she had yet to take any action to address it.

For her part, Louisa updated Asha on the emerging job opportunity in Amsterdam, Peter's continuing objections to it, and the revelation that his apartment had indeed been on a short-term lease. A mix-up by an assistant, supposedly. Louisa shook her head in disbelief. She spoke of the surprise meeting with Robert at the airport and the ensuing dinner with her old flame. And, no surprise, Peter's arsey reaction.

Asha laughed. 'Well, it's good that he's jealous, honey.' The big smile was suddenly replaced by a deadpan expression. 'And knowing your past with Robert as I do, I guess he has reason to be.'

Ouch! Louisa blinked but said nothing. She moved the conversation on.

'But here's the thing. When I told Peter about the funeral arrangements – well, it was awful. As if it was all just some bloody great inconvenience. There was no empathy, not a trace of any compassion or care for me, for how I was feeling about losing my brother. I got angry with him.'

'I'm not surprised.'

Louisa grimaced. 'So, I told him I wanted a divorce.'

Asha stared at her. 'Oh my God, babe, do you mean it?'

'I dunno really. It's not my preferred choice. I'm desperate to avoid it, in fact. But I've tried so hard to get him to see what he's become, what *we* have become. And there have been flickers of hope, but then we just revert to the dull, jaded, loveless marriage we've both endured for too long.'

Louisa leaned forward and tapped her friend's hand for emphasis. 'Maybe, just maybe though, the threat worked.'

'Go on.'

'Well, he sent me the most enormous bunch of flowers. So I messaged to thank him, obviously, but I was quite cool about it. And then he called, pleaded with me not to leave him.'

'Okay! And you said…'

Louisa shrugged. 'I was non-committal. I told him I wasn't interested in empty promises. That there was a lot of healing to do. We'll see, won't we?'

Asha winced. 'I hope it all turns out okay for you, babe.'

'So do I. Oh, and Robert has been in touch, too. Says he wants to talk to me about a job opportunity.'

'Hey, that's great. What is it?'

'He couldn't tell me over the phone.'

'Couldn't or wouldn't?'

'I don't know,' said Louisa. 'But we've arranged to meet for a walk in Richmond Park – tomorrow.'

'Hmmm. Interesting… in so many ways.'

***

Asha tapped her card on the machine as Louisa nodded towards a table.

'Shall we sit over there?'

'Sure.'

As Louisa put down her glass, she caught sight of a man watching her from the far end of the bar. A man she recognised. He smiled and came over.

'It's Louisa, isn't it? Mikey's sister?'

'That's right. George?'

'Correct.' They shook hands, and Louisa introduced Asha before putting a hand on his arm. 'Look, George, can I buy you a drink? I would love to have a chat if you can spare the time.'

A couple of minutes later, George solemnly dipped his head as the three of them chinked glasses.

'To Michael.'

'Michael.'

The conversation unfolded easily, the three of them soon joined by others as Louisa's identity became known. Some pulled up stools, some stood beside their table, Louisa brushing away the occasional tear as her new friends regaled her with stories about her brother. Sometimes the group was smiling and laughing, then melancholy would settle over them as they reflected on the fact that Michael was gone forever, cruelly taken. A wave of joy followed by a trough of depression, the sequence replayed again and again, as if on a loop.

Louisa looked at the faces around her, two conclusions forming in her mind. First, her brother had been a popular and well-liked figure. The strength of feeling here about his shocking death was clear. Secondly, no one had any idea who would want to hurt him, let alone kill him. Michael didn't have any enemies. He was always open to meeting new people, always looking for the positives. He would be missed. The best theory that anyone could come up with was that this was a random attack, possibly homophobic, carried out by someone with serious psychological problems. Why else would a life have been needlessly taken?

Comfortable now with those around her, Louisa steered the conversation onto a topic about which she had some privileged knowledge.

'Was my brother in trouble, do you know? Did he have any financial problems?'

George answered for the group, all of them nodding in sympathy with his assessment.

'I think money was quite tight. As a scriptwriter, his income was precarious, to say the least. He was always moaning about his credit-card bill, but with a smile, if you know what I mean. He never gave the impression – not to me anyway – that he was in serious trouble of any sort. I think he would have told me. He was useless at hiding things, keeping secrets.'

'That was Michael.' Louisa jerked upright. 'That reminds me. His funeral.' She fumbled in her bag and produced an index card. 'Here are the details, and my email address should you need it.' She looked around the group and pleaded, 'Do you think any of you will be able to make it? I really hope you will.'

George spoke for them. 'Oh, that's such a relief to hear. As soon as I recognised you, I was determined to ask. You might be surprised by how many will want to come.'

Louisa smiled. 'Can I ask you a couple of favours, George?'

'Of course.'

'First, make sure all of Michael's friends know about the funeral. And having put the word out, if you could give me some idea of the numbers we can expect, I can make sure that no one goes away hungry or thirsty.'

'Agreed.'

'Thank you.' Louisa looked around the group. 'And another thing – please would one of you be so kind as to talk about Michael at the service? My daughter Sophie will speak for the family, but it would be lovely if someone would do so on behalf of his friends.'

One of the men standing to the side smiled at her, then nodded to George.

'He's your man, Louisa. He's a stage actor… done the National, the Old Vic *and* the West End too. Marvellous at working a crowd. Aren't you, my love?'

George smiled and looked down. He spoke softly. 'Thank you. I'd be honoured to do it. Mikey was a very special person.'

# 25

Thursday's fine weather did little to allay Louisa's sense of guilt about meeting Robert. Her husband's flowers and subsequent pleading had only served to complicate matters. On Tuesday, she had told him they were going to divorce. A decision made. But her surprise at his reaction had made her think again. Maybe Peter had finally got the message, and was prepared to change his ways. It would take more than words, but perhaps he'd needed a shock to get him to understand just how bad things had become between them.

Louisa and Robert soon found each other in the Petersham car park, the embrace a replay of the one they had shared in the terminal at Heathrow. Only this time Louisa's eyes were open, as conflicting emotions coursed through her mind. Just two days ago it had been made up – she had told Peter she wanted a divorce. And the prospect of meeting up with Robert had lifted her spirits, as she contemplated the opportunity to spend some time in the company of a man who evidently cared for her.

Then just yesterday, she had relented in the face of Peter's unexpected but welcome promise to change. She had to allow him to prove he could – consequently, regrets about the arrangement with Robert had surfaced. Keen to put her confusion aside, she detached herself from him and asked what the plan was for their walk.

He suggested they head off past the ponds and on to the Royal Ballet School, before making their way back and having tea in Pembroke Lodge. As they walked, Louisa shared an update on the police investigation into Michael's death, together with the result of her visit to Bar Seventeen with Asha. There was no mention of either her loan to Michael, or her faltering plans for a divorce. Robert listened carefully, showing interest and concern, both for his goddaughter and for Louisa herself. She was relieved that he made no attempt to question her about Peter's reaction to their dinner in Amsterdam.

Once outside the entrance to the ballet school, they stopped and turned to face south.

'Anyway, I think we've earned a cuppa,' said Robert. He nodded towards the trees and lowered his voice. 'If you like, we can head back through Spankers Hill Wood.' He turned to Louisa, one eyebrow raised. 'I thought you might like that.'

Louisa blinked furiously, her expression deadpan. It worked for about five seconds before they simultaneously exploded into fits of juvenile laughter, Louisa going red-faced and whacking his upper arm with the back of her hand. She took a deep breath as they set off. My God. That was, what – twenty-five years ago? She needed to change the subject.

'So, moving on. This mysterious job. Tell me all,' she said.

'Ah, yes. Well, there's this privately owned company that's growing fast, and the founder has decided it's time they appointed a proper finance director. So I wondered whether you might be interested.'

'Well, I think I've had my fill of multi-nationals for a while, so I may well be. Are you able to tell me who they are?'

'Sure I am.' Robert turned to Louisa as they walked. 'It's my business. I want you to come and work with me.'

***

At home that evening, Louisa lounged on the sofa, half-watching a repeat of a food programme. Only it wasn't really about cooking, it was more like a prelude to an orgy. She wasn't sure whether she wanted to emulate the sultry goddess presenting it, or throw a bucket of cold water over her.

Her thoughts turned away from the food porn to her afternoon in the company of Robert. Equally evocative, but for very different reasons.

As they headed back from their walk, Louisa had asked plenty of questions about the job, and Robert's plans for the business. She knew he had built his company from scratch, and that it was doing very well. But she was surprised to learn how big it had grown, Robert and his rapidly expanding team having earned a strong reputation for organising and managing top-tier events. Conferences, exhibitions, and his favourite: lavish corporate functions with their eye-watering budgets.

It all sounded great, and under normal circumstances she would have jumped at the opportunity. But several issues were screaming for attention, getting in the way of a swift acceptance.

First, the job was in the UK, and Louisa had made up her mind that spending time in Amsterdam with Peter was critical to saving her marriage. Unless, of course, he was able to undertake the bulk of his work from home. But even if that possibility were genuine, and not some throwaway comment designed merely to appease her, actually implementing it seemed a long way off.

Or was she being naïve about Peter's apparent epiphany? His begging for forgiveness, his admission of his failings, had been a welcome surprise. Time would tell if he'd meant any of it. There was a real possibility that she might reject Robert's offer now, only to regret it bitterly should she and Peter indeed go their separate ways. She tried to assure herself that the regrets would be confined to the lost job opportunity.

Finally, if there was indeed hope for her marriage, then that would likely be compromised by any decision to go and work for Robert. Peter would struggle to accept it, always fearing the worst. Okay, he'd never found out about her one-night stand with Robert while he was briefly back from Canada, but Peter *was* aware that for nine months she and Robert had shared a bed. And his hostile reception of the news that Louisa and her former lover had dined together in Amsterdam made clear his understandable discomfort at any hint of them being together. Because Louisa and Robert had form.

So what did she do now?

***

The following morning, Louisa sat at the kitchen island with her tablet, exploring catering options for her brother's wake at the rowing club. She needed George to get back to her about the number of friends who might attend. The funeral was next Friday.

She was interrupted by her phone, her heart skipping as she stared at the screen. Her mother's nursing home. They weren't in the habit of calling to tell you everything was just fine.

Ten minutes later, she rang off, rested her elbows on the worktop and buried her face in her hands.

***

Within the hour, Louisa was sitting opposite the manageress of the home as the facts were gently explained to her.

As was usual, a staff member had gone in to attend to Barbara first thing that morning. She had been concerned to find the elderly woman face down in bed, and had been unable to rouse her. The on-site nurse was summoned immediately, but couldn't detect a pulse. An ambulance had been called, but Barbara Bruce-Gardiner was confirmed dead on the crew's arrival. The police had been summoned, and two uniformed officers were subsequently joined by a detective.

The police could see no signs of foul play, but whilst the death of a woman in her eighties was hardly surprising, it had not been expected. The body was now under the jurisdiction of the coroner. A post-mortem was likely. Louisa winced as she addressed the manageress.

'Did they say anything else? Any ideas as to how she died?'

'They couldn't be sure. But there was no obvious trauma. She was old, she was frail, and when the nurse found her, Barbara had her face buried in her pillow.' The woman sighed. 'We don't know what went on in her mind, but the tragic death of your brother may have had an impact. I know you felt she hadn't taken it in when you broke the news, but afterwards she was weeping and muttering about Michael. We thought she knew, on one level at least. Old and sick people can sometimes just give up after a blow like that.'

'Oh, God. Perhaps I should have kept it from her completely, even if I did lie about the circumstances.'

'It can be hard to know what to do. Barbara was a wonderful lady and we shall all miss her. But I believe she led a good life and that she is at peace now. Hopefully, you can find some consolation in that.' The manageress leaned closer and cupped her hand over Louisa's. 'But how are you, Mrs Hedley? You've been through two deeply traumatic events in close succession.'

Louisa felt her eyes well with tears. 'Thank you for your kind words. And your concern.'

'Look, I'm going to fetch us some tea. Naturally, we shall arrange for your mother's effects to be sent on to you. But is there anything else we can do in the meantime?'

'Well, while you're organising the tea, do you mind if I pay a last visit to Mum's room?'

'Of course not. I'll see you back here when you're ready.'

Moments later, Louisa stood motionless, one hand resting on her mother's armchair. She fingered the bed jacket draped over the back, and gazed at the slippers tucked under the bed. Her eyes moved to the framed photos, neatly lined up on top of the dresser. The little vase of flowers, wilting now, as if in sympathy with Barbara's passing.

Louisa drew a deep breath and whispered to the empty room: 'Goodbye, Mum. Love you.' She made her way out and eased the door shut.

***

Once home, Louisa made herself a coffee and drifted around the kitchen, reflecting on her changed circumstances. It was just two weeks since Michael's horrific murder. Now her mother had slipped away at the end of a long and (mostly) contented life. No fuss, no bother. That would be entirely in character for Barbara, the way she would have chosen, if indeed a choice had been afforded her.

Louisa wondered if, beneath the veil of dementia, her mother had registered what had happened to her son and simply decided to die, as the manageress of the home had suggested. The last two weeks of her life must have been lived in some hideous fog of bewilderment and pain at the loss of her darling boy. And it was her daughter who had chosen to deliver the devastating news.

Why, oh, why hadn't Louisa kept it from her? Who knows how much longer her mum would have gone on for? A few months? A couple of years, perhaps? Bumbling around in her confused world, images of a good life well-lived occasionally flashing in front of her. Content. Safe. In blissful ignorance of her son's shocking and premature death.

Whatever was going on in her mother's mind, one thing

was certain. In almost the blink of an eye, Louisa had lost the only two people connecting her to her family. The one into which she had been born and had grown up. A couple of weeks ago there were three of them. Now it was just her. A page had been decisively turned in the metaphorical book that catalogued her life; one that it was impossible to ease back for one last, loving look. She would never again share a nostalgic discussion with a close relative who had experienced the same childhood events as her. There were no more Bruce-Gardiners. Not from their family, anyway. It was the end of the line.

A weepy ten minutes was followed by Louisa giving herself a stern talking to. There were still so many things for her to do. She reached for her notebook and started making lists. She was good at that. The task completed, she rewarded herself with another coffee.

She sipped and studied the names of the people she needed to contact. She reached for her phone and paused with her finger on the contact entry for Sophie. She reasoned with herself that her daughter and Barbara were blood relatives. So it was natural that Louisa should tell her first. But that logic failed to mask a somewhat damning conclusion – that most spouses would instinctively turn to their other half for comfort at such a time. It's what couples automatically did, for God's sake. But not in their case, it seemed.

Louisa's voice faltered as she delivered the news to her daughter, both of them crying as they consoled each other, one mourning the loss of a mother, the other a gran. Then Louisa felt guilty as, without hesitation, Sophie insisted she would catch a train home that afternoon.

'No, darling, you're coming home anyway for Michael's funeral on Friday. You have work…'

'Mum, it's no problem.'

'But I worry about you. What if the ferry people think

you're letting them down? You don't need to be here. I'll be fine.'

'When's Dad coming home?'

'I haven't called him yet.'

Louisa instantly regretted her spontaneous reply. She could have avoided the question, given some dismissive response about having left a message. But it would have been a lie. And Louisa refused to lie to her daughter. In the briefest of pauses that followed, Louisa was sure she could hear Sophie's brain working. The girl's voice was firm.

'I'll be there this evening. And now you had better get hold of Dad.'

Having done as Sophie had instructed, Louisa lowered her phone. She was pleasantly surprised. Peter had picked up straight away. He had been kind. He was coming home.

***

The weekend played out as expected. On Friday afternoon, Louisa made a pie with a bag of mixed fish pieces liberated from the icy depths of the freezer. She had preferred to keep busy rather than succumb to the grief that could easily overtake her.

Once again, she collected her daughter from Barnes station and was grateful to have her to herself for a couple of hours before Peter arrived from Amsterdam. But he did seem to be making an effort, and the short evening they all spent together around the kitchen table was relaxed and congenial, despite the renewed trauma that had overtaken their lives.

Before they ate, Sophie lifted her wine glass.

'I should like to make a toast to my gran. A wonderful woman. We all loved her and will miss her. To Barbara Bruce-Gardiner!'

The ceremony completed, Louisa silently raised herself

from her chair, wrapped her arms around Sophie's neck and kissed her. She paused to dab at her face with a handkerchief before she kissed Peter in his turn. He patted her hand and topped up her glass. No great demonstration of feeling, but that was always his way.

On Saturday they settled on the idea of a walk, Peter's proposal of Richmond Park was hurriedly rejected by Louisa, who suggested taking the tube over to Hyde Park instead. To this, Sophie added a subsequent mooch around the shops in Kensington, a condition to which Peter agreed, providing he could leave 'you girls' to it and return home to watch the racing on TV. Dinner would be eaten in a restaurant at the bottom end of Castelnau, one of Sophie's favourites, given its strong vegetarian offering.

At just before seven, sweet-smelling and ready for the evening, Louisa poured drinks for Peter and herself as they waited for Sophie to join them. She nodded to his flowers on the coffee table between the sofas.

'What do you think? You haven't mentioned them.'

He glanced in their direction. 'Gorgeous. Really nice.' He lowered his voice. 'I meant what I said, you know. About us.'

Louisa pretended not to hear. 'The colours are summery, but they don't jar like some arrangements do.'

'So are we okay?' A pause. A sip of his drink. 'Can I show you I love you? Later.'

She flashed him a weak smile.

'Peter, my mother died yesterday.'

Keen to close off the discussion, she lifted her wine glass and turned to gaze out of the window. Despite the clumsiness of his timing, she knew she should be pleased by Peter's apparent desire to have sex with her. But still, the doubts lingered.

***

On Monday morning, and once again feeling lonely in the empty house, Louisa took a call from Janna in the Netherlands. The client wanted to meet Louisa in Amsterdam on Wednesday week. If she were keen to pursue it, she would need to sign, scan and return a confidentiality agreement. Louisa was. She did.

Janna then sent over the details. It sounded perfect. Apart from periodic meetings in Amsterdam, the work could be done from anywhere that enjoyed a good broadband connection.

But what to tell Peter? She could call him now, full of enthusiasm, though she doubted he would share it. Or hold off from revealing her hand and deliver the news when he was home for Michael's funeral. In the meantime, she would book her flight. Out on Tuesday, home on Wednesday. She would make a reservation at the same hotel as last time, but ensure she could cancel. Just in case Peter had once more moved without telling her, and she could miraculously stay with him.

The arrangements made, a tell-tale noise announced the arrival of a WhatsApp message from her husband. He asked how she was and told her he would come home on the Thursday night for Michael's funeral, not Friday morning as originally planned. He hoped she was pleased, and said he loved her.

Louisa lowered the phone and stared out of the sitting-room window. The blackbird had been busy on the bonnet of the Passat again. Despite Peter's nagging, she had given up hosing it off all the time.

Peter. Her husband. Now she felt a sense of shame. For doubting him at the weekend when all he'd wanted to do was to make love to her. For denying him the opportunity to do so. Her guilt was made worse by the upcoming visit to Amsterdam, her deviousness in not telling him about it contrasting with his thoughtfulness in arranging to come home earlier than planned. He wanted to be with her. He'd repeated that he loved her.

Maybe, just maybe, it was all going to be okay.

# 26

## WIM

Wim smiled as he watched Sibel and Laila clearing the table, carrying the dirty plates over to where Caria was loading them into the dishwasher.

'I feel guilty, not helping.'

Caria glanced up at him. 'It's okay, we would all get in each other's way if you did.'

Wim waited for the girls to drift off to their room.

'That's why we need a bigger place. And I made some progress last week, an important step in releasing that money I was telling you about.'

Caria continued arranging things in the dishwasher. 'Good.'

'Is that it? You don't seem too bothered.'

She straightened herself, her hands on her hips. 'Of course I'm bothered, but as I don't know anything about it, it's hard for me to comment, isn't it?'

'I get that, and it is complicated. But I take my responsibilities seriously.' He rose and came over to where she stood, wrapping his arms around her. 'I'll do anything for you and the girls. You know that, don't you?' He detached Caria's hands from her hips and rearranged them around his waist.

'I know, I know.' Now she leaned back and frowned up at him. 'And I do worry about you, you seem to be so preoccupied lately. Don't go overdoing it, or working too hard. Okay?'

***

A little later, Laila sat cross-legged on her pillow, studying the cover of her book. Opposite her, Sibel lay back on her bed, reading. Her feet were up on the wall, a pair of earphones clamped firmly on her head.

Wim grinned and lowered himself to sit next to Laila. 'How's Reynard been doing?' he asked.

Laila nodded. 'Fine. I looked at the pictures, but I need you to read the words for me.'

'It won't be long before you're reading them for yourself.'

Laila frowned. 'No, Reynard is for you to read to me. You like him, don't you, Papa?'

'Well, I do, yes. He's very clever. He makes me think.'

'But he does bad things. You don't do bad things, do you, Papa?'

Wim smiled as he patted her leg. 'Of course not, little one. Of course not.'

# 27

# LOUISA

On Tuesday Louisa took a call from the coroner's office. The post-mortem on her mother had concluded that she had died of either suffocation or heart failure as a result of old age, or a combination of both. Whilst it was impossible to be certain, there was no medical evidence to suggest that the death was anything other than natural.

The police had confirmed that they had found nothing suspicious, and an inquest was not therefore deemed necessary. Louisa was relieved to be able to go ahead with organising the second funeral. The plan was to replicate Michael's ceremony – Mortlake Crematorium, followed by a wake at Putney Town Rowing Club. Louisa would contact the nursing home and offer to lay on a mini-bus for staff and any residents who were able and willing to attend. She dreaded the task of trying to inform distant relatives and any surviving friends of her mother's family. An announcement in *The Times* perhaps? In her day, her mother would have insisted on it. Very proper.

Then there was a phone call with the solicitor. The one who, following the death of Louisa's father, had organised her mother's affairs.

Barbara's will was clear, and there was a sizeable legacy

on her passing. Sophie, as the only grandchild, would receive a generous lump sum. But following the death of her husband, the bulk of Barbara's wealth had been transferred to a bloodline trust. Although, as Detective Inspector Griffiths had correctly identified, with Michael's childless demise, his interest in the arrangement would cease, so now only Louisa and her children could benefit directly. She and the solicitor were the trustees. As with the powers of attorney, Barbara had chosen to keep her improvident son well away from the management of her affairs.

Then there was a call from George, who broke the news that some fifty friends and acquaintances of Michael's planned to attend his funeral, if that was alright? Louisa tried and failed to hide her emotion – she'd had no idea that her brother was so popular. George's compassion came to the fore as he spoke once again of 'Mikey's' wicked sense of fun, and of his consideration for other people. And now they wanted to pay their final respects to their friend. In their droves, it would seem.

Louisa sobbed as she rebuked herself for never really showing much of an interest in her brother's private life. Whilst there was no doubting her love for him, he'd been so frivolous and mercurial that she had never taken the trouble to see and appreciate what lay beneath. Shame on you, Louisa Hedley, she told herself. George's soothing words to her were kind and well-meaning, but they couldn't drive away the guilt.

***

Thursday. Funeral day minus one. Louisa's tension had been building during the week, but now she finally believed that everything on her lists had been ticked off.

Sophie arrived home in the late afternoon. Glasses of wine in front of them, they sat at the breakfast bar as she rehearsed her tribute to: 'My uncle Michael. An eccentric but much-loved man who defied convention and did things his way.'

Louisa sat with her head in her hands, staring down at the worktop, deliberately facing away from her daughter as Sophie's words painted a picture of the man just as surely as if she had been working on a canvas. Louisa could see him now: the bright eyes, the naïve optimism forever reflected in his face. It was beautifully observed.

The stillness that followed Sophie's wavering conclusion was eventually broken by Louisa, who slowly eased herself from her stool and, without words, hugged her tearful daughter.

Peter arrived home at around nine, and under Louisa's gaze, poked at the vegetarian lasagne that she had earlier plated up for him as she served Sophie and herself.

Later, in bed and at Peter's initiation, they talked about their marriage, even if Louisa found the timing a little odd. He was insistent that he loved her, that he was trying to be a better husband and hoped she could start to see a difference in him. He pleaded for her to abandon her threat to divorce him. Louisa reached over and turned out the bedside light. She chose her words carefully as she lay on her side, facing away from him.

'You know I don't want a divorce. I want us to get back to the loving and fun couple we once were. But as I have said many times now, we have to be together. And once we have got through tomorrow, I'll tell you about an opportunity that could help us achieve that.'

It was quiet for a minute or two before she felt him slide over and press up against her. His hand on her hip, his breath on her neck as he began to kiss it. His groin flexing, nudging her, signalling his intentions.

He eased the nightdress up, then wrestled with his briefs before caressing her. She hesitated as he manoeuvred himself into position. It wasn't what she'd expected, and it felt somehow inappropriate under the circumstances. But she would not deny him, not with everything that had been said of late. She drew her thighs up and pushed her bottom out.

***

The last family funeral was seven years ago. Seven years since Louisa's father had died, and she had gently but firmly supported her mother through her grief. By then, dementia had, for the most part, rendered Barbara Bruce-Gardiner's life a confused blur, interspersed with periods of remarkable lucidity. But the task of taking care of her mother at the funeral had given Louisa a sense of responsibility, an important mission, helping to distract her from her own sorrow.

Today, she thought she might concentrate her attention on Sophie, but it quickly became apparent that the girl had similar ideas regarding her. Louisa wondered how long it would be before her daughter was the stronger, the more capable of the two of them, as the ability and confidence of the parent was overtaken by that of the child. It was all happening so quickly.

But for now, they fulfilled their roles well, Louisa in awe of Sophie's involvement in the organisation of the day, albeit remotely. Mother and daughter had worked as an informal but efficient team, seemingly reading each other's minds. Louisa tried to avoid contrasting their easy cooperation with Peter's apparent lack of engagement. But then, neither had she tried to include him in the preparations.

The funeral director nodded to Louisa, she nodded back, and to the sound of 'Bitter Sweet Symphony' by the Verve, she, Peter and Sophie followed the coffin into the hall at Mortlake Crematorium. Louisa gasped. She had expected around twenty attendees from their circle. She was sure that

George was being optimistic, so to that had added perhaps thirty of Michael's friends. But the hall held just over ninety, and it was full. Nobody likes the idea of a sparsely attended funeral, but now the wave of gratitude that washed over her was quickly offset by mild panic about the catering she'd arranged at the rowing club.

Her incredulity gave way to joy and relief. This was going to be a proper send-off, attended by representatives from both sides of Michael's life. Their cohort was, for the most part, dressed in sombre tones, Asha and Robert amongst them. As for Michael's friends, the ones that Louisa never really knew about, the colours of the clothes they wore could have been taken straight from a Caribbean artist's palette. And despite the warmth of the July day, as far as Louisa could tell, they all wore a scarf of the type that had become Michael's trademark.

Louisa felt strengthened as the proceedings unfolded. The celebrant was true to his word and made sure that this was a thankful and joyous acknowledgement of her brother's life, as well as an expression of sadness at its premature passing. The choice of music was the result of a collaboration between Sophie and George. At Louisa's request, they had cooperated via a messaging app on the selection of songs that would punctuate the service, together with the production of a playlist that became the backdrop to the wake in the rowing club.

Sophie's eulogy was preceded by 'I'll Stand by You' from the Pretenders, the assembled mourners following the words from the order of service in front of them. They then watched while the young woman recounted events in her uncle's life, interspersed with anecdotes and humorous observations. Sophie finished by sharing the messages of love and respect that they had received for Michael, her hands gripping the lectern as she read.

As she stood down to applause and tears, the mourners

took to their feet and joined in 'Heroes' by David Bowie. Michael always had a soft spot for Mr Bowie.

George then took to the lectern and, true to his classical training, gave a masterclass in oratory. Louisa thought he should do this for a living, before reminding herself that, as a stage actor, he did. His tribute spoke of a kind and generous man, one whose moral courage was the envy of his large circle of friends. Louisa sat in awe throughout, remembering the kindly lady who had asked her if she was okay as she stood before Michael's makeshift shrine on Clapham Common.

*'Knew him well, did you, love?'*

*'Not well enough, I'm afraid.'*

As George closed his speech, the song 'Spirit in the Sky' caused people to spring from their seats, the gyrating and clapping more redolent of a southern states gospel congregation than a humanist West London funeral.

Finally, Louisa stood at the front, thanked everyone for being there and insisted they join the family at the rowing club opposite, where she hoped to meet all of Michael's friends.

They left the hall to the uncompromising instruction 'Don't You Forget About Me' by Simple Minds.

In the rowing club, Louisa's panic about the food was quickly swept aside by the spread before them. No one would go hungry. George greeted her as if they were old friends. He and Sophie hugged each other on their first meeting, their remote work on the music for the funeral having established a friendship already. Louisa was both relieved and happy to lose herself in the embrace of Asha, there with Samuel. She longed for a private catch-up with her friend and told Asha so.

With a little skip of the heart, she caught sight of Robert, tall and imposing in a well-tailored dark suit. He embraced her, the brief but pointed eye contact between them an acknowledgement of things that could never be undone or forgotten. Their past relationship. That reckless one-night stand. Events to which they could now add their recent covert but innocent walk in Richmond Park.

But whilst Peter knew nothing about the last two, his behaviour with Robert suggested otherwise. The greeting he offered was dispassionate, lacking any warmth. Louisa didn't understand why he had distanced himself from his former best buddy, but today was hardly the time to go into it.

The wake unfolded with Louisa spending much of her time in the company of Michael's friends, keen to learn as much as she could about the brother whose adult life was mostly a mystery to her. Some of them were regular patrons of Bar Seventeen, many of them appeared to know each other, but all the people with whom she spoke had responded to the police appeal to come forward with any information they had about Michael. Not that it had amounted to much. There was real anger and distress at his death, but no clear theory as to why it had happened. No one could point to any person or event that might have precipitated the killing.

One somewhat awkward attendee explained that he was an old friend of Michael's but hadn't seen him for a while. He had heard about the death on the police TV appeal. Louisa thanked him for coming before she was distracted by Sophie, who pulled her to one side.

'Do you know him?' her daughter whispered.

'We just met. Why?'

'Well, it seems odd, but when we came out of the crem, there was a car opposite the front entrance, parked a little way off. I'm sure I saw a man with a camera inside. One of those with a long lens.'

Louisa frowned. 'How strange.'

'Yes, but the thing is, that chap you were talking to just now, I saw him go over and have a quick word with him – the cameraman.'

Louisa looked around. The awkward man had disappeared. She went over to the club entrance and peered outside, but there was no sign of him. A theory had formed in her mind, one that she would put to the test next week.

***

As they were getting ready for bed that evening, Peter asked Louisa about 'the opportunity' she had referenced last night. The one that could help bring them together as a couple.

Louisa took a slow, deep breath.

'You remember I met with Janna, the recruitment consultant? Two weeks ago in Amsterdam.'

Peter had his back to her. Louisa couldn't see his face, but noticed him pause his work on the tie of his dressing gown.

'I do.'

'Well, the company wants to meet me.' She winced, and then was cross with herself for doing so. 'I've got an interview.'

Louisa wasn't expecting a loud cheer or a punching of the air, but a bit of enthusiasm would have been nice. Instead, there was a pause while Peter removed his watch.

'Okaay, but you seem to be forgetting that I'm trying to get my boss to agree to my working from the UK. It would be a bit silly if I'm back here just as you end up working over there, wouldn't it?'

'True, but *you* seem to be forgetting that I can do the work from anywhere. I'd only need to visit the Dutch office from time to time.'

'Oh, they all say that.'

Louisa felt her enthusiasm deflate. But she kept going.

'It's a one-year assignment. I'll be over there on Tuesday. The interview is on Wednesday. You said you're in the office all week, so I've booked us that hotel again for Tuesday night.'

'Seems a bit extravagant, don't you think? Staying over

just so we can spend the evening together. I'll be home again a week on Monday for your mother's funeral.'

'On the Monday? The funeral's on Tuesday. So why wouldn't you come home the Friday before, spend the weekend here and fly back to Amsterdam on the following Wednesday? Make a proper stay of it.'

'Because that's two work days lost. So I'd need to work the weekend before to make up for it. I've already decided I'll fly back to Amsterdam tomorrow, to try and catch up on today.'

'But tomorrow's a Saturday!'

'I plan to work on Sunday. As I say, catch up. And you should think seriously about that hotel. The cost of it, and the flights…'

'Peter, my interview is at ten o'clock. The earliest flight from Heathrow gets me into Schiphol at nine. There's no way I can be sure of getting there on time. So the company have said they will pay for a hotel for the night before. It's perfect, don't you think?'

Louisa studied his reaction. He smiled. 'Of course. We can have dinner together. What's happening with your compromise agreement, by the way? When do you sign?'

'I've kind of set that aside for now, what with everything else that's been going on. The lawyer has queried one or two things, but says it's a very good offer.'

'So sign it.'

'I will, but I still don't like the wording around the termination. That both parties have "agreed" to end the employment contract. It's insulting. *They* want to end the employment contract, not me.'

'Christ, that's there for your benefit. What's the matter with you? Just sign the bloody thing! Let's get the severance money into our account. Soon.'

# 28

Peter's hurried return to the Netherlands had allowed mother and daughter to unwind after the traumatic events of Friday and relax in each other's company. Over a mushroom Stroganov on Saturday evening, Louisa explained about the Amsterdam opportunity and how it would enable her and Peter to spend more time together. Sophie's response had been telling.

'Well, I hope that's what he wants. He seemed keen to get away from here just as soon as he could. Or from me, anyway.'

Louisa wondered what it was with parents. Some programming that mysteriously takes place when a couple have kids. The tendency to excuse the behaviour of the errant spouse in front of the child. To defend the indefensible. She ran true to form.

'Sophie, he is very busy at work. Perhaps he felt left out these past couple of weeks, that's all. And he does love you, you know.'

Sophie had given one of her doubtful shrugs. The matter was left there.

***

On Tuesday morning, Louisa was putting the last-minute touches to her list of interview questions. Her carry-on bag was packed and in the hall. The two-ten flight out of Heathrow would get her into Schiphol at four-thirty, plenty of time to make her way over to the 'usual' hotel before Peter joined her that evening.

She smiled to herself, quietly satisfied with her growing familiarity with Amsterdam, even if that was mostly confined to matters such as the geography, restaurants and the transport system. Oh, and the red-light district. This was exciting, fun even. And Louisa had decided that a bit of fun was something she would like more of. She was hopeful that the interview tomorrow would go well.

As she busied herself with an uncooperative printer, she was distracted by the crunching of the gravelled forecourt to the front of the house. Shit. Detective Inspector Griffiths. Not someone she had hoped to see today. To start with, he made her uncomfortable. She wished he had a colleague with him, even one as frosty as DS Lynch. Furthermore, she had a plane to catch. And finally, she had yet to prepare herself for the confrontation that she fully intended to have with him. He raised his hand and waved to her through the big bay window. She could hardly avoid him now and made her way to the front door.

'Mrs Hedley, good to see you again.' He glanced at the wheelie bag behind her in the hallway. 'I hope I'm not disturbing you?'

Louisa glanced at her watch. 'I don't have long, I'm afraid.'

'Going somewhere, are we? Not a *permanent* departure, I take it?'

My God – was he suggesting that she might be fleeing from the UK to avoid the long arm of the law? She forced a smile, maintained her hold on the latch and took a deep and calming breath.

'If you're worried about your prime suspect fleeing to foreign parts, then I can assure you it's merely a brief visit to Amsterdam. So, how can I help you, Inspector?'

He didn't respond to the sarcasm, but flashed an equally unconvincing smile in return. 'Well, I was wondering if you picked up on anything or anyone unusual at your brother's funeral. I believe it was held on Friday.'

'Yes, we should compare notes on that, I suppose.'

'I'm sorry?'

'Come now, Inspector. You had someone there working the crowd, didn't you? And a photographer. You could have told me in advance, you know.'

His expression gave nothing away. 'As you would expect, Mrs Hedley, we are keen to catch your brother's killer.'

'Does that mean I'm no longer a person of interest?'

She could see him mulling over his reply. He gave her a smile she could have done without.

'Well, that depends on what you mean.'

Louisa paused while she considered the ambiguity in his words. Was he toying with her again, to see if she would rise to the bait?

'Now it's my turn to look confused,' she said, preferring to gloss over her discomfort.

'Ah.'

She glanced at the wheelie bag. 'Was there anything else?'

'No, but don't forget my offer. If there's anything I can do to help. Anything at all.'

'Thank you.'

He stepped down onto the driveway before turning his head, 'How's your husband, by the way?'

***

Louisa was in their hotel room and studying her notes for the meeting tomorrow when Peter arrived.

A quick shower was accompanied by a debate about where to eat. Peter proposed trying the hotel's restaurant, whilst Louisa was determined to experience more of the city. Her plan would result in them taking the metro three stops towards the city centre, then walking across the Amstel river and on to a wooded square intersected by tram lines. This gave way to Utrechtsestraat at its northern side, described in her guidebook as a 'bustling and festive street lined with shops and informal restaurants'. Perfect. They could dine wherever they fancied.

As they sat on stools in the hotel's bar, Peter asked her about the upcoming interview. She told him about her preparation and the extensive research she had undertaken into the company.

He nodded. 'You're serious about this, then?'

'I am. And you know why.' She raised her eyebrows. 'Do I have your support?'

She blinked in surprise and gratitude when he leaned closer and kissed her on the mouth.

'Of course you do.'

'Thank you. Now, do that again.'

He raised his eyebrows and obliged.

Louisa gazed down as he slowly leaned back, one hand resting on her thigh. She could feel her skin warming under his touch, through the thin material of the summery wrap dress. Her pulse was increasing and her neck felt hot; she knew both it and her cheeks were reddening. She gently rolled her shoulders and toyed with the idea of proposing that they visit their room before going out to eat. The sort of thing that, twenty years ago, she would have done without a second thought.

What the hell. She moved her mouth closer to his ear.

'Let's go upstairs. Now.' She pulled back a little so she could study the expression on his face.

'Mrs Hedley, are you trying to seduce me?'

Shortly afterwards, she was lying face down on the duvet,

the dress pulled up around her hips, her right hand alternately scrunching and releasing the soft white bedding beneath it.

***

The following morning, they were both awake early. Louisa made them coffee before Peter disappeared into the bathroom.

She tidied the cups away and reached for her cabin bag, intent on a final review of her interview notes whilst waiting for the shower. As she hauled the wheelie onto the bed, it caught Peter's jacket, arranged over the back of a chair. It fell onto the floor, with what appeared to be a letter partly spilling from an inside pocket. It had an official appearance and was from an organisation called the 'SVB'. Louisa couldn't speak Dutch, but the language had something in common with German, which she could. The SVB appeared to be similar to the UK National Insurance scheme, but more than that, Louisa was unable to discover.

Except…

Maybe she was wrong, but whilst the letter was intended for Peter – 'De heer P. Hedley' – the address didn't match the one he had given her for his new digs – his friend's house.

Louisa raised her eyes to the bathroom door. Beyond it, she could hear the noise of teeth being brushed. She reached for her phone and took a picture of the letter before returning it to his jacket pocket.

***

At eleven-twenty, Louisa emerged from her interview, confident that she had done a good job, but concerned that she was one of three people under consideration. Not a done deal, then. Get used to it, she told herself. You might think you're bloody marvellous, but there are plenty of other capable candidates around. As promised, she phoned Janna and gave her an update. Now she just had to wait until the company made up its mind as to who they wanted to hire.

But in the meantime, she had something to do. Her original intention had been to spend a couple of hours exploring Amsterdam, expanding her knowledge of the areas where she and Peter might take an apartment. That should usefully kill a bit of time before her flight home at five-thirty.

However, the plan had changed. Consulting her map, she worked out that she could easily walk to the metro at Amsterdam Zuid. From there, it was a couple of stops to an area called De Pijp – according to her guidebook, an enclave famous for its lively mix of cultures. Then a short stroll would take her to the address on Peter's letter.

By midday, she had made herself comfortable in a café opposite the mystery dwelling. The street in which it was situated consisted mostly of residential buildings several storeys high, their tall gable ends featuring prominent hoists on beams that jutted out over the pavements beneath. Cars and bicycles vied for the limited space along one side of the road, the line broken here and there by the trunks of pollarded trees, with a welcome splash of green above. The odd shopfront added to the sense that this was a buzzing yet neighbourly area.

A man with a ponytail took her order for coffee. She asked him if it was okay to work on her laptop whilst she sat there. He smiled.

'You're a Brit, right?'

Louisa wondered where this was headed.

'I am, yes.'

'You're so damned polite, you guys. Most people don't give a shit and wait for us to tell them either to buy something or leave.'

'I promise I won't take advantage.'

The man laughed and laid a hand on her shoulder. 'Don't worry, lady, you're fine. Do you have a man?'

'I'm sorry?'

He laughed again. 'Relax, I'm joking with you. But you're really nice. You let me know if you need one, right?'

Louisa felt redness flooding her cheeks. 'I will, thank you.'

'*Ja*!' The man clapped his hands and went back to work. He soon reappeared with a cup of coffee, an individually wrapped biscuit and the code for the wi-fi.

Louisa eyed the building across the street as she sipped. There were three floors in addition to the basement, which appeared to serve as some sort of workshop. At the left-hand end of the terraced building, a steep flight of stone steps led up from the pavement to the imposing front door. Louisa could see what looked like an intercom panel with buttons and nameplates. The address on Peter's letter had the suffix 'A'. Presumably the apartment next to the main entrance, thought Louisa.

An hour passed and she had just ordered another coffee whilst falling victim to a bit more chatting up from her pony-tailed admirer, when a woman turned up the steps of the house and let herself in through the front door.

Moments later, Louisa caught sight of her in the entry-level apartment. But the line of sight from the café was at an upward angle, offering restricted views of the occupant as and when she appeared behind one or other of the two huge windows. Louisa imagined a single large room serving as a kitchen, dining and living area. The bedrooms must be at the back.

Louisa thought the woman to be in her early to mid-thirties. Hard to tell from here, but the dark hair and olive skin spoke of the eastern Mediterranean. Turkey perhaps? She disappeared from view for a while before once more busying herself with something that afforded Louisa only occasional glimpses of her.

Louisa's protesting stomach resulted in an order for a ham and cheese toastie, accompanied by some exaggeration of the truth when her nosy waiter enquired what it was she was working on.

'Just catching up before another appointment later on.'

His thoughtful nod was followed by a broad smile. 'My name is Gerrit, by the way. And you are…?'

'Louisa. My name is Louisa.'

'Nice name, I like that.'

It was now two o'clock. Peter would be unlikely to finish work for at least three hours, and she would have to leave to catch her plane well before then. And perhaps this was all a waste of time, the address on the letter merely for the receipt of mail. A favour from a work colleague, perhaps. Louisa wished she had considered that possibility before. Perfectly sensible, if you knew you were going to be moving frequently, as Peter had. Maybe he was right when he accused her of being paranoid.

But maybe he wasn't. She was here, and might as well see this through to a conclusion. Either put her mind at rest or maybe learn something about her husband's nomadic tendencies. She logged in to her BA account and searched for a later flight, finding one that left Schiphol at just after nine o'clock. Ouch. How could they charge that?

Louisa was just returning from a rushed visit to the washroom when she saw the woman leaving the apartment, returning not long afterwards with a child in tow. Judging by appearances, they looked as if they could be mother and daughter, the girl perhaps nine or ten years old.

Louisa looked at the time. Three-thirty. Another drink, tea this time. She regretted not sticking with coffee. Louisa wondered why she had never quizzed Peter about the people with whom he was lodging.

Four-fifteen. Louisa's anticipation was growing. She sat

up as a younger woman arrived with a second child, another girl. This one looked to be about five, with a paler complexion and brown hair. They all congregated in the front room for a few minutes, before the woman who had recently delivered the youngster left. Could be a child-minder, thought Louisa.

Five-twenty. Louisa stiffened and hid her face behind her hand as she recognised Peter, walking towards the apartment. Letting himself in with a key. Not an occasional visitor, then. She craned her neck, trying to get a better view through the two windows, catching only fleeting glances of her husband and the woman. No sight of the youngsters, but they would be shorter and harder to see. She saw nothing untoward, but that didn't stop Louisa from feeling light-headed. Her breathing was shallow, her heart rate up. And where was Peter's friend? *It's this guy I know from work.*

Shit. Now they were all coming down the steps. Louisa hurriedly packed away her laptop, signalled to Gerrit and fished out twenty-five euros. She blinked when he bestowed a friendly embrace on her, calling out: 'Louisa, come back and see me soon!'

Keeping her distance and with her sunglasses firmly in place, she followed the little group from the apartment and down the street. They walked a hundred yards or so before turning left. Moments later they entered a park: paths, grass and trees offset by a rather grand monument to someone or other. Peter and the woman sat on a bench whilst the children made use of a poorly equipped play area.

Louisa felt exposed here, vulnerable. It was easy enough to avoid being spotted on the streets, especially when no one was expecting to see you there. But here she had to lurk behind bushes with her wheelie bag, aware of some odd looks from passers-by. She pretended to be messing with her phone before adding to her sense of unease by taking some photos of her husband with the dark-haired woman.

The children appeared to be enjoying themselves, but Louisa's attention was firmly fixed on the two adults sitting together, chatting away. One of whom was her husband. There was no physical contact between Peter and the woman, and Louisa had just concluded that she had to leave when she saw him saunter away and take out his phone.

Seconds later she froze as her own rang in her hand. Her heart lurched. Oh, Jesus, it was *him*. Trembling, she stabbed at the button to reject the call, looking up in horror at her husband. Had he heard her ringtone from where he was? Had he spotted her lurking in the shrubbery and decided to confront her? Relief swept over her as she watched him pocket his phone, apparently none the wiser. He looked over to where his female companion sat and ambled back towards her, at which point she got up and started beckoning the children.

Shortly after, they set off in the direction from which they had arrived earlier. Her direction. Louisa turned around and hurried up another path, away from the group. She paused on a corner and turned, catching a glimpse of the little girl reaching for Peter's hand before they disappeared.

# 29

# PETER

In the privacy of the toilet, Peter tapped away at his phone.

> Tried calling earlier. Not sure what time yr flight? How was interview? Will call tmrw. x

Half an hour later, he was rewarded with a return message.

> Interview good. One of three. Now have to wait. Lost track of time exploring Ams so changed flight. At airport now. xx.

Peter lowered his phone. One of three. At least she wasn't the only candidate, but then again, few people would have prepared as well as his wife. And if she did get the job, then hopefully they wouldn't want her to start until early September. Because of the mass exit for the beaches and campsites of France, Germany and Spain, non-urgent Dutch business activities tended to die a death during the summer holiday season.

Even so, that would put him under pressure sooner rather than later. He needed more time. He needed to slow Louisa down. Because she mustn't get to Amsterdam.

# 30

# LOUISA

Thursday. Louisa eased herself down in her chair, aware of a tenderness in her lower back, a heaviness in the legs. She had given it everything at her class this morning – the upside of being unemployed was that you had time in the day for things other than work. Such as exercise.

But her physical discomfort was nothing compared to what was going on in her mind. For she had no idea what conclusions to draw about what she had witnessed the day before. She opened her notebook, ready to set out her observations, in the hope that studying the written facts might help. After all, she had built a career around objectivity.

Then she hesitated. This sort of personal stuff must never be read by others. So she took a sheet of paper from the printer and started listing what she knew.

So, to start: Peter had given her his new address. He had messaged it at her insistence, when forced to reveal he had moved out of the dull apartment where she'd stayed with him just a few weeks ago.

But the letter she'd seen in his pocket featured a different one. In De Pijp, on the city-centre side of the river. The address where she had spied on him from the café. So was that a simple error on his part, or a deliberate attempt to deceive her?

On arrival at the De Pijp apartment, Peter let himself in with a key. Without knocking. Surely then he must be living there?

Peter had accompanied the woman and (her?) children to the park. Now, if you live in an apartment, you have to go to a public space to get some air. But as a lodger, you wouldn't accompany your host family unless you were very familiar with them. More evidence that this was indeed his home away from home.

And whilst Louisa only had a fleeting glimpse of it, the little girl had reached for Peter's hand as they headed back to the apartment – something he'd seemed surprisingly comfortable with. That wasn't like him; he was never brilliant with Sophie when she was young, and avoided other kids like the plague.

But, to her immense relief, and perhaps most important of all, Louisa had seen nothing to suggest that her husband and the woman were anything more than friends. She raised her eyebrows. A bit like his life back here, then.

So, she reasoned, those are the facts. Now for the conclusions. And there was only one. Peter lived in that apartment. But more than that, he appeared to have quickly become an integral part of the family. So why lie to his wife and give her a different address? Could it be that he felt awkward about living in a household such as the one Louisa had witnessed? That he suspected his wife might be uncomfortable with the arrangement and consequently had lied to her, to save the embarrassing discussion that might ensue, should he tell her the truth?

Entirely possible. Plausible even. For she did find it odd. And then a realisation hit her. She had not seen another man there. The 'man of the house', as her mother would have grandly described him. Perhaps Peter's embarrassment was because he was lodging with a woman. Someone from work. A single mother, maybe. Ah, *now* we're getting somewhere. It would make sense for a household with just one income to be under pressure financially. The prospect of a lodger providing extra money could be welcome. And, yes, Louisa would be uncomfortable with the idea of her husband living with an unattached woman. Bloody uncomfortable.

The more she thought about it, the more sense it all made. She breathed deeply, took her sheet of paper and leaned over to the shredder. Mystery solved.

She rose from the desk, her face softening as she saw her handsome blackbird flying out of the holly tree. She had earned a coffee. Now all she had to do was decide how to confront Peter about it, extract the truth from him – but without revealing what she had learned for herself. Because none of this spoke well for their marriage. Husband lies to his wife about where he lives and with whom. Wife spies on husband and secretly follows him.

Was there any hope for them?

***

On Friday Louisa met Asha for lunch, as before offering to collect her friend from outside her office. The place where Louisa used to work, until about seven weeks ago. They would once again visit the garden-centre café.

Asha wrestled with her seatbelt before turning back to Louisa, who was staring up at the uninspiring office building through the windscreen, hands on the steering wheel. Asha followed the direction of her friend's gaze.

'Do you miss it, babe?'

Louisa sighed. 'I do, yes. The work, the buzz, the people. But not that cow in Atlanta.'

'The lovely Christine. We do need to talk about your compromise agreement, though. If we can do it without spoiling lunch, that is.' Asha wagged a finger. 'But the good news is that this is officially a business meeting, so lunch is on the company.'

Louisa grinned. 'There is a God!' The grin disappeared. 'But as for the agreement, I won't sign it as it is. The company needs to acknowledge in writing that it was wrong to fire me, that it failed to follow due process and that it apologises. Then I'll sign.'

'Shit, babe, do you think our friend in Atlanta will agree to that?'

'If she wants to avoid me taking the company to a tribunal, she will.'

Asha winced. 'What about the money?'

'This isn't about money. The severance offer is fine. It's a matter of principle.' Louisa turned briefly to her friend as she drove. 'But I don't want to be a pain and cause trouble for you, so I'll have my lawyer write to the company, making my position clear.'

Asha looked glum. 'Don't worry about me. I've started contacting some recruiters myself. I've had enough.'

It had been a week since they had last seen each other. That was at Michael's funeral. Over lunch, Louisa brought Asha up to date on her Amsterdam visit. The interview. The letter in Peter's pocket. And then her covert staking out of the apartment. What she saw.

Asha stopped chewing. 'Whoah, this is all getting a bit heavy, don't you think? What will you do? Are you going to have it out with him?'

'Well, that's the thing. I don't know. The address he gave me is certainly different from the one that was in the letter, the one where it looks like he's living. It's hard to believe that's an error, don't you think? And the whole business of him moving from one flat to another without telling me, then the "mix-up" over the last place. Either it's a catalogue of highly unlikely cock-ups, or it's something rather sinister. And I don't know which version to believe.'

Louisa turned aside, blinking. Her jaw clenched. She felt Asha's hand on her arm.

'Maybe you can find some way to ask him about the address without it sounding like you are accusing him of anything.'

Louisa shrugged. 'Well, if you've got any bright ideas, I would love to hear them. We spoke yesterday on the phone, but it was all very uninformative. I talked to him about the interview and then lied to him about how I spent the afternoon wandering around Amsterdam. But there's nothing to suggest he wants me over there with him, even if he's trying harder since I told him I want a divorce.'

'Well, that's progress, isn't it?'

'Yes, but I'm not sure it's genuine. I'm not sure I believe him.'

'Maybe you're just feeling a bit insecure. A lot of shit has come your way lately.'

Louisa sighed and gave Asha a pained smile. 'That's precisely the sort of thing Peter keeps saying to me.'

She looked down at her plate. Maybe the problem was with her after all.

***

Louisa spent Saturday alone. Again. She strolled alongside the river to Barnes village, where she had a mooch around and a coffee, before visiting the fishmonger and pointing to a hideous but horribly expensive monkfish. She would make a seafood curry for Sophie on Sunday, a treat ahead of Barbara's funeral on Tuesday.

As she walked home, Louisa brushed aside the feeling of guilt that accompanied her pleasurable anticipation of having her daughter to herself for a bit. Peter would arrive on Monday evening.

The shopping trip was followed by a couple of hours at the piano. It had been a long time since she had played, and Louisa was determined to fulfil her promise to start exploring some of the more contemporary, jazzy music of which she was becoming increasingly fond.

The evening dragged, another M&S meal for one accompanied by most of a bottle of wine and a movie, one of her favourites. Her exasperation came to the fore as she cursed Stevens, the meticulous but repressed butler in *The Remains of the Day*. 'You bloody fool! For God's sake, tell her you love her. Give her a big snog!'

Louisa's anticipation mounted as Sunday wore on, and that evening she was once again overjoyed to wrap her arms around her daughter outside Barnes Station. At home, they sat in the kitchen and drank some wine, Louisa shaking her head as Sophie, tasked with delivering a second eulogy at the funeral of a close relative, offered to read it to her mother.

'No, darling, I would rather hear it for the first time on Tuesday. Then, hopefully, your next visit home will be under more cheerful circumstances.'

'Here's to that.' Sophie raised her glass and sniffed the air. 'How's that curry doing? I'm starving.'

Peter's homecoming on Monday was accompanied by a heightened sense of tension for Louisa. Partly ahead of her mother's funeral, and partly because the last time she saw her husband, she had been spying on him, hidden behind a bush in an Amsterdam park. It was surreal. Comical even. This wasn't what married couples did, it was bloody ridiculous.

She found herself avoiding his gaze, afraid that some superhuman power might result in him being able to read her thoughts. He'd sneer as he addressed her. 'Ah, I know what's going on here. You've been following me, haven't you? I can see it written on your mind. You conniving bitch!'

Fortunately, there was no evidence of any such ability, and the evening passed without incident. Louisa feigned a headache at bedtime lest Peter attempt any ill-timed attempts at lovemaking. Well, sex anyway.

He didn't.

***

On Tuesday afternoon, Louisa breathed a sigh of relief and filled the kettle. She took another look at the Order of Service for her mother's funeral, pleased that it was all over and everything had gone to plan. Peter and Sophie had headed straight upstairs to change, but Louisa was desperate for a cup of tea. She cursed as a knock on the front door interrupted her work with spoon and mug. Oh, no.

The unwelcome visitor nodded at the doorbell. 'Still not fixed, then?'

'Inspector Griffiths. Good afternoon.'

'Ah, good afternoon, Mrs Hedley. I'm sorry to disturb you, but I was passing your door and wondered if you'd had any further thoughts on the matters we discussed?'

'Meaning?'

'Well, anything you might have picked up at your brother's funeral, any further ideas as to whom he owed money – that sort of thing.' He looked down the hall towards the kitchen before turning back to Louisa, his eyebrows raised.

'I'm sorry, Inspector, I won't ask you in. We have just returned from my mother's funeral. But no, I don't have any new information for you.'

Louisa thought he hid it well, but there were still tiny indicators that gave away his surprise. An almost imperceptible widening of the eyes. A slight stiffening of his body. A long, slow breath.

'I see. Well, I'm very sorry to hear that. Your mother... her passing...'

'Yes?'

'You didn't think to let me know?'

'Excuse me?'

'Well, given our previous discussions. And the cause of her passing was... if I may enquire?'

'My God. You accused me of having my brother murdered. And now you appear to be suggesting...'

'Mrs Hedley, please. I never accused you of anything.'

'Look, Inspector, she died in the nursing home where she lived. There was a post-mortem. Natural causes, okay?'

'Okay, very good, I can see...'

'Very good? What the hell do you mean? She died. My mother died!'

'Mum?' Sophie was coming down the stairs.

'It's alright, darling. The inspector is just leaving.'

Louisa could see his eyes taking in her daughter. He flashed a smile at her and raised his eyebrows.

'We haven't met.'

Louisa glared at him. 'No, you haven't. Will that be all?'

The inspector took a deep breath and held it, as if about to say something profound. What came out was anything but.

'My apologies for the interruption, and your loss. I'll wish you a good day.' He made to leave before stopping and turning back to Louisa. 'Oh, one last question. Your mother's funeral. Would that have been a burial or a cremation?'

Louisa shook her head. 'Cremation. Why? Does it matter?'

A forced smile. 'Good evening, Mrs Hedley.'

# 31

On Thursday, Louisa was wondering if there was any progress with the Amsterdam job when her thoughts were interrupted by a call. But not from Janna. She stared at her phone for a couple of seconds before answering. Robert.

'I thought I would call to see how you are. I know you haven't had an easy time of it lately.'

Louisa reflected on how effortlessly kind some people can be. A timely show of concern. A reassuring and caring tone. They chatted for a couple of minutes, Robert keen to hear how his goddaughter was coping with it all.

'Anyway, there's something else I want to ask you. It relates to the job I talked to you about. What are you doing tomorrow?'

'Let me see.' Louisa clicked on her calendar, well aware that she had absolutely nothing lined up for the Friday. But she needed time to think. She had yet to tell Robert that she wouldn't be pursuing his job offer. Nor had she worked out how to do so. She could hardly tell him the truth: 'Oh, the job sounds fantastic. The only problem is that my marriage is shit, and with us working together I might struggle to contain my affection for you.'

Equally, she was feeling bruised after everything that had happened of late, and dreaded the idea of drifting around on her own with nothing to do whilst waiting for news on the one position that she had actively pursued. Maybe Peter was right. Maybe she needed to start taking her employment search more seriously.

'I'm free most of the day.' A lie. She was free all day. The evening too, if it came to it.

'Good. We've got an event on – we're organising a travel awards dinner tomorrow evening. Park Lane Hotel. I have a crew setting up during the day. It would be a great opportunity for you to see what we do, and get a taste of some of our work. And it includes a free lunch. What could be better?'

'Well, I know I haven't…'

'Let me stop you there. This isn't optional.' Robert laughed. 'Come on, Louisa, what's the worst that could happen?'

***

Louisa tilted her head back to allow some air to circulate around her neck. Despite the stifling heat, the Piccadilly line was relatively quiet, the Friday morning rush having been replaced by something a little calmer. She even had a seat.

Emerging from the sweaty, subterranean world at Hyde Park Corner, she headed north before crossing over to Mayfair and its decidedly upmarket environs.

On arrival at the hotel, she followed the directions of a receptionist towards the function suites. Once there, a woman with both a radio and a clipboard (clearly very important) pointed to a door, behind which Robert could be found.

Broad grins and embraces were exchanged before he gestured around him.

'Welcome to our makeshift office-cum-storeroom. It's a bit of a mess, but secure. You have to be careful with all this gear.'

For the next hour, Louisa was given a tour of the function

room and backstage areas, the whole resembling a colony populated by frenetic ants. Tables (twenty-seven of them – Louisa counted) were being laid with cutlery, glasses and flower arrangements by an army of waiters and waitresses. Around the periphery, a group of gorgeous young things were busy erecting showy stands of the sponsor's expensive luggage. On a circular stage, sound engineers were wrestling with yards of errant spaghetti that trailed between speaker cabinets and mysterious boxes with lots of knobs. A grand piano in the centre dared anything to try and upstage it.

Robert nodded to a tall woman in a striking multi-coloured headband, restraining an abundance of black hair. Hands on hips, her stern expression was accompanied by an almost constant scanning of the room as she sought to keep track of all that was going on around her.

'That's Serena. She's one of ours, and this is her gig. From start to finish, it's all down to her.'

'Wow, big job. How long has she been with you?'

'Joined as a runner about eight years ago. Got promoted to assistant and then, about a year ago, she became a producer. That's what we call them, anyway.'

'Wow, good for her. So how many producers do you have working for you?'

'Four on the payroll and several more self-employed. There's a lot going on. As I very much hope you will soon come to discover.'

He smiled. As did Louisa. She wasn't ready to tell him. Not just yet. She watched as Serena greeted a man dressed all in black. The shoes, trousers, and despite the heat outside, a black polo-neck top. Her eyes widened and she tugged at Robert's sleeve.

'Oh, my God, look who it is.'

Robert grinned. 'Got to have a cool band at these events.'

'Do you know him?'

'Sure, we've used him quite a bit. A real professional, but pleasant and relaxed with it. Come and say hello, and to Serena.'

Louisa grabbed his arm. 'Don't be silly, they're busy.'

'Trust me. He's a nice guy.'

Robert was right. He was. Louisa could feel herself reddening as they chatted about music, about what she liked to listen to, and the tune she most liked to play on the piano.

'Perfect, let's do it together. Grab a seat.'

A few minutes later, Louisa looked up in surprise and embarrassment. She had been so absorbed by the challenge in front of her that she had failed to notice that everyone had stopped what they were doing to listen, and now they were all clapping. Her new friend stood to one side of the piano stool and, flourishing an arm towards his accomplice, proceeded to join in the applause.

***

Louisa and Robert ate lunch in a little bistro a few minutes' walk from the hotel. Calm, unpretentious, and with a simple but good menu. The surroundings, the company and a bottle of crisp, chilled wine, induced in her a gentle slide into a tranquil and dreamy state, as if half-dozing on a shady terrace overlooking a peaceful Mediterranean vista.

She knew the question was coming at some point. She studied his face as Robert attempted to mask his anxiety with a breezy smile.

'Look, I don't want to appear pushy, but I was wondering if you've had any further thoughts about the job? Whether today might have helped.'

Louisa extended a finger and slowly brushed the single, delicate flower in the tiny vase before her.

'Robert, the last thing you are is pushy. And, yes, I would love to come and work for you. But I don't think I can.'

He winced. The disappointment was obvious. 'And why is that?'

Louisa studied his face. She knew him well enough, why not just come clean about it? Tell him that she was struggling with her marriage and didn't trust herself in his company. Not a good idea.

'Let's just say I'm holding out for the opportunity in Amsterdam. Because to do otherwise would be a betrayal of the promise I made to myself.'

A nod. Not one of agreement, but acknowledgement. The nod was followed by a frown.

'What promise?'

A pause.

'To do everything I can to save my marriage.'

Robert took a deep breath. 'I'm very sorry it's come to that.'

She looked down and poked at a crumb on the table. 'I don't think you're surprised. You must have worked it out. Surely?'

He gave a weak smile. 'And if you can't? Save it, that is?'

Louisa shrugged. 'One step at a time, I think.'

They sat silently for what seemed like an age before Robert spoke again.

'About the job thing, then.'

Louisa nodded and raised her eyebrows, glad to be moving out of the danger zone. The place where mistakes could easily be made when old, half-suppressed feelings quickly got the upper hand. 'Go on.'

'Well, if I can't persuade you to join me, can I ask for your help in defining what I need? I have some ideas, but it's not my area of expertise.' Robert lifted his voice as if trying to lighten the mood. 'Finance, uurgh! A job description, candidate profile… that sort of thing. Would you do that for me?'

Her answering smile was warm. 'Of course I will. It's not as if I haven't got the time.'

'Thank you. I can let you have my notes, my thoughts, and the list of tasks that I've put together. But it needs the attention of a professional, someone who understands exactly what's required.'

'You're flattering me. And thank you so much for lunch, it's been lovely. But now I think we should probably get going.'

'Okay. Before you head home, let me show you those notes on my laptop. I can talk you through what I have and then email it all to you.'

***

Shortly afterwards, they were back at the hotel's function suite. Louisa waited as Robert had a quick discussion with Serena before relieving her of the key to the storeroom.

Once inside, he arranged two chairs in front of a small table and fired up his laptop. He took her through his initial impressions of what he thought he needed from a finance director. Louisa found herself nodding with approval, offering feedback and encouragement. But even as Robert explained his thinking, she felt herself drifting. For this was an indulgence, the enjoyment of a special moment spent close to someone for whom she still harboured profound feelings. Louisa had worked hard to suppress these in the early years of her marriage, certain that she should and could make them disappear over time. And even if they had never died, she had done a good job of papering over them with the joys of motherhood, the building of a beautiful home and the pursuit of her career.

But she knew that in one area of her life at least, she had not been successful, her marriage to Peter having withered to the point where its continuation hung in the balance. In consequence, she was vulnerable, and right now she was struggling mightily with her feelings for Robert. In the cramped and stuffy little room, she was unable to concentrate, her eyes drawn back again and again to his face. He was right there – this man whose skin, whose touch, whose very being she was so familiar with. She felt herself slipping back into the trance that had overtaken her in the restaurant. The screen no longer held her attention. It was all on him. Oh, Christ.

Now his finger was pointing at his notes, his mouth was moving, but she could recognise no words. He looked at her and paused; her dilated eyes connected with his. He had stopped talking. They sat there silently before she angled her head and inched it towards his. As if in slow motion, their faces came together. Their lips touched, and for a second they both froze, a silent acknowledgement of a seismic event, one that would change everything between them.

Louisa delighted in the softness of his hand on her cheek, the gentle movement of his mouth on hers, marvelling at just how pleasurable a kiss could be. Without parting, they both slowly rose in mutual recognition of their awkward posture and manoeuvred themselves up against the table. Now Robert was holding her hips, she was pulling him onto her, his growing excitement evident against her belly. Louisa moaned as she felt him lifting her dress.

'Hold this up.' The instruction was delivered softly but assertively into her neck.

She did, then watched as he lowered himself onto his knees and slid her panties down to her ankles. She laid a hand on his shoulder and lifted first one foot and then the other, the redundant knickers cast aside. He then took her left calf in both hands and eased it sideways. She gasped as she saw him lean forward, close his eyes and put his mouth to her.

Her free hand went to the back of his head, caressing,

pulling him in, as she gazed down at the scene unfolding beneath her. The arousal that came from watching Robert pleasuring her in this way seemed strangely disconnected from the sensations that seared through her with his every movement. It was as if they were two separate events – very different, but equally sublime.

Together, they resulted in an inexorable build-up of feelings, as if shaking a champagne bottle with a thumb over the top, in the certain knowledge that the contents will, at a certain point, explode in a euphoric release. Which they did.

Shortly after, and with the fight for breath having subsided, her head flopped down to see Robert's face resting against her trembling thigh, his eyes closed.

She lowered her hand, cupped his chin and raised her eyebrows at him.

The words were whispered. 'And what would you like?'

He smiled softly, slowly got to his feet and turned her around, so that she faced away from him. He kissed her neck, then eased her over the table before raising the dress and touching her.

'To be inside you.'

Louisa heard the jiggling of a belt buckle, a zipper being lowered and the rustle of clothing. She rested her head on her folded arms and closed her eyes.

# 32

Louisa nearly missed the Hammersmith stop. She'd stood in a trance on the tube, there was no seat at this time of day. Her goodbyes with Robert had been surreal. He had been caring, kind – studying her face closely, his hand on her arm.

'I don't regret it, and I'm not sorry it's happened. And I don't want you feeling bad, either. What we did was beautiful, Louisa. You're a beautiful person.'

She had cried: 'But I'm *married*, Robert. What have I done?'

'No. It's what *we* have done. Together. I say again, it was beautiful. An expression of how we both feel. Don't you dare go beating yourself up about it.'

Louisa had sniffed and nodded. 'Okay. But we'll have to talk about it some more… another time. I don't know what's going to happen, and I can't deal with this right now.'

'Do you want me to come back with you?'

She sounded cross. 'No, of course not.'

'Do you want to meet up tomorrow? Over the weekend?'

'But… your kids. It's hardly… I just don't know. Look, I'm going now.'

He peered into her eyes. 'Remember what I said. We're in this together. If I need to speak to Peter…'

'Oh, Christ, let's not go there. We'll talk tomorrow, okay?'

Louisa hung onto the overhead rail as the train rocked along, the deafening roar and that characteristic sour smell pouring in through the open window that separated her carriage from the next.

Well, you've done it now, girl, she told herself. Her previous fling with Robert had felt justified by the temporary break from Peter. But not now, not after all this time. Why did she have to fail after so long – her principles, her integrity, tossed aside in a single, selfish moment of indulgence?

She looked around the carriage, sneaking glances at her fellow passengers. Were they all at it, too? Cheating on their partners? You could never go back from it, she realised. It was like being a virgin, only the other way around. You were, until you weren't. And she, Louisa, wouldn't stop being an adulterer next week. It wouldn't go away. And she wasn't a teeny-weeny bit of an adulterer either. It didn't work like that.

She remembered her father scolding her once. She had used the phrase 'it's very unique'. He had harrumphed, as befitted a senior diplomat who had built himself a formidable reputation through his skilled use of words.

'Silly girl! It's either unique or it isn't. There are no degrees of uniqueness.'

He had been right, of course. And here she was. A fully-blown adulterer. Because there was no other kind.

***

Louisa wondered when Robert might call. Ten o'clock on Saturday morning was the answer. She could hear the sound of his kids in the background, then Robert shooing them out of whatever room he was in.

'Sorry about that. How are you this morning?'

The pleasantries were never going to last long. Louisa

launched into a tirade of self-loathing for her betrayal of her husband. Robert's intervention was kind, it may even have been true, but it didn't make her feel any better.

'Look, I know you have problems with your marriage. I don't think it's anything new, and I saw it again when we had dinner in Amsterdam. And on our walk in Richmond Park. There was even tension between you and Peter at Michael's funeral.'

'Oh, God, I hope I didn't say anything I shouldn't have?'

'Of course not. But you'd make a lousy actress, that's for sure. Anyway, that's not the point. The point is, you're in a bad place and sooner or later it's bound to spill over. What we did was not a betrayal, it's a reflection of how things are between you two, and how you and I feel about each other.'

'And I should tell that to my husband, should I? I don't think so.'

Robert lowered his voice. 'My actions were, and are, a genuine expression of my feelings for you. I want you in my life, Louisa. I want you to leave Peter and be with me.'

'Robert… I made a promise when I married him. I even remember the bloody words I used. And you're right, my marriage isn't working. But I have also made another promise. Which is that I shall do everything I can to sort it out. And only if I conclude that I can't, will I walk away.'

'I understand that. And despite my feelings in all of this, I wish you well in your efforts. I want to see you happy. But you've made it clear that you don't want to live a lie. And neither do I. I love you, Louisa, and I want us to be together. Remember that, won't you?'

She said that she would, aware that she could hardly get him out of her mind after their moment of madness. But that was all it was, or could ever be. Her first duty was to her husband, however distant and inattentive his behaviour of late. He had told her he loved her and wanted their marriage to last. She owed it to him to give their relationship one final chance.

***

The following day, she called Peter. She knew what she was going to say and had even rehearsed her little speech. It didn't help when, as usual, he failed to pick up. Louisa could understand it when he was at work, but this was a Sunday morning, for God's sake. What *was* he doing?

He returned the call around lunchtime. There was a brief and strained exchange as she asked him what he had been up to, Peter's reply appearing both vague and mildly resentful of her questioning. His previous pleading with her not to pursue a divorce seemed hollow given this lack of engagement. But even if his failure to ask about her was depressing, it was also a relief. For Louisa's anger was tempered by graphic flashbacks to the events of Friday.

And whilst there could be no doubt that her adultery was very wrong, it might also be the source of their salvation. For at least it had brought things to a head, and now, surely, was the time for closure.

'So, Peter. When you come home on Friday, you and I are going to have another good talk. We said that, in order to save our marriage, we would both change. Well, it isn't working. There is something fundamentally wrong. I don't know what it is, but since you've been working out of Amsterdam, our relationship has fallen apart. Wouldn't you agree?'

A sigh. 'You know I think you're exaggerating the problem. It's not easy with me being away, and I can see that I have been detached and remote. But I am trying, and I'm not prepared to give up.'

'Good. But this is our last crack at it, Peter. You're going to have to tell me why you've lost interest in me. Because the healing has to be preceded by a diagnosis. Up to now, we've tried to fix the symptoms without understanding the root of the problem. Only if we share that, can we hope to solve it. Does that sound fair?'

'Yes.'

'Right. Because if you're honest with me, I'll be honest with you. We need to lay everything out on the table. It might be painful for both of us, but it's the only way.'

'Okay.'

'So are you prepared to be truthful, to explain what's caused you to go off me?'

'Yes. I promise.'

Louisa felt better for having taken the initiative. Again. Ten out of ten for bloody effort. Patron saint of lost causes. Marital ones, anyway. She tried hard to dismiss the niggling suspicion that was gnawing away at her. The suspicion that she might have been better off telling Peter that it was over, and then jumping into the car and driving over to Robert's.

As it was, she had five days to wallow in her misery before she would have the opportunity for a showdown with her husband. And this time there would be a clear decision, one way or the other. The default position for her was divorce. There would have to be a compelling reason to overturn it.

***

Louisa looked at the kitchen clock. Peter's flight would get him into Heathrow at seven-fifteen. Home around nine, then. There were earlier flights he could take on a Friday evening, but the ones at peak time were always more expensive. And despite the pressing and fundamental nature of the discussion he had agreed to have with his wife, Peter was not a man to spend more than necessary on an aeroplane ticket.

A moussaka and Greek salad awaited his arrival, but

the wine would not. Louisa poured herself a glass, sat at the breakfast island and reflected on the past week.

Her heart jumped as she heard the key in the door. Christ, she was so on edge. Her mind flashed back to Amsterdam, when she had watched Peter from her vantage point in the café. When he had inserted a key into the lock of the apartment opposite.

Louisa wondered what it would be like for a 'normal' couple coming together after one of them had been away for well over a week. Okay, they were in their late forties, but hardly over the hill. Big smiles, surely, kisses and soft touches accompanied by the unspoken promise of further intimacy to come. After dinner. Or maybe sooner.

But that wasn't going to happen here. Weak smiles betrayed their mutual nervousness, the greetings were civil, but lacking in warmth. Like opposing generals meeting to discuss a much-needed cease-fire, thought Louisa. The pre-dinner conversation was bland, both Louisa and Peter judiciously avoiding anything controversial, an unspoken agreement that wine would be drunk and food eaten before they got down to business.

# 33

# PETER

Peter studied Louisa over his glass as she cleared away the plates. He took a fortifying sip of red wine. Not long now. Whilst he was confident that he had prepared well for this evening, he knew that there was no room for complacency. He was acutely familiar with his wife's frustration at the state of their marriage, but unsure of the tack she would take in attempting to explore his lack of interest in her. But he had a few tricks up his sleeve, a toolbox into which he could delve, depending on the way their conversation unfolded.

But the imperatives – his goals – remained clear. No divorce, and no interference in the life he enjoyed in Amsterdam.

Here we go. Louisa retook her seat and studied his face. Don't look away, he urged himself. Lots of eye contact.

'Peter,' she began. 'You promised me honesty. Does that commitment still hold?'

He rolled his eyes. 'Jeez, you sound like a priest or something.'

She didn't reply. Her raised eyebrow was enough.

'Yes, of course it does.'

'Okay. Thank you. Let's start with the apartment where you're living now. You gave me the wrong address, didn't you?'

Peter's expression didn't register anything, but his mind was racing. Fuck. Where did that come from? He switched on a puzzled look.

'Really? What address did I give you?'

Louisa shook her head. 'Let's just make sure I've got the correct one, shall we?'

A shrug. 'Of course. No problem.' He reached for his phone before holding it up in front of Louisa. 'Isn't this the one I gave you?'

'No. Could you spell it out for me, please?'

'Of course.' Peter obliged, watching as she tapped away at her screen. The task done, she turned back to him.

'Okay. So why don't you tell me who you live with? A friend from work, you said.'

Peter reached for his drink. He looked back at Louisa and smiled.

'That's right. There's Wim, he's the guy who works in our office. His partner Caria, and their two girls, Sibel and Laila.'

'Lovely names. They sound nice.'

'They are. I think money's quite tight for them. Rent in Amsterdam is hugely expensive, as you know.'

'Right. And you have a room there?'

'Well, yes. As I explained, it's tiny. But it does me, and it's a hell of a lot cheaper than renting an apartment.'

'So what do you do about meals?' asked Louisa.

Okay, he thought, let's build a picture for her.

'Breakfast I buy from a convenience store at the Bijlmer Arena station, on the way to work.' A shrug. 'A yoghurt, maybe a croissant… that sort of thing. Eat it at my desk. Lunchtimes I have a main meal in the canteen at work. It's not bad. Then something light in the evening. Usually in a café. Wim and Caria have invited me to eat with them, but I don't like to impose.'

'Understandably.'

Peter raised his eyebrows. 'Tell you what, next time you're over, you'll have to meet them. That would be good for everyone. Faces to names, and all that.' He watched Louisa's shoulders relax. He could see the aggression, the tension, draining away, to be replaced by relief. Now that, he thought, was bloody inspired.

'Thank you. That would be great.' Louisa smiled. 'I would love to meet them. Yes, please.' She peered at him and laid her hand on his. 'You're my husband. It's important I know where you live, who you share your life with when you're over there, okay?'

'Absolutely. I get that.' He overlaid her hand with his own. The nod was accompanied by a sincere expression. He inwardly smiled to himself.

'So, I'm going to refill these glasses,' said Louisa, 'and then you can explain why we have been so distant. Why you never hold me, show me any love. I need to know what's wrong, Peter, so we can put it right. Because if we can do that, we can stay together. If not, we can't. Do you understand?'

Looking down again, he nodded. 'We have to stay together.'

'Then you must come clean with me.'

He watched her make her way to the fridge. How the fuck did she get the address of the apartment?

***

Louisa swallowed and put her hands on the table, palms down. 'So, tell me.'

Peter knew what she was expecting. This whole charade had been designed to expose his inadequacies, his failings as a husband. Okay, he might highlight things about her that could conceivably have turned him off. Her bossiness, her obsession with detail. She was probably anticipating that.

But they would be things that she would have little trouble dismissing. Things that would invite the perfectly reasonable retort: 'So why wouldn't you tell me, rather than allowing the problem to fester over many years?'

But he was smart. He was going to subvert her expectations. She was in for a surprise. He took a sip of wine and then slowly returned the glass to the table. His expression was pained. He studied her face before speaking, alert for any signs that his tactic was working.

'Louisa, have you ever been unfaithful to me… betrayed me? Either when we were engaged, or since?'

There it was. That tiny intake of breath through the nose. Not a sniff, just a modest inhalation, caused by an involuntary tensing of the muscles in her chest. He had seen it before.

She had given him her answer with her expression. She gave him a different one with her words.

'No.'

A pause. His voice was deadpan. 'Okay. I see.'

Silence.

He raised his eyebrows. 'Aren't you going to ask about me?'

Peter watched his wife take a deep breath, then glance at her wine, as if desperate to grab the glass and gulp it down in one. Bitch.

'Of course I am,' she said. 'So, have you ever been unfaithful to me?'

Peter resisted the urge to grin. To raise a pretend fishing rod and start reeling her in. This was going exactly to the script he had prepared.

'Yes,' he said. 'I have.'

# 34

# LOUISA

Louisa liked to think she was pretty organised. Good at planning, at preparing for a range of eventualities. Covering all the bases, so to speak. But now she realised that, in this matter, she was terrifyingly exposed.

Her plan had been simple enough. To put the identical, direct question to Peter. And if he admitted that he had been unfaithful, then she was going to do the same. No names or dates, of course, but his admission of guilt must surely be followed by hers. And then the playing field would be levelled. It wouldn't make the adultery go away, but at least they could take some comfort from their mutual admissions of guilt. It would be a start.

She still wasn't sure how she would feel if Peter owned up to infidelity. And neither did she know how he would respond to an admission of hers. But honesty would have prevailed. And then, perhaps, the healing could begin.

But she wasn't prepared for him to ask the question of her first. She hadn't even considered that possibility. This was *her* show, it was Peter who was on trial here. Did he know about her and Robert? Of course not. How could he?

'No.'

Even as the denial left her mouth, Louisa knew that she had just descended deep into a pit of deceit. Her ethics, values and morals had been stripped away. She felt sickened by the depth of her betrayal of him.

She heard him say, 'Okay, I see'. Heard him ask if she was going to put an identical question to him. Louisa thought back to the time when, in front of DI Griffiths, Peter had given the impression he knew all about the twelve thousand pounds she had lent her brother. The ease with which he had hidden his true feelings and coped effortlessly with the shocking revelation. And lied. So she was fully expecting a denial of any infidelity. Only it didn't happen. Because he admitted to it.

***

Louisa looked to one side, unable to meet his eyes. Her hand shaking, she raised the glass and emptied it. For the second time in as many minutes, she had been blindsided.

So, they had each betrayed the other.

But he had owned up to it, whereas she had lied. It was all relative, of course, they had both cheated. But it was Peter who now occupied the moral high ground, chest out, back straight, the standard held proudly aloft. For he had told the truth.

And she, Louisa, was grovelling at his feet, wallowing in the stench of her lies and cowardice. She thought she sounded like some lame counsellor when she squeaked out the question.

'Do you want to tell me about it?'

He sighed. 'It's complicated. I found it tough being on my own in Amsterdam. And not long after I began working there, I started developing this weird feeling.'

Louisa's voice croaked. 'What weird feeling?'

His eyes bored into her. 'That there was something you weren't telling me, keeping from me. Something important.'

Louisa opened her mouth, but the words caught in her throat. 'How do… like what?'

Peter held up his hands. 'That's the point… I don't know. It sounds ridiculous, but I became trapped, fixated – constantly wondering what it was. And it affected me. Badly.' He looked away. 'I started visiting prostitutes.'

Louisa slowly lifted her hands to her mouth. 'Oh my God.'

'It went on for some time. And then I decided to get help. Therapy.'

'When was this?'

'The therapy? A few years ago.'

'And?'

A weak smile. 'It worked. No more prostitutes. But another problem appeared.'

'Which is?'

'My crippling sense of guilt. Every time we're together, I feel completely unworthy. That I have no right to either show you love, or to receive it.'

His shoulders slumped. The next words were muttered. 'I've failed you, haven't I?'

Louisa stared at him, wide-eyed. She could feel the tears running down her face. She moved around to his side of the table, where they came together in a tight embrace. Peter was shaking, moaning.

'I'm so sorry, Louisa, I'm so sorry…'

She enveloped him in her arms, like a mother consoling an overwhelmed child.

'It's okay Peter, my love. It's all out now. We're going to get help, okay? We're going to get over this. My poor man. My brave man.'

***

Louisa lay on her back, staring up into the darkness. Peter was snoring softly at her side. They hadn't said a great deal after his confession. It was all mutterings, crying and reassurances, followed by tender kisses and promises of a new start together. Emotionally exhausted, they had wearily climbed the stairs, got ready for bed and, with the lights out, held each other in silence.

And now, nowhere near ready for sleep, Louisa was trying to analyse her feelings about the revelations her husband had made. Her conclusions were a jumble, relief on the one hand, new anxieties on the other.

Relief that he had been truthful. Louisa was surprised by her ability to cope with the shocking image of Peter pushing himself into one of those Amsterdam whores they had gawped at. She much preferred the notion that he needed to have sex with a stranger to one where he entertained a lover, someone who meant something to him. Someone she knew, even.

And however unsavoury his behaviour had been, surely the very process of sharing his awful secret represented the first stage in overcoming the barriers that had caused so much damage to their relationship. And she, Louisa, would rise to the challenge. She would be strong, she would take him by the hand and guide him through it all.

But her resolve to cure the sickness failed to answer the question of what had caused it. Why had Peter's move to Amsterdam created the feeling in him that there was something she wasn't telling him? How on earth could the two events be connected? For ten years their marriage had been fine. Not brilliant, but fine. Louisa knew very well that she had not married the most romantic man on the planet. But that was alright – they were doing well, life was generally pleasant, and the sex wasn't bad either.

Okay, there was the option of some gentle probing around what had triggered his unease, but Louisa had always been cautious about stirring things up unnecessarily. Sleeping dogs were generally better let to lie.

But whatever had taken place between them earlier wouldn't make her deceit, her spinelessness, go away. And if she ever wanted to regain her self-respect, she knew she would need to find the courage to do what Peter had done that evening. She would need to tell him about her recent infidelity.

# 35

## PETER

It was a slow start to the day, Peter's leisurely shower giving him time to reflect on the events of the evening before. Under different circumstances, he might have hummed a tune as he stood under the streams of water that invigorated his body. But not today. That wouldn't fit with his act.

Instead, he thought about Louisa's reaction last night. It had all worked perfectly. His revelation about his 'weird feeling', that there was something she wasn't telling him, had clearly caused her discomfort. And with good reason.

As a result, she had been suckered into seeing his fictitious visits to whores as some sort of psychological problem. One for which she shared responsibility; one they had to overcome together. 'Poor Peter. My poor man.' Marvellous stuff. A masterstroke, he told himself.

So now he sat with his elbows on the breakfast island, his coffee cup held between his hands. He sipped noiselessly as he stared at her. He knew Louisa's mind would be in turmoil, wracked with shame. For she had watched her husband break down in front of her, confess to his failings and beg forgiveness for his tawdry indiscretions. A shining beacon of remorse.

But she... For years now, he had known that she had

made a fool of him. And during that time, he'd had ample opportunity to decide how and when she would pay. So, whilst her stupid idea of muscling in on his life and coming to live with him in Amsterdam had altered his master plan, he still intended to see it through. But in a way that would now be far more beneficial to him.

In the meantime, he could enjoy watching her squirm, the guilt only worsened by her open deceit of the night before. The delicious irony of her witnessing *his* apparent remorse, feeling desperately sorry for him, whilst all the while shame was gnawing away at that vision of her perfect, bloody self.

He took another sip and smiled at her.

'So, what shall we do?'

Louisa took a deep breath.

'Well, I think we need another talk, I should...'

'No.' He shook his head and then nodded in the direction of the garden, the outdoors. 'I meant today. What shall we *do*?'

'Ah. I see.' A pause. Louisa raised her eyebrows. 'Well, it's a lovely day. We should definitely make the most of it.'

# 36

## LOUISA

The problem with a place like London was that you could become blasé about what there was on your doorstep. Louisa couldn't remember the last time they had visited Kew Gardens. She knew they had been there with Sophie, perhaps when she was around seven. But today it would be just her and Peter. She booked tickets online.

Louisa was sure that under what might euphemistically be called normal circumstances, she would have loved their visit. Hundreds of years of the discovery, cultivation and husbandry of ornamental and exotic plants, laid out before them in a magnificent spectacle. It was easy to knock colonial era Britain, to see only the things one's country had got so wrong. But this surely was a cause for pride. She was, however, struggling to concentrate on the botanical splendour around her. Because of what she was about to confess to Peter.

Her opportunity came as they stood on the bridge over the lake, admiring the swans beneath them. Their serene gliding contrasted absurdly with her inner turmoil. Heart rate up, breathing shallow. She gripped the awkward uprights of the parapet and turned to face her husband.

'Peter?'

'Mmm.' He continued his observation of a swan.

'Yesterday, you were honest with me. But, I'm ashamed to say, I wasn't with you.'

He nodded down towards the water. 'I read somewhere that they typically mate for life. Can you believe that?'

'Peter, please. Look at me.'

He did, his face expressionless.

Louisa was mentally prepared this time. There would be no repetition of yesterday's failure to anticipate his questioning. She had decided what to share, even if it didn't represent the full extent of her deceit. As a result, she chose her words carefully.

'I too, am guilty of adultery. It happened when I was feeling particularly low. I was convinced that you didn't love me. It was a terrible spur-of-the-moment mistake, and I deeply regret it. I'm not going to go into the details, because they don't matter.'

He studied her face.

'Okay. I'm glad it's come out. Thank you.'

'You don't sound surprised?'

He smiled at her. 'Because I already knew.'

Louisa felt her grip on the situation sliding away from her. She looked down, expecting to see it dribbling between the wooden planks beneath their feet. Was he having her followed? Did he know about Robert, their visit to Richmond Park, the Mayfair hotel? Had Robert confronted Peter and told him what had happened in some bizarre attempt to get him to desert his wife? She needed to stay calm. Regain control.

'How?'

'Your face, yesterday. The guilt was written all over it.'

Louisa took a deep breath. 'I see. And now that you have my confession, does that change anything?'

'Absolutely. Of course it does.'

Louisa felt her chest tighten. Oh, God, he's going to

punish me, cast his cheating wife aside. And it will all be my fault.

'In what way?'

He slipped an arm around her waist.

'It means that we have both done wrong to each other. That we have both owned up. And now we can start again.'

Could it be that easy? They had both admitted to infidelity within their marriage. So on the surface, they were quits. Together, they could get on with the process of healing. But her profound sense of shame remained. Because, whilst what she had told him was true, she had failed to tell him everything, and her betrayal ran even deeper. She began to cry.

He folded both arms around her, albeit a touch awkwardly. But she was relieved by the contact, and they stood like that for a minute or two until her composure returned. Then Peter spoke up.

'Tell you what. How about we have some lunch here? Then we're going to go home. There's a bottle of champagne that's been lurking in the fridge for a while. We can toast our future, take it upstairs, and then I plan to make love to my wife. How does that sound?'

# 37

Louisa sipped her morning coffee, scanning the holly tree for her absent friend. A new week. A new beginning. A leisurely morning the day before had been taken up with a trawl through the *Sunday Times* and then brunch, before Peter had left for Heathrow at midday. This time, they had enjoyed a proper kiss on the doorstep, Louisa looking around to see if any passers-by had seen them. She rather hoped so.

In the afternoon, she took a walk alongside the Thames, filled with relief at the way things had turned out. She now knew what Peter had done, and how the rot had set in to their marriage. What she didn't understand was the catalyst, the cause of his turning to the Amsterdam sex workers, something that he, too, seemed unable or unwilling to explain. But so be it. They both needed to move on.

She was relieved that she had matched his confession with her own. And, critically, Peter had taken it on board without any of the destructive interrogation that could so easily have set them back to where they were. It was over, done with, the slate wiped clean.

So now, surely, they could get back to the way things used to be – the Louisa and Peter who loved and supported each other. She didn't doubt there would be some hiccups along the path to healing. You couldn't exorcise demons like theirs without some deep reflection and further questions. But those questions had to be introspective, there was nothing to be gained by raking over the coals with each other anymore. So she would accept, expect, some further moodiness on Peter's part, in the hope that he too would respect her bouts of contemplation. Because the idea that you could just breeze ahead and pretend these things had never happened was ridiculous.

Her thoughts were interrupted by her ringtone. Louisa stopped and turned to face the muddy River Thames. Her heart skipped. It was Janna calling. That lovely Dutch accent.

'Hello, *Louisha*, how are you?' The pleasantries were quickly dispensed with. 'I'm calling with what I hope is good news.'

***

Louisa left an excited message for Peter before sending another to Asha.

> Got the job! Thx for intro with Janna. Going to Ams Thurs to see company! Talk soon. I owe you. xx

Peter called at around five, his congratulations were followed by Louisa's suggestion for a possible timescale.

'Apparently, everyone in Amsterdam will be on holiday in August, so they don't want me to start until the sixth of September.' She winced as she spoke. 'Now I know that you normally deign to take a bit of time off in the autumn, but how about we pull it forward to this month, before I start the new job? Maybe we can find an adults-only hotel. I was thinking Crete.' Her voice lowered. 'It will be good to get away. After everything.'

'Ah, that could be a problem. I'll see what I can do, but we have a big project in Poland that's about to kick off. Precisely because August is quiet.'

'Oh, Peter, please can we? I don't want to have to ask for time off just as soon as I have started the new job, now do I?'

Louisa could almost hear him counting to ten.

'Darling, please? You're always quick to have a go at me about *my* work getting in the way of our lives. You haven't even started your new job, but already it's more important than mine.'

Louisa bowed her head in resignation, aware of Peter's restraint and her own selfishness. She took a deep breath.

'No, you're right. I'm sorry. Let's leave it for now. But the company do want me over on Thursday afternoon. To go through the job details, sign contracts, that sort of thing. So I'll come over in the morning and head home on Sunday – I can book that same hotel.'

'But why come for three nights? That won't be cheap.'

'Because I would like to view some apartments on Friday. And if I see something I like, then you can take a look, too. It will be fun, Peter. This is what we have been working towards, right? Being together. And now it's going to happen.'

'Okay, but I think I might have a clash… let me see.' A pause. 'Ah, yes. I'm in Italy again at the back end of the week, I won't be able to join you until Saturday, I'm afraid.'

'Okaaay. Maybe we could look at some flats together then? A shortlist of the ones I will have seen on Friday. Oh, and you can introduce me to your hosts.'

'That will be a bit tricky, they're off to France, camping. Like I say, it's August.'

Louisa tried to push the doubt from her mind, but failed. There it was again, that same evasiveness. There were always barriers and reasons why things weren't possible. It was no wonder she struggled to trust him.

He continued. 'But I could show you their place, if you like.'

Louisa was sure he could hear the relief in her voice. 'Oh,

right. Yes, I would love to see it. Great idea. Perfect.'

She cursed herself. Why did she always assume the worst where Peter was concerned? Her nasty, suspicious mind. What the hell was wrong with her? After all, he was the one who had talked openly about his failings, and exposed his mental challenges. Owned up to visiting prostitutes. And despite her subsequent admission of adultery, the confession had only come about because of, and following his. But she had revealed nothing about when it took place, or critically, with whom. No – when it came to hiding the truth, she trumped him.

***

On Tuesday, Louisa busied herself booking flights. Pleasingly, these would be courtesy of her new employer. The hotel was no problem, they had a room available. Louisa briefly toyed with the idea of booking a slightly flashier one, before reminding herself of her husband's habitual caution when it came to money.

She looked at the screen as her phone rang. Oh, Christ.

'Hello, you.' Robert's voice. Soft. Provocative.

She cursed as she felt herself begin to respond. She could not allow that to happen – not now that she and Peter had committed to making their marriage work.

Louisa screwed her eyes shut as she forced herself into denial. She and Robert had never been true lovers. Hadn't he put his career ambitions before any feelings he'd had for her? And that steamy one-night stand in Paddington all those years ago – a drunken and irresponsible act, hardly meaningful. As for the recent episode in Mayfair, an aberration born of her vulnerability and despair. She would force it from her mind and press the 'delete' button. Gone.

Because the important thing here, the only thing that mattered, was her own and Peter's determination to wipe the slate clean and start again. If Robert's feelings were hurt by that, so be it.

'Robert, how are you?'

Louisa didn't wait for a response, determined not to fall victim to his charm. This conversation was to remain anodyne. Two old acquaintances being civil to one another, and no more than that.

'Look, I'm glad you've called, because I have something to tell you. I got that Amsterdam job. Peter and I have had a good talk, and we're going to find an apartment over there. Together.'

'Hey, well done. Congratulations! That's great news, I'm pleased for you.'

Louisa exhaled sharply, unaware that she had been holding her breath. Maybe Robert sensed her desperation not to be dragged back to the place they had so foolishly visited. The place where, in a moment of madness, former lovers abandon their principles, judgement and control in steamy acts of betrayal. Her optimism was quickly dented.

'But I shall always regret I couldn't persuade you to be with me.'

Louisa's voice quavered. 'I have to do this, Robert. I made a promise when I married Peter, twenty years ago. I recently broke it. With you. Now I've made myself another promise. Either to make my marriage work or to walk away. And it looks like I'm making progress. Peter and I hit a bad patch – we didn't make time for each other. But we've thrashed it all out and believe we can make a go of it. I hope you understand.'

There was a pause while Robert digested everything she was saying, and slowly found his voice.

'I understand and respect that, and I wish you all the luck in the world.'

'Thank you.'

'How's Peter? Thrilled, I hope.'

Louisa felt her front teeth pressing down on her lower lip.

'Of course. We both understand how important this is.'

'And what about my goddaughter? How does she feel about it?'

'I called her last night. Sophie's over the moon, as you can imagine. She knows it's not been easy. We'll plan our visits back to Barnes to work in with her uni plans.'

'I'm glad to hear that, Louisa. You've done a great job with her.'

Louisa shut her eyes tight and struggled to keep her voice even as she replied, 'Thanks, Robert. And I'm sure you'll understand that I'm going to be rather busy for a while…'

'I do. And I wish you all the best, both of you. I hope Amsterdam is the new beginning you deserve. And if it's not… you know where I am.'

***

Louisa's alarm was set early on Thursday morning; the ten o'clock flight out of Heathrow should get her into Schiphol by twelve-thirty. If time allowed, she would drop off her bag at the hotel, before making her way via the metro to her new company offices in the south of Amsterdam. There she would meet with her future colleagues.

This was almost becoming routine, her fourth visit to the city in less than eight weeks. She now knew her way around the airport, the train lines and the metro, and was starting to get a feel for the layout of the centre, too.

The plan for Friday was simple. She had six apartment viewings lined up, with an expectation that any properties that appealed could be revisited on Saturday with Peter.

And there was an additional item in the diary. The project she would be leading was to be supported by one of the so-called 'big four' consultancy companies, an organisation with which Louisa was familiar. As was usual, they would assign lots of ambitious and devastatingly intelligent young people to it, all of whom would boast MBAs from good universities. These worker drones would do the heavy lifting, putting in incredibly long hours, in the hope of rising through the ranks and one day attaining a partnership in the firm.

This was the prize, where the big money awaited. Very big money. And a piece of work such as this routinely boasted a partner at its head, a man Louisa had been told about and whom she would meet this afternoon. A man she would join for dinner, along with her new boss.

Everything went smoothly. The meetings with her new employer and the consultants went well. The partner responsible for the project was a polite Dutchman in his mid-forties, perhaps ten years junior to the man to whom she would report at her new company.

Louisa also had a good discussion with the HR manager, an efficient lady who took her through the details of her contract and the process for obtaining the necessary permits. All seemed in order ahead of the sixth of September start date. Signatures were added to documents, Louisa departing with her copy just after five o'clock.

As planned, the partner from the consultants picked her up in a taxi outside her hotel at seven-thirty. Dinner was both pleasant and useful, although eaten without her new boss, who had cried off for reasons unknown. Louisa had earlier messaged Peter, updating him and explaining the dinner plans with some new colleagues. She had felt guilty about creating the impression that there would be quite a few of them. Despite their promises of a new start, she had no intention of revealing the truth. It wouldn't help. She knew him too well.

***

The apartment viewings on the Friday were undertaken in the company of Tess, a pleasant but typically direct young Dutchwoman. Louisa enjoyed the experience, even if she realised that renting in the city was going to be hugely expensive. The properties were visited in what turned out to be ascending order of cost, with the best kept until last. Perhaps unsurprisingly, that was the one with which Louisa fell in love. It was on a quiet street alongside the busy river, and directly opposite the luxurious Amstel Hotel on the far bank.

On parting from Tess, Louisa spent an hour exploring the area. The location would work well for both Peter and herself, the Weesperplein metro station was within a few minutes' walk on the other side of the waterway. From there, they could quickly travel to their respective offices.

Utrechtsestraat too, was a short stroll away, with its quirky shops and plethora of restaurants. Louisa enjoyed wandering down it, recalling the dinner they had enjoyed there on her last visit just over three weeks ago. It would be fun to make this 'their' corner of the city, she decided.

That evening, Louisa headed down to the public area of the hotel. It was too early to eat, but she was ready for a drink. She took one of the easy chairs to the side of the bar where she leafed through the apartment details and reflected on the meeting with her new employer. And enjoyed a little surreptitious people-watching.

Over dinner, she thought about the apartments she had seen. Six in total. The appearance of the one she favoured was not dissimilar to the one where Peter stayed now, although this one looked to be bigger and on the next floor up. But, my God, those stairs were steep. A pair of glazed doors to either side of a huge bay window overlooked the street, which ran directly alongside the river. Each doorway boasted a small balcony, just big enough for a couple of small chairs. Perfect in the summer.

The occupants weren't at home, but the plethora of cardboard boxes suggested they were packing up. Apparently, they would be out by Sunday evening.

There were two bedrooms, a good-sized double with a huge bed and a small one with a single. But it still meant that Sophie could come and visit them, and two bedrooms seemed like a luxury in the city. The other apartments she had viewed had only one; it must be hard living in the characterful centre if you had a large family.

And as this thought crossed her mind, she wondered about Peter's hosts. The apartment was almost certainly on one floor, the row of intercom buzzers and nameplates confirmed that. Could there be three bedrooms? Hard to see how you'd create three in a place like that. Louisa had a vision of the two girls either sleeping in with their parents or in the living area, just so the family could scrape an additional income from a lodger. That didn't sound much fun. She felt a pang of guilt for her comfortable existence.

But all would become clear when she visited the flat with Peter. Tomorrow.

# 38

## WIM

Friday evenings were Wim's favourite. They tended not to vary much. It being the prelude to the weekend, he would get home in good time, reach for a cold bottle of Heineken from the fridge and sit chatting with Caria at the table. He would then change out of his work clothes before taking his family to a nearby Italian restaurant. Nothing fancy, but the kids liked it. Sibel and Laila would eat way too much pizza, whilst Caria and he would typically choose a pasta dish.

But this evening he was feeling guilty. Because the next day, he would once again have to leave his family. Caria had scolded him when he broke the news earlier in the week.

'Wim, please. What is it this time?'

He rolled his eyes. 'That big refurbishment project we've got on. We are close to launch, but there seems to be one problem after another. It's just a quick visit. But…' He called over to the girls, produced some tickets from his pocket and announced that their mother would be taking them to the Artis Zoo on Saturday afternoon. Whilst their excitement was obvious, Caria looked at him and shook her head gently.

'You might have asked me first, you know.'

'Nonsense, it will get you all out of the apartment. It's a treat.' Wim shrugged, 'compensation for my being away.'

***

Once back from the restaurant, Laila had a bath and then came over to Wim, clutching her book, her hair damp and tangled.

'Please, Papa. More Reynard?'

'Okay, little one, ask Sibel to brush your hair, then get into bed and call me when you are ready.'

Caria smiled at him. 'I'm not sure who enjoys those stories more – you or Laila.'

Wim patted her leg. 'Reynard is very clever. I like him. He knows how to get what he wants. Lessons in life.'

'Don't go frightening her, that's all.'

Moments later, Wim was installed with his daughter. She snuggled into him, wide-eyed, as he prepared to read more about the cunning fox and his exploits. Laila tapped the picture on the page.

'A big hen.'

'That's a cockerel. Look at his colourful feathers. He thinks he's very grand and very clever. But he's no match for Reynard. Oh, no!'

Laila looked up at her father's face. 'What's Reynard going to do to him, Papa?'

'Well, we'll have to read on and find out, won't we?'

Ten minutes later, Laila's eyelids were drooping. Wim laid down the book and gently tucked her in. He kissed her forehead and gazed down at her for a moment or two; she smiled softly back and emitted a contented sigh. His precious girl. For the sake of his family, he must be even more cunning, more daring, than quick-witted Reynard. The fox always won. And so would he.

# 39

## LOUISA

On Saturday, Louisa was waiting in their hotel room, having received a message that Peter should be with her in about thirty minutes.

That was a positive sign – keeping her informed. Her intention (she corrected herself, her hope – they needed to decide these things together) was that after Peter had dropped his bag, they could head off into the city centre. There, they could have a late snack lunch, wander around for a while, and then he could show her the flat where he stayed with his host family. She reminded herself to pretend she had never seen it before.

Following that, it was about a fifteen-minute walk to Sarphatikade, the street where Louisa would anxiously introduce Peter to her preferred apartment. Tess, the letting agent, would meet them there.

They would then have the late afternoon to spend 'at their leisure', as a tour guide might put it. Louisa was hopeful that they would spend it here, in their room. Perhaps followed by a post-coital snooze in that lovely bed. The perfect interlude before a cocktail or two and dinner.

On his arrival, Peter smiled widely, kissed her on the

lips and even briefly held her. Louisa fleetingly glanced at the bed. She had avoided sitting or lying on it as she waited for her husband, preferring not to disturb its 'come-hither' appearance.

Peter pulled a few things from his wheelie bag as Louisa explained her plan.

'The agent will meet us at the apartment at three o'clock, so I thought we could have a snack before we go and see where you stay.'

'Okay. I'll just use the bathroom before we head off.' He picked up his phone. Louisa frowned at him.

'Not work, I hope?'

'A quick message I forgot to send. No big deal.'

Ten minutes later they were on their way. Not long after that, they were installed outside a café close to the street market they had explored in June. Only weeks ago, but an awful lot had happened since then. They took their time over a cold beer and a sandwich before Peter looked at his watch.

'Right. Let me show you where I live.'

'Is it far?' Louisa's eyebrows were raised. Liar, she told herself.

He grinned, donning sunglasses and a baseball cap. 'About two minutes, max.'

As they approached the address, Louisa glanced nervously over the street to the coffee shop where she had spent the afternoon spying on her husband. The last thing she wanted to do was bump into her pony-tailed admirer, the man who had served her during her protracted stake-out. She was relieved when they were obscured by a large white van, parked outside the apartment entrance.

Peter stopped and pointed up. 'There you go. It's the one next to the front door. What do you think?'

'I like the street. Very Dutch. Let's go inside.'

Peter smiled as he shook his head. 'I really don't think we

can. I wouldn't feel right bringing someone into Wim and Caria's home while they're away.' He looked back up at the building. 'Not bad though, is it? Great value, too.'

Louisa struggled to hide her exasperation. 'But, Peter, I thought you were going to show it to me. Your room, anyway. Surely Wim and… thingy wouldn't have a problem with that?'

'Caria. I just don't think it's right, that's all.'

'But didn't you think to ask them before they went away? You knew I wanted to see it. I'm sure they wouldn't mind. Two minutes, that's all. Please?'

'We mustn't.'

'Peter?'

'Look, next time you're over, you can meet them. Okay?'

Louisa shook her head in frustration, her hopes of laying to rest any lingering doubts about her husband's lodging arrangements suddenly dashed. All she wanted was to visit the room where he slept, and see his things spread around. Clothes, toiletries, and the photo she had given him a couple of months back. Then her curiosity would have been satisfied, and she could move on. Was it too much to hope for? Apparently so.

She stormed off along the footway and then marched diagonally across the street, nearly stepping into the path of an oncoming cyclist. The young girl shouted at her as she wobbled past. Louisa glanced over her shoulder as she mounted the pavement on the other side, before crashing into someone. A pedestrian, this time.

'Oh, God, I'm so sorry, please…'

Surprise was instantly followed by alarm as she recognised Gerrit, apparently heading for his café.

'Hey, it's my Brit friend. How are you, lady?' His greeting was enthusiastic and loud. He put his hands on her shoulders. 'You came back to see me!'

Louisa froze. Peter would be behind her somewhere, no doubt watching the scene unfold.

'Louisa, isn't it? Yes, that's it…' Gerrit's smile turned to an expression of anxiety. 'You okay? You look surprised. Do you want a coffee?' He gestured towards the café. 'On the house.'

He stopped talking as the Englishwoman in front of him stared back wide-eyed, her lips pursed, making a 'shushing' sound. Louisa flicked her eyes up and to the side. It appeared to work, Gerrit glancing along the street before turning back to her.

'Please, Gerrit. Please?' she whispered, her face creased with anxiety.

Louisa could see him scanning the scene, as if wondering whether he was about to get mixed up in something unpleasant. She wished he hadn't done that; it just underlined the fact that she had told him something controversial. Peter wouldn't have missed it.

Then Gerrit relaxed into a show of embarrassment. He raised his arms and laughed.

'Oh, my God, silly me! You look just like someone I know. I'm so sorry.'

Louisa's eyes closed for a second, the feelings of gratitude and relief almost overwhelming her.

'No, no, *I'm* sorry for crashing into you like that. My fault.'

She turned away, expecting Peter to be there, to confront her, to challenge her. Louisa looked around, but couldn't see him anywhere. She crossed back over the road, before catching sight of him lurking behind the corner of the white van. He took her arm none too gently and bundled her away from the scene.

'Peter, please, you're hurting me.'

'What's going on?'

'I just bumped into some man, that's all. Nearly sent him flying.'

'You know each other?'

Louisa's head jerked. 'Of course not.'

Peter spoke sharply. 'So how come he spoke to you in English?'

'Well, I guess he has an English friend who looks like me. How else?'

Peter stopped. He still had hold of her. Louisa gave a little shake of the head. She frowned down at her arm.

'Peter, will you let go, please?'

He scanned her face, his expression giving nothing away. He released his grip and turned to look behind him. Louisa watched as his eyes moved slowly back and forth between the café and the apartment, as if connecting the two.

# 40

Peter peered out of one of the two sets of french doors and then walked across the room to the other, where he stood gazing down at the river.

'I agree, it ticks all the boxes.' He turned down his mouth. 'But it's way too much.'

'Peter, nice apartments cost a lot over here – you know that. And we need a decent place to live.' Louisa lowered her voice, conscious that Tess was watching them. 'But the new job pays well, and the settlement from my last one will represent over a year's salary.'

At this point, the young rental agent coughed politely, excused herself and told them she would wait outside. Peter held off until she had left.

'I get that, but this is insane. Why don't we take our time to have a good look at what's available, maybe some areas further out of the centre?' He shrugged his shoulders. 'This is so damn expensive and there's no rush, after all.'

Louisa breathed in deeply. She could feel her nostrils flaring.

'I'm not prepared to go over this again. No more delays, no more procrastination. I've viewed six apartments, and this one is perfect. If you don't want me here, tell me now.'

'It's not that, it's...'

'No, Peter. Choose – in or out. The place is ideal and we

can afford it. It's not about the cost, it's about whether you want us to be together. We either do this, or it's over.'

Louisa turned away, her chin raised. She could feel herself shaking. He remained silent. Seconds later, she heard him walk towards the door and step out of the apartment.

***

A minute later he was back, with Tess.

'Your husband tells me you will take it. I'm very happy for you. Congratulations.'

Louisa smiled, shook the proffered hand and then walked over to Peter. She put her mouth close to his ear. 'Thank you. And I'm sorry for losing it just now.' She kissed him on the cheek.

Tess stepped forward.

'So, the occupants will be gone by tomorrow evening. The engineer will visit on Monday to service the boiler, and the apartment will be thoroughly cleaned. We shall need to do a handover with you. Shall we say the following Monday – the twenty-first of the month? The rental would have to start by then.'

Louisa looked at Peter and then nodded. 'Perfect.'

'Good. I'll get the paperwork over to you on Monday.' Tess smiled. 'I'm afraid it's in Dutch.'

Peter shook his head. 'No problem. Email it to me and I'll have someone at work go through it.'

***

They ate dinner at an Italian restaurant. The conversation was laboured, Louisa trying but failing to lift her husband's mood. Surely they should be excited, celebrating the fact that they had just committed to a beautiful apartment in this wonderful city? But no, the old Peter was back, the one she was desperate to leave behind.

She concluded that he was punishing her, partly because she had bullied him into taking the apartment, and partly because he was uncomfortable about her earlier encounter outside the café. Louisa consoled herself with the knowledge that whatever apprehensions Peter might harbour, he couldn't know about her spying on him, and neither had he heard Gerrit using her name. He had been too far away at the time.

Glumly, she watched him twirl some spaghetti around his fork, and returned her thoughts to the fundamental issue. She had thought that by coming to live with him here, they would rediscover what they once had: a sense of connection, love based on a close and shared life.

But she could only get his agreement to the proposal by repeatedly playing the divorce card. She had done it again today, in the apartment. And once more, Peter had caved in, clearly determined to avoid the break-up of their marriage. Six weeks ago he had begged her not to leave him. And just last weekend, they had both admitted to terrible wrongdoings and resolved to start afresh. Which *had* to mean he loved her, surely?

So why did he still seem so reluctant for them to share a life in this fascinating city? And then the biggest question of all. If his motivation was based purely on her threats to end the marriage, what was the point? She reminded herself of their earlier discussions. Being physically together wasn't enough. He had to *want* to be with her. Without his emotional investment in them as a couple, it wouldn't work. Louisa was starting to think she might be making a terrible mistake.

They finished the meal, if not in silence, then something close to it. As they strolled towards Waterlooplein and the Metro, the sound of Celtic folk music grew louder, and they found themselves peering through the windows of an Irish bar. Inside, a folk trio was giving it everything they had, the fiddle player stamping her foot as she swayed around, the red hair flying, her right arm frantically working the bow. The place was packed – sweaty bodies jigged up and down, while condensation tracked down the inside of the glazed door.

Peter smiled for the first time in a while. 'How about we have a drink in here?'

'Your Irish ancestry coming to the fore, is it? Peter, you've hardly said a word all evening and the place is rammed. I'd rather not, to be honest.'

He shook his head slowly. 'Christ, you can be so selfish. I give in to you on the apartment, but you won't even do this for me? Or are you afraid we might bump into someone else you know?'

# 41

Back home on Sunday, Louisa had plenty to occupy her mind. She had met her new colleagues, everything was set for the start of her job, and she was excited about the prospect of spending time in Amsterdam. The only doubts in her mind centred around Peter's mood swings over the weekend. An unwelcome and retrograde step.

In the meantime, there was news to share with her best friend. A couple of messages and it was all arranged. A Tuesday lunch with Asha at the garden centre café. Life in the fast lane, thought Louisa. But it would be good to catch up.

Then it was an eagerly anticipated call to her daughter. Sophie wanted to know all about the apartment and was thrilled at the idea of visiting Amsterdam.

'But in the meantime, how about I come home next weekend? I'm off duty and could turn up on Saturday.'

'Oh, Sophie, that would be marvellous. Of course, darling.'

'Great. Will Dad be there?'

Louisa's laugh masked a recurring sense of unease. 'No, you'll have to make do with your mother, I'm afraid. A bit of girlie time together. But why not come up on the Friday evening?'

'Mum, I'll try, but my shift doesn't finish until seven. If

there's any way I can change it, I will, but I don't hold out much hope.'

***

Monday was spent doing a bit of shopping, followed by a bout of gardening. Best get the place into shape now, Louisa thought, there would be less time to devote to it in the future.

At around four, and before taking her second shower that day, she messaged Peter to get an update on the apartment. Did he have the paperwork? Was it all in order?

The reply came soon enough. Yes, he had the paperwork. But there was a problem. The engineer had called to service the boiler as planned, but had discovered a fault that rendered it unsafe. It was an old model and a part had to be ordered, although its availability was causing concern. There would be a delay whilst the replacement was procured and then fitted. The best estimate was a few weeks.

Louisa tossed her phone down. There was always bloody something. Okay, this wasn't Peter's fault, he was only the messenger. When she had finally dared to believe that all the hurdles had been overcome, this popped up at the eleventh hour.

She stomped off for her shower. Whilst rinsing shampoo from her hair, she had an idea. Once clean, dry and dressed, she sat at her desk and Googled the cost of replacement boilers. Okay, these were UK prices, but surely they wouldn't differ that much around Europe? By her reckoning, the cost of a new boiler, plus allowing the same again for installation, would be less than the rental income that the landlord would lose whilst the existing one was being fixed. And the boiler that was there was apparently old. So why not simply replace it with a new one and be done with it? Bloody obvious, really.

She looked at the clock. Too late to call now, but she

would contact the letting agency in the morning and suggest it. Anything was better than drifting around in a state of paralysis, at the mercy of the prevailing wind and tides.

***

On Tuesday morning, as Louisa held the line for Tess, she wondered if she was being a bit silly. Her impatience to get things moving was starting to look childish. Ah, no going back now, Tess was speaking to her.

Greetings exchanged, Louisa came to the point of her call and shared her plan for the replacement of the boiler. Tess listened in silence before asking her to hold the line. Louisa sat watching through the bay window as the last of the rush-hour traffic passed on Lonsdale Road, her regret at making this call mounting. Eventually, Tess returned.

'I'm sorry, *mevrouw*, but I've just spoken to my colleague. There is no problem with the boiler. We took a call yesterday from your husband.' Tess cleared her throat. 'He told us that you had changed your plans and will not now be renting the apartment.'

# 42

Louisa pushed herself out of her chair and marched into the kitchen. Then she marched back into the sitting room and picked up her phone. Shaking, she held it poised in front of her before lowering it and drifting back into the kitchen. There, she sat on a stool at the breakfast island and cried.

She hadn't believed Tess, saying there must be a mistake. Would she please check with her colleague? Because, as Louisa explained in a quavering voice, *'The consequences of what I have just been told are going to be considerable.'* Tess had quietly and firmly said she understood. Louisa believed her – Tess had realised that a significant deception between a man and his wife was unfolding before her. Another minute had passed before the agent came back on the line, sounding apologetic but firm. There was no misunderstanding.

This was it. The story about the boiler was a blatant lie. Peter had shown his hand, the upturned cards there on the table for all to see. How might he have explained it to her when she subsequently found out that the apartment had been let to someone else – that he had been lying? He must have known it would all come out. He must have!

Even as this question presented itself, Louisa knew that she could, if she wanted, play along and find out. See what the bastard came up with. Because at some point, he would have to advance a cock-and-bull story to her. But there was no way she was going to wait that long. She had to take the initiative. She wanted that divorce. And quickly.

She wiped her eyes and looked at the clock. She would need to leave in ninety minutes to pick up Asha. God, she needed to talk to her. The only question was whether to confront Peter now, or after she had shared the devastating news with her friend.

Whatever the decision, she had been made to look a first-class fool. But in this sick game of her husband's, she finally had the advantage. A temporary one at least. Peter didn't yet realise that she knew about his lies, his cruelty. But that advantage would not last long. She needed to act. Fast.

***

Louisa's forced smile was never going to convince. Even as she got in the car, Asha frowned at her friend.

'What's wrong, babe? Tell me.'

Louisa's voice was shaking, her eyes full. She looked in the rear-view mirror and flicked the indicator switch.

'Just let me drive. We'll be there in ten minutes. I can't speak until then. Okay?'

'Okay, hun. But take it nice and easy, right?'

Once parked, Louisa turned to her friend and, for the next twenty minutes took her through everything. Well, nearly everything. There was no mention of the sex with Robert. Asha was characteristically unflappable. She looked at her watch and picked up her phone.

'I'm just going to call the office and tell them something's come up. We're going to need a bit more time while you decide what you're going to do.' She nodded to the café. 'Then we'll get some food inside you.'

Over tuna and cucumber baguettes, Asha discussed Louisa's options with her. They were pretty much as she had figured. Call Peter, and have it out with him on the phone. Or go over to Amsterdam and make a scene. Either at the apartment or maybe even his place of work. Or else hold off completely until he next came home. Louisa's response to that was unequivocal.

'Well, I'm certainly not going to wait. I have to strike whilst I have the advantage. Neither do I want to talk to Peter on the phone, it just allows him to lie some more. I'm done with that. What I need is clear evidence of his double life. Certainty that the woman in the apartment where he lives is his lover. It makes no difference to the outcome, because I won't take any more of his deceit. But at least I will have arrived at the truth behind this whole bloody charade. I need that – for me.

Asha nodded. 'Sounds like another covert trip to Amsterdam then.' She winced. 'And if you get categorical proof that Peter is shacking up with this woman, you're done?'

'Of course. At that point, I can calmly explain to him that we're divorcing. No debate, no need for any more of his bullshit.'

'And if there is no visible proof?' asked Asha.

'Then I think I will bang on the apartment door when Peter isn't there and confront the lady in question. Caria, apparently.' She winced. 'I doubt she shares my husband's ability to scheme and lie. That has to be unique.'

Asha sat back. 'Sounds like you have your plan, babe.'

'I need to get on with it, though. Peter told me he's off to France on Thursday evening. I'll fly over tomorrow. Then I'll have the evening and most of the next day to catch the bastard red-handed. And this time, I'll be better prepared.'

***

On Wednesday, as Louisa made her way from Schiphol to the hotel, she contemplated the perversity of her situation.

Her efforts to find work in Amsterdam had borne fruit. And for the next year, during the life of the project that she had been employed to lead, she would need to visit the city regularly and often. And whilst she was whizzing in and out of the place that she had grown to love, her (soon to be) former husband would be in the same city, carrying on with whatever arrangements he had worked so hard to hide from his wife.

It sounded silly, but she was prepared to make a bet that sooner or later she would bump into him. On a flight, in the airport… She would need to plan what to say and how to behave when it happened. Louisa didn't like being unprepared.

And then sadness swept over her. It was going to be horrible. The house in Barnes would have to go, a casualty of the divorce. Everything that they had chosen together, cherished, would be up for argument, picked over. She was glad that she had kept her promise to herself, to try and do everything she could to save the marriage. She may have failed, and been made a mockery of, but better to fail trying than not to try at all. Because the alternative was so final. Divorce. A decree absolute.

Having checked in, she made her way to the room. She looked around, recalling the excitement of her previous visit. It had all been an illusion, a cruel sham. She opened her bag and took out her sunglasses and a wide-brimmed hat bought especially for her mission. The summer blouse, too, was new – not that she expected Peter to recognise anything she wore. Better safe than sorry, though.

Thirty minutes later, she approached 'her' café in De Pijp, where she rather hoped to find Gerrit. She owed him both her thanks and an explanation, there being little point in hiding the truth. Despite her disguise, she kept one eye on the apartment opposite. She didn't expect to see or bump into her husband at this time of day, but couldn't rule it out on his home territory.

The door to the café was wedged open in the warm August air. Gerrit had his back to her, his ponytail bobbing up and down as he talked with a customer. She took a seat near the window. Shortly afterwards, he turned to the new arrival and greeted her in Dutch. The disguise worked then.

With a glance over towards the apartment to make sure she was not being watched, she slowly removed her sunglasses.

'Hello, Gerrit.'

'My God.' He quickly glanced around, as if expecting someone to march up and confront him.

Louisa smiled, trying to look reassuring.

'It's okay, I'm alone. But I owe you my thanks for last time, and an explanation.'

His expression eased. 'You don't owe me anything. But I'm really glad to see you. Are you okay? I was worried about you.'

Louisa assured him she was fine and thanked him for his concern. Gerrit looked relieved.

'Now, what would you like? On the house, of course. On me.'

'Oh, no, I insist it's on me. I don't know if you can sit down for ten minutes, but if so, I'll tell you why I'm here.'

Gerrit smiled. 'Of course. Coffee, was it?'

Louisa nodded.

'Two coffees it is, then.'

He addressed an attractive young woman working behind the bar before taking the seat opposite Louisa's. They made small talk until the coffees arrived. Gerrit smiled up at his colleague, then at Louisa.

'This is my daughter, Ilse. Ilse, meet Louisa. A friend.'

Louisa could have hugged him for the way he introduced her. Right now, in this city, she felt exposed, vulnerable. Having a friend here would be a comfort to her.

For the next thirty minutes or so, Louisa took Gerrit

through the salient parts of her Amsterdam story. Her husband's continual and increasingly extreme attempts to stop her from coming to stay there with him. Her fears that she was being duped, and that Peter was living with his lover in the apartment opposite. Gerrit nodded knowingly as Louisa told him her story.

'I just want the lying to stop. I've told him we can divorce, but he keeps insisting that there's nothing wrong. That nothing's going on. We can't continue like this.' She nodded through the window.

'I need to know. If they are lovers, so be it. I can cope with that.' She hoped she wasn't lying to herself. 'What I can't cope with is the deceit.' She turned back to her new friend. 'Does that make sense?'

Gerrit breathed deeply, then nodded over to the apartment.

'I recognise the man who lives there. I've seen him often enough. On his own or with the woman and the kids. I don't know his name, but we'll nod to each other in passing.'

'And is there another man who lives there? My husband has told me that he lodges with a man called Wim and his partner, Caria. And their two kids, Sibel and Laila. I've seen her, I've seen the kids. But not another man. This Wim fellow.'

Gerrit frowned. 'Well, there could be, I suppose. I can't say I've paid them much attention.'

She had another question. 'The family are supposedly on a camping trip. Or were last week. Any thoughts on that?'

'No way. They were certainly around all last week. A woman, maybe a childminder, brought the younger girl in here. I think she was dropping her off to her mother, who wasn't yet home. When they arrived, the mother and the older girl joined them.' He nodded to a table. 'They sat there.'

He tensed a little as he looked through the window.

'Here they are, now.'

Louisa quickly put on her sunglasses. Sure enough, Caria and Sibel were mounting the steps to the apartment. Seconds later, they could be seen through one of the two large windows. Louisa looked at her watch. Four o'clock.

Gerrit excused himself to do some work. After thirty minutes or so, another woman arrived with the smaller child, Laila. They both joined Caria until the childminder left shortly after.

Louisa continued her surveillance, frequent glances at her watch accompanied by pointless speculation as to when Peter might arrive. If he did, of course. Once more Louisa recognised the random approach of her sleuthing. This may well be a total waste of time. Gerrit stood alongside her now and again and asked for updates as the minutes ticked by. Louisa smiled to herself. Her pony-tailed admirer seemed fully invested in her mission.

At five-forty, Gerrit came and sat next to her.

'Louisa. You need to know that we close at six.'

'Ah. Of course.'

'But don't worry. I live directly above here. You are welcome to stay and watch out of the window. In fact, it will be better from there because you will see down into the apartment opposite. And while you watch, I shall cook us some dinner. You can sit by the window and eat there, if you like.'

Louisa blinked at him. 'Well, that's very kind of you, Gerrit, but I don't want to be a nuisance. If I don't…'

He held up his hand. 'I promise you, I wouldn't ask if I didn't want you to stay. It will be my pleasure. I'm not the best cook, but I won't poison you either.' He leaned forward. 'And I respect women, okay? You don't have to worry.'

He spoke briefly with his daughter before escorting Louisa out of the café, in through an adjacent door and up a typically steep flight of stairs. Louisa's faint discomfort at her intrusion was quickly displaced by her appreciation of the unimpeded view she had into the apartment – the one where Peter stayed, though in what capacity she was still uncertain.

There were no blinds on the windows opposite. Apparently, this was quite normal in the Netherlands. She recalled, as part of her research, reading about the Calvinistic attitudes of many Dutch people. Frugal, hard-working, law-abiding. And the extension of those attitudes into the idea that honest citizens have nothing to hide. Hence, fewer curtains and blinds. Although, despite the bare windows, the concept of nothing to hide clearly didn't apply to her husband.

Presumably Gerrit felt differently when it came to domestic privacy. Louisa screened the chair he offered her behind a part-drawn curtain and settled down.

She didn't have to wait long. At around six-fifteen, Peter walked up the steps to the front door opposite and let himself in. Louisa was aware of a feeling of light-headedness as he dropped his messenger bag onto a chair and kissed Caria on the lips, his hands on her waist. Exactly the way he used to greet his wife when he came in from work. In the old days.

They were then joined by the two girls who also received kisses, the younger one clinging to Peter's thigh for a minute or two before they both scampered off. At this, he walked over to the window where Caria was working at the sink.

Louisa moaned as Peter positioned himself close behind her. His hands came into view and he began to fondle her breasts. Caria tipped her head to one side, a smile on her face. She was looking directly out of the window towards the point where Louisa sat, motionless, not daring to move. Time stood still.

Louisa was jerked out of her trance when she heard a key in the lock. Gerrit appeared, cradling a paper bag stuffed with groceries. He kicked the entrance door closed behind him and nodded to the window.

'How's it going? Seen anything useful?'

Louisa burst into tears.

***

Louisa sat down at Gerrit's table, nursing a large glass of white wine. The curtains had been drawn at her request. She had seen enough, and neither did she want to risk being spotted by her husband. This was a turning point. No further proof was needed, ongoing discussion was pointless.

Gerrit must have sensed her mood.

'Look, you wanted certainty. You have it. Now you can get on with the rest of your life. That's good, *ja*?'

Louisa gave an emphatic nod. 'Ja.'

He stood. 'A toast. Louisa and her future!'

She stood as well, they chinked glasses and sipped. Then she thanked him and kissed him on the cheek before sitting again. He clapped his hands together, as he had when they first met.

'Oooh là-là.' He took his wine over to the small kitchen area.

'Okay, Lady Louisa. Let me show you what this weird Dutch guy can do in the kitchen.'

Around two hours later, she sat slumped in her chair, somewhat the worse for wear. As well as several glasses of wine, Louisa had polished off a mighty skewer of Gerrit's chicken satay. This was accompanied by a serving of noodles, some Asian slaw and a dollop of homemade peanut sauce. She smiled at her host.

'You've been very kind to me, thank you. And the food was amazing.'

'It's my pleasure. I appreciate your company.'

Louisa pushed herself up on her chair and looked around for her bag.

'And now I must leave you, but thank you so much for all you have done for me. I'm very grateful.'

He raised his eyebrows. 'You don't have to go, you know. If you want, you can stay the night with me. I would love that. You're very pretty. We can just lie together, or we can fuck. Your call, Lady Louisa.'

Louisa felt her cheeks and neck reddening. She laughed. 'Oh my God. I love you Dutch people.'

'Why? What's so funny?'

'You're just so damned direct.'

Gerrit looked confused. 'In what way?'

'We can just lie together, or we can… fuck.'

'*Ja*? What's strange about that?'

Louisa shook her head.

'Nothing. Its greatest virtue is its honesty – something I haven't encountered very much of, recently. But I won't stay, thank you, Gerrit. I need to get home as soon as I can. I need to set the wheels in motion.'

# 43

Louisa's trip home on Thursday morning was spent reflecting on the last forty-eight hours. On the one hand, she felt relief that the truth had finally emerged. She recalled the essence of the saying, if not its source: that the certainty of pain is preferable to the pain of uncertainty.

And at least she now had that certainty. She knew Peter was living a double life with his lover in Amsterdam. That he had been lying to her, deceiving her, even if she had no idea for how long. And whatever he said, however much he tried to deny events and wriggle out of things, they were going to divorce.

But the relief of knowing what he was up to was matched by a profound regret that their marriage had ended like this. She had failed as a wife, her husband preferring the company of another woman.

The question 'why' still hung over her. Why had he chosen to look for love elsewhere? There was no doubt that the past ten years of their marriage had been dull, but a big part of that, pretty much all of it in fact, had been down to him. And if it wasn't for her recent efforts and yesterday's revelation, then Louisa was sure that Peter would have carried on with his parallel life exactly as it was. For reasons she did not understand, the arrangement suited her husband.

So, what were the next steps? First, see a solicitor. Whilst waiting for her ten-thirty flight out of Schiphol, she called the firm that advised on her mother's affairs. Following her arrival at Heathrow, Louisa would go straight to their offices in Richmond. There she would meet with a specialist in family law.

She would then confront Peter and explain what she knew. Brush off his denials and the lies that would surely follow, and get straight on with the business of winding up the marriage.

At this point, she winced. She was about to inherit from her mother's will. A few hundred thousand initially. Sophie would receive a generous legacy, but Inspector Griffiths had been right in his analysis. With Michael gone, the rest of her mother's assets would now pass to Louisa. Presumably, Peter would get half of whatever she eventually received in the divorce settlement. Jesus!

But she did take comfort from her mother's natural caution and the solicitor's wisdom. Because years ago, before the dementia had fully set in, the bulk of her mother's wealth had been transferred into a trust – and only Barbara's blood descendants could benefit from that. Distributions of income and capital were solely at the discretion of the trustees. Louisa was one, the solicitor the other. As her husband, Peter would of course have benefitted indirectly when his wife came into her inheritance from the trust. But he was unaware of its existence. As Michael had been. For Barbara had been adamant: it was nobody else's business what she did with her money, and only she and her trustees were to be made aware of her plans.

Louisa wondered if Peter assumed that, with Michael and her mother dead, Louisa would inherit Barbara's wealth directly and in its entirety. And, hey presto, half would then automatically come to him in the divorce. If so, he was in for a disappointment. She allowed herself a rueful smile.

Louisa's other decision was that she would make her position on their divorce clear to Peter before breaking the news to Sophie, who would be home on Saturday.

She now had a plan. Solicitor first, Peter second, then Sophie.

As for how things would unfold over the coming months, she would do all that she could to keep Peter away from the house. She didn't think for one minute she could stop him being there, but surely his desire to spend all his time in Amsterdam with his lover would only be reinforced by their impending divorce. She hoped so.

And what of more recent events? She allowed her head to rest against the back of the seat as she gazed out of the aircraft window at the Netherlands coast slipping away beneath her. Gerrit. Just at the point where she was at her lowest, rejected and betrayed, her value as a wife shattered… he had gently lifted her up and brushed her down. His admiration for her had been so patently sincere, and his easy acceptance of her choice to remain disengaged so refreshing. Why weren't there more men around like him? And Robert, of course. She hadn't forgotten their recent encounter, even though she'd tried to banish all thought of it from her mind. With a smile on her face, she closed her eyes.

***

This was it. The meeting with the solicitor had gone as well as could be expected. The process for winding up the marriage was carefully explained to her by a young woman who approached Louisa's situation with a strange cocktail of professional detachment and female empathy.

The path to becoming a single woman appeared technically straightforward, and there was nothing that Peter could do to ultimately prevent it. His cooperation would make the whole process simpler and cheaper, but Louisa knew that this was by no means a foregone conclusion. But for now, she would not tell him of her consultation with her solicitor. The advantage of her newly acquired knowledge would be temporary. In dealing with Peter, she realised she needed all the advantages she could get.

At lunchtime, she left him a voicemail and then messaged him for good measure. There was no ambiguity in the wording of either communication. He called back shortly afterwards and listened in silence whilst, in a shaking voice, Louisa delivered her prepared script.

'Peter, I want a divorce. It's not up for discussion. And the reason is that you are leading a double life in Amsterdam with Caria. I know it's true, so please don't insult my intelligence by denying it.'

He was silent for a while before replying. 'I have never insulted your intelligence, and I don't intend to start now. But what makes you so sure? Had me followed, have you, had a private detective tailing me?'

'Sort of. Me. You and Caria are living together. You're not her lodger, you're her lover. Her partner Wim is a figment of your vivid imagination.'

Peter's tone changed. He snapped at her: 'Wim *is not* a figment of my imagination. Don't you say that, okay?'

She sighed. 'Oh, for Christ's sake, Peter. I've seen you holding her, caressing her, when the children weren't looking.' Despite her best efforts, Louisa's voice cracked. 'You used to do that with me. So please don't deny it. Don't try and wriggle out of this with more of your lies.'

'Hmm, I thought you might have done a bit of snooping. The café opposite the apartment. Your encounter with the owner. You know him, right?'

Louisa instantly regretted not playing along with the private detective idea. Why the hell hadn't she thought of that? The prospect of Peter exacting some sort of revenge on Gerrit was not a pleasant one. They were neighbours, for God's sake.

'He recognised me, that's all. I spent quite some time in that café, watching you.'

'No, you saw Wim.'

'I know what I saw, Peter. Look, I'm tired of this charade. But tell me this. If you weren't happy with me, with us, why not simply tell me it's over and be free?'

A sigh. 'Well, I had my reasons. Driven by you, of course.'

'I don't understand.'

'Really? Would you like me to explain it all to you, dear wife?'

'I think I've had enough of your lies.'

'No lies. The truth will have to come out, now that we are to part ways.'

'Go on, then. Let's hear it.'

Another pause. 'Not over the phone. I want to see your face when I do. On Saturday. I'll fly over then. We can sit down together and go through it all.'

'Well, sorry to spoil your sick game, but Sophie's coming home on Saturday. We can't do it then.'

'What time will she arrive?'

'Late afternoon.'

'Right. I'll be there Saturday morning, ten o'clock. And then we can have our little chat. But there's a condition, okay?'

'What's that?'

'You don't go blabbing to her, or Asha, or anyone else beforehand. You can tell them whatever you like afterwards, but until then, our intended divorce remains private. This is our business, okay? Just between us for now. Do I have your word on that?'

'I don't gossip, Peter. This is between you and me.'

'Right. While I'm there, I'll pick up a few of my bits and

pieces. I can arrange to get the rest of my stuff another time. Don't worry, nothing of any value. You can stand over me whilst I pack.'

Louisa rested her forehead on her hand. This was already getting unpleasant, and they hadn't properly started yet.

'Will you still be here when Sophie gets home?'

Peter gave a little laugh.

'You want to be able to poison her mind without me around, is that it? No, you can have your wish. I'll be gone by twelve at the latest.'

# 44

# PETER

Peter cursed as he put his phone down. Where did all that come from? Okay, things were a bit strained when they parted on Sunday; he should have been on a charm offensive over dinner the evening before. But he didn't feel up to it – the episode with the café owner had rattled him, and he hadn't been convinced by Louisa's assurances that they didn't know each other. Turned out he was right after all.

And then Louisa's blackmail at the overpriced apartment: playing the bloody divorce card again, trying to force him into renting it. Well, he wasn't a man to be forced into anything. Who the fuck did she think she was?

But something about their telephone conversation just now had stuck in his mind. On Monday, she had appeared to accept the story about the dodgy boiler – a story that should have bought him the time he needed. But her suspicious mind must have got the better of her. Presumably she had spoken to the letting agent about it. That had to be it – there was no other way his wife could have learned the truth. But then there had been that reference to her seeing him with Caria. Louisa was emphatic about that, it wasn't a bluff. Had she been back to Amsterdam this week? Or did she pay someone to gather evidence for her? How else could she be so sure?

But whatever Louisa knew, the critical issue here was whether she had shared her findings and conclusions with anyone else. Did Asha or Sophie know that she had now resolved to divorce him? That was the last thing he needed. Thank God the bitch had promised to keep quiet about it until after they had their little chat. All he could do was hope she'd meant it. She probably did, it wouldn't be in her character to promise him discretion and then go blabbing to all and sundry. She was too fucking superior for that.

So, the agreement was for the shit to hit the fan on Saturday morning. The big showdown. And then Sophie would turn up that same afternoon. And there was no way Louisa would keep the situation from her daughter once *they* got together. Yak, yak, yak. The intended divorce would be common knowledge by Saturday evening. Sophie, Asha, that smug bastard Robert – they would all know. And that didn't suit Peter at all.

In which case, he would just have to surprise her. Change plans. Take back the initiative. Fortunately, much of the preparatory work had been done. He relished the prospect of getting closure.

# 45

## LOUISA

Louisa spent Friday in a haze. She resisted the temptation to start making lists of who would get what, but did Google some estate agents to try and work out which firm would be best placed to handle the sale of the house. She would need Peter's agreement, of course.

A guarded phone call with Asha the evening before reinforced Louisa's determination not to become the victim of manipulation or brainwashing by Peter. He had done enough of that lately. She knew the discussion with him would be emotionally draining, but at least they would then be able to move on to the practicalities of the separation. And God knows, that would be hard enough.

At three-fifteen her phone went.

'Hi, it's me.'

'Peter?'

'Yes. Different phone. A temporary one. I can't find mine anywhere.'

'Oh.'

'Look, I know this is short notice, but are you home – right now?'

'Well, yes. Why?'

'Okay. Got anyone coming around or anything? It's just that I caught a flight over from France today, there's nothing early enough in the morning to get me to you by ten. If we have our talk now, I can head back to Amsterdam tonight. Save me staying over, which I would rather avoid.'

Louisa wasn't sure where he had planned to sleep and felt a wave of dread at the idea of him being in the house with her, even if she knew there was nothing she could do to prevent it. She had to force herself to think in terms of 'their' house. It already seemed like he didn't belong there.

She could hear the noise of traffic, and his breathing as he walked. 'So where are you?'

'I'm on Lonsdale Road, two minutes away.'

Louisa felt a surge of apprehension, but kept calm. 'So what were you going to do if I didn't answer?'

'Leave you a message, get what I need now and come back in the morning as planned. I have a key, remember.' His voice softened. 'Don't worry, I'm not trying to spook you, and I really would rather not stay in the house.'

Louisa felt the tightness in her chest ease. 'Er, well… yes, okay. See you in a minute.'

She looked around her, as someone might before the impending arrival of an unexpected and unwelcome visitor. This was getting weird.

***

Louisa stood in the hallway as she heard the key turn in the lock. She could see a man's outline through the stained-glass window to the side of the front door. Even this early in the process, it felt like an intrusion. Christ. She wondered how long it would be before she had her own place – one for which Peter would not have a key.

'Hi.'

Louisa frowned at the appearance of the man before her. 'Shit, Peter, what are you wearing?'

He looked down at himself through tinted wraparound sunglasses. 'The distribution centre in France was always going to be grubby. It's in the middle of a major refit.'

'And the bucket hat… when did you get that? It's so not you.'

He shrugged. 'Dunno.'

She stifled her instinct to voice some objections about his unflattering and inappropriate choice of clothing. It was none of her business now. Instead, she heard herself resorting to sarcasm.

'Of course, there's a lot about you I don't know, isn't there?'

Louisa watched as he stuffed the offending headgear and shades into a rucksack. He was dressed like a festival goer. Faded jeans, dirty trainers. A plain grey hoodie, although lightweight, seemed inappropriate for August. She nodded over her shoulder. 'Let's sit in the kitchen.'

He followed her in and dumped his rucksack next to him. Something else she hadn't seen him with before.

Louisa reached for a glass. 'Do you want some water?'

He nodded to his pack. 'Got some in there.'

Louisa sipped hers, watching him. She barely recognised her husband. This wasn't the conservative Peter she was used to. It was as if her discovery of his double life meant that he could finally stop pretending. He was clearly living in two very different worlds.

'So, Peter. I'm not going to get angry or make a scene, but I do want to know why you did what you did. Things between us used to be okay. And then, after you went to Amsterdam, it all fell apart. Was that when you met Caria?'

'It's not like that.'

'What caused it then? And why, when you decided that

you wanted to be with her, would you not just tell me? Come clean. You owe me that much, at least. It happens, Peter. People meet someone and then decide they don't want to be with the person they married anymore. They'd rather be with their new love.'

He said nothing but sat back and folded his arms. He looked at the ceiling, as if contemplating the meaning of life.

'Hmmm. There are a couple of questions in there.' He lost interest in the ceiling and trained his gaze on her. 'And I, lovely Louisa, will answer them truthfully – if you promise to answer mine in the same way. Deal?'

She paused; this felt like a replay of their confessional of exactly two weeks ago. She stared at him before replying. 'Fair enough. Okay.'

It was quiet for what seemed to her like a long time. She was conscious of Peter's shoulders hunching, the hoodie riding up behind his head as his neck shrank into his shoulders. His eyes narrowed. Louisa waited for him to speak, sensing that something profound was about to play out.

'Sophie.' He leaned forward, his lips had receded to reveal bared teeth. '*So-feee!* You know perfectly well she's not mine, don't you?'

# 46

Louisa sat at the breakfast island, taken completely by surprise. Even as she did, she knew the game was up. The only plausible behaviour from an innocent woman in this situation would have been an explosion of laughter and incredulity, swiftly followed by a vehement denial: *'Why on earth would you think that? Of course she's bloody well yours. Jesus, Peter.'*

But the opportunity for that was already gone, all she had left was the truth. Feelings of relief and shame battled for supremacy. Her head hung forward, the answer spoken softly, towards the floor.

'No, I don't *know* she's not yours.' Now she looked up at him, this man who was her husband. The man with whom she had built a life. 'But, equally, I can't be certain she is.'

Peter was staring at her. She could see him inhaling slowly. The traces of a cynical smile played about his eyes, his teeth visible in a triumphant smirk. Her momentary relief that there was no outward show of rage was quickly undermined by a recollection of his ability to mask his fury with benign and innocent behaviour. As he had when DS Lynch had dropped that bombshell about Louisa's loan to her brother. So she knew that Peter was capable of being two people at once. And was suddenly afraid. He hissed at her.

'Twenty years. Twenty-fucking-years.'

'Peter, I'm…'

His hand shot up, palm in her face. The classic 'stop' sign.

'Don't you dare fucking apologise! Just don't, okay?'

'I wasn't going to. I was going to ask what made you think Sophie wasn't yours?'

Peter pulled a bottle of water from his backpack and took a swig. 'In a minute. Is she Robert's?'

'Well, she's either yours or his. There's nobody else who could be her father.'

'My, how restrained of you. Does he know?'

'Of course not.'

Peter smirked. 'Not yet anyway. No doubt he'll want to thank me for raising her, for feeding, clothing and educating his illegitimate daughter.' He wagged a finger at Louisa. 'Must remember to send him an invoice.'

She looked away. 'What's your agenda here, Peter? Who are you trying to hurt?'

'Who am *I* trying to hurt? That's bloody rich. You fuck up everyone's lives with your cheating, your deceit, then accuse *me* of trying to hurt people?'

'It wasn't cheating. If you remember, we had split up when Robert came back from Canada for a visit. You and I had broken off our engagement. I wasn't cheating on you.'

'And it took you – what? – all of five minutes to part your legs for another man?' Peter shook his head. 'The high and mighty Louisa Bruce-Gardiner. You're just another fucking slut!'

Louisa briefly closed her eyes. She had nothing to say in response. She didn't need Peter to point out her failings, they had been torturing her for years now. She addressed him once again.

'So, back to my question. What made you think Sophie might not be yours?'

'Well, I know Robert high-tailed it home from Canada

with indecent haste as soon as you and I broke up. Maybe you encouraged him. And then when we got back together, you insisted I didn't need a condom. Right at the end of your cycle, you said. You had never, ever done that before, you always made me use the damned things. So, with the enormous benefit of hindsight, I am bloody sure you were worried that you might have already conceived with my old mate. And a heat-of-the-moment and unprotected shag with dopey Peter would remove any concerns about there being a different father on the scene.'

'But you still married me, knowing I might be carrying another man's child?'

'Fuck, no, I was too slow to work it out at the time. I had no idea then that you had slept with him, had I? But a few years later, Asha let it slip that she, you and Robert had dinner together while you and I were separated. But *you* never told me about it, did you? So I became suspicious. I wondered what else you might be hiding from me. And then as Sophie grew up, I started to think she was developing a remarkable resemblance to her godfather. Couldn't see it when she was small, of course, all babies look like ET to me. And those blue eyes of hers... I don't have them, neither do you.' He smirked. 'But that cunt Robert does.'

'So is that it? Just a bunch of suspicions and her blue eyes? There's a six per cent chance that parents with brown eyes will have a child with blue ones. It's perfectly possible.'

In that instant, Louisa wanted to snatch the words back. Too late. Peter grinned at her.

'Aaah, gotcha! And how, dear wife, would you know that very specific biological fact? What caused you to go and research it? Panicking, were you? I'll bet you were... bitch! Anyway, I know she's not mine.'

'I don't believe you. How on earth could you know?'

'Duh, it's not rocket science, is it? I had a DNA test done in Amsterdam. Not long after I started working over there.

When I was home, I took some hair from Sophie's hairbrush. They needed follicles, though. That's where the accessible DNA is. I had to repeat the exercise three times before they had a good enough sample. Cost me a fortune. So now I know for sure she isn't mine.'

Peter gazed into the distance. He appeared to have drifted into another world. Louisa watched in horrified fascination as he avoided looking at her and calmly addressed one corner of the room.

'Yes, you're a lying, cheating whore. They used to whip women like you. Strip them naked, parade them around the town square, everyone jeering, pointing their fingers.' He swung his head in an exaggerated nod, eyes shining. 'I've read about it – seen illustrations.'

Louisa's instincts got the better of her. She felt it was important not to show the fear that was welling up inside her. He had clearly done some sort of grudge-bearing research while contemplating his wife's deceit. Now his unmasking into this medieval monster was frightening her. She took a deep breath and went on the attack.

'Oh, and here's Mr Righteous passing judgment on everyone. The man who leads a double life with his lover in Amsterdam, and visits prostitutes to satisfy the dirty urge he can't control.'

'I never visited a prostitute. Why would I pay for sex?'

'But you told me you did!'

Peter sighed. 'Yes, dummy, because I needed to create the circumstances in which you would own up to your own cheating. I wasn't sure if you would ever tell me about Sophie's real parentage, but I was mightily surprised when you revealed your adultery. More fucking deceit, whoring around. Yes, you dropped straight into my trap there. Presumably that too was with Robert? I don't know why you didn't marry him in the first place.'

'Neither do I,' hissed Louisa. 'And was it the proof that

Sophie wasn't yours that caused you to take a lover? Was Caria your first?'

'I don't need to sleep around like you do.'

Louisa watched her husband. Peter's face twisted, as if he were in pain. He looked to one side again, as if back in his alternative universe.

'Wim and Caria got together about seven years ago.'

'Peter, are you all right? You look unwell.'

'I'm fine.' He reached for his water and gulped greedily. He tossed the bottle back into his pack.

Louisa continued. 'So what happened to this Wim? Did he and Caria split? When did you and she hook up?'

Peter looked puzzled. 'No, they are still together. Very much so.'

Louisa's smile was one of confusion, of disbelief. 'So you're Caria's lover, but she's still with Wim? Christ, Peter, this is getting…'

Louisa stopped talking. She slowly leaned back on her stool, the blood thumping in her ears, a tingling sensation in her back and neck. At that moment, she realised she didn't know this man at all. She managed to force out the words.

'Are you telling me that *you* are Wim?'

His smile was benign. 'Don't be ridiculous. I'm Peter. Your Peter.'

Louisa opened her mouth and tilted her head. She was working out what to say next. But Peter wasn't done.

'But in my other life, my *better* life, yes, I'm Wim. And soon, Peter will no longer exist.' He threw his hands in the air. 'Boof! Gone.'

Louisa ran a hand over her forehead. She chose her words carefully. It would be easy to deride him, to ridicule his concept of two parallel, but very different lives. But she was afraid, fearful of the consequences of challenging the beliefs of a dangerously disturbed mind.

'So, you said you… Wim and Caria… got together seven years ago? And you've been living together in Amsterdam all that time?'

'Yes.'

'So how old is the younger girl… Laila? She doesn't look much more than…'

Once again, her words stuck in her throat. Louisa's mouth, her face, her entire body froze, as the realisation hit home.

Peter nodded and smiled, raising his hands and miming applause.

'That's right. Peter doesn't have a daughter. But Wim does.'

***

Louisa sat gazing into space, briefly lost for words.

Peter looked on, arms folded, a sneer transforming his face into that of a stranger. Wim.

'Right. My turn now,' he said.

She slowly lifted her head, as if it weighed a great deal.

'For what?'

'To ask questions. I have one for you.'

'Go on.'

'You knew that Sophie might not be mine. Maybe you were sure she wasn't.'

'I told you, I didn't know. Unlike you, I had no proof, one way or the other.'

'So you say. But you never told me, never so much as hinted. How could you do that?'

Louisa rolled her eyes.

'It was really difficult, Peter, I was scared. You and I were back together, and it became obvious very quickly that I was pregnant. I couldn't be certain whose it was, and I didn't know what to do. We were in love, had always agreed that we would have several children. The idea of us living a full and happy life, with the chance that one of them might not be biologically yours, seemed the best option at the time.'

'For who?'

His lip curled, the sarcasm not wasted on her. Despite that, Louisa chose to keep her voice calm. She hoped her words sounded reasonable.

'I tried to do what was best for all of us under the circumstances. The hysterectomy after Sophie's birth was a terrible shock to me – living with the knowledge that I could never become a mother to more children – your children – was horrible. I even researched the idea of you fathering through a surrogate mother.' Louisa gave a weak smile. 'Although that proved unnecessary in the end, didn't it?'

'Hah! Still oozing your fucking superiority, even though it was *you* who fucking cheated on *me*!'

Louisa reached for a tissue from her pocket. 'I'm sorry if I made the wrong call.'

'I told you earlier, don't you dare apologise. It's way too late for that. It just makes me even angrier.'

For the first time since she'd known Peter, Louisa was truly afraid of him. And of what he might do next.

***

Her water glass replenished, Louisa stood at the sink, trembling as she sipped. Her desperation to de-escalate the situation, to calm things down, was matched by her hunger for the truth. For there were still unknowns that needed to be addressed. She retook her seat.

'So, now that the truth about Sophie and your alternative life has come out, please will you answer my other questions?'

Peter sneered. 'Try me.'

'Firstly, why didn't you come clean? Tell me that you

knew Sophie wasn't yours, and that you had found this other woman you wanted to be with. Why on earth would you perpetuate this weird lie we've been living?'

'Payback, of course. I've spent a load of my money raising someone else's kid. I think I deserve proper compensation.'

'What? You mean from Robert?'

'Oh, no, I don't suppose he's going to be writing me a big fat cheque when he finds out that I brought up his daughter for him.' A smirk appeared on her husband's face. 'Although Reynard is considering how to make him pay in other ways.'

Louisa covered her face with her hands. 'Oh, Jesus, Peter. Please stop! And who is this Reynard? Where does he come into it?'

'Oh, don't fret, my darling wife. Peter's not going to do anything that will get him into trouble. And Reynard's a fox. A very cunning one. My inspiration, in fact. The fox will come up with a suitable punishment for Robert, don't you worry. No, the compensation, the *financial* compensation, comes from you. For being the cheating, lying whore that you are.'

Louisa struggled to suppress the panic that was welling up inside her. His words were bad enough, but the way he curled back his top lip in a snarl was frightening her. And what was this about a fox? Was Peter genuinely sick, disturbed? Were his thoughts, his actions, being driven by some vision of an animal, one that spoke to him, guided him? And what hideous plan was he hatching for Robert? *Stay calm, stay calm*, she repeated to herself.

'I don't see how,' she said, deliberately keeping her tone of voice level.

'Well, they say that revenge is a dish best served cold, right? And Peter, the wronged husband, has been very patient. Like he was with Barbara, for instance. Your dear mother. It was obvious she wasn't going to last forever, although the old cow considerably exceeded expectations, shall we say?'

Louisa looked to the floor, shaking her head. 'I can't believe I'm hearing this. So you deliberately delayed any discussion of a divorce so you could share in her estate. Is that it?'

Peter's face wore an expression of triumph. 'As I say, I'm due some payback. Bloody well entitled to it!'

Louisa surveyed the man sitting opposite her. His behaviour was becoming increasingly alien to her previous idea of him. His eyes were glinting, not with benevolence or love, but with the glee of someone who has waited a long time for the opportunity to crush the one he hates. Beads of perspiration dotted his temples and upper lip. His previously languid movements had become skittish, jerky.

And on top of his worrying behaviour, he looked so odd. Despite his explanation about the work he was doing in France, his clothes didn't seem right for someone of Peter's age. So why was he dressed like this? Louisa felt she no longer recognised him. No longer saw him as the man to whom she had devoted the past twenty years of her life. Her heart was thumping in her chest, each exaggerated beat trying to pump more blood into her head than it was able to take. She gripped her left hand with her right. Both had started to shake.

But her brain was screaming a very clear message to her. *Do not mention that most of your mother's estate is in trust.* That it can never become your husband's. Because if you do, the consequences could be terrifying.

So she left the words unspoken, the ones that would have ruined his moment of glory. Instead, she moved the discussion on to the last question that was haunting her. What did Peter's Amsterdam partner believe was going on when he was back in the UK, or on the occasional holidays he deigned to take with his wife?

'Caria. What does she know about me and our life here? You have been deceiving me for a long time, and very effectively. But what does she think is going on, would you answer me that?'

A shrug. 'She knows Wim has a wife and a home here. She always has. And that his wife has a daughter, although she's not his.'

'So how come she puts up with you and your perverse double life? Why doesn't she insist that you commit to her and abandon me? It's what typically happens, right?'

'She's not like that. And she accepts the reasons that Wim gave her. Very noble reasons.'

'Which are?'

He narrowed his eyes. 'None of your business.'

'What have you got to lose by telling me?'

'I don't owe you any explanations. I don't owe you anything. It's the other way around, remember?'

Louisa watched Peter reach over to his backpack, lift out the water bottle and take another long drink. The tiny beads of perspiration from earlier were now merging into something more obvious. He pulled out a handkerchief and wiped his brow and neck. She could tell he was stressed by her question, that this was a subject he didn't want to get into. But Louisa's curiosity got the better of her, even though she knew she was on dangerous ground.

'You've lied to her, haven't you, Peter? You've conned her, deceived her. It's what you do, isn't it? Of course, I could ask Caria myself. Yes, that's it – how about I pop round when I'm next in Amsterdam and we can all have a little chat? Then she'll find out what her lover is really like.'

'Oh, shut the fuck up, will you? You know nothing about it.'

He stepped over to his rucksack and began rummaging around inside it. Louisa carried on berating him, but he was ignoring her, intent on whatever he was looking for. Some fumbling was followed by snapping noises before Peter withdrew his hands. They were now wearing blue surgical gloves, and in the right one was a large and vicious-looking knife.

***

Even if her body remained paralysed, motionless, Louisa's mind started working overtime. The knife... Where had he got it from? It wasn't one of theirs. It didn't come from the kitchen drawer. Why have a knife with him at all? And those blue gloves. Why blue? When she last had a doctor examine her, the gloves were a sort of beige... Maybe these were different, maybe they had something to do with the odd clothes he wore? Ah, he was coming closer, she'd ask him what...

Louisa watched as Peter transferred the knife from his right hand to his left. Phew. A fleeting sense of relief. He's right-handed. If he was going to do something silly with it, he wouldn't have moved it. So there must be another explanation...

And then there was a flash and her head jerked up and to the side and her neck hurt as did her cheek and she didn't know what had happened until she looked at Peter and could see his face in front of hers with his teeth bared and his mouth set into a predatory snarl.

His right arm was held in front of him, as if in an invisible sling. Louisa stared at his hand, at the red smears on the blue of the glove, and wondered if he was about to strike her again. Instead, he leaned right in front of her face and spat out the words.

'I said, shut the fuck up.'

The knife was returned to his right hand before being held up in front of her eyes, as if for her inspection. Louisa took in the brand name, the same make as the ones she used in her kitchen. Oops – *their* kitchen. This one looked brand new. And huge – bigger than any of the ones she used. The blade itself was a dull silvery-grey, with a purposeful indentation on the top. Presumably for pressing down upon, for extra leverage whilst you cut away at whatever it was…

'…or you'll get some of this.'

Louisa stared straight ahead as the knife and the arm that was wielding it moved around to the left side of her face, where the pain was pulsing across her cheek. She felt something cold touch her neck, below her ear.

'Understand?'

The word came out in a whimper. 'Yes.'

'Now then. Time's getting on and I have to leave soon. So you're going to do exactly as I say. Okay?'

'Peter, please…'

'No! For fuck's sake. You do as I say, or it's all over for you.' He jabbed his index finger towards the ground. 'Right here, right now.' His face was up against hers, his left hand snaking round to the back of her neck where it took hold of her hair and gave a sharp tug, jerking her head back so that her face was upturned. Louisa emitted an involuntary cry as she looked along her nose at him. A clown-like expression of mock sympathy had replaced his snarl.

'So the best thing is for little Louisa to do just as the big, bad fox tells her.' He gave a series of exaggerated nods as he spoke. 'Got it?'

She whispered: 'Yes.'

'Right. First thing, get your purse and take out all the money. Just the notes.'

Louisa made to turn her head towards her bag, where it lay on the floor at the foot of the sofa. Peter's hand didn't let go of her hair but moved with her, and seconds later the bag was on the breakfast island where a trembling Louisa struggled to extract the cash.

'Okay, now get a freezer bag and put it in there. A big one. We aren't finished yet.'

He marched her to a kitchen drawer where she did as she was ordered.

'Right. Upstairs. The bedroom.'

Once there, he continued his instructions.

'Jewellery, watches. All of it. Now!'

As before, Louisa obeyed, lifting her jewellery case from her dressing table. Once the contents were removed, and with some difficulty, she twisted off her wedding ring.

Peter smirked and nodded at her hand. 'I wasn't sure it would come off.'

Louisa glared at him as she rubbed her sore finger. 'One way or another, it's coming off, Peter.'

His grin disappeared. He nodded over to his side of the bed.

'Now my best watch.'

'You want to steal your own watch? I don't understand…'

He sighed. 'Let's just do it, shall we?'

Still gripping her hair, he marched her over to his bedside drawer. Louisa retrieved his watch with a shaking hand. It went into the bag with the other items. The bag was shoved into his pocket. The task completed, he grabbed the drawer and ripped it from the unit, the contents spilling onto the floor.

'Oops!' He grinned again. 'Right, over there. Your drawer.'

'But there's nothing of value in there.'

He shook his head. 'For fuck's *sake.* A fucking burglar doesn't know that, does he?'

Once more, Louisa was taken by the hair, and once more the drawer was wrenched from its housing, Louisa's things scattered beneath her feet.

'Okay, we're done up here.'

They made their way out of the room, Peter releasing his

grip on her hair as they approached the top of the stairs. Louisa reached for the handrail, but as she did, she experienced a sensation of everything in motion, flying up into the air around her, as if a giant had picked up a dolls' house and shaken it around, with herself, the unfortunate resident, bouncing around inside, smashing off the walls. Stabs of pain accompanied fractured images that flashed before her eyes until, mercifully, the giant appeared to lose interest and set the doll's house down.

***

It was quiet. Louisa lay still, blinking at a scuff mark on the skirting board inches from her face. She made no attempt to move, intent on processing where she was and what had just happened. She rolled her eyes around, realising that her head was resting on the cold floor tiles at the bottom of the stairs, while her body lay splayed out behind her on the lower treads.

She presumed she had fallen the length of the long single flight and was now lying on her side, her right arm stretched out beyond her head.

That was it! On TV, they always made you wiggle your toes. If you could, you hadn't broken your back. She tried it. It worked. But her head hurt like hell, and she had no means of assessing the injury. Blood seeped into her eye. Although in an awkward position, her left arm felt unencumbered. Perhaps she could use it to help lever herself down onto the hall floor. The attempt caused an explosion of red light before her eyes, followed by a shock of pain the like of which she had never experienced. She froze, clenched her teeth and breathed deeply through her nose, trying to ride the wave of nausea that was intent on drowning her, rendering her unconscious. Was she fainting? No, it was passing, but there was something very wrong. She made herself a promise not to move that arm again.

A little rest, that was the thing. She tried to work out what had happened. A fall, obviously, but what had caused it? And then she froze as, from behind her, she heard the unmistakable squeak of the eighth tread. And it all came rushing back to her. Peter…

So, had she fallen or was she pushed? She tensed, her breathing quickening as she considered the possibilities. He would either come to her aid – or… Or what? Then she remembered. The jewellery. Yes, surely he had got what he had come for and would now leave her alone. But she needed medical attention. In a weak voice, she gasped, 'I can't move. I need help. Please… call an ambulance.'

There was no reply. Instead, she heard him manoeuvre around her and make his way towards the kitchen. He returned almost immediately, following which there was the sound of his rucksack being lowered to the floor nearby. When he spoke, it was in a conversational tone that sent a chill down her spine. He seemed completely unmoved by the sight of her, broken and helpless at the bottom of the staircase.

'I'll be off soon, but first I need to finish feigning that break-in. We don't want the insurance company coming to any inconvenient conclusions, now do we?'

Louisa still didn't understand. What was her role in all of this? If Peter was going to steal their valuables and make it look like a robbery, then surely he would explain to her what he wanted her to say. Be patient, she told herself. Don't antagonise him, whatever you do. She craned her neck to watch him, anxious not to disturb her damaged arm. A bolt of pain accompanied the movement, and she groaned.

'Just hold tight, old girl. Won't be long now, then I'll be on my way.'

With that, he donned his hat and sunglasses, eased open the front door and peered around its edge. He then slipped outside, pulling the door behind himself, but without shutting it. Louisa heard his footsteps on the gravel, the sound fading. Her gratitude for his absence was short-lived; moments later the crunching noise returned, and she could see his blurry image through the stained-glass panel to one side of the door. She jumped as a loud bang was accompanied by shards of coloured glass tumbling into the hall.

Seconds later, a maniacal face grinned at her through the jagged hole. 'Heeere's Reynard!' – a poor imitation of Jack Nicholson in *The Shining,* a film Louisa had reluctantly sat through with her husband more times than she could remember. And that *Reynard* again. Peter's fox, his guru, the sinister manifestation of a disturbed mind.

He came back inside, closed the front door behind him and removed his sunglasses. Louisa watched his head moving around as he peered through the smashed pane. Appearing satisfied that his efforts had gone unnoticed from the street, Peter lowered a lichen-stained brick onto the hallway console. He froze as he caught sight of his wife watching him in the mirror hanging above it, and they stared in silence at each other's reflection for what seemed to Louisa like an age. She briefly wondered if he was going to relent, to show his broken wife some compassion.

But her hopes were in vain, her heart sinking as Peter switched on a manufactured smile – one that failed to reach his cold eyes. She shuddered, the mirror adding a dehumanising barrier between them. It was as if she were viewing some psycho movie on a TV screen, with her husband playing the unhinged lead role. When he spoke, his tone hinted at modest regret for an inconvenience.

'There. All done. Sorry about the noise.'

He laid the bucket hat and shades beside his rucksack

before nodding over his shoulder towards the broken glazing. He tutted loudly.

'Nice panel, original feature and all that, but no good at all for preventing a break-in. I'm sure the insurance company will insist on a toughened version when it's replaced.'

'What about me?' Louisa muttered through clenched teeth. 'Will you call for help when you're gone?'

'Darling, everything will be taken care of, okay?'

'Thank you,' she wheezed. And heard him snigger in response.

He reached over to his pack, Louisa watching out of the corner of her eye as he retrieved the knife. She hadn't even been aware he had put it in there. Why the hell did he still need that? She was hardly in a position to disrupt whatever plan he was working on, was she? Even as this thought spun around her mind, she felt her body go cold, her skin hot. She had read somewhere that just before a major heart attack, victims often experience a profound sense of dread. Right now, she felt the same – a feeling of utter hopelessness, of impending doom.

So this was it. Forty-eight years, twenty of them spent married to the man who was about to kill her. Suddenly, the narrative her husband was trying to construct became clear to her. A domestic break-in. Some crazed drug addict looking for the money to buy his next fix. He tries the doorbell. Unknown to him, it doesn't work, so he assumes no one is home and forces his way in. He disturbs the woman of the house and threatens her. He steals the jewellery she's forced to reveal to him, then pushes her down the stairs. Or maybe she falls. Who cares? But the knife… Would an opportunistic burglar use a knife?

Unlikely, thought Louisa, clinging to hope. A break-in is one thing, murder is something else. Most burglars aren't stupid, they try to avoid violence. Because harming people dramatically increases the length of any jail term if they get caught. Peter must know that. A wave of relief. He wasn't going to kill her. He wouldn't risk using the knife.

But the reasoning was quickly brushed aside, to be replaced with something very different. Because now her husband was coming towards her, pointing the blade at where she lay defenceless on the hall floor.

# 47

Once more, he eased past her, this time mounting a few stairs. Louisa heard and felt him sit down next to her feet. He patted her bottom.

'You're a tough one, aren't you? How do you feel?'

'It hurts like hell. Will you call an ambulance, please? Or are you going to stick that knife in me?'

'I promise you, that's not in my plan. Unless you force me to, of course.'

Louisa's sense of dread at the prospect of being murdered with that hideous blade was replaced by another. She was growing weaker and wasn't sure how long she could remain conscious. She ran her tongue over bone-dry lips.

'I don't think I'm in any position to force you to do anything. I need help. What are you trying to do here?'

'I'm not *trying* to do anything. The fall – there was always a chance that it would kill you. Equally, it might not. Reynard's bad luck, that's all. So the fox is going to have to help you on your way. Lift your head and smash it down on the floor. Rather hard. That might do it. If not, he'll have to break your neck and snap your spinal cord. Death will be instantaneous, but unfortunately it's not easy to achieve. In the movies, you see these tough guys grab someone around the head, and with a quick twist, it's done. That's crap. In reality, it's nothing like that. The victim instinctively tenses their muscles and resists. But in your case, you'll be unconscious, so you can't. And neither will you feel anything. Oh, and if that fails, then yes – it's the knife, I'm afraid. But the fox will try and avoid that, because then it really will look like murder, rather than injuries sustained whilst falling down the stairs. And that doesn't fit with the break-in scenario, does it?'

Louisa summoned all her failing energy, appealing to the man she prayed was still inside this nightmarish creature that had usurped his body.

'Peter, please don't do that! Please don't kill me. And the police are going to know you've been here. You're bound to get caught. You'll be in jail for the rest of your life. Think about your daughter, think about little Laila.'

'Jeez, I've told you. Peter doesn't have a daughter. Laila is Wim's daughter.'

As with an overly complicated TV drama, Louisa was struggling to follow the twisted narrative.

'But anyway, this break-in here was done by some low-life junkie,' he continued. 'The best the police will get from any local CCTV cameras are hundreds of ordinary people going about their business, including some nerd in a bucket hat and shades. They won't see the fox – he knows how to cover his tracks. Furthermore, Peter's in France, in Lille. He's nowhere near here, Louisa.'

'But you have plane tickets, you've been through passport control.'

'Ah, you underestimate me, my love. But then again, you always did. I have tickets to get me over here tomorrow morning, as you and I agreed. And I bet you've told Asha all about it, correct?'

Louisa said nothing.

'There you go. And that's helpful, by the way. But as for today, Peter has an alibi that puts him in France all afternoon and this evening. It comes from a sales lady who works for an equipment supplier of ours. Someone I've been cultivating for a while. Grooming, in fact. I award her very profitable contracts for the Lille project we're working on, and in return, the little whore has sex with me.

'Now, I don't need the sex. In fact, she rather disgusts me. But I may well need the alibi. And in order to keep the lucrative flow of business coming, my sporty Lolita – that's what I call her – will swear to anyone who asks, including the police, that she and I were working together all this afternoon on the project. She will explain, with red cheeks and her face averted, that Peter Hedley and she are secret lovers. And that after the meeting, we went back to her apartment in the city, where we had athletic sex before she cooked me dinner. We then had more sex – this will be amazing for my reputation, by the way – following which I left my rampant little pet, exhausted, sore, but content. I return to my hotel, where, at around ten-thirty this evening, I shall meet my team at the bar. They, aware of the rumours surrounding my bit on the side, will exchange knowing glances amongst themselves whilst never daring to raise the matter with me.'

Louisa was keen to keep him talking. He seemed typically proud of the details surrounding his plan, and having him talk was better than the alternative. But she could feel what little strength she had left ebbing away. She forced out the words.

'Very clever. But you will have overlooked something. They will catch you.'

He rubbed her buttock as he remonstrated with her, the sensation of his hand upon her making her flinch in disgust.

'Just like they caught Michael's killer, right? I don't think so.' He paused his rubbing.

'Anyway, my darling, you should have more faith in me. It's a brilliant plan. My Lolita and I even had sex twice this morning at work. In the disabled toilet, she sat astride me. She now has a plastic bag containing two used condoms. Plenty of DNA, both hers and mine. They'll go into the bin in her bathroom as soon as she gets back to her apartment this evening. A bin she will forget to empty for some time. Excellent forensic evidence, don't you agree? Evidence supporting the story that I was with her earlier in the evening. She also has my phone – hence the temporary one that I used to call you earlier. Lolita will make a couple of calls with mine a bit later. The data will of course appear on the cellular network there – more evidence that I was in France. And my apologies for this, but one call will be to your phone, at about seven. A loving husband calling his wife.' He sighed. 'Only you won't be able to pick up, will you?'

Louisa's nausea was getting worse. She struggled to speak.

'But it will take the police just minutes to find out you've entered the UK today. You can't cover up your journey.'

'I don't have to. The person who travelled today took the one-thirty-five Eurostar from Lille. He arrived in St. Pancras at one-fifty-seven local time. His name is John Peter Healy, and he travels on an Irish passport. One he easily procured some years ago, on account of his father having been born in Ireland, with the surname Healy. Once they'd moved to the UK, my grandparents registered themselves here under the name Hedley, mindful of the discrimination that Irish immigrants typically experienced over here. They didn't want that for their family, they wanted an English-sounding name for them, and a proper English upbringing.'

Louisa could hear the note of triumph in his voice. He had worked this out so bloody well. How long had he been planning her murder? But that realisation was as nothing to the sense of hopelessness that overwhelmed her then. She thought of Sophie. That was all that mattered. She didn't want to leave her daughter, for her to be alone. What hideous revenge would Peter's twisted mind bestow upon the girl, in the absence of her mother?

Her attention shifted back to him, still crowing about his clever plot.

'And the beauty of it is that there is nothing to link the two characters. Apart from some early testing to make sure it worked, I have only used my Irish identity and passport twice before today.'

Louisa's eyes were starting to close. Must stay with him. Must keep him talking.

She croaked, 'When?'

'Well, very recently. The first time was when I came over to take care of Michael. Did us all a favour there, didn't I? Useless fucker. I'd never thought about it before, but when you told me about your plan to meet for dinner in Clapham, I thought, hang on a minute, there's an opportunity here. Why allow the prick to inherit from your mother and get half her money? You told me exactly where you and he would be. So that one's down to you. Thanks for the inspiration.'

Louisa struggled against a strong craving to close her eyes and drift away as the full horror of this confession sank in. She moaned. 'No. Oh, Peter, no. You murdered my poor brother?'

'Er, yes. Well done. But it wasn't all plain sailing, I can tell you. I had to hang around outside whilst he dragged you into that gay bar – Jeez, I didn't envy you that. But I knew at some point he would have to walk back over the common to get home. I bided my time, and the fox's patience was indeed rewarded. And there's nothing to link me to the events of that night, of course, since Peter Hedley was in Amsterdam at the time, as I'm certain the police will have checked.'

Louisa felt herself slipping into a fog of hopelessness. Her last moments of life stained by the revelation that the man she had married had brutally murdered her kind and harmless brother. She thought back to his earlier revelation, and a terrible idea crossed her mind. She strained to speak.

'Twice. You said you had only used your Irish passport twice.'

Peter sounded like a teacher congratulating a small child. 'Aaah, very good. You've worked it out, haven't you? My clever girl.'

'No… no. Please, no.'

'Oh, yes. The second time was when I paid a visit to your mother in the home. And once again, that was down to you. Because your plan to come to Amsterdam was gaining traction. You forced my hand, didn't you? We needed her gone quickly so you could inherit her money before I took care of you. Twenty-eight days is the default. You have to survive her for twenty-eight days to inherit from her will. Well, you've exceeded that by two weeks. So whilst the legal process may take some time, your death will not prevent your mother's money from making its way to your estate. And from there, of course, to Peter Hedley, the grieving husband and primary beneficiary of your will.'

He exhaled loudly. 'It was a bit touch and go, but all's well that ends well, eh?'

Louisa thought she would faint at the horror of it. Already, flecks of black were whirling and dancing before her eyes. It was a struggle to haul air into her tortured lungs, their movement restricted by the bottom stairs and hard floor tiles on which she lay crumpled. She wheezed out the words. 'You're sick, Peter. You're a sick man.'

'Oh, come on. Barbara was the sick one. It was high time she went. Remember when you and I last visited her, to tell her about Michael's unfortunate demise? Ironic, really, when you think about it. Well, we borrowed the key to her patio doors to get some air. Remember? I went to hand it back whilst you sorted out your mother. Only I never did. So, a second trip over to the UK for John Healy. I just hoped to God the home had another key, which presumably they had, otherwise they would have changed the lock. Anyway, I let myself into her room, took her pillow and… well, you get the picture. And, hey presto, my wife inherits all of her mother's considerable estate. You should thank me.'

'You utter bastard. You're going to rot in hell…'

'Unlikely, I think. Life for me will be rather sweet from now on. Your mother's money, your pension fund, the sale of this house… And our joint life insurance policy means there'll be another six hundred grand on top – amazing. Anyway, no time to lose. John Healy needs to catch that Eurostar. At seven-thirty-four.' He looked at his watch. 'I might even make the earlier one.'

Louisa was aware of him getting to his feet, then making his way down the few stairs to the hall. She moaned as she heard him lower himself to his knees behind her head, then tensed as she felt the rubbery touch of his gloved hand on top of her skull. She pressed her head down as hard as she could against the cold tiles while the fingers of his other hand tried to work themselves under her ear.

She could feel the panic wash over her, her last remaining seconds of life evaporating in despair. The pleas came out spasmodically through gritted teeth. 'No, Peter… Peter, please… you don't… don't have to do it… please…'

He lowered his mouth towards her and spoke softly. 'I take no pleasure in this. I did love you once, you know. I worshipped you. But you drove me away with your deceit and lies. You shouldn't have done that. You forced me into this.' He took a deep breath. 'Shush now. Just relax, it'll make it easier, it'll all be over in a few moments…'

Louisa was aware of a gurgling sound emerging from her mouth as she screwed her eyes shut and focused all her fading energy on tensing the muscles around her neck. She tried to picture a beam of seasoned oak – hard, rigid, unbreakable. But the image wouldn't stay with her, replaced instead by a drifting sensation, not unpleasant – a sensation that beckoned her along, inviting her on a dreamlike and tranquil voyage of discovery. She could feel her awareness retreating from her body, sliding backwards as if she were separating into two parts. This Louisa, and that one over there.

But the journey was brought to an abrupt halt as her head jerked. Not violently, and neither was this a movement of her making. A moment elapsed as Louisa's consciousness flooded back. Her eyes snapped open. She could feel Peter's rubbery hands releasing their grip on her head. Something had disturbed him.

Now she heard it too, the sound of a key being turned in the lock. She could feel him reaching past her, fumbling for something on the stairs. He began carefully to lift himself from his kneeling position, like an animal preparing to spring forward in attack. Louisa could see the cold steel of the knife blade over her head as he slowly raised both it and himself.

The front door eased open.

'Dad? Oh my God. Mum?'

Sophie stood there, her blue eyes flickering in shock at the scene before her.

Peter continued his sinuous movement. 'You! What are you doing here?'

Louisa grunted as she twisted her head, pain shooting down her chest.

'Run, Sophie. Knife…'

The girl froze in her tracks, Peter never taking his eyes off her as he slowly advanced.

'It's okay, Sophie. Hey, it's okay. Stay calm. Your mother's…'

Then he lunged forward. Louisa managed to lift her right arm high enough to catch his ankle. She felt a kick to her hand as she screamed out: 'Run, run!'

Peter stumbled, falling onto one knee, the knife clattering across the hall floor in front of him. Sophie turned to the tall ceramic pot that was home to several umbrellas, grabbed one, and holding it with two hands, thrust it at Peter as he was getting up. The point caught him in the shoulder, causing him to shriek and slap a hand over the injury.

'Aah, shit! You little bitch. I'll fucking kill you.'

Peter staggered towards her as Sophie turned and launched herself back through the door and down the steps. Louisa was aware of him picking up the knife. She listened as the sound of two pairs of feet running over the gravel melted away, along with the remains of her consciousness.

# 48

It all seemed real at the time. Louisa was lying on the stairs, surrounded by people in masks and gowns. She turned away from the dazzling light above her head. There was Michael with his big, carefree grin. Was that a new scarf? He was standing next to their father. Dad looked the way he always had when she was small. A towering figure. As a child, she had been in awe of him. In response to her pleas to 'be a horsey', he would bounce her up and down on his knee and make the appropriate noises: clip-clop, barump-barump! And there was Robert – a gentle smile for him. Don't tell my dad what we got up to, for God's sake! Then Gerrit, his ponytail stuffed under a surgical cap. Hello, you randy Dutchman. But here, bless her, and stroking her mother's hand, was Sophie, bare-legged and with her spiky running shoes protruding from under the hospital scrubs. And, weirdly, over there, the barman from the Amsterdam hotel. How did he get in here? Made sense though, she did feel very thirsty.

They all appeared to be tending to her whilst they talked amongst themselves, Louisa nervously watching those blue surgical gloves. She suddenly panicked and looked around for Peter, but mercifully he wasn't there. She wanted to shout at them, explain that her husband had taken his own watch, it wasn't a burglar, they mustn't believe that…

***

Now she felt parched. Where had that barman gone? She ran her tongue over cracked lips and opened her eyes. Sophie was leaning over her. Big smile. Lovely girl. Had she been crying?

'Mum?'

Hard to speak. 'Mmm. Darling?'

'I'm just going to call the nurse. Don't try to move, okay?'

'Thirsty.'

***

This time she lay thinking about the events of… when was it? Friday? Yes, that was it. So what time was it now? Her head ached. She eased it in the direction of the window. Bright sunlight. Saturday perhaps? Louisa's left arm was heavily bandaged, and she couldn't move it. A clear plastic tube led from it to a device somewhere behind her that buzzed gently, stopped, and then did it again. She could feel something above her left eye, whatever was holding it in place pulling slightly at her temple. She looked down at her right hand. Heavily bruised. Another tube, this one secured with an adhesive strip. She tentatively raised both the hand and its plumbing to her forehead. Big, padded dressing. A wound-closure strip on her cheek. She wondered if she would have a scar.

Sophie was slumped in a chair beneath the window, apparently fast asleep. Louisa lay there, watching her daughter's rhythmic breathing and thinking just how much she loved this caring, thoughtful child. She shuddered as she pictured that brutal knife. Whatever had become of Peter, Sophie was safe. And that was the most important thing. So right now, Louisa could allow herself to worry about a couple of other pressing matters. She needed some water, and she needed a wee. In that order.

She glanced down and lifted a wedge-shaped thing with a cable and a red button. A nurse was soon at her side, helping her to drink from a cup that looked like it had been designed for a hyperactive toddler.

Sophie had woken and was standing next to her, smiling. She had her hand on her mother's shoulder. Louisa drank greedily, before the nurse took the cup and explained that he would have the doctor come and take a look at her.

'Thank you. But I do need a wee.'

The nurse winced. 'Can we have the doctor examine you first? Can you wait? Then I'll bring you a bedpan.'

Louisa laid her head back and closed her eyes. 'Oh, God.' The idea of being helped to pee by a male nurse was a new one for her. She wondered how long it would be before she could visit the bathroom.

***

It was just the two of them. Sophie sat on the side of the bed, holding the fingers of her mother's right hand, anxious to avoid touching the cannula. The left arm was definitely off limits, having sustained a compound fracture as Louisa crashed down the stairs.

Louisa had learned from the doctor that the bang to her head had not resulted in any fracturing of the skull. So far so good. But she had lost some blood and had undergone emergency surgery to repair the radius and ulna, the two bones in her forearm. Compound fractures were complicated, with careful management of the wound essential to avoid infection.

Louisa smiled weakly at her daughter. 'Are you okay? Tell me what happened.' She sighed. 'Then I need to explain a few things to you.'

Louisa listened intently as her daughter took her through

the events of yesterday. Her delight at having swapped her shift at work, enabling her to come home a day earlier than planned.

'I know I said I would try, but I didn't think there was much chance of actually doing it, of getting home on the Friday. So I thought I would surprise you.'

And then her panic when she saw the smashed glass to one side of the front door. The scene that greeted her as she opened it. Her temporary confusion as she tried to register what was going on.

'Why did he have the knife? Was he trying to kill you? And if so, why?'

Louisa took a slow and deep breath. 'He was, yes. I'll tell you everything later.'

Sophie covered her mouth with her hands. 'Oh my God, Mum. Why?'

'Later, okay? Go on with your story.'

Sophie studied her mother's face. 'Okaay. But it was only when you shouted and he brandished the knife, that I realised what was going on. And your tripping him up saved the day. I was hoping that stabbing him with the umbrella would incapacitate him, but it just made him mad, and he came after me. So I ran.'

'I'm very glad you did, my love.'

'Yes, but even as I legged it across the driveway, I developed a plan. There was no way he was going to catch me, but neither did I want him to think that. If he'd given up on me, he might have come back to the house and…'

Sophie looked over to the window, tears streaming down her face. Louisa slid one hand towards her.

'Come here, my love.'

They shared an awkward hug, Sophie careful not to disturb the broken arm. She reached for some tissues for them both before continuing.

'So I started running, but then pulled up, pretending I had hurt my ankle. I limped up Lonsdale Road, getting further from the house, allowing him to gain on me. When I felt we were far enough away, I came to a halt, clutched my ankle and turned to him. He was wheezing, panting, his arm outstretched towards me, telling me to wait, telling me it wasn't what I thought.'

'Oh my God, why did you stop?'

'Well, I could see he didn't have the knife anymore. I guessed he had ditched it over a garden wall or something. He was clearly knackered, so as he approached, I kicked him hard, right between the legs. His knees came together, he doubled up and went purple in the face. That's when I called the police.'

Louisa gently rubbed Sophie's leg. 'My brave girl. But you should have run as fast as you could.'

Sophie looked defiant. 'No, Mum, I told you why I didn't. Anyway, Dad had obviously had enough and staggered off towards Hammersmith.' There was a look of triumph in her eyes. 'So I started following him, all the while talking to the police on my phone. They were there so quickly! And I was screaming at them, pointing to Dad.'

'So what happened then?'

Sophie grinned. 'He was finished, gulping for air. The police put him in handcuffs, two more cars turned up, they took him away, and then we drove back to the house. I think by this time you'd blacked out. I was really frightened, but the policeman took your pulse and confirmed you were still with us. The ambulance arrived shortly after, but they had to stabilise you before you could be moved. It took ages. I came with you – sirens and everything. And then while they were attending to you in A&E, I phoned Asha. She went round to the house and set about finding someone who could do a temporary repair on the window.'

Louisa gave a gentle shake of the head. 'So brave, so calm.'

Sophie continued. 'Whilst they were operating on your arm, the police questioned me here. They want to talk to you as soon as they can, and there's a policewoman outside your room who has to call them once you come round. In the meantime, we are both witnesses, so we aren't supposed to swap stories until they've interviewed you as well.'

Louisa raised an eyebrow. 'Okay. Then you'd better tell my minder I'm awake.'

***

At around eleven o'clock, two familiar figures entered Louisa's hospital room. DI Griffiths and DS Lynch. Despite feeling tired, Louisa gave them an account of Peter's actions of the previous day, the events that led up to it, and his sickening revelations regarding Michael and their mother.

At Louisa's suggestion, Sophie had taken a taxi back to the house to shower and change. She would also pick up some things Louisa would need in hospital. Not least her mobile phone. The doctor had earlier indicated that, assuming no complications arose, she could be discharged as early as the following day.

She was grateful that the detectives expressed little interest when told of Peter's allegations surrounding Sophie's parenthood. Whatever complications blighted the family's affairs, they were not of a criminal nature, and therefore of no interest to the law.

Whilst the police had found Peter's second passport and Eurostar tickets on him, DI Griffiths seemed disinclined to dwell on the subject, as if embarrassed for not having looked into him more carefully when investigating Michael's murder. They had also relieved Peter of the plastic bag containing the jewellery and watches.

Prior to DS Lynch snapping her notebook shut, a date was agreed for Louisa to attend the police station and give her formal statement. Not long after the police left her alone, she was fast asleep.

***

Louisa woke to see her daughter back in the visitor's chair, prodding at her phone. Apparently the doctor planned to visit soon, at which point it was hoped that the cannula could be disconnected and Louisa would be encouraged to get out of bed and move about. The buzzing box would stay with her, housed in a small shoulder bag.

In the meantime, there were things that Louisa needed to share with her daughter. She asked her to sit on the bed. Sophie obliged, her solemn expression suggesting she knew that something serious was about to be revealed.

Louisa spoke slowly and, to the best of her ability, dispassionately. There would be plenty of time for emotion later, once the whole sordid tale was laid out.

She recounted how losing her job had led to the idea of spending more time with her husband in Amsterdam. Working there. How Peter had baulked at this, and deployed increasingly obvious attempts to thwart her ambitions.

'I couldn't understand why he was against it. So I did some digging. I spied on him, Sophie. I still can't believe I did it, but I had to know the truth.'

Her daughter replied in a whisper. 'Which was?'

Louisa covered her mouth with her fingers. 'He's been leading a double life. He has another family over there. It's been going on for years.'

'Oh, my God. So how… why… why would he do that?'

Louisa's head flopped back against the pillow. Her mouth had gone dry. She asked Sophie to pass her some water and studied her daughter's face whilst sipping slowly, trying to put off the inevitable just a little longer. Before the girl's youthful world was rocked by a life-changing revelation.

Louisa chose her words carefully. 'He told me that he knows you are not his daughter. He had a DNA test done in Amsterdam some years ago that proves it. He says he took hair from your brush.'

Sophie was staring at her mother, her brow creased in confusion. She shook her head from side to side. 'Is he mad? Why would he even think that?'

Louisa watched as the instinctive denial faded. She could sense the thought process going on in her daughter's mind. Louisa knew what was coming next. It was inevitable. Sophie took a deep breath.

'Is it true?'

Louisa's eyes dropped momentarily, before re-engaging with her daughter's pained, blue gaze.

'I think it probably is. Yes.'

Sophie gave a brief laugh. Of astonishment, disbelief. 'You *think*? Christ, Mum. You must know, surely?'

'No, I don't.'

'So, do you have any idea who my father might be? Or was he just some stranger passing in the night?' Sophie raised her voice. 'One of a number, perhaps. Did you keep count in your bloody notebooks?'

Louisa flopped her head back on the pillow and closed her eyes. She spoke softly, in a resigned tone.

'All right, my love. I understand your anger.'

Sophie headed over to the window and stood with her hands on her hips, silent as she gazed out. Louisa watched her intently, wondering what was going through her daughter's mind. For nineteen years, she had lived with the perfectly reasonable assumption that the man she called 'Dad' was indeed her biological father. How does a young mind deal with the discovery that this isn't so? She could see Sophie wiping a tear from her cheek.

Louisa spoke to her back. 'There is only one other man it could be.'

Sophie walked over to the bed, shame-faced, and gently put her arms around her mother.

'I'm so sorry, Mum, for what I said. That was hateful of me.'

'No, darling. You aren't capable of hate. It's completely understandable. But I can't tell you who I think your father is until I have spoken to him. Peter knows who it is and will want to hurt him, me and you, as much as possible. So we need to confront it ourselves, in a way that works for us. But in the meantime, you need to know what Peter tried to do to me… and what he has done to others.'

Then Louisa started crying, as the horror of her husband's revelations pierced the fog of painkillers and anaesthesia. Uncontrollable sobs punctuated the words that she forced out. 'And it's going to hurt, Sophie… I'm so sorry, but you need to learn the truth.'

For the next ten minutes, Louisa's voice faltered as she took her daughter through Peter's dreadful deeds. She paused often to draw deep breaths, summoning the will to keep going, to get through this ordeal. Throughout, Sophie sat motionless on the side of the bed, her hands clasped tightly in her lap, her face pale and blank, her eyes never leaving her mother's.

She listened in silence as Louisa explained her husband's determination to exact revenge and secure the compensation he felt he was due. How he'd initiated a plan to kill first Louisa's brother, then her mother, and finally Louisa herself. Following which, the undiluted wealth of Barbara Bruce-Gardiner would make its way into the hands of a grieving and much-pitied widower, along with a substantial life insurance payment on his late wife.

Only when the whole, sordid tale was out did mother and daughter let go, the raw emotions overcoming them in bouts of crying, whimpering, hugging and reassurance. It went on for some time.

***

A little later, Sophie was half-reclining beside Louisa on the pillow, her head resting against her mother's. Hands clasped together, they were staring blankly at the ceiling, both of them red-eyed, exhausted.

Eventually, Sophie broke the silence.

'I hope he rots in hell, and I really hope he is not my father. But how can we be sure? Because I need to be certain that *creature* is not my dad.'

'Well, we could ask him to supply a DNA sample. Then we can match it with yours.'

'Do you think he would?'

Louisa pulled a face. 'No idea.' She forced a laugh. 'I thought I knew him. But, assuming you want to know who your real father is, and assuming he wants you to, then you two can do a test.'

'Do I know him?'

'Speculation isn't helpful. Let's just take this one step at a time. But know this.' Louisa turned towards Sophie, smiling to reassure her. 'You were conceived in love. Of that much, I am certain.'

# 49

At her mother's insistence, Sophie had gone home to some well-earned rest. Louisa had poked at a surprisingly edible hospital dinner with her good hand, grateful for a little time on her own before Asha turned up that evening.

In the meantime, she had chatted with the cheerful woman who came to collect her tray, seemingly delighted that this patient at least had enjoyed the food. Louisa had detected a reticence to instigate any discussion around the cause of her injuries. *So what happened to you, love?* Louisa suspected her new friend was well aware of the police comings and goings during the last twenty-four hours.

The reunion with Asha kicked off with tears and hugs made awkward by Louisa's fragile condition. The cannula was gone, but the buzzy little machine was not, and she had been dismayed to learn that it would be her companion for the best part of two weeks. Its purpose was to create negative pressure in the wound on her arm and so reduce the chance of infection.

It was no surprise that their conversation mostly revolved around Louisa's recent, traumatic experience. But she was delighted to learn that Asha had secured a new position and would be handing in her notice on Monday.

'Well, congratulations, my darling,' she croaked. 'You

certainly didn't hang about, did you? And who is the lucky new employer?'

But here Asha was uncharacteristically close-mouthed 'Babe, you will be the first to know, I promise. But I have been sworn to secrecy for now.'

Louisa nodded, stifling a yawn. 'Oh, God, excuse me. It's suddenly hit me, I feel blitzed. But this job sounds intriguing. I can't wait to find out more.'

***

Louisa rolled her eyes in frustration at the news that she was not to be discharged on Sunday. The consultant who would take the eagerly anticipated decision would not be at work again until Monday, and the doctor on duty for the weekend was unable to act in his place on such matters. Patience was required. In the meantime, there was another difficult discussion to be had.

Robert had already spoken to Sophie, who had briefed him as best she could, but without going into the lurid details of Peter's motivation. That much would remain secret for now. Robert was deeply shocked and wanted to know when he could visit Louisa. Sophie arranged for him to come to the hospital early on Sunday morning. When she heard of it, Louisa was grateful that she would have him to herself for a while, before her daughter arrived later on.

With Robert at her bedside, Louisa once more recounted the tale of Peter's double life, his determination to keep it a secret and his decision to murder his way into inheriting his mother-in-law's wealth.

Louisa took a deep breath as she looked at Robert, sitting forward in the visitor's chair, his expression incredulous. And with good reason: this was Peter they were discussing. The man who was once his best friend.

'But there is something he alleges he discovered, which has had a profound effect on his state of mind,' she continued. 'Something he learned not long after he started working out of Amsterdam. And that something concerns you.'

Louisa watched Robert frown, tense up.

'Me? Oh, God, what have I done? What is it?'

Louisa shook her head, the gentlest of movements. She closed her eyes briefly.

'You haven't done anything wrong.' She was still unsure of the words that she was going to use. 'The thing is, Peter says he had a test done. One that compares Sophie's DNA to his. And that there is no match.'

Robert was silent. He kept his eyes fixed on her, but seemed unable to comment on what he had heard.

'There's only one other man who could be her father – and that is you. That night we spent together when you briefly came back to London, just after Peter and I had split. I think that's when Sophie was conceived.'

Robert was usually a calm and polite man, not given to rage or uncontrolled outbursts of emotion. Louisa studied him intently, painfully aware of how badly she had misjudged her husband.

She could see Robert's features changing. The muscles in his face relaxed. The tension previously apparent in him had eased.

He brushed a hand over his eyes, now moist and glinting. He got to his feet and moved over to the window, his hands on his hips. Louisa gasped – that was exactly what Sophie had done, how she had stood when, the day before, Louisa delivered the news that Peter was unlikely to be her father.

She was desperate to ask Robert how he was feeling, but good sense got the better of her and she waited for him to speak first. Eventually, he swung around. Tears were rolling down his cheeks.

'I already love that girl as her godfather. And if what you have said turns out to be true, as I desperately hope it is, I will love her as a father. She's the most wonderful child, and I couldn't be a happier, prouder man. The idea that you and I share a daughter is something quite beautiful. Thank you.'

Afterwards, Louisa thought back on these moments again and again. The warmth of Robert's reaction, the gentle hug he gave her and the way he kissed the top of her head. It was all so unselfish. It wasn't about them as individuals, it was about the realisation that they were joined together in a way that only parents can be. Their DNA fused in the creation of a new human being, a new life. It was as if, there in that hospital, a daughter had just been born to them, a tiny, bruised, pink thing, eyes scrunched against the light, the shock of entering the world written on her wrinkled face.

But for now, there were many questions to answer. Important ones, mostly from Robert.

What does Sophie know? Only that Peter alleges he is not her father.

Does she have any idea who her biological father might be? She might hazard a guess, that's all.

What will her reaction be? She loves you, Robert. But it's all a huge shock, so who knows?

So when do we tell her? Very soon. She wants answers.

And what about your children, Robert? How and when should they be told?

And then the biggest one of all. How can we be sure? How do we establish this for certain? Because the pain, if it's all a cruel trick of Peter's, would be awful.

***

Sophie helped her mother to exit the taxi and then held her

breath as, motionless, Louisa stared at the plywood fixed over the broken window. Her eyes filled.

Sophie eased an arm around her. 'Are you okay, Mum?'

A sigh. 'Let's get this done with. The sooner I confront it, the better.'

Louisa moaned as she stood at the foot of the stairs, her eyes fixed on the blood-stained stair carpet. Sophie set down the overnight bag and patted her shoulder.

'I'll get someone round to give it a good clean. I'm sure it will be fine.' She smiled at her mother. 'As will you.'

They were soon sipping tea in the kitchen, Sophie brushing away protests as she explained that she would not be returning to her summer job.

'Mum, they were fine about it, and they'll be happy to have me back next year. Term starts in just over four weeks, but for now, I can stay and look after you. So, how about some lunch? I was thinking scrambled eggs.'

'Darling, that's so kind. But before we eat, would you like to know who your father is, assuming of course it isn't my husband?'

Sophie's body stiffened, her expression solemn.

'Yes.' A deep breath. 'Yes, I would.'

Louisa watched her daughter steeling herself.

'Robert. It has to be your godfather, Robert.'

Sophie's face screwed up, the expression held for a few seconds before she exhaled loudly. She stood and leaned into her mother, Louisa wrapping her good arm around her and pulling her tight. Sophie's body began to tremble as the muffled words escaped her.

'I so hoped it would be. Now I just want it to be true.'

'Darling, we both do. But it is something we have to think about very carefully.'

A minute or two later, mother and daughter both wiped their faces with tissues.

'So what happens now?' asked Sophie.

Despite her puffy eyes, Louisa smiled. 'Well, that's for father and daughter to decide.'

Sophie spluttered a brief and snotty laugh. 'I suppose it is, yes. But you must have discussed it with Robert when you told him. And I want to know his reaction, by the way.'

'Of course.' Louisa took Sophie's hand in hers. 'He was over the moon. He already loves you very much, and there was no mistaking the joy and pride he felt. It was written all over his face. You are both very lucky people.'

Louisa explained what Robert had said. That before telling his children, he felt it made sense for him and Sophie to undertake a DNA test. They still couldn't be sure whether or not Peter was playing some last evil trick. But they need only go ahead if that was what Sophie wanted. After all, she might choose to live her life in blissful ignorance.

Sophie said she understood. Robert had already done some research. A kit could be ordered online for next-day delivery, at which point the tests would be completed and posted without delay. The results would be sent via email the following afternoon.

Over lunch, they talked about his children and how they might take this news. Sophie was no stranger to them; Robert's thirteen-year-old daughter Lily held her in awe – 'like a big sis' – whilst Josh, aged eight, was convinced that Sophie was destined for the England women's team, such was her ability with a football.

Having cleared away the lunch things, Sophie watched as Louisa called Robert to update him. Her daughter had stressed that she preferred to await the results of the DNA test before engaging with the man she hoped was her father. At which point, she would either greet him as such, or else he would remain her much-loved godfather.

Robert said he was relieved. He felt the same way, but

lacked the courage to express his thoughts as clearly as Sophie had.

Feeling tired, Louisa went upstairs for a lie-down. Sophie had tidied the bedroom and returned the drawers to their rightful places. Louisa was pleasantly surprised that they appeared to have sustained no damage. On closer inspection, she could see lines of glue where the front panel of one had been re-attached to the sides and base. She lowered herself and her buzzing companion down onto the bed and stared at the ceiling, thinking how much she loved her beautiful, sweet and caring daughter. No matter who the girl's father turned out to be, nothing could ever change that.

# 50

Behind her desk on Tuesday morning, Louisa peered through the window, looking for her friend, the blackbird. Maybe he'd be back later. In the meantime, there was a new list to start. It was going to be a long one.

First thing, order the DNA test. Then call her new employer in Amsterdam and calmly explain that, following her husband's failed (obviously) attempt to kill her, she was somewhat incapacitated and could she please delay the start of the new job? Although, come to think of it, perhaps she would just stick with telling them she had fallen down the stairs and broken her arm.

The page began to fill. The practical tasks included organising a repair for the stained glass. The replacement would need to be much more robust than its fragile predecessor.

And there was a litany of discussions she would need to have with the bank, financial institutions, service providers and the like. She imagined the recording that might greet her when she telephoned: 'Your call is very important to us. Please press one for sales, two for customer service and three if your husband is on remand for your attempted murder and you don't know what to do.' Maybe an initial call to the solicitor would be a good idea.

By lunchtime, she had made progress. Whilst the 'to do'

list continued to grow, the DNA test should arrive tomorrow, and another appointment with her solicitor had been arranged.

But there was a problem with the job. She had spoken to Janna, and to the company directly. They had both expressed sympathy for Louisa's predicament, but her prospective employer was committed to launching this project on time. If Louisa was forced to materially delay her start, then regrettably they would need to make alternative arrangements. She was frustrated by the news, but understood their position. It would be weeks before she would be able to work. Back to the drawing board, then.

***

The following morning, a metallic rattle of the letterbox caused Sophie to head for the front door. Louisa eased herself from her stool by the breakfast island, hoping her expression did not reveal the anxiety that was welling up within her.

Sophie flicked through the mail before holding something aloft. Her voice mirrored her mother's nervousness.

'I'm guessing this is it.'

They both adjourned to the kitchen, where they sat and examined the contents of the envelope. The process appeared simple enough: Sophie and Robert would both need to complete the test. A stick was rubbed around the inside of the mouth and then pressed onto a patch on a special card, which afterwards was sealed. Assuming the samples arrived at the laboratory the following morning, the results would be emailed later that afternoon.

Louisa had agreed with Robert that he would call round at one-thirty to complete his part of the process. As she had previously made clear, Sophie would not be at home.

Louisa finished reading the instructions and turned to her

daughter, who was standing at the end of the breakfast island, her hands covering her nose and mouth.

'Darling, what's wrong?'

Sophie shook her head slowly, her eyes brimming. 'I don't want to do this, Mum.' She came over and leaned in.

Her mother's right arm wrapped protectively around her. Louisa had seen her daughter crying too much of late. Her uncle's violent death, her grandmother's too. And now this terrible choice – whether or not to test Peter's assertion.

'But why, my love?'

'Because that murdering monster insists it isn't him, and if that's true, it has to be Robert. So let it *be* Robert. Do you think he would agree to that? If he would, why don't we take it as fact that Robert is my father, and then I can just forget about that bastard behind bars?'

Louisa took a deep breath. She hadn't prepared herself for this reaction, but could completely understand where Sophie was coming from. She took her daughter's hand.

'If I've got this right, you're petrified of learning that Peter is, after all, your biological father. Is that it?'

Sophie nodded as she wiped at her eyes. 'Yes. That would be too much to bear. And the more I think about that man, the more I think he might be playing some sick game. Having killed you and got away with it, he would have told me that I wasn't his daughter, just to be rid of me. Even if I was. And then I would have spent the rest of my life wondering who my father really is. He's evil.'

Louisa studied Sophie's face. What a choice. What must be going through her daughter's tormented mind? Because on this particular point, a girl who loved science – grounded and pragmatic – was prepared to brainwash herself into believing what she desperately hoped was true, without a shred of proof.

But then, Louisa reasoned, billions of people the world over did precisely that, committing to something they could never establish as fact. Belief born of a vision of a meaningful life, with a better one to follow. An act of faith. Was her daughter's craving so unusual?

'I understand that. All I would say is that Peter's story sounded convincing to me. The detail he gave about having to do three DNA tests with your hair, because the first samples weren't complete. Would you make that up for no good reason? But, yes, it's a gamble, and I totally understand where you are.' She paused. 'Might it help to have a chat with Robert? To see where his mind is on this?'

Sophie looked up at her mother, the torture evident in her eyes. 'It wouldn't be fair on him. This is a decision I have to make. To be certain, I'm required to roll the dice, and I don't think I have the courage to do it. Because it's all or nothing, Mum, and I am terrified of getting the wrong result.'

Louisa hugged her weeping daughter as best she could, whilst cursing her broken arm. Cursing her husband. Cursing herself. Sophie shouldn't have to suffer like this. That was Louisa's responsibility. She had made a huge call all those years ago, and now she needed to do it again. She pulled her head back, peering into Sophie's eyes.

'Sophie. Listen to me. It will be alright, do the test. Robert is your father.'

'But you don't *know*, Mum. You've said he might not be.'

'Do it, please. Otherwise, you will never be free from the doubt. Do it, Sophie. For both of us.'

'Mum?'

'I promise you, darling. Robert is your father. I know he is.'

***

Louisa often reflected on this afterwards. Whether she had done the right thing. Unsurprisingly, Sophie had pushed back, demanding to know whether this was some 'instinct' on the part of her mother, or a hard fact. Because, as she wisely pointed out, their emotions were all over the place right now, and there was a danger that hope might override good judgement.

Louisa examined her daughter's face before rising from her stool. She extended her good hand to her child.

'Come with me.'

They made their way into the sitting room, where Louisa ran a finger along the long line of notebooks before taking one down from the shelf. She perused it briefly before sitting alongside Sophie and tapping her thigh.

'This is woman-to-woman stuff. Mother to daughter. If you want, I'm going to show you when you were conceived.'

Sophie smiled, as if in disbelief. 'Really? You have that recorded in one of your notebooks?'

'Yes. But it's in a sort of code, so no one else would understand it.'

Louisa showed Sophie a table, hand-drawn in blue ink. She explained the rows representing the days of her cycle. Then the columns: dates, the letters indicating her period and when it ended. Her likely ovulation date.

Sophie pointed to an exclamation mark. 'What's this?'

'That's when Robert and I made love. He was on a brief visit home from Canada. After *you know who* and I broke up.'

'But looking at your chart, that's five days before you would likely have ovulated.'

'Yup. It was a shock to me, too. Maybe I was early. And I had no idea then that sperm could live so long inside a woman's body.' She nudged her daughter. 'Something to remember.'

Sophie winced. 'Given my current preferences, it may not be relevant.'

Louisa looked into the distance, her face sad. 'I should like to be a grandmother someday.' She turned to her daughter and shook her head, albeit with a smile. 'Not yet, mind.'

Sophie nodded, her eyebrows raised. 'It's possible, I guess, so who knows? Anyway, back to your records.'

'Well,' said Louisa, 'here's where Peter and I got back together. I told him we didn't need to use protection, partly because I knew that I was at the end of my cycle. But partly because, even then, there was a tiny, nagging doubt in my mind.'

'By this time, of course, the fertilised egg that became you was already implanted inside me, although I wasn't aware of that. I missed my period, but held off for quite a while before telling Peter that it was late. I did a test and – hey, presto.'

'So when did you work all this out?'

'Only after you were born. You were two by then, and your features were starting to resemble Robert's. So I got a bit panicky. That's what prompted me to do a bit of research, revisit it all and set it out like this. Because up until then, I hadn't appreciated the science around conception timings.'

'So how come you remembered all the dates so precisely?'

'I didn't. But I made a note of the date of my last period at the time I suspected I was pregnant.' Louisa nodded towards the shelves. 'It's in an earlier notebook somewhere. And it was easy enough to check back and establish the dates on which Peter and I broke up, Robert and I slept with each other, and when Peter and I got back together.'

Sophie nodded slowly. 'Okay, I get the dates and everything. And that you weren't sure at the time. But once you had set it all out like this, once you *knew*,' Sophie looked to the corner of the room, as if choosing her words carefully, 'what went through your mind, then?'

Louisa's smile was weak but appreciative. Partly an acknowledgement of her deceit, and partly in gratitude for her daughter's tact in the way she'd phrased her question.

'You mean, how could I live with the lie?'

'If you like, yes.'

'I wasn't sure I could. Peter and I were married. You were a little girl, you were loved, and we were both happy enough. So I knew we could carry on, with you and Peter in blissful ignorance, or I could come clean. I knew a bit more about my husband by then, and I was afraid of the consequences.'

Louisa closed her eyes and rubbed her forehead, as if reliving the terrible decision.

'I was petrified of being reviled and rejected. By Peter, by my parents, by everyone, really. Life could have become very difficult. Peter would most likely have stormed out, and I would have been left as a single mother, trying to balance the demands of a small child and a full-time job. Neither did I think it fair to tell Robert at that point. The opportunity had been lost – he was engaged to be married by then, and I didn't want to ruin his life, either.'

Louisa took a deep breath. 'So, I began to convince myself that your father could indeed be Peter. It was the only way I could deal with it. Over time, the belief grew, suppressing what I was previously sure was the truth.'

Louisa's trembling hand reached out for her daughter's. 'I took the coward's way out, Sophie.'

'You're not a coward, Mum. Did you ever subsequently think of telling me and Da… *him*?'

'Only very recently. When I discovered he was living this double life with a lover and a child of his own. But then events overtook any decision on my part.'

'Okay. And now there is another decision to make.'

Louisa raised her eyebrows.

Sophie nodded at the notebook in her mother's lap. 'Do you want me to put that back on the shelf, or are you going to take Robert through all this?'

'Ah.'

***

Sophie had made them both a sandwich before hurrying out of the house, determined to honour her pledge not to encounter Robert until the test results were known. But the hug she gave her mother before heading off was accompanied by a reassuring smile. One that spoke of understanding, respect and above all, love.

It had taken the two women only a short while to run through all the arguments and conclude that Louisa's secret should remain just that. There was nothing to be gained by tormenting Robert with the knowledge that for the past seventeen years she had been privately convinced he was Sophie's father.

Sophie's completed test was waiting on the breakfast island in the kitchen. It merely needed Robert to undertake his, for the truth to be established.

On Thursday, at four-thirty, it was.

At six-thirty on the same day, Robert returned. Louisa stood in the kitchen doorway, tears in her eyes as Sophie launched herself into her father's arms, nearly knocking the chilled bottle of champagne from his hand.

Seated on the kitchen stools, they drank a toast to new beginnings. Louisa glanced between Sophie and Robert over the rim of her glass, thrilled by the beaming faces and animated chatter that sparked around their little group. She contemplated the extraordinary chain of events that had unfolded these past weeks. How, despite Peter's evil nature and terrible crimes, something good had transpired. For the truth regarding Sophie's father had emerged, she had been freed from living in the shadow of a monster, and both she and Robert were overjoyed by the revelation.

You could see it in the way their eyes shone – partly as a result of the tears of relief and joy that crept into them from time to time, and partly at the prospect of sharing the good news with others. Robert was clearly excited by the opportunity to tell Lily and Josh that they had a big sister, one they knew well and adored. He would deliver the news tomorrow, and on Saturday, Sophie would visit their house, where the four of them would have a celebratory dinner together. Mary Poppins would cook; Robert would collect Sophie from her home and line up a taxi for her return.

He was cross about Louisa's refusal to join them. No, she had said, this was an important time for a father and his children, a chance to mark a very special moment. Together. She didn't budge on that point. But Robert did extract a promise from her to have dinner with him on their own and proposed a day next week. Louisa had nodded at the sling and her buzzing companion, stating that it was a bit soon.

At this point, Sophie intervened, insisting that 'Dad' should come for supper before then. She beamed at her mother and father, who exchanged rueful smiles, fully aware that they'd been outmanoeuvred. A date was set for one week's time.

***

Louisa had plenty to keep her occupied, but found herself taking frequent naps as the days unfolded. Both her physical and mental selves were in recovery mode, the damage to the former being the most apparent. Naked, and with one hand, Louisa washed her bruised and battered body whilst standing in front of the mirror. She eyed the bath, longing to enjoy a warm soak in its comforting embrace, but was not capable of lowering herself into it with one arm. She regretted her modesty. Sophie would of course have been more than willing to help.

As for her mind, she found herself alternating between

moments of unexpected euphoria, offset with interludes of great sadness and anger.

She was alive. Peter had failed in his diabolical plan to kill his wife, thanks to the intervention of the daughter Louisa had brought into the world nineteen years before. For now, her husband was behind bars and likely to remain so for some considerable time. Meanwhile, Sophie knew who her real father was, and was surrounded by love.

But then the bitterness of Louisa's loss would hit home. Of her dear brother, his chaotic but valuable life snatched away in a cruel and ruthless act. The only shred of consolation was that she had discovered Michael had a wonderful collection of friends, people who had cared about him deeply. And then their own poor, harmless mother, sent early to her death in Peter's single-minded pursuit of the *compensation* he believed he was owed.

Louisa made no mention of it, but wondered how events might have unfolded had his plan to kill his wife succeeded; for Peter could never have benefitted from her mother's bloodline trust. Only Sophie and her heirs would have been able to enjoy the proceeds of that. Louisa shuddered as she contemplated what evil he might have dreamed up by way of retribution, on learning the truth.

But for now, she would dwell on the positives, and on Tuesday, she was delighted with the outcome of a hospital visit – her arm was healing well. She celebrated with a glass of wine as her daughter prepared the evening meal for them. Sophie was already planning something special for tomorrow night when she would cook for both her parents.

# 51

Louisa and Robert sat at the breakfast island and exchanged surreptitious grins whilst Sophie darted between her recipe, a chopping board and the oven. All offers of assistance had been politely but firmly declined, and they were minutes away from enjoying baked salmon with a creamy yoghurt and dill dressing, new potatoes and a pickled cucumber salad.

After dinner, Louisa sat with her elbow on the breakfast bar, her chin in her hand, and smiled at the sight before her. Sophie was gently bossing a bemused Robert as he helped his daughter to clear away. The work done, Sophie returned her apron to the drawer, glanced up at the kitchen clock and announced that she was meeting a couple of friends for a drink in Hammersmith. She grabbed her bag and was gone.

As the front door closed behind her, Louisa and Robert looked at each other, bewildered expressions on their faces. Louisa nodded to him.

'So, did you put her up to this?'

Robert shrugged. 'No, but I wish I'd thought of it. Did you?'

'No.'

'Hmm. Do you think she's playing games with us?'

'Probably.'

He nodded at her empty glass. 'Can I pour you some more wine?'

'Just a little.'

Robert studied her face.

'How are you feeling?'

'Better, but a bit tired. Thank you for asking.'

'Would it help if I kissed you?'

'Yes, very much.'

***

Louisa took Robert's arm as they strolled alongside the Thames. As she had pointed out to him, the last thing she wanted in her condition was to trip and fall over.

He had frowned. 'So if it wasn't for your injury, you wouldn't hold on to me, is that it?'

She looked up at him and smiled. 'Damn. You've got me there.'

It was the first of September, a Friday, and Robert had taken the day off to be with Louisa. He would see her again tomorrow, but then it would be with Sophie, Lily and Josh in tow. They had planned a family outing – a sightseeing boat trip on the Thames accompanied by a ride on The London Eye, and then an early-evening meal at an Italian restaurant. Robert would leave his car at Louisa's house, and they would all head into town from there.

He had explained that today he wanted some time with her by himself. She didn't argue. They had yet to discuss what they were going to do. On Wednesday, when they kissed in the kitchen at Barnes, after Sophie had adjourned to the pub, there had been no reference to their feelings. And neither of them had tried to take things further. Louisa was grateful; she knew that she was emotionally vulnerable and respected Robert's reticence. But she was sure he wanted to say something, and if he didn't, she would. He didn't disappoint.

'Look,' he began, 'I can't imagine what's going through

your mind right now, how you must be feeling. I am in awe of your strength and composure. So I want you to know two things. First, I don't want to get in the way of your healing. You need time. Your daughter…' he smiled – '*our* daughter is there for you, and so am I. As your friend. Okay?'

They stopped walking. Louisa turned to face him, scanning his expression.

'Thank you, Robert. That's very thoughtful.'

'The second thing is that I don't want you to think my other feelings for you have changed.' His expression became more serious. He lowered his voice. 'When we made love in the hotel. I told you then that I loved you, that I wanted to be with you.'

Louisa looked briefly down at the ground before regaining eye contact. Robert wasn't done.

'Since then, my conviction has only grown stronger. But I know that you've been dealt some extraordinarily cruel blows. And you need time to recover. So I'm not going to pester you. But please don't think either my feelings or hopes have changed, because they haven't.'

Louisa brushed her hand over his cheek. She thanked him for his sensitivity, and his patience. It made no sense to rush into anything, not with her mind all over the place. After all, she had recently made some appalling errors of judgement. And before that, come to think of it. So, for now, she would allow herself to get over the trauma. And then see how she felt.

# 52

Late September, and autumn was making itself felt. The Amsterdam air had a distinct nip to it. Louisa looked at her watch as she took her seat in Sarphatipark, glancing around at the children, the parents, and the lovers. It was just over ten weeks since she was last here, spying on her husband and the woman she was now expecting to meet. Caria.

It felt odd. Louisa had easily found the contact details for Gerrit's café on Facebook. He had been thrilled to hear from her again, even when he realised that she was not about to relent and fall into his arms. Instead, she had another favour to ask.

Louisa gave him a potted version of recent events and said she was anxious to reach out to Peter's (or was it Wim's?) partner, Caria, who, as Gerrit knew, lived opposite. Would he please pass on Louisa's details and ask if the two women might meet?

The invitation had been accepted. Now Louisa pulled her coat around her as a woman she recognised approached her. A woman she had last seen standing in the window of her apartment, while Peter fondled her breasts. The greetings between the two women were understandably awkward, but they agreed to repair to a nearby café.

Over the next hour or so, they calmly shared their stories, Louisa constantly reminding herself of the shock that Caria must have experienced on hearing that her man, the father of her second child, was in prison in England, charged with two counts of murder and one of attempted murder.

But the big revelation for Louisa came when she asked Caria what was her understanding of *Wim's* familial arrangements in England. The woman had calmly explained that he had told her that Louisa, his wife, had a daughter by another man. But, despite this, they had been happily married until Louisa's early and rapidly accelerating dementia had struck. Caria had been told that Wim's wife was now in a home in Sunbury, to the south-west of London (apparently the very one where Louisa's mother had lived).

Wim had solemnly insisted that he would not turn his back on his wife, especially given her prognosis. She was unlikely to survive for long, and it would be very wrong of him to abandon her. So, ever the dutiful husband, he would return to the UK as often as he could, and even occasionally take his confused wife on trips to the seaside and to her family home in Norfolk.

His wife's daughter, Sophie, had now attained her majority. But, as Wim had explained to Caria, despite there being no legal obligation, he made sure to visit her regularly and check that she was okay. Yes, Caria stated firmly, Wim was a caring man and a loving father.

She gazed into the distance as she explained how Laila, denied any knowledge of the *allegations* against Wim, had taken his absence particularly badly.

'Laila loves her father to read to her. *Reynard the Fox* is her favourite book. I find the stories in it quite disturbing, but she couldn't get enough of them. It was something they liked to share.'

Louisa inhaled sharply at this reminder of Peter's twisted mind. She recalled how he had morphed before her eyes into the human embodiment of that cunning beast – the heartless, ruthless hunter who would not stop his onslaught until he was stained with the blood of his prey. Thank God for Sophie's timely intervention. And poor Laila, idolising the father who had brought her up on tales of cunning and cruelty. Not that the child's mother seemed to find anything wrong with that.

'I have to tell you,' Caria continued, 'we shall be fighting for justice for Wim. I don't think for one minute he would ever deliberately have hurt you, and neither do I believe he harmed your family. Yes, he lied about you and your mental state, but that's because he wanted to take care of you and your daughter. I know he was under a lot of pressure. Trying to juggle two families, to provide for us all as best he could. That must have been so hard for him.'

Louisa smiled, but made no attempt to counter Caria's view of Peter, or rather of Wim. She must still be in the denial phase, refusing to believe that her man, *their* man, was suffering from a dangerous personality disorder. And the eventual fallout for her and her two girls would be dreadful. Emotionally and financially. Maybe one day she would see things differently, realise the danger she and her daughters had been in. But for now, in her eyes, Wim remained a good man. It was not Louisa's responsibility to change her mind for her.

The goodbyes were harder than the introductions. What the hell do you say to someone who remains deluded under such circumstances? The clumsy farewells were conducted with little expectation that they would meet again.

And now there was only one thing left to do in Amsterdam. Louisa allowed a few minutes to pass before she headed off in the same direction as Caria had. Louisa wanted to visit Gerrit in his café.

The hug he gave her was genuine, reiterating his pleas for Louisa to abandon her life in England and come and live with him here. For a moment, despite everything that had happened, she could see the attraction. Nevertheless, she told him he was a wonderful man, touched her lips with her index finger, pressed it to his and was gone.

***

The following Monday, Louisa stood by the front door, frowning at an envelope as she turned it in her hands. It was marked 'The estate of Michael Bruce-Gardiner'. It bore the address of his studio apartment in Clapham – since let to a new tenant – but had been forwarded to Louisa by the service to which she had subscribed. Despite his debts, or perhaps because of them, she felt it important that her brother's affairs were wound up as best they could be.

Louisa was surprised to discover that the letter was from his agent. She had never given any thought to the idea of Michael having professional representation, but with hindsight, it made perfect sense – how else do creative types get their work in front of those who might buy it?

In the opening paragraph, the agent apologised for the impersonal nature of the communication. She was aware of Michael's passing, but had no idea who his next of kin was. The letter presented two pieces of good news. Firstly, Michael had received an offer for a television drama that he had written. Whilst the agent thought it fair, its acceptance would require the agreement of Michael's legal representative.

Furthermore, the prospective buyer was a fledgling production company in which Michael had invested twelve thousand pounds in April. The company was apparently doing well, and had already pre-sold Michael's output to a popular TV channel.

Louisa lowered the letter and gazed into space. Twelve thousand pounds! Michael was clearly unable to make the investment from his own funds – he had none, so he must have borrowed the money. The pressure to repay it, and with no obvious means of doing so, had resulted in his approach to his sister. Even if she was unaware of the provider of the original loan, the mystery appeared to have been solved. Louisa looked forward to passing the news on to Detective Inspector Griffiths. Game, set and match.

But several thoughts were now flying around in her head. First amongst these was that Michael had succeeded in writing a script that would be aired on mainstream TV, and his violently truncated career would be judged a success as a result. Louisa imagined her brother's name prominently displayed in the credits, as they rolled up the screen.

Additionally, and even if he'd borrowed the money to do so, Michael had the foresight and courage to invest in a business that he believed had good prospects. Not quite as flaky as his sister had judged him to be, then.

And furthermore, the proceeds of the sale of his work would easily cover the repayment of his debts. Louisa was unsure if clearing them was a legal requirement, but doing so would enable Michael's affairs to be closed off with dignity. He would depart this life owing nothing.

But even as she considered this welcome news, Louisa's attention turned to her own loan to her brother. There was no way she wanted the twelve thousand pounds back, preferring that the surplus that would result from the winding up of his affairs should be directed to a better cause. And then an idea began to form. One she regretted she had not had sooner. A bold idea, but one that would involve a meaningful sacrifice on the part of Sophie and herself. An idea that would ensure her brother's memory was forever associated with kindness and the care of others – a fitting tribute to a man whose life was cruelly snatched away in an act of greed and loathing. A snub to the perpetrator of the crime, Louisa's husband.

On an emotional phone call with her daughter that

evening, Louisa and Sophie agreed to the establishment of a foundation in Michael's memory. It would support and champion the work of those individuals and organisations that acted to combat hatred and bigotry. It would be funded by a sum of money, the equivalent of that which, had he lived, would have been available for the benefit of Michael as a result of his mother's legacy. The trustees of the foundation would include Sophie and, should he agree to serve as one – Michael's good friend, George.

***

Two weeks after her brief return to Amsterdam, Louisa was in the kitchen of a beautiful and tranquil holiday rental on the south coast. She kissed Robert before sitting down opposite him.

'You're doing too much,' he warned her. 'Just take it easy, will you?'

'I'm fine, don't fuss.' She smiled at the sound of furtive giggling coming from another room and looked towards the door to the hallway. 'I'm not sure who's leading who astray in there.'

The weekend break was always going to be rushed, Robert whisking Lily and Josh straight from school on Friday before hightailing it down to East Sussex. Louisa had collected Sophie from Southampton, and they'd all met up in this wonderful house within sight of the chalk cliffs, Cuckmere Haven and all the incredible scenery this part of the coast had to offer.

Louisa had woken that morning to see Robert smiling at her. She had closed her eyes again, rolled onto her back and grinned as she felt a hand wander over to her side of the bed.

'Stop it,' she hissed. 'I can hear your two trashing the place already. We can't stay in bed all day.'

And so they had taken full advantage of the Saturday to do all the things that families were supposed to do on a weekend away by the sea. Or a *trainee* family, as Robert had quietly described them. And now, seated at the table and with dinner behind them, there was the prospect of a gradual wind down before another blissful sleep.

Louisa spoke softly. 'This works. All of us together on neutral territory. But at some point, we have to float the idea of a merger.'

Robert lifted his glass, grinning. 'A merger? Now you do sound like a bloody finance director. These are our families we're talking about.'

'I know, but hopefully, this break has set the scene. It's the first time they've seen us sleeping together.'

'Progress, then. So we need to decide how to…' He stopped talking and beamed as Josh and Lily came into the room, looking decidedly guilty. Sophie followed, crossed her arms and glued herself to the doorframe. Robert looked between the three of them, sensing they were up to no good. Josh was clutching something, which he now held up before dropping it onto the table and rushing from the room, hotly pursued by a giggling Lily. Sophie didn't flinch.

Louisa looked at Robert. He shrugged and looked at Sophie. She shrugged and looked at her mother. They all looked at the offering on the table. Robert lifted it and turned it in his hands. It appeared to be a home-made envelope of sorts, held together with sticky tape. The names 'Robert' and 'Louisa' had been written on the front, surrounded by hearts. Josh's work for sure.

He smiled and passed it to Louisa. 'You can do the honours.'

The card inside was a folded sheet of paper, a single, beautifully drawn heart adorning the front. Lily's contribution, this time. Inside were the words: *We love you both. Please can we all be a family together?*

It was signed by Josh, Lily and Sophie. Louisa started to count the kisses but lost track and gave up.

***

Louisa had found parting from Sophie hard after the fun-filled weekend. Dropping her daughter off in Southampton, they had hugged tightly, both of them thankful for the way their lives had changed over the past few months. Before leaving their temporary seaside home, Louisa, Robert and their offspring had all solemnly promised that the five of them would be together by Christmas, whether that be in Marlow, Barnes, or somewhere else entirely.

And now, as Louisa set off towards London on a Sunday evening, she scolded herself. Get a grip, woman. It wasn't wise to drive with teary eyes. But despite the emotional parting from Sophie, the week ahead was filled with promise. For tomorrow, she would start her new job as the finance director of Robert's company. She was also very much looking forward to seeing her new colleague – Asha's mystery new position having turned out to be as HR director of the same business. She would begin work on the same day, her last act at their old company being to send Louisa the final version of the compromise agreement, acknowledging and apologising for the organisation's failings in the nature and handling of her dismissal.

On Wednesday, she and an enthusiastic George would meet with the lawyer tasked with setting up the foundation in Michael's honour. Sophie would join them via a conference call link.

On Thursday evening, Louisa would cautiously resume her fitness classes. And next week she would have her first piano lesson in thirty-two years, delivered by a rather dishy jazz aficionado. Yes, there were big changes afoot.

Two hours later, she parked the Passat in the driveway, looked up into the holly tree and unloaded her bag from the boot, careful not to put any strain on her still fragile left arm.

She always enjoyed coming home. Selling the Barnes house would be a wrench, but that's what tended to happen when couples divorced. In the hallway, she leaned against the closed door and eyed the stairs. Those stairs… The stain on the carpet had just about come out, but now would be a good time to move on. The future looked bright. Who knew where she, Robert and the family would end up next? Wherever it was, she would make sure their lives were filled with love, fun and hope.

Louisa's eyes fell on the box of old notebooks awaiting someone strong enough to carry them away to be shredded. All sixty-eight of them. She smiled. Her new life had begun.

I really hope you enjoyed this book. Either way (yes, really!), I would be very grateful if you would kindly leave a review on the site where you bought it, and share your feedback with others. A couple of lines is all it takes, but it's so important to emerging authors like myself. And if you drop me an email when you have done so (robbie@robbievale.com), I'll be sure to reply and thank you in person.

And don't forget to visit my website, where you can sign up to access all sorts of bonus materials and info related to this and my other titles. There's even a free short story!

Input the website address or use the QR code below.

robbievale.com

# ACKNOWLEDGEMENTS

Firstly, thank you to you, lovely reader, for choosing this book amongst the (literally) millions out there. Your opinions and feedback really matter, so please do leave a review.

I would like to extend my sincere appreciation to my advanced reader team. Your willingness to preview the book ahead of its publication (and with no idea as to whether or not it was any good!) shows considerable generosity and a wonderful leap of faith. Your feedback is critical. Thank you all.

I should also like to offer my heartfelt thanks to my editor. Lynn Curtis is a superstar, and although unseen by the reader, her contribution to this book has been profound.

Big thanks to Chloé Messinger of Troubador Publishing for her cover design. I hope you like her work as much as I do!

Finally, sincere thanks to my long-suffering wife, Heather. Your support, encouragement and patience are truly amazing. You never doubted me, and I'm a lucky man.

Made in United States
Cleveland, OH
12 March 2026

34405280R00204